A COLD MIND

"SUPERIOR . . . A TENSE, MOUNTING MYS-
TERY WHICH COMBINES A POLICE PROCEDURAL
WITH A FIRST-RATE CAST AND DRUM-TIGHT
SUSPENSE."

—*John Barkham Reviews*

A COLD MIND

"AN ASTONISHING BOOK."

—Michael Gilbert

A COLD MIND

"A solid, literate thriller with one extra grabber: the murderer's truly creepy *modus operandi.*"

—*Kirkus Reviews*

A COLD MIND

"A SUPERIOR CRIME NOVEL of grim realism. The
characters are alive, and they carry the suspenseful plot
to its inevitable conclusion. The author shows a shrewd
mastery of his chosen genre."

—*Atlanta Constitution*

A COLD MIND

David L. Lindsey

PUBLISHED BY POCKET BOOKS NEW YORK

The lyrics to "Força do Amor," on pages 198, 199 and 200, are used courtesy of Edições Musicais Helo Ltda.

The lyrics to "Eu Te Amo," by Chico Buarque, on pages 252 and 253, are used courtesy of Polygram Discos Ltda. and Chico Buarque.

POCKET BOOKS, a division of Simon & Schuster, Inc.
1230 Avenue of the Americas, New York, N.Y. 10020

Published by arrangement with Harper & Row Publishers, Inc.
Library of Congress Catalog Card Number: 82-48682

ISBN: 0-671-49933-5

First Pocket Books printing August, 1984

10 9 8 7 6 5 4 3 2 1

Printed in the U.S.A.

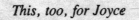

This, too, for Joyce

Acknowledgments

For enabling me to conduct specific background research regarding certain portions of this book, I am grateful to the Houston Police Department for its generous cooperation. Especially, I wish to thank Homicide Division Captain B.F. Adams, who made it possible for me to know, and work with, Detectives Tom Ladd, Mike Kardatzke, Kenny Williamson, and Jimmie Ladd.

And for introducing me to the richness of an unfamiliar culture, I am indebted to Mike Quinn, a man who lives in Austin but whose soul resides in *a musica brasileira*.

. . . clinical analysis must not be used to obscure the moral problem of evil. Just as there are evil and benign "sane" men, there are evil madmen and benign madmen. Evilness must be seen for what it is, and moral judgment is not suspended by clinical diagnosis. But even the most evil man is human and calls for our compassion.

Erich Fromm
The Anatomy of Human Destructiveness

But the line dividing good and evil cuts through the heart of every human being. And who is willing to destroy a piece of his own heart?

Aleksandr Solzhenitsyn
The Gulag Archipelago

1

Roland Silva was driving, a wrist draped limply over the steering wheel as he slouched against the door so his face caught the full blast from the air conditioning vent. He was eating crushed ice from a Pepsi cup.

"Kothman must've drawn this cruiser on the swing shift," he said sourly. "The air coming out of this thing smells like a sewer."

Peter Walther shook his blond head. His lanky frame was also slouched against his door, while his eyes scanned the small wood-frame houses in the smutty darkness. Even at the end of his shift, when the last thing he wanted was to stumble onto a drunk or a family brawl, he conscientiously watched the serrated edges of the shadows where ninety percent of everything that shouldn't happen took place.

It was less than an hour before they were due in and Walther's and Silva's meandering drift through the Mexican barrio of Magnolia Park never strayed far from the lights of Navigation Boulevard, the umbilical cord that connected them to the downtown police station, nearly five miles away.

The two men had been partners for the past nine months—long enough to have a baby, Walther thought—and they had learned each other's moods and flash points. Recently Lenny Kothman, a cocky cigar-smoking bear of a patrolman who could throw a softball like a cannon shot, had become Silva's thorn in the flesh. Ever since Kothman had learned that Silva, who usually knocked everything out of the park during their Saturday-afternoon games, couldn't hit what Kothman had come to call his "greaser ball," the thorn had worked itself into a festering sore.

"You know," Walther said, his voice bouncing back at him from the window in front of his face, "you've gotten so you blame everything on Kothman."

Silva looked at Walther sharply and lowered the volume on the radio.

"What do you mean by that?" he snapped.

"I'm just saying it's noticeable," Walther said.

"Shit." Silva shoveled the last chunk of ice into his mouth and tossed the empty cup onto the seat. He chewed furiously, sulking as they cruised past the Immaculate Heart of Mary Catholic Church.

Walther smiled to himself. This time when they reached Navigation, Silva would make a violent left turn and roar into the lights of the main thoroughfare, driving the speedometer needle to ninety in a surging release of pent-up frustration before he slowed to the legal speed. That would put them a third of the way to the car pool and Silva would feel better for it. Little things meant a lot to him.

But instead of turning, Silva calmly continued on Seventy-sixth Street toward the smelly crotch of the wharves that lined the Turning Basin of the Houston Ship Channel. When Walther looked questioningly at him, Silva shrugged and said, "A little variety."

The streets became tighter nearer the public wharves. Tankers and freighters draped with sparkling lights lay in

2

the docks and waited at a distance in the basin, their exotic voyages having come to an end amid the rancid stench of the chemical plants across the harbor and the oily fumes of diesel fuel from the barges that plowed the bayou. A ship's horn groaned across the channel.

"You picked a real scenic route for variety," Walther said. "And you made a big mistake."

"Naw, we'll just make a quick turn. Won't stop for nothing less than a cutting or shooting in progress."

They crept along a potholed street where darkened storefronts were crowded against silent bars whose neon signs were dark in this last hour before daylight. A single, sallow-faced whore watched them with dopey eyes from a doorway that emitted soft, hazy blue light.

Silva followed the street to the last warehouse on the west end of the basin and then turned back along the wharf fronts, playing his spotlight over the rusted warehouses, where even the newer buildings seemed aged and decayed from the constant assault of acidic air and brine.

At the far end of the headlight beams, they saw something move in the weeds at the base of one of the loading docks. Silva threw his lights on bright and accelerated as Walther sat up in his seat. They both watched as a rangy cur came out of the shadows and loped across the street in front of them, his head held high with a ropy wad of viscera dangling from his mouth as he disappeared down the sloping embankment toward the channel.

"Mother Mary," Silva said in disgust. "America the Beautiful."

And then suddenly the woman came at them out of the weeds from the direction opposite the warehouse. Her eyes were wild and rolling, her mouth flung open, making a gaping black hole where her face should have been. She ran directly at the headlights.

"Goddamn!" Silva yelled, hitting the brakes. They felt a

3

slight shudder against the front fender and Walther leaped out of the car, leaving his door open, as Silva slammed the gears in reverse.

Before Silva could get out, he saw Walther jump backward into the glare of the headlights, his hands fumbling for his revolver. A dark gash glistened high on his left cheek; his face registered astonishment. Then the woman was up, staggering in a flurry of wild hair and fluttering skirt as she bolted into the dusty weeds toward a chain-link fence that ran out from the last warehouse along the top of the sandy embankment above the channel.

Silva swung the spotlight in her direction and jumped out as Walther, regaining his presence of mind, buttoned the strap on his revolver and plunged after her.

Running flat out, the woman smashed headfirst into the fence as if she hadn't seen it. It knocked her down but she was up instantly, running halfway between the fence and the dead-end street. Suddenly she careened blindly into the fence again.

"What the hell's *wrong* with her?" Silva yelled.

Walther was on her before she could get up a second time and was struggling to pin her down in the weeds and sand when Silva got to them.

"Cuff her ankles," Walther yelled as he pinned one of her thrashing arms under his left knee and snapped his cuffs on her other wrist. Blood poured from his cheek and dripped off his chin into the woman's hair.

Silva grunted as he finished with her feet and stood up.

"Shit, man. She cut you real bad!" he gasped, looking down at Walther. "Where's the knife?"

Walther shook his head. "No knife," he said, checking the cuffs. "She bit me."

"She *bit* you?"

"Yes, dammit," Walther said impatiently. He was

4

breathing heavily and had sat back on his knees to look at the writhing woman and catch his breath.

"Wonder what she took? Ten to one it's angel."

"I don't know," Walther wheezed. He took his handkerchief from his hip pocket and touched it to his face. There was a raw depression; she had actually bitten away a part of his cheek. He felt queasy, light-headed.

As the two of them watched, the girl gasped and began to convulse. Walther quickly rolled her over on her side and tenderly pulled her hair away from her face. Strings of saliva streaked his hands and matted in her hair with his blood.

For the first time, they got a good look at her. She was a Mexican girl, maybe twenty-five years old, with strong Indian features. It was hard to tell if she was pretty. Her face was pulled into a distorting rictus as she choked on her saliva, which poured from her mouth in curious overabundance. Suddenly her head arched back in seizure and the muscles in her throat jerked taut.

"Hey, man?" Silva stepped back. "She's checking *out!*" He wheeled around and ran back to the unit radio.

Walther, still straddling the girl on his knees, watched intently. He tried to check her tongue but she tore at him again, viciously, bringing blood from a bite to the outside of his hand below his little finger. He swore, confused. Tentatively he put his other hand on her shoulder and then gripped her tightly as if to reassure her, to tell her she wasn't alone. Silva had turned on the flashers to make it easier for the EMS to find them, and the cherry light hit the girl's face every other second like the pulsing bursts from an inner fire that threatened to consume her.

"I don't know," Walther said out loud to no one. "I don't know." He had forgotten about the wound in his cheek and the entire left side of his face was slick with blood, which was still splattering the girl's face and hair, unnecessarily soaking her with gore.

5

The voices on the radio barked dispassionately, harsh with static. Far away in the sparkling city, a siren stretched across to them.

In the darkness twenty yards away where the fence ended and the embankment fell to the muddy channel, the cur returned. Half crouched in the dry weeds, his bloody muzzle raised slightly, he scanned to and fro in the night air for some clue to explain the strange scene he watched in the flashes of red light. Suddenly he snuffled, the short hair along his bony spine rose all the way to the back of his neck, and he turned warily and disappeared down into the dark margins toward the water.

2

Stuart Haydon stood back from the sluggish green water of Buffalo Bayou and watched the bars of early-morning sunlight break through the pines and play across the white coveralls of the three men as they wrestled the woman's body onto the bank. A thin, steamy veil hung over the water. Haydon thought of the Lady of the Lake. Modern version.

He glanced over his shoulder at the three figures standing silently in the damp grass a few yards up the gentle slope. Leo Hirsch was supposed to be getting statements from the two boys who had found the body, but now that the woman was stretched out on the bank, the three of them had turned to look at the soaking corpse. One creamy breast lolled seductively out of the woman's shirtwaist dress and the soggy skirt was bunched up around her waist, revealing the patch of matted black hair between her long waxen legs. A dark smear of bayou mud crawled up the inside of one thigh.

The police photographer, who had gotten several shots of the body while it floated in the water, now circled the dead woman like a vulture, concentrating with voyeuristic thoroughness as he moved in for close-ups. When he finished, the coroner's assistant, with a peculiar sense of decency, put a small towel over the woman's face.

Haydon looked behind him again. "Talk to them, Leo," he scolded, and walked over to the body and squatted down. The coroner's investigator was trying to unwad the dress from around her waist.

"Just leave it that way," Haydon said. "You see anything? Ligatures? Maybe something we should look around for?"

"Nope." He was a young man, pudgy, with a razor haircut stiff with hair spray and a wispy mustache that would never be anything but wispy. "And it doesn't look like she was knocked around." He picked through her stringy hair. "Probably hasn't been in the water more than three or four hours. Her fingers and the soles of her feet are wrinkled, but she hasn't soaked up much. She's in good shape."

"Okay. Go ahead and load her in the van before the reporters show up."

Haydon watched them get her onto the stretcher and cover her with a disposable paper sheet, which quickly soaked up the water on her body in dark spreading blotches. They strapped her down and started up the slope through the greenbelt of pine trees that separated the bayou from the homes just above them; the ambulance was parked on a dead-end street up there. Haydon turned and stared at the edge of the brackish water where it disappeared into a swampy stand of cattails. His eyes narrowed in preoccupation, not really seeing what they were looking at as he stood alone on the wet grass where the woman had lain in a death sprawl of mute provocation.

Abruptly he reached down for a dried pine branch that lay near his feet and proceeded to walk along the bank, probing idly in the heavy grass and cattails. There was no telling where she had gone in. Probably not here. He looked across to the dense woods on the other side. Houston's fifteen-

8

hundred-acre Memorial Park lay straight ahead. He could hear the traffic on Loop 610, which cut across the western edge of the park six or eight blocks away through the forest.

He threw down the stick and walked over to Leo and the boys. The two kids looked to be about twelve years old. They were dressed in the uniform of the upper-middle-class Tanglewood adolescent: Adidas jogging shoes, Izod tennis shorts, and imitation Oiler football jerseys.

"Rickey here was just explaining how they came to find the 'deceased,' " Leo said, and winked at Haydon. "This is Detective Haydon," he said to the boys. "Why don't you start over, Rick?"

"Yes, sir," the boy said. He looked at Haydon from under a shock of woolly blond hair that badly needed cutting and gave a smart-ass little grin. Haydon took an instant dislike to him. "We were hunting frogs along here." He held up a sharpened bamboo stick. "There's lots of them in the bayou. We use them for experiments."

"What kind?"

"Just ordinary old frogs. I don't know."

"I mean what kind of experiments."

"Science experiments," the second boy said. His voice was deep and somber. He wasn't grinning.

"This is Doug," Leo said.

"We were just walking along over there," the first boy continued, "sneaking up on them, when we saw this paper plate floating under the water. We started throwing our javelins at it until we finally hit it."

"Only it wasn't a paper plate," Doug said grimly. "It was her buttocks."

"Buttocks?" Leo raised his eyebrows.

"Right," Rick said. "I speared her in the butt."

Leo made a note and shook his head.

"Course I knew it wasn't a paper plate then," Rick continued quickly. He didn't want the story to get away from

9

him. "So I jabbed it again and then pushed hard. That's when the back of her head came out of the water." He imitated the way she leveraged to the surface by stiffly bending over at the waist and coming up slowly with a frozen expression. "Her hair had been tangled in some of those reeds or something and when I pushed, it pulled her loose or something."

"Then we went up to my house because my mom's gone out to the airport, and we called the police," Doug said.

"Why didn't you go to Rick's house?" Leo asked. He referred to his notes. "It's closer."

"No way," Rick said.

"His mom's super strict," Doug said. "She wouldn't have let us come back down to watch."

"Did you get a look at the woman's face while she was on the bank over there?" Haydon asked.

They nodded, a little embarrassed because her face wasn't what they remembered most about her.

"Had you ever seen her before?"

Only Doug nodded.

"You know her?" Leo asked. He drew a line across the bottom of his note pad.

"No, sir. But I know where she lives."

"Where?"

"Up there on Pinewold."

"The dead-end street?"

"Yes, sir."

"You live close by?"

"Yes, sir. On Pine Hollow."

"Does she have a family? Any children?"

"I don't think so. I don't think she's married."

"Why's that?"

"Well . . . I see lots of men there, you know. I think maybe she's divorced."

"Maybe," Haydon said. Kids don't miss a damn thing,

10

he thought. "I guess we parked right across from her place, didn't we?"

"Yes, sir."

Without saying anything further, Haydon turned and started up the dark path made by the stretcher bearers in the dewy grass. The others followed.

When they got to the barrier at the dead-end street, a television cameraman was filming the coroner's assistants as they closed the back door to the van and walked around and got inside. The cameraman followed them a little ways as they drove off. A young woman in a snappy summer suit stared after them, her hands on her hips in a petulant stance. Behind her, a man with an unkempt beard leaned against a rusty Volvo, grinning. When he heard the two detectives and the boys approaching, he turned toward them. His grin widened when he saw Haydon.

"I told her it'd be you," he said to Haydon, who ignored him and kept walking.

The girl turned around and Haydon recognized the new anchorwoman from a local television station. She strode decisively toward him and introduced herself as she extended her hand. Haydon stopped, shook her hand, and nodded.

"You're Detective Haydon?" she asked.

He nodded again.

"Can you tell me what's going on here?" She gestured toward the bayou with her stenographer's pad.

Haydon shook his head.

"Oh, come on now," she said, forcing a smile. "You can't expect to keep something like this a secret. What happened here?"

"You know as much as I do at this point," he said.

"Sergeant Haydon," she said. "I don't even know if it was a man or a woman under that sheet, for Christ's sake. Those assy coroner's assistants wouldn't tell me anything." She couldn't hide her exasperation.

"That's right," Haydon said, and walked past her toward his unmarked car.

The bearded reporter laughed. "I told ya," he said to the girl. "Nobody talks on Haydon's cases."

"Now wait just a damn minute," the girl said to Haydon's back. "You don't control the coroner's office. You've no jurisdiction." She followed him a few steps before Hirsch and the two boys pushed past her as they followed Haydon up to the car.

"Hey, you two. Boys. Did you see what happened down there? Want to be on television tonight? Hey!" She turned to the cameraman. "Bennie, shoot their backs!" she snapped.

The strobe lights came on and Haydon whirled around.

"Bennie! You like your job? You want to keep it?"

The lights went out.

"Bennie!" the girl shrieked. "Shoot them! Turn the goddamn thing *on.*"

"There's nothing to *shoot,*" the cameraman argued defensively. "Four backs. What's that?"

"You little prick!" the girl screamed, flinging her steno pad down on the pavement. "You just lost your job anyway."

The newspaper reporter threw back his head and crowed and slapped the hood of the Volvo.

The girl stormed past the cameraman and got into the television station's white compact, marked with giant red call letters on its doors. She slammed the car in reverse, swiveled backward up the hill, and roared away.

"You silly bitch," the cameraman yelled. He shot her the finger when there was no chance of her seeing it. "She don't know her hole from an ass in the ground," he said.

The reporter was still laughing as he motioned for the cameraman to get into his car. They drove away together, waving to Hirsch as they passed the two detectives and the boys, who had not missed the import of what had happened. When Haydon spoke to them, they listened with new attentiveness.

"That's her house over there?"

Doug nodded. So did Rick, though he didn't know.

Haydon opened the car door and slid under the steering wheel. He radioed the station for the resident listing and computer name check, then stared across at the house as he waited for the information. Leo thanked the boys for their help. He gave each of them one of his cards and told them to call him if they thought of anything else the police might want to know. They walked away up the slight incline of the street, glancing back once before they disappeared around the corner.

"What do you think?" Leo asked as he looked around at the thick woods that provided seclusion for the surrounding homes. The woods were a desirable amenity much touted by the realtors.

"She wasn't wearing any underwear," Haydon said, still looking at the house.

"Yeah. I half expected to find them stuffed in her mouth."

"Lewis said she hadn't been in very long. Maybe we should drag the bayou along here."

Leo shrugged.

The night's coolness was quickly fading to warmth. In half an hour you could call it hot and in another hour you could call it sweltering. Above them the Gulf clouds drifted swiftly inland from the coast, fifty miles away to the southeast. It wasn't going to rain, but by noon the stifling humidity would make you wish it would.

Leo pulled off his sports jacket and threw it across the hood of the car. He wiped his oily forehead with a handkerchief and took out a pack of Certs. He'd been eating breath fresheners like candy since he'd quit smoking.

Haydon remained on the car seat, staring out the opened door. He wore a parchment-colored suit by Uomo with a crisp white shirt and a dun tie. Later in the day, when the heat would be lethal, he might remove his coat but the tie would stay firmly knotted. There were streaks of gray at the temples of his sable hair and if you looked closely, concentrating on the brown eyes flecked with amber, you would see the beginnings of creases angling in toward the outer corners, which turned downward when he smiled—which, lately, was seldom. He was olive-complected, with a good straight nose, and a mouth that could not be described as either full or thin. He was exactly six feet tall, and lean.

Leo turned to Haydon. "Why didn't you take the promotion?"

Haydon continued to stare across the street, but Hirsch thought he saw a flicker of a smile rise, then die out, at the edge of his mouth.

"I miscalculated," Haydon said. "I thought you'd ask me in the car on the way over here."

"I'm learning restraint," and Hirsch grinned. At twenty-six, he was ten years younger than Haydon and looked even younger, with his penchant for Bass Weejuns and Oxford-cloth button-down shirts. He wore the same Ray-Ban aviator sunglasses he had worn in college and was typical of a new breed seen with increasing frequency in the police academies. He hadn't stumbled into police work on a fluke, like many of Haydon's contemporaries. Rather, he had deliberately anticipated his career by taking a degree in psychology and two years of criminal law at the University of Texas Law School before he entered the academy. His attitudes about law enforcement were more like the Peace Corps attitudes of the Kennedy era than those of the men who had come out of the academies in response to the rampant rebellion of the sixties and seventies.

Haydon did not answer Hirsch's question or even act as if

14

he remembered what they had just said. Then, just as Hirsch was about to ask him again, Haydon said, "I thought I'd wait until I was forty."

"What?"

The radio hissed and Haydon leaned over and turned it up. Homicide's air frequency was separate from that of the rest of the department; the transmissions were usually informal and quite clear.

"Haydon?" Lieutenant Dystal's voice was slow, with redneck intonations. "I got a resident for you. A baby doll named Sally Steen, that's S-t-e-e-n. Forty-two years. Got a purty long sheet for prostitution. Mostly high-class call-girl stuff. Looks like Ed Mooney's dealt with her more'n anybody else in Vice. I guess he could give you a good rundown on her."

"Could you get me a printout on her and leave a message for Mooney to call me?"

"Will do."

"Would you also get the paperwork started on a search warrant so we can go through her place over here?"

"Okeydokey."

"We're going to see if anyone's home. If not, we'll go down to Ben Taub and see what happened to her."

"See you later," Dystal said, and the radio went dead.

Nobody answered the doorbell. Leo prowled around the edges of the house, trying to look in the windows without success. The place was expensive. If Sally Steen had bought it with the rewards of her profession, it was a cinch she didn't spend her time hanging out on street corners.

Reluctantly, the two detectives left without even sticking their heads in the door.

3

Ben Taub General Hospital sat on the northern edge of the vast Texas Medical Center complex across from Rice University and the green expanse of Hermann Park. As a charity hospital having the largest emergency facilities in Houston it caught the majority of the city's violent action. The green room of Ben Taub was the next best thing to an actual war for the young interns trying their hands at trauma cases.

The two detectives drove to the rear entrance of the hospital and turned into the driveway that gave access to the emergency room and morgue. They double-parked behind a car they recognized as belonging to one of the interns on duty and walked across the drive to the ramp where the morgue vans loaded. The morning air had already become oppressive as it bounced off the asphalt and hovered within the dank cement walls of the ramp. The gray metal elevator doors opened and they entered a battered cubicle that sank with glacial motion into the white-tile-and-stainless-steel world of the morgue. They stopped at a desk just inside the shiny swinging doors and introduced themselves to a girl

Hirsch thought was too pretty to work in a morgue. Haydon told her what they wanted and asked for Dr. Vanstraten.

"He's in autopsy right now," she said, taking a clipboard off the wall and flipping through the pages with long, ruby-nailed fingers. Her roan hair was shoulder length, swept back on both sides and held in place with tortoiseshell combs. Her speech was crisp, her lips cutting each word with exactitude. Hirsch fell in love with her mouth.

"Let's see," she said. "It's a Jane Doe, our second one this morning, marked 'possible homicide.' She's probably yours. You can go in. He'll be about halfway through. He got on her as soon as she came in."

Hirsch winced at her choice of words.

"We'll get a cup of coffee and come back," Haydon said. "Would you tell him, please?"

"Sure," she said, and smiled.

"She's new," Hirsch said as they retraced their steps.

"There's a new one almost every time we come down here," Haydon said.

"True."

By the time they had ridden the sullen elevator up to an automated snack bar, where they stoically sucked vending machine coffee from paper cups and then rode the elevator down again, Vanstraten had finished his autopsy and was talking on the telephone.

He sat on the corner of a second desk and talked in the confidential tones that Haydon was used to hearing from doctors, and that came naturally to the self-assured coroner. When he finished, he stood and shook hands with them, smiling easily.

"They're getting your samples ready," he said. "I hope you're not expecting something obvious with this one." Vanstraten's caramel coloring and fine Nordic features had always reminded Haydon of the luckless German theologian Dietrich Bonhöffer. Vanstraten was taller than Haydon by

17

three inches and had a solid frame that gave him the strength he needed in his daily wrestles with corpses. He was a natty dresser, given to three-piece suits with a distinctly Old World cut that drew attention in Houston's fast-paced haut monde, where he enjoyed a rather macabre popularity.

"I try never to expect anything," Haydon said.

"A very safe philosophy," Vanstraten concurred, not taking the remark too seriously. He glanced at Hirsch, who flicked his eyebrows noncommittally. Touching the clean part in his blond hair, Vanstraten said, "The report will be typed shortly after lunch, but I can give you an overview."

He folded his arms across his chest, exposing porcelain cuff links and a new, wafer-thin Concord Delirium on his stout, hairy wrist. Some of the homicide detectives referred to Vanstraten as the Gaudy Ghoul of Ben Taub, but Haydon saw him differently. He would have to. The chief medical examiner was hardly more elegant than the detective himself. They liked each other and had more in common than an unusual interest in cadavers.

"The woman is probably a prostitute. She's in her middle forties though she has the physique of a woman ten years younger. Her cervix is scarred from abortions, probably several of them, and she has herpes lesions around her genitalia and one at the right edge of her mouth. Not necessarily the same virus, of course. She has one bruise about six centimeters below her groin on the inside of her left thigh and a smaller one on her left calf. I think they're incidental to cause of death. The only other evidence of violence are several curious postmortem wounds on her buttocks. . . ."

"A couple of kids found her," Leo explained. "They poked around at her before they realized what they'd found."

"Mmm. Well, she seems to have died of acute asphyxia with fatal hypoxia," Vanstraten said. "Did she drown? I don't know. Maybe."

18

"Maybe? You can't tell?"

Vanstraten frowned slightly, a puzzled notation of Haydon's impatience. "It's not that simple," he said.

"You've never told me that about a drowning before."

"That makes sense. I don't recall you've ever brought me a suspected drowning before," Vanstraten said pointedly. "The fact is, there's no anatomic or chemical finding that's distinctly and uniquely characteristic of drowning. It can only be established by history, the circumstances surrounding death, and a complete autopsy to exclude other causes of death. It's a process of elimination. No one thing 'proves' drowning."

Vanstraten gestured outward with his crossed arms. "She was floating in water, her lungs were edematous. But a lot of things cause pulmonary edema. Like pneumonia. Often in drownings there are large quantities of foam protruding from the victim's mouth and nostrils. But this is also true with some drug-associated deaths. There was none here. However, there *was* a considerable amount of highly viscous saliva. About sixty percent of drowning deaths result in hemorrhaging in the middle ear. There was none here. There was no water in the stomach, also a common occurrence in drowning deaths. There was only a trace of alcohol. In short, we did find 'symptoms' of drowning and she *was* found floating in water, but other common attributes of a drowning death were not present. And she was a prostitute, which makes everything suspect. That's part of the history I mentioned." Vanstraten stopped. "You want me to go on?"

Haydon ignored the rhetorical question. "What about poison, then?"

"I don't think so. But I've taken tissue sections and we'll run toxicologic studies." Another smile. "Then I'll be able to give you a 'probable' cause of death."

One of Vanstraten's dieners came out of the autopsy

room with a small styrofoam box containing the samples required by the police laboratory and a manila folder with the pathologist's photographs. Hirsch took the container and sat down at the second desk and checked the contents against Homicide's Autopsy Sample Request form. Then he rolled the multicopy form into the typewriter and began filling it out.

"We got a rundown on the woman just before we came in," Haydon said, moving away from Hirsch's typing. "You're right. She's a prostitute. Leo will give you everything we know on the forms. What about narcotics?"

"If she used them, she didn't take them with a needle," Vanstraten said. "She was clean. Not even a hint of old scars. No olfactory signs of cocaine use either." He read Haydon's thoughts. "The gross anatomy was clean. If there was foul play we'll discover it in the laboratory, not from the body."

"That's terrific," Haydon said.

"Look at it from my point of view, Stuart. These sort of cases relieve the world of its most tedious occurrence: the unimaginative death. It's amazing. Unquestionably the most significant event after beginning life is ending it. Yet I am constantly reminded how little serious consideration people give to it. If Ms. Arendt believed evil was banal, she should have hung around death awhile."

Haydon waited tranquilly through Vanstraten's theatrical pause.

"Every day I see people who've abruptly traded this existence for another with apparently no more creativity than is required to turn on the tap and get a glass of water. If the poor woman died of disease, or accident, or suicide, then I can respect the cosmic implications. On the other hand, if someone devised her departure without resorting to the obvious, well, I can only be grateful for the diversion. As long as the whole matter is in the past

20

tense," he said, absolving himself of the moral faux pas of relishing too much what he should have wished prevented in the first place.

All this was said with a mixture of facetiousness and sincerity that could not easily be distinguished. Harl Vanstraten was the most unabashedly intuitive man of science Haydon had ever known.

Haydon's pager beeped at his waist. He snapped it off and looked around for a phone. The girl who was too pretty to work in a morgue pushed hers across the desk. It was Ed Mooney. Haydon told him what had happened and they agreed to meet at a drugstore on Montrose in half an hour.

Hirsch finished the form and ripped off the yellow copy to give to the roan-haired girl. He took a little extra time with her, asking if his corrections were legible on her copy, if she saw anything he'd missed.

"Okay," Haydon said to Vanstraten. "How soon can you let me know about the tests?" He knew, give or take a few days, but Leo was trying desperately to make a good impression with the girl. He could use another couple of minutes.

"The drug results, tomorrow. The tissue sections, five days, maybe a week. The toxicological tests, two to four weeks if they're put into the rotating schedule with everything else. If it's urgent, vital, I could make it closer to two weeks than four."

Haydon shook his head. "It's not urgent." Then, "That's a shame, isn't it?"

"What?"

"That it's not urgent."

A smile of amusement formed slowly on Vanstraten's face as he reached into the breast pocket of his coat and withdrew a gold cigarette case. He offered a cigarette to

Haydon and took one himself. He lit them both with a matching lighter.

"That's a melancholy observation," he said.

Haydon inhaled deeply of the filterless Dunhill. He turned to look at Hirsch and the girl too pretty to work in a morgue.

"Nevertheless . . ." he said.

4

The Grove Pharmacy sat in the middle of the block between Montrose and Roseland and was flanked on either side by a neighborhood washeteria and a secondhand bookstore. Hirsch let Haydon out at the curb and continued downtown to do the paperwork on Sally Steen, who had now become HPD Homicide Incident number 6-14-82-01.

Ed Mooney was waiting at a black-topped dinette table in the coffee shop and grill at the back of the pharmacy. He was chewing on a hard doughnut and drinking milk. Haydon sat down and Mooney raised his milk in a toasting gesture and washed down a cud of doughnut.

"Better have one," he said, stretching his thick neck to swallow. "They'll never be any fresher than they are now."

The coffee shop had only four tables and a six-stool lunch counter. Haydon looked over to the counter and was caught by the riveting stare of a broad-faced girl with a complexion like raw hamburger. "Coffee," he said.

"I can't drink that crap anymore," Mooney said. "No more. Ulcer." He pressed the fingers of one hand into his

23

stomach and Haydon noticed with surprise, because he hadn't noticed before, that Mooney was getting fat.

"I thought milk was bad for ulcers. Sours in the stomach or something."

"It's controversial," Mooney said with authority. "It seems to do okay by me."

The girl brought Haydon's coffee and Mooney took the last bite of his doughnut as he turned in his chair and leaned back against a display rack of Dr. Scholl's foot pads. The plastic packets rustled as he shifted his weight.

"So what's the matter?" he mumbled through the doughnut before he swallowed. "What happened to Sally?" Mooney's bushy ginger eyebrows were raised attentively and Haydon noticed his ruddy complexion was beginning to suffer from the intense Texas sun. A craze of tiny blood vessels had appeared on the upper parts of his cheeks.

"Some kids found her floating in Buffalo Bayou. There's nothing to go on immediately. Vanstraten's running tests."

"You mean she wasn't shot or stabbed or anything?"

"No. Van didn't see anything wrong from the gross examination."

Mooney fixed his eyes on the white tessellated tile of the old drugstore. "You know, sometimes when those gals get around Sally's age they see more problems ahead than good times. They'll live through rough-ups by pimps and tricks, live through bad trips with drugs, live through a dozen desertions by guys they just knew were going to love them forever—survive worse treatment than a Viet vet—and then suddenly snuff their own candle. Maybe Sally was just worn out by it all."

"Was she the sort to give in like that?"

Mooney thoughtfully gathered his bottom lip in his fingers and slowly shook his head. "No, really; she wasn't."

"How long had she been in the business?"

"She goes back a long time. Never able to marry out of it,

24

which is what usually happens to those who get out grace-fully. She used to be top-of-the-line, worked the major hotels. But the call-girl market is hard on the ego. You have to look like you stepped out of a *Penthouse* double-pager. High-riding tits, tight skin, no wrinkles. That means you got to be between eighteen and twenty-five.''

''Vanstraten said she was in great shape.''

''Good for her. Sally stayed at it longer than most because she used to work her ass off in a spa over on San Felipe. She was plucky, but it eventually caught up with her. She dropped out of sight for a while; I think she tried to break into the same level of action in Dallas. When she surfaced again she'd taken one step down the ladder and was doing 'spots.' ''

''How could she afford the fancy house? Or was it hers?''

Mooney grinned. ''She was smart, Stuart. Working spots may be a hard life, moving from city to city and putting out for an unpredictable clientele, but if a girl's sharp she can pull down two thousand a week in that business. Sally made a deal with herself. Ten months on the circuit and not a day more. For the first time in her life she began socking it away like a miser. At the end of ten months she had a bundle banked away. She bought that place on Pinewold because of the seclusion and the high-class address.''

''She couldn't have made enough to buy the house and re-tire too. What was she doing?''

''The benefit of working spots, aside from the money, is the chance to make contacts.'' Mooney suppressed a belch. ''When Sally came back to Houston and bought her little re-treat, she left the whoring life behind. That is, attitude-wise. Now she was just a nice-looking woman with a good address and lots of company. When her old tricks came to Houston, which was often enough to keep her calendar full, she had guests. Just like any other swinging single having a friend

25

over for a fuck. Only these friends left big bucks on her fancy wet bar when they left. It was good times all around.''

Mooney drank the last little bit of milk in the squatty ribbed glass and winced as he pressed one hand into his stomach at the beltline. ''No, as I think about it, things were going real good for Sally. I don't think she would have dunked her life away in that stinking bayou.''

''Who'd she work with when she had a weekend set?''

''Only one girl. Judith Croft. Judith, not Judy. Sally used her exclusively when she had combos. They worked well together. Personal friends.''

The girl with advanced acne came over and poured more coffee into Haydon's cup. He hadn't wanted any more but he thanked her. He poured two packets of sugar into his cup and stirred it solemnly.

A young Vietnamese girl holding tightly to the hand of a small boy came in the front door and timidly approached the lunch counter. They stood behind the stools silently, studying the menu displayed in red plastic letters above the grill. The waitress looked at them without speaking. After a brief, soft-spoken consultation with the little boy, the girl ordered a single ''brakon sahn-whis.''

''To go or eat here?'' the waitress asked.

The Vietnamese girl nodded.

The waitress hesitated a beat, started to say something, then shrugged and turned away to start the sandwich.

When the strips of bacon hit the overheated grill with a searing hiss and the smell of salty pork reached the two detectives, Mooney looked at Haydon and said, ''I heard you turned down lieutenant.''

Haydon didn't know what to say. He shifted in his chair.

''Different strokes . . .'' Mooney said. There was more than a trace of bitterness in his voice. His puffy hands twisted a paper napkin into a tight screw.

Haydon sipped the damned coffee. It was better than having to say something.

"Six years is a long time to be on the shelf," Mooney said.

They had made detective third together. Mooney had been a hotshot. He was savvy, alert, and aggressive. He moved quickly to second and first while Haydon seemingly stood still. Then Mooney's career hit a wall. Young men who move fast in any organization make enemies they will have to watch out for the rest of their careers, and the police department is no exception. Somebody put the brakes on Mooney's hard-driving rise up the ladder.

Looking back, they both saw the inevitability of what had happened. Aside from being sharp, Mooney had no influence, no personal friends in advantageous positions to look out for him when his aggressiveness rubbed the wrong people the wrong way. He was too busy doing what he did best to play politics, and suddenly he found himself way out front . . . all alone. He was bounced around from department to department until he ended up more or less permanently in Vice.

"Those fuckers," Mooney said. "I guess if I hadn't been such a bad-ass I could've been there too." He sighed a fat man's sigh. "But look at Dystal. Hell, he was no shrinking violet. He went on up. Didn't have special buddies." He shook his head. "Those fuckers."

Over the years Haydon had watched Mooney's stalled career eat at him like a strong acid, and yet Mooney stubbornly refused to get out or tame the wild Irish temper that contributed to his unpopularity with a cautious administration sensitive to cops who might someday drag the force into the headlines with charges of police brutality. Haydon used Mooney on loan to Homicide whenever he could, but otherwise his career wasn't going anywhere. All of his wars were

27

merry and all of his songs were sad; he was his own worst enemy.

"Why'd you turn it down?" Mooney asked. "I'm just curious."

"I'm not sure myself," Haydon said. "It didn't seem to be the right time for it."

He was staring steadily at the muddy coffee and could feel Mooney's eyes on him. When he looked up, Mooney turned away, a scornful smile fixed uncomfortably on his mouth.

5

Judith Croft lived in an expensive condominium complex less than two miles from where Leo Hirsch, search warrant in hand, was now going through the personal effects of Sally Steen. Haydon stopped his car at the empty gatehouse and squinted at a bright Plexiglas-covered map showing the village-sized streets, all of which started with Briar: Briarwood, Briarlane, Briarmeadow, Briargrove. Very cute.

He found the Briarcliff address at the end of a cul-de-sac on the farthest side of the complex. The condo was a decent French style, which was at least one step up from the imitation Elizabethan half-timbering that had been done to death by the apartment builders a few years back. He followed a brick sidewalk through a gate in a box hedge and around a bank of oleanders into a private courtyard. The bricks in the courtyard had been recently washed and a humid, loamy odor from the flower beds hung in the air. He stood in the shade of the recessed doorway and rang the bell.

There was a moment's wait before the door opened a few inches. Haydon held up his shield.

"Miss Croft?"

"Oh, Christ!"

Haydon could see only a pale-blue eye and short straight black hair. He caught the fragrance of shampoo.

"Miss Croft?" he repeated.

"Yes, yes," she said with resignation.

"I'm Detective Haydon. May I come in?"

The door opened a little farther to reveal a face with a remarkably beautiful structure and marble-white skin.

"Do you have a search warrant?"

"No, but then I don't intend to search anything. You don't have to let me in, but I think you ought to."

"Oh, come on, dammit."

The door swung open and Haydon stepped into a bright, sunny room overlooking a lawn that sloped to the bayou in back. The room was furnished in yellows and greens, with perky plants in wicker baskets placed occasionally among the furniture, which was arranged toward the lawn and the bayou.

Judith Croft closed the door behind him and led him around to the collection of sofa and armchairs. She was tall and wore a tea-rose peignoir that reached to the floor and was so sheer it was transparent in the bright room. As he followed her he could clearly see she had no suntan at all. He could even see the dimples above her hips. She turned, aware of herself, of her high breasts with dusky areolas pimpling the gauzy peignoir, and settled in an armchair upholstered in a wheaty fabric. He caught a glimpse of the dark triangle between her thighs before she gathered the folds of the peignoir in her lap.

She gestured toward the sofa. "Go ahead, sit down," she said impatiently.

He sat across from her as she picked up a sweaty glass with an orange slice floating in ice and what must have been vodka or gin. He guessed her to be in her early twenties. She was delicious to look at, her shiny hair framing her face in

30

the sharp angles of a one-length bob. Her movements were lithe, and reflected the confidence of a woman who had long ago realized the intimidating power of her beauty. She was sophisticated. Très chic. There wasn't a detective on the force, except himself, who could afford to spend the night with her.

She tucked one leg under her in the plush chair and looked at him over the top of her glass, the sweaty rim of which she caressed softly against her pale lips.

"You work with Sally Steen, I believe," Haydon said.

She didn't respond, but sipped from her drink. Her fingers were interlocked around the tall glass.

Haydon saw no profit in playing games with her. He'd cut right through the shit.

"She was found dead this morning, floating in Buffalo Bayou not a hundred yards from her home."

The ice in the glass shuddered and the passive expression Judith Croft had chosen to hide behind froze into a stupefied blankness.

"It's not yet apparent how she died. We're hoping the medical examiner will be able to establish the cause of death. In the meantime we're trying to learn as much as we can about her movements during the last few days."

Judith Croft set her glass on an end table of copper and jade tile. "Are you sure it's her?" She had to clear her throat.

Haydon nodded. It was odd how often people asked that question.

She tossed her head to clear the bangs from her forehead. "This is incredible." She swallowed hard. "Good God." She spoke only to herself.

"Had you seen her recently?"

Haydon waited while the girl's thoughts chased the intruding concept of death. She heard his question, like a delayed echo, from the far side of a long silence.

31

"No." Her eyes came back to him. "No, I hadn't seen her for three or four days."

"When?"

"When. Oh, God, let's see." She ran a milk-glass hand through her straight raven hair. "Four days ago."

"A working visit?"

"What does it matter?" she said coldly. "Are you with Vice?"

"No."

"I didn't think so. Homicide?"

"That's right."

"Then you've talked to Ed Mooney."

"Yes."

"Mooney's nice. He's not a goon."

Haydon wondered what that meant, from Mooney's perspective.

"Why were you over there?"

"She called me. She had the blahs, was running a fever and was coming down with something. We had a few drinks and watched a Redford movie on HBO. By the time it was over she was getting headachy, so I came home."

"That was the last time you saw her?"

"Right. Well, it was the last time I *saw* her. I talked to her again the next day. The day before yesterday."

"What time?"

"Midmorning. About ten o'clock. She was still feeling rotten and wanted me to entertain one of her people."

"And you did?"

"Yes, I did. I didn't call her yesterday. It just wasn't convenient." Her eyes lost their focus on him and she grew thoughtful again. "But I called her today. To see how she was doing. When she didn't answer I assumed she was feeling better and had gone out."

"Do you know of anyone who might have been in contact

with her since you? Someone who might have seen her yesterday?"

"No. I'm not familiar with her . . . schedule."

"Do you know if any of her acquaintances have ever given her trouble? Anybody ever harass her?"

"Sally didn't put up with that sort of thing. If somebody got the least bit rough, she simply wouldn't be available to them anymore. She let the S and M crowd take care of that."

"How long have you known her?"

"Two, nearly three years now."

"You've been working with her that long?"

"Just about."

"And you can't think of anyone who might wish her harm? Someone with a volatile personality, maybe?"

"Volatile? Was she . . . shot or something? I thought you said you didn't know how she died."

"We don't. I'm guessing that maybe someone had something against her. Maybe someone hotheaded enough to have killed her. When you don't have any facts you do a certain amount of guessing and see where that gets you."

She thought about that. "Well, sure, you meet all kinds. This isn't the same as spots or being on the street, but you still meet a lot of different kinds of people. Odds are you're going to get some peculiar ones occasionally. But I can't say I could give you the name of anyone you could quiz for murdering Sally. I just can't feature anyone like that."

Two perpendicular creases had appeared between Judith Croft's embossed eyebrows, and these alone constituted a frown on her smooth face. Both hands lay in her lap, and she unconsciously flicked together her pink thumbnails.

"This is incredible," she repeated. "You really think she was murdered?"

"I didn't say that. We're just trying to find out what

33

happened." He watched her features. "She could have drowned accidentally."

She gave him an oblique glance.

"She wasn't drunk," he said. "There wasn't enough alcohol in her blood. She could have committed suicide."

"No. I think I knew her well enough to rule that out. I can't see it."

"She could have had the wrong combination of pills."

"No way," Croft said flatly. "No dope. That was anathema. It was nothing moral with her; it was just that she made good money, better than good, and she wanted to keep bringing it in. She wouldn't touch the stuff. Alcohol, sure, lots of it. A little toke to mellow things out. Fine. But that was all. No more than that."

Haydon waited.

"What about her illness? Could she have died from that?" she asked.

"Sure, I suppose. But why was she floating in the bayou?"

"Was she raped?"

"If she was, it wasn't obvious from the initial autopsy examination. And considering her occupation, the presence of sperm wouldn't mean anything."

Judith Croft's eyes hit space again as she mulled over the direction the conversation was taking. Haydon looked around the clean, bright room, which merged into a formal dining room and, beyond that, a glimpse of a kitchen. She was a very neat woman with excellent taste. He looked at her again. She was gorgeous. His gaze went back to the rosettes of her nipples beneath the peignoir. He had been staring at them for several moments when he felt her eyes on him.

He pulled his notebook from his jacket pocket.

"Could you give me the names of the clubs Miss Steen frequented the most?"

Miss Steen. Jesus. He was amused at himself. Formality was always his knee-jerk reaction to getting caught at being an average red-blooded human being.

"Club Bragança. Maxie's. The Boulevard. Copa's. La Brasilia."

"Three Latin clubs?"

"Brazilian. Sally loved Brazilian music. Those places have live bands."

"Did you go to these clubs with her?"

"Sometimes. We both like the Brazilian thing."

"Did you pick up tricks at these clubs?"

"Sometimes."

"Do you think you know most of her regulars?"

"I would say so; yes."

"Would you be willing to go over her list of tricks with us, give us some idea of the personalities of these men as you see them? It would be confidential, of course."

"Where did you get a list of her tricks?" She watched him closely.

"If we get a list."

She took her drink from the end table. She sipped slowly until the clear liquid was half gone. Haydon knew what he was asking. It could mean the end of a very lucrative career for her. She and Sally Steen charged rates that eliminated the vast majority of men who lived in, and traveled through, Houston. Their clientele, therefore, included prominent men willing to pay a high fee not only for their entertainment but also for the assurance that their fun remained totally secret. No detective could guarantee an informing call girl protection from the press. Secrets about murder are hard to keep. If Croft's name hit the papers, former tricks wouldn't want to admit they even knew a call girl, much less continue business as usual. If word got out, Judith Croft's fast-lane living would come to a screeching halt.

"I'll have to think about it," she said.

"Fine." Haydon stood and put his notebook back into his pocket. He handed her one of his cards. "If you think of anything else that might help, would you give me a call?"

She nodded, stood, and followed him to the front door. He opened it, stepped outside, and turned for one last question.

"She didn't have any family?"

The girl shook her head. "Her parents are dead. That's it as far as I know. She never talked about anyone else." Then tentatively, "What about a funeral?"

"If there's no family, no friends"—he looked at her—"the county will take care of it. Pay for it out of her own checking account." It was a bleak conclusion to a life on the sunny side of the street.

Judith Croft's eyes reddened as she stood in front of him, her naked body illuminated through the peignoir by the sun-lit room behind her.

"My God," she said huskily. "You would have thought it would have ended so differently."

The situation, the girl, and the remark suddenly struck Haydon the wrong way. He spoke before he knew what he was going to say.

"Just how did you think it was supposed to end?" he snapped. "Did you think you two were supposed to live charmed lives, that you were entitled to good times right up to the end?"

The girl looked shocked, puzzled, then sober, in rapid succession. Her eyes locked with his and became as opaque as lapis stones as she slowly closed the door between them.

6

"Sally Steen was a very organized woman," Hirsch said, lifting the cardboard box of things he had brought from the home on Pinewold onto the adjoining desktops.

Leo had gotten the search warrant from Lieutenant Dystal and had spent the afternoon going through the house. When he finally got back to the office with his cardboard boxes, it was late afternoon. Haydon had called Mooney over from the Vice section to go through Steen's things with them. He would be the best man to interpret what Hirsch had found.

Haydon and Mooney shoved the CRT screens and overflowing wire baskets against the wall and put the telephone in the top basket. Haydon took out a tablet of paper and a pencil to record the items as Hirsch threw them on the desk in front of the other two detectives.

Hirsch slapped down a manila packet. "American National health insurance and hospitalization. Strong policy. The premiums cost her a fortune, but she wouldn't have had to pay out a cent to go to the hospital."

He pulled out another manila envelope and dropped it. "Metropolitan World life insurance policy. Twenty thousand dollars. Beneficiary: Judith Croft. TransContinental life insurance policy. One hundred thousand. Beneficiary: Judith Croft."

Mooney whistled.

Hirsch dropped a white legal-sized document. "A photocopy of her will. It's pretty straightforward. Judith Croft gets everything."

"No shit?" Mooney reached for the envelope and took out the document. He read it quickly, scanning the formalities. "Isn't that something?"

Another envelope hit the desk. "Three business contracts verifying that Steen owned percentages in three clubs: Copa's, La Brasilia, Club Bragança. The percentages vary and they aren't big. The most is twenty percent in La Brasilia. The other two are ten percent each."

Hirsch pulled a long fat envelope with a glassine window from the box. "And she owned property. These are mortgage papers for a condo she leases on Quenby in West University Place."

"I underestimated Sally's business ah-cue-men," Mooney said. "That's near Rice, in your area, Stuart."

Haydon opened the mortgage papers. "Looks like she bought it about a year ago, fourteen months."

"And now for dessert," Hirsch said. With both hands, he reached into the box and pulled out two heavy photo albums and slammed them down. On top of them he placed a black five-by-seven Guilford address book.

Initially the photographs did not portray actual sexual activity, but there was little doubt about what was going on. Nude women were in many of the shots and while Sally herself showed up in only a few of them, Haydon saw the gloriously delicious body and smile of Judith Croft much more often.

The three detectives went through the two albums together. From the appearance of the clothes and cars in some of the backgrounds, all the photos were recent. The settings were varied: ski slopes, swimming pools, beaches, interiors. They studied the men's faces carefully. It was the part Haydon hated the most. There was still a lingering dread that carried over from his own days with the vice squad. Too often there were familiar faces, faces you had seen on television, sponsoring benefits for crippled children or breaking ground for new buildings or running for office. Faces that didn't fit their public images in their present context, and faces that were unfamiliar but belonged to prominent men you had heard of though never seen until they surfaced in the ignominious little colored squares of a prostitute's private collection.

By the time they had gotten to the last half of the album, Haydon's neck muscles had tightened sufficiently to give him the first dull throbbings of a headache. Mooney, sitting on the right side, was lifting the large pages and peeping under them in anticipation.

"Okay, boys, here come the squirm shots," he said, and spread open the next pages with a proud smirk. In a series of a dozen five-by-seven pictures, three different groups of naked men and women were photographed through separate red, blue, and yellow filters. The pictures were taken from an angle slightly above the revelers, who writhed in fleshy contortions upon a large round bed. Liquor bottles cluttered a bedside table and the flash from the camera had been caught by numerous mirrors on the walls and ceiling, causing star bursts to careen into the camera lens and appear in unpredictable parts of the photographs, occasionally obscuring a face. The naked bodies captured by each of the colored filters shimmered in the Day-Glo brilliance of ruby, sapphire, or gold.

"Look at that, will you?" Hirsch said.

"Quit slobbering," Mooney said. "For two hours of

onesies and twosies like that, Leo, you'd have to cough up about three-quarters of your monthly paycheck.''

"It might be worth it," Hirsch said.

"Sure as shit. Then you'd have nice photos like these floating around for every con artist in the city to blackmail you with."

"You're jaded, Mooney."

"You're damn right. This is as close as you can get to these people without taking a risk. All you can do is look. Anything more than that and you're going to get burned."

Haydon opened his desk drawer and took out a magnifying glass. He played it up and down over the photographs. "I wonder if all these pictures were taken in the same room."

"Probably." Mooney leaned down close. "You'd be surprised how creative these baby dolls can be with that junk. Strobe lights, black lights, mirrors, reflective materials. I don't know what-all kinds of crap."

"Leo, is this room in Steen's house?"

"No, I didn't see anything like it."

Mooney took the magnifying glass from Haydon and pulled the album over in front of him to get a better look. He took his time concentrating on a red picture, then a blue one, and then a yellow one. He went back to the red one, breathing heavily as his stomach pressed against the edge of the desk.

"Stuart," he said after a prolonged silence. "You may have something. Yeah." He rubbed a fat thumb against one of the pictures as if he would wipe away the monochromatic effect that prevented the distinction of detail. "Yeah, you may have it. And I think the *furniture* is colored. The same color as the filter."

Haydon and Hirsch looked at the pictures again while Mooney elaborated.

"In the red shots everybody's skin is pink, which is what

40

it should be if you shoot white skin with a red filter," he said. "But the furniture is a uniform shade of a darker red. If this was an average room, some of the furniture would be lighter or darker depending on whatever the color was that mixed with the red filter. Right? Same with the other pictures. The bodies are yellow, but the furniture is a uniform darker gold; the bodies are blue, but the furniture, the whole room, is a uniform darker blue."

"Sure, that's right," Hirsch said slowly, following through with Mooney's reasoning. "If everything in the room was white, all of it would more closely match the lighter shades of the naked bodies. But the rooms and the furniture are consistently much darker."

"Exactly," Mooney said. "What we got here is a red room, a blue room, and a yellow room shot through filters of corresponding colors."

"Or flooded with lights of corresponding colors and shot without colored filters," Haydon said.

"I don't know if that'd do this," Mooney said, looking down at the photos again.

"I'll check it out with Murray down in the lab. We'll want blow-ups anyway."

"Wait a minute," Hirsch said. "It *is* the same room. The furniture's identical, it's in the same arrangement, same pictures on the walls, same clothes chests, closet doors, everything."

Again the three detectives crouched over the album together, passing the magnifying glass back and forth and taking turns getting down close to the garish photographs. Finally Haydon straightened up and tossed the magnifying glass on the pictures.

"They're three different rooms," he said.

"Bullshit," Mooney said doubtfully.

"Look at them." Haydon used his pencil and pointed at a clothes chest in the red room. The pencil lead touched the handles of a middle drawer. "Curved pulls, the kind you hook your fingers through. The other drawers in the chest have these round pulls." He moved the pencil lead to another drawer. "It's the same in all the red pictures, but not in the blue and yellow ones." He pointed to the alarm clock amid the clutter of liquor bottles on the nightstand in the yellow room. "Little wind-up thing with the bells on top. Look in the other two rooms. Electric clocks. The nightstand in the blue room is shorter than the bed. In the other two rooms they're slightly higher."

"They're obviously intended to appear identical," Hirsch said.

Haydon nodded. "Someone has a quirky mind."

Mooney gave a consenting grunt. "And the quality of the furnishings ain't ticky-tacky, that's for sure."

Haydon stood and let Mooney and Hirsch go through the photographs, trying to one-up each other by finding additional discrepancies in the rooms. He thought a moment, then picked up the address book and thumbed through it. It contained only first names, and all the telephone numbers had out-of-town area codes. There wasn't a single Houston number in the book.

"Leo, where'd you find this stuff?" he asked.

Hirsch looked up. "In a filing cabinet behind a bunch of dresses in her bedroom closet. I guess it was her bedroom. It was the only one of the three that was actually lived in."

"Wasn't locked?"

"What, the filing cabinet? Sure. I had to go out to the car and get a tire tool to pry it open."

"Was this all that was in there?"

"No. I've got another box here with all her canceled checks, receipts for purchases, things like that."

"I don't think we have it all." Haydon tossed the address book on the desk and Mooney picked it up. It didn't take him long to see what Haydon meant.

"Maybe this is just her old spot list. Maybe she just saved it for . . . whatever."

Haydon walked around to his side of the desk and sat down. He absently fiddled with the keys of the CRT.

"A lot of those pictures were made out of town," he said. "Some out of state. You think *any* of them were made in Houston?"

"Maybe not," Mooney said. He looked at the insurance policies and other legal documents that had already been carefully labeled and put in individual manila folders when Hirsch found them. "She was careful, all right. If she didn't incriminate locals by leaving their names and numbers laying around, it seems consistent she wouldn't have an album full of their photographs either."

"Let's say none of the pictures were taken in Houston. I thought she'd quit working out of town."

"Who says she was working in these shots?" Mooney said. "Hell, even a whore needs a vacation."

"Those shots don't look like vacation."

Mooney shrugged and took the magnifying glass again. He started with the first series of monochromatic photographs.

Haydon looked up at Hirsch. "Leo, why don't you go through that second box and see if you can find out who her lawyer is. If Judith Croft doesn't know about her beneficiary role in Steen's will, I'd like to keep her from finding out for a while. We need to find out who's leasing the condo too."

Hirsch stood and pulled his arms forward in a stiff stretch. "First thing in the morning?"

Haydon glanced at his watch. "Sorry. First thing in the morning's fine. Thanks, Leo." It was nearly six-thirty.

Hirsch got his coat, told them goodbye, and walked out through the nearly empty squad room. Haydon watched him go, suddenly feeling tired.

"Well, bless my ass," Mooney said. He was standing,

43

one knee in a swivel chair as he bore down close to one of the blue pictures. Haydon looked across the desk.

Mooney put a thick forefinger below the face of a laughing blonde sprawled across the circular bed. A muscleless man was on his hands and knees over her and had buried his face in one of her heavy breasts. The bodies of another couple covered her left side, and her face was visible only in a little wedge of space between the other girl's back and the back of the muscleless man's head.

"Her name's Sandy Kielman. She died recently from an overdose. She was expensive, but she was laying down a lot of mileage. I'd known her for about a year, but I didn't know she knew Sally."

"An overdose?"

"Yeah. She really wasn't a doper, not many of these call girls are, but a girl friend said she'd been sick for a few days with some kind of respiratory thing. I guess staying cooped up was giving her the heebie-jeebies or something, so she took some yellow jackets to calm things down." He snapped his fingers. "That was it. It wasn't much, but she wasn't that big a girl." He looked down at the photograph. "Except for her tits."

"When was this?"

"About three weeks ago. Some of your people looked into it. Wallace and Jenkins, I think. Wallace filled me in on it." Mooney nodded at the pictures. "She's in all four of these blue-room photos, but that's the only one where her face is showing. I wouldn't even have seen her except for that one shot. Funny."

"Kielman's girl friend said she'd been sick a few days prior to her death?"

"Yeah. Flu bug or something."

"That's what Croft said about Steen. Said she was running a fever, headachy, coming down with something."

Mooney turned and sat down in the swivel chair and faced

Haydon. "What's the matter? You think you got a roll going here?"

"It's possible. How many call girls have died in Houston during the last few years?"

"Just call girls? No spots or streetwalkers?"

"Just call girls."

"Well, none that I know about."

"Now we have two within three weeks. The photographs make me think Steen had something going a lot more complicated than an expensive toss in the sheets for executives. I can't help feeling there's a new twist in here somewhere."

"A new twist." Mooney was unimpressed.

"You said Sally worked almost exclusively with Croft, but here's Kielman and some other girls we haven't even identified yet. And I don't see Croft in any of these colored-room shots."

"But neither is Sally. Maybe she didn't have anything to do with these people. Maybe somebody just gave her these photos." Mooney tapped the colored pictures with the end of a pencil. "Hell, nothing says she's connected to all this."

"You just said you didn't know Kielman knew Steen. *You're* making the assumption they knew each other."

"I just said it. I didn't give it any thought."

"Gut feelings," Haydon said. "That's even better than logic. And what about Kielman and Steen having similar symptoms before they died?"

"Stuart," Mooney said. "Those symptoms are as common as dirt. Everything from a head cold to the bubonic plague starts out with headaches and fever."

"There's more to it than that. There's enough here to make you wonder." Haydon leaned forward in his chair and looked across his desk to the album of photographs in front of Mooney. Sandy Kielman's upside-down face laughed up at him.

"There's enough here to make *you* wonder, Stuart. The

45

thing with you is you have a devious mind. That's why you stay in this fuckin' business. But I'll tell you something: You get carried away and let your intelligence show through. You outdo these people, give 'em too much credit in the brains department.''

"I want to know how they got sick."

Mooney grinned. "You think there's a Typhoid Harry out there in the cement jungle giving our little hometown girls pneumonia?"

Haydon was quiet, then he reached across and closed the album. "I think I'll sleep on it."

"I think that's a good idea," Mooney said.

7

Haydon's route home did not require him to travel the freeways that embraced Houston like tentacles of sargasso reaching in from the Gulf of Mexico to strangle the city with congested veins of shimmering cement. Instead he turned from the blistering downtown canyons of steel and glass with their constant reverberation of new construction and entered the old neighborhood of Montrose, where a boulevard lined with palms led through an inner-city community as eccentric and aberrant as any in the distended metropolis.

Houston has no zoning laws. The supreme authority is money. It is the impetus for manic growth, growth so uncontrolled and uninhibited that it approaches the obscene. The city lies wide open like a promiscuous and greedy woman who gives herself with abandon to anyone who can afford her and wants her. Many can and do. Montrose is one of the countless offspring of her debaucheries.

It had been an upper-middle-class neighborhood of the thirties and forties. Two-story homes with porch swings and green, neatly trimmed yards sat quietly on oak-shaded streets where the only distractions in the languid summer af-

47

ternoons had been the occasional slapping of screen doors and the thrumming of metal-wheeled roller skates on sidewalks.

It was, incredibly, still that, but it had become much more too. The young mothers of the 1940s had become the widows of the 1980s. Rather than lose the big homes they could no longer maintain, they had converted them into boardinghouses and apartments for college students and young career seekers who weren't yet earning enough to move to the more expensive apartment complexes farther downtown. Convenience stores sprang up in the middle of quiet blocks and some of the old homes were converted to art galleries with trendy beauty salons upstairs, or into stylishly laid-back offices for hard-driving young lawyers who wanted to be near the action downtown.

In addition, the gay community had alighted on Montrose like a gaudy butterfly on a fading rose; and Westheimer, the main artery which cut through the area from downtown west to Loop 610, had become a cheesy strip of massage parlors, coo clubs, body-art shops, and funky restaurants with hanging plants, neon artwork, and topless waitresses. The crime rate had undergone changes too. Montrose now saw a good portion of the city's homicides.

But the bohemian life of Montrose stopped cold in the steady, righteous stare of Broad Acres, its neighbor, where Haydon lived in a world that had not changed, and never would. Older than River Oaks, the enclave of the nouveau riche, Broad Acres was exclusive, with the patina of history saving its mansions from ostentation. Life here was understood in terms of a different reality. There was no moil of humanity searching insanely for that elusive something which could only hope to be grasped through incessant movement. Here serenity was pervasive. The families in these stately homes knew exactly who they were, where they were going, and most importantly, where they had come from. Old money.

As Haydon rolled down his window to let the fragrance of freshly mown lawns wash away the heat and staleness the car carried with it from downtown, the tolling of the tower bells of Rice University a few blocks away drifted over the oak-arbored lawns. He stopped at the pillared entrance of his drive, pushed the remote-control button, and waited for the wrought-iron gates to scrape open. His eyes caught a lichen-green stain running down the Belgian slate roof to the limestone lintel above a third-story window. He wondered if he should have it checked. How long did slate roofs last? Forever, probably.

He drove through the gates and circled the brick drive to the porte cochere, where he parked the dun-colored department car behind his own royal-blue Jaguar Vanden Plas. Getting out of the car, he walked over to the edge of the lawn to wait for the old collie who was already making his way from his hideout beneath the gnarled wisteria that grew over the front wall. Cinco managed a bit of a canter, then slowed to a measured hobble. Though each passing summer took its toll on the old dog, his white-tipped tail still swung metronomically as he approached Haydon, who patted and talked to him as he ruffled his mane. Haydon regarded the collie with sad affection. His muzzle was graying in a codgerly way and small scaly spots were appearing on the ridge of his nose and on the tips of his ears, like liver spots on an old man's hands.

The two of them walked around to the side of the house and followed a gently curving arbor, covered with trumpet vines, to a broad walled-in lawn crowded with citrus trees. In a daily ritual, they wandered through the grassy rows of trees while Haydon checked the nubby beginnings of summer fruit and made a mental note to remind Pablo to change the fertilizer ratio. A mourning dove soughed in the ebony

49

trees as they turned back toward the house. They climbed the terrace steps, Cinco with careful, arthritic movements and Haydon leisurely, in consideration of the old dog. Once at the top, they made the rounds of the mammoth terra-cotta urns that stood at intervals along the balustrade. Cinco waited sleepily as Haydon stopped at each urn and took a single blossom from the lavish bougainvilleas, whose dazzling cerise flowers burned like fireworks in the shadows.

Cinco gratefully stretched out on the cool terrace while Haydon unlocked the French doors to the wide hallway that led through the house to the front. He picked up the mail from a small table where Gabriela had left it and went into the kitchen. A tray covered with a starched white cloth sat on a butcher's block in the center of the square room. Haydon put the mail and the bougainvilleas on the tray, got a small glass from the cabinet and a half-empty bottle of Chablis from the wine rack, and took everything into the library. He put the tray and glass on a refectory table and opened the French doors from the library to the terrace. Stepping out, he filled the small bowl that sat next to Cinco's paws with Chablis. The collie's tail fluttered slightly in appreciation before he began lapping at the wine without even bothering to stand. Haydon went back inside, uncovered the tray, and began peeling the bowlful of pink shrimp, which he dipped in Gabriela's rémoulade sauce as he ate.

When he finished, he sat back to go through the mail while he sipped wine. There was a large manila envelope from his lawyer. It was approaching the end of June and there were third-quarter decisions to be anticipated, stocks to reevaluate, finances to arrange. There was a bill from Federico Sodi for the last two suits he had made and a bill from the nursery for the new shrubbery Pablo had ordered. He stared a moment at a colorful postcard with a picture of cherry blossoms reflected in the Tidal Basin, with the Lincoln Memorial in the background. He turned it over and saw it was from Pearson, a homicide detective who had taken his family on an early vacation to Washington. There was a brochure from a new pizza place on Audubon Street and a letter from the police department in Baton Rouge.

He put the mail aside without opening it, and stared out to the terrace, where Cinco had moved to the head of the steps. The old dog lay with his forepaws crossed at the wrists in that aristocratic way of collies, his ears erect as he watched a squirrel on the lawn below. The soporific drone of cicadas came through the French doors like the audible soul of summer, ancient and timeless.

He thought about the question both Hirsch and Mooney had asked, and why he hadn't answered them. The fact was, he had only recently realized what the change that had been coming over him during the last six months had meant, and he didn't know what to do about it. It was a goddamned shame. He was chagrined. And angry. When a man became a cliché he was already on the lip of his final descent. Maybe he was even irredeemable at that point. For a long time Haydon hadn't wanted to believe it. He was supposed to be different, the exception to the stereotyped cynical cop.

But he had had to admit it. After eleven years his emotions had been cauterized. It was true; there were no more astonishments for him, no more marvels or mysteries or revelations. There was only a suffocating predictable finality to life, which he regretted in a fatalistic way that made him feel foolish, the way a stubborn smoker must feel when he is told he is dying of lung cancer: no hope and no one to blame but himself. His idealism had indeed vanished. It had been replaced by an analytic eye, glaucous and filmy gray, that clouded his vision and protected his own sensitivities from the relentless malevolence of others, from the cuttings, the shootings, the beatings, rapes, and mutilations. He was possessed of an overwhelming disappointment, a disappointment that weighed upon him to the exclusion of all else.

When the telephone rang he turned away from the terrace and took the instrument off a tea table next to a red leather armchair.

"I've an invitation to a wine tasting tonight," she said. "Compliments of Manuel Canovas Fabrics. Seven sharp. We could go to Bernie's afterward. I'm in the mood for Bernie's."

He visualized Nina at the drawing board in her studio near the university. Her light-cinnamon hair would be pulled back like Evita Perón's, her silk sleeves rolled to her elbows, and her fingers smudged with the pastels of colored pencils as she cradled the telephone on her shoulder and sketched in the highlights of an atrium design. The north light in the studio would be going soft, too dim to work.

"Bernie's requires some concentration," he said.

"Exactly," she replied. "We can savor it."

"Something special?"

"Yes. Us."

"I have to work tonight."

"Oh, for . . . You're kidding."

"No, I'm not."

"Emergency?"

"No."

"Then get someone else to do it."

"I can't," he said, which was true. But aside from that, he didn't want to go to the wine tasting or to Bernie's. He knew it wasn't something Nina had her heart set on. She was only trying to draw him out, gently.

"Maybe tomorrow night," he said. He felt like a heel.

"Maybe so." Her voice had gone flat and he imagined she had stopped sketching and was gazing out at the same fading light he saw beyond the opened doors.

"I'm sorry," he said. "Look, I shouldn't be later than midnight. Why don't you go on; no use sitting around here alone. When I get in, we'll have a glass of something and talk. Okay?''

"No. I don't want to go to Bernie's without you. I'll go to the Canovas thing, though, and grab something to eat on the way home. Try to get back earlier than midnight, can't you?''

"I'll try," he said. He put down the receiver and looked around at the book-covered walls. It was a big room, the best in the house. His father's lawbooks took up one entire section of shelves near the doorway that opened into the hall of the west wing. If Webster Haydon had had his way, his son's lawbooks would have taken up an equally large section beside them. But it hadn't worked out. After one year of law school, Haydon had turned into a cop instead. A cop with a master's degree in English literature, which resulted in something more akin to a gargoyle than the lawyer his father had wanted.

In rejecting the legal profession, Haydon had broken four generations of family tradition, but it was a tradition his father had first weakened by leaving Boston when he was a young man, to take his law degree at Columbia instead of Harvard. Then, instead of going into the family's firm, he went to Britain to study English law. He married a Scots woman, shattering his family's dreams of strengthening old family alliances back in Boston, and moved to Mexico City to study the Mexican legal system. His family had given up hope and could only shake their heads in corporate pity by the time he finally settled in the steamy gulf city of Houston in the early 1940s.

In the final analysis, however, it seemed that Webster Haydon had made all the right decisions. His eccentric intellect and his social contacts in Mexico City and Houston had enabled him to become the legal adviser to oil magnates on both sides of the border. He acquired immense wealth. In retrospect, it was a brilliantly engineered career.

53

But Haydon's total departure was a distinct disappointment, even to his father. And yet it was not a disappointment that built a wall between them. The old man saw too much of his own independent thinking in his son to believe it was a bad thing. He became Haydon's most creative colleague. In this library, surrounded by the collective knowledge of both their perspectives, they had talked through many long nights, their dialogues ranging to the edge of what was known, and beyond, to theory and speculation.

Haydon missed him. More now than at first, more than he had ever imagined he would.

8

Copa's was a small club a block off North Main, where it cut through the sprawling Latin neighborhood north of downtown. Its white stucco facade was mostly hidden, except for the green neon sign, behind a courtyard that fronted the street and was choked with banana trees and large fan-shaped palmettos. Haydon parked at the curb and pushed his way through the overgrown courtyard to the green-lacquered door of the club.

Inside, he stood by the door and let his eyes adjust to the dim green haze. There were about two dozen tables with wooden chairs, and candles burned under green globes set in coconut shells. There was a small empty dance floor in the center of the room and at its edge a skinny youth wearing a dark three-piece suit with an open-collar shirt sat at a piano playing moody interpretations of Barry Manilow to a scattered, disinterested audience.

Haydon walked over to the bar, which was covered with bamboo matting, and asked for a Scotch and water. The bartender, a short, chunky man in his late thirties, with thinning black hair and dark smudges under his eyes, got Haydon's drink with bored efficiency. When he set the drink on the bar Haydon paid him with a five-dollar bill and watched him get the change.

"I thought you had Latin music here," Haydon said.

"Except on *Tuesdays*," the bartender said testily. "Tuesdays are slow, see"—he pointed an open hand toward the tables—"so we let this jerk moan mainstream for us. Latin bands are expensive. The jerk does it for about nothin'."

Haydon sipped the Scotch. It was too watery. The bartender walked to the other end of the bar and mixed three drinks—something with grenadine, a Screwdriver, and something with gin—for an impatient barhop whose fishnet stockings were sagging at the back of her thighs. She was gaunt and breastless, with chronic cocaine sniffles.

When the bartender finished her drinks, he came back toward Haydon with a handful of lemons, which he sliced and dumped in a glass embedded in crushed ice.

"You know where I can find Larry Shaver?" Haydon asked.

"Who wants to know?" the bartender said. He put both hands on the bar, arms straight out, and sighed. He chomped once on a piece of gum.

Haydon pulled out his shield. The bartender bent down and looked at it, saw what it was, and swung his head to the side in disgust.

"Now what the hell did Larry do?"

"Nothing. I want to talk to him about someone else."

"And what'd this somebody else do?"

"Is he here?"

The bartender looked Haydon over. "You don't dress like a cop."

Haydon did a palms up apology.

"Okay. I'm him."

Haydon's smile said that Shaver hadn't been fooling anyone and Shaver gave him a low-lidded look of tired indulgence.

"You know Sally Steen?" Haydon asked.

"Of course."

"Have you seen her lately?"

"Couple of nights ago."

"Where?"

"Here."

"Can you be more specific about the night?"

"Maybe. What's the deal?"

"She was found floating in Buffalo Bayou this morning."

Shaver's eyes popped open and he thrust his head forward in shocked inquiry. Haydon thought his reaction was genuine enough.

"Dead?"

"We don't know if it was homicide. We're checking into it."

Shaver swallowed. "You sure it's her?"

Haydon nodded and sipped his watery Scotch.

"Can you believe it!" Shaver said to Haydon as if Haydon should share his incredulity. He pulled a pack of Barclays out of his shirt pocket and lit one. "Well. Yeah, I can be more definite when she was in here. It was, uh, Saturday night. Yeah, three nights ago."

"Early? Late?"

"Early. 'Bout ten-thirty."

"Was she with anyone?"

"No. She came by herself and left by herself. Sat with some people while she was here. Several different people. She was just . . . cruising." He seemed to wish he hadn't said that.

"She owns part of Copa's, right?"

Shaver narrowed his eyes and cocked his head in an attitude of suspicion.

"She's dead," Haydon said. "We don't know why. We look into everything."

"Okay, yeah, I can see that," Shaver said uncertainly. "She was into it ten percent."

"How did that come about?"

Shaver pulled on his Barclay. "I knew Sally from when I owned another place, out on the Gulf Freeway. It was a kicker place. It did all right until that damned Travolta movie came out. The whole damn thing blew apart then. People started building fucking *barns* for nightclubs. Put those mechanical bulls in them. Sixty thousand square feet! Five hundred tables! Two bands playing at one time! Shit! Ever'body and his dogs wanted to do kicker business. Turned it into a carnival. I was a little operation and those big places sucked me dry as a country gourd."

He shook his head, thinking about it. It still pissed him off.

"Hell, that stuff's dying out, though," he said. "It's a passing fad. Won't last. You got to look ahead in this business. Who remembers disco, right? Got me something a lot stronger here. Latin's going to be big. I'm talking serious big."

Haydon looked at him blankly until Shaver responded to the silence.

"Oh, yeah. Sally, well, she came into the Broken Spoke all the time. That was my kicker place. She found out I was having troubles and offered to spot me a little something to keep the place floating. But it was too late. When I opened Copa's I needed a little capital and I remembered her offer. I called her up and traded her ten percent for a little boost."

Haydon finished his drink and Shaver reached for the glass.

"No, thanks," Haydon said. "You have other co-owners besides the two of you?"

"Two more. Businessmen. Both have fifteen percent."

"You own sixty percent, then?"

Shaver nodded.

"How long have you known Sally?"

"Way back."

Haydon gave him another blank look.

"Okay. Since, uh, 1966. She was working hotels then. The good ones. I was working out at a gym, thinking I wanted to be a power lifter. It doesn't show now, I know, but in those days some people thought I had potential. Anyway, she worked out there too. Shit, let's face it. Sally and I both looked a lot better back then."

"Do you know anyone she might have gotten crossways with? Anyone who could've killed her or wanted her killed?"

"Naw, shit. No idea. But, really, I mean, in her business . . ."

It was Haydon's turn to nod. "How about her other business interests? Do you know anything about the other two clubs she owns part of?"

"What?"

"The other two Latin clubs."

"She owns a piece of two other Latin clubs?"

"You didn't know that?"

"Hell, no, I didn't know that," Shaver said indignantly, as if Haydon had accused him of something enormously indecent. "How do you like that? God dog! What clubs? No, let me guess: Club Bragança and La Brasilia."

Haydon nodded again.

"Can you believe that broad? That's conflict of interest. She's been jockeying customers to three clubs. No wonder she didn't bring much in here. *Son* of a bitch. I'll bet all I got was the seeds and stems."

"Do you know the other two places?"

"Oh, yeah, sure. One's nice and the other one's nicer."

"In what order?"

"La Brasilia's the best. It's swanky. I mean, it's over on Post Oak. You couldn't want it any better, right?"

"Do you know the owners?"

"No. I don't know them," Shaver said tersely. His forehead knitted in thought, he made a swipe at the already clean bar with a damp rag he had tucked in his hand. He was ticked off about Steen's selling her co-ownership around the way she had her body.

"Do you know Judith Croft?" Haydon brought him back to the present.

"Yeah."

"And?"

"I just know her from being here with Sally."

"She never came to the Broken Spoke?"

"Well, yeah; there too."

"Were they close?"

"Yeah, I guess so. They were pretty much a pair."

"Have you ever been to Steen's house?"

"I don't even know where she lives. Look, let's get this straight. I don't know her all that good. Just through the clubs, you know. Her business brought her around a lot. Okay, I laid her a couple of times back in the muscle man days. Free of charge, I might add. I couldn't afford her for hire. She kinda took a liking to me but it didn't last, and neither did the nooky. It was just a brief little deal. A couple of months. Since then it's been a strictly across-the-bar kind of relationship. And then this business thing, like I explained. That's all. She had lots of money, so I wasn't afraid to take her offer. That's all. Honest."

The Barry Manilow songs were beginning to get on Haydon's nerves. It was time to go anyway; Shaver had run out of gas.

"Could I have one of those lemon slices?" Haydon asked.

"Huh?"

60

"Lemon slices. Could I have one?"

"Sure. A lemon slice," Shaver said dumbly. He jabbed his paring knife into a slice and pointed it at Haydon, who removed it gingerly and got off the barstool. He squeezed some of the juice into his mouth.

"I appreciate your help," he said.

"Hey, listen," Shaver said, reaching out and touching Haydon's arm. "Is this going to throw a kink in my business arrangement?"

"I don't think so. I'm sure her lawyer will be contacting you."

"Her lawyer?"

"It'll have to be cleared up."

Shaver ducked his head again, shaking it as if he couldn't believe his luck. "This'll probably cost me some kind of legal fee or something. God doggit. Just one more hassle. I swear, there's no end to the shit in this business, you know. Her lawyer. Jesus. Every time I get within ten feet of a lawyer it costs me something. Talk about a bunch of hustlers."

Haydon started toward the door and was almost to it when Shaver called to him.

"Oh, hey, listen."

Haydon stopped and turned around.

Shaver twisted his shoulders awkwardly and shifted his feet. "I'm real sorry about her being dead and all. That's bad. You know?"

Haydon nodded and let himself out into the hot, humid night.

9

They sat side by side in the warm purple night, sipping gin limes in a slush of crushed ice, their feet stretched out to rest on top of the terrace wall. Haydon shifted his bare back against the cool mesh of the wrought-iron chair and looked at the mauve cast of the night on the baggy white Mexican *calzones* he used for pajamas. Nina's bare legs were darker, with lavender highlights reaching toward her lap, where the pearl silk teddy bear hid the shadows of her groin.

"I didn't actually think you'd be in before twelve," she said. "Good for you." She squeezed his hand.

"I barely made it."

"Barely's good enough for me," she said, and reached her leg over and laid it across his and rubbed the inside of his foot with the tops of her toes.

He liked her to do that. Sometimes in bed, after they had exhausted themselves, they would go to sleep that way, with her rubbing the inside of his foot with her toes. It was, he thought, a simple but genuine gesture, something from the very heart of what people needed from each other.

The faint, spinning hum of the city was softened by the trees and hedges surrounding them and nearly lost in the rhythmic stridulation of crickets in the grass. Fireflies bobbed like the lanterns of tiny boats below them in the lime trees.

Haydon could sense that Nina wanted to talk. She was not going to be content to sit there and drink another gin lime and then another and another until her mind was as moist and sated as the night. That was what he wanted to do, until it all slipped away and there was no difference between reality and something he might dream. Morning would come as a surprise and he wouldn't have had to wait for it.

But Nina didn't like to lose control. It was, in fact, her control that had made their marriage as rich and fulfilling as it had been. People who knew them would have characterized them both as reasonable persons, which they were. Only it was in Nina's soul to be reasonable, it was as natural to her as her sensuality, which she was aware of and accepted matter-of-factly. Even her passion was a measured, deliberate appetite, and because of this Haydon often felt she experienced a greater, more profound dimension of their lovemaking than he. She let nothing slip away from her in the fog of delirium, but consumed it all and went beyond him through sheer intensity of concentration to a wide-eyed metaphysical cognizance that acted upon him as an aphrodisiac. Nina's reasonableness was a gift.

For Haydon, on the other hand, reasonableness was a learned discipline. He understood it as the best way to survive, to get through life, but it did not come easy for him and there were periods during times of prolonged stress when he would reject it altogether. These times—his black seasons, when he turned his back on everything that held his life

63

together—were his bane and his best-kept secret. His and Nina's.

She had seen him do it first just two years after they were married. They had had a quarrel, so she was misled as to the reason for his disappearance and had the presence of mind to tell his lieutenant he had a stomach virus when he called to see why Haydon had failed to show up at the office. She didn't want their squabbles bandied about among the detectives. When he did not come home after the second day and well into the early-morning hours of the second night, she knew something was wrong and doubted his disappearance had anything to do with their argument.

Haydon had come home at three in the morning, followed up the terrace steps by a sympathetically morose Cinco, whose tail was tucked contritely between his legs. He collapsed trying to open the library doors, and Nina, bracing herself against the shock of his appearance, helped him upstairs. Though he was still wearing his suit, with loosened tie, it was filthy beyond redemption. He was unshaven, gummy with perspiration, and moaning uncontrollably with a migraine. Gaunt, cadaverous, and unable to focus his eyes, he lay helplessly on the bed as she undressed him, bathed him all over with a wet cloth, and pulled a cool sheet up to his waist. She gave him a double dose of Fiorinal and sat with him until it began to take effect. He had said only, "Don't tell," before he went under.

He slept for twenty-seven hours without rousing. Nina watched him closely, called the doctor to see if it would hurt him to sleep so long, and waited. He woke at six, as he did every morning, and reached out for her. She was already looking at him, having awakened when she felt him stir. Facing her, he smiled only with his glistening eyes and traced a slim hand across the rise of her naked breast to her hip, where it rested.

"I do this sometimes," he said simply. "It's nothing to do with us." His mouth was dry after the fever and he swallowed.

"Sometimes?"

"Rarely," he said.

"Not since we've been married."

"Just before."

"It'll happen again?"

"Yes." He closed his eyes, then opened them again. "But afterward everything's fine. It'll take me a couple of weeks to get my weight back." He tried to smile with his mouth then. "I'll have a gargantuan appetite."

Nina had started to speak, but without warning her eyes filled with tears. His long, elegant fingers touched her mouth.

"We can talk about it later," he said, and she put her arms around him and drew him close. They lay together, not talking but communicating a complex of emotions through their embrace as the morning sun traveled to them across the room and gilded their bed.

They hadn't talked about it later, not the way he had made it sound they would. She never learned what had happened during those two days or any of the other days during the years that followed when he would disappear unexpectedly and then return too haggard and sick to do anything but sleep it off like a drunk after a colossal binge. But it wasn't that. She had already learned Haydon had inherited a stomach so sensitive and touchy that it had precluded his ever being an alcoholic. His system rebelled before he swallowed enough to addict him. He liked a few gin limes every evening, but he had never built up a tolerance for it. For him, a binge was four or five drinks before passing out. Sometimes he drank too

65

much deliberately, in substitution for sleeping pills when he had seen more than he wanted to see during a long shift. Drugs were out of the question for the same reason. Haydon's metabolic system was fast, which kept him trim, and he had a low tolerance threshold for stimulants, which probably kept him healthy.

They had been married more than a dozen years now and he had been right. His disappearances had been rare, infrequent but regular, and inevitable. The years diminished them in no respect or intensity. And Nina had stoically become a part of the conspiracy. She had, mercifully, refused to harry him. For a week after that first episode she had looked after him with an unconscious frown and he had often caught her staring at him with heavy, doleful eyes. Cruelly, he never explained anything, never enlightened her to lessen her suffering for him. His silence in those weeks was to set the pattern on these occasions for the years to come. They both agonized over it, but her silent empathy was an eloquent declaration of faith. It was the one great anomaly of their marriage. Her silence on this subject was the solitary sacrifice of exception she made to her reasonableness, solely for him. He had accepted the offering with all the gravity and solemnity with which it was given.

All this played over in his mind as they sat together in the darkness. He sensed that she was restless.

"Penny," she said suddenly.

He was not surprised. "Nothing," he said. "Just relaxing."

"What's bothering you?"

"A few mosquitoes."

"Come on," she said. He could tell she was smiling.

"Something else, you mean?"

"Something else, yes."

66

"Nothing."

"Come on, Stuart."

He drank before speaking. He had squeezed extra lime into this one and the clean, sharp citrus acid made his jaws ache momentarily before he swallowed.

"Well, I guess I'm losing my touch. Bringing my work home with me."

"You've always done that. You never had a touch to lose." She nudged the inside of his foot and he saw her dark figure from the corner of his eye as she, too, drank. She moved smoothly and comfortably and, he thought, a little sadly.

Cinco shifted on the tile beside her chair.

"Then I'm bringing it home with me a little more than usual, that's all."

"Anything in particular?"

"Everything in particular."

"Ever think about doing something else?"

It had never been a question before, even remotely, and he was surprised that she had even considered it a possible query now.

"No," he said.

"Never for a fleeting moment?"

"I don't think there's anything in this world that I haven't considered for a fleeting moment."

"But not now?"

"Not now." He didn't know why he lied about it.

"I thought perhaps you'd been thinking of it lately." She gave his foot another nudge, and then a slow caress that traveled on the underside of his foot from his toes to his ankle.

He could see her long, firm leg bend upward at the knee as she did it and suddenly he wanted to make love to her more than anything else in the world. He looked at her in the cobalt night with an emotion that was as fresh and exciting as the first night they had made love. He set his drink on the tile and leaned over and pulled her long hair away from her face and lightly kissed her. She shrugged to him and bent her head to let him nuzzle the soft hair at the back of her neck. There was the fragrance of Je Reviens.

"Let's go inside," she said.

10

The casement windows were thrown open to the night and the ceiling fan pulled in the heavy coastal air and scented it with Nina's perfume. She was asleep in the crook of Haydon's arm as he lay on his back feeling the even rise and fall of her soft breasts against him. She was sticky-hot; they both were, but he didn't care. He had wanted the room open tonight, to ward off the creeping claustrophobia that seemed to be smothering him. He watched the spider shadow of the fan blades and wondered at his deepening sadness in the sweet air that swirled around them. His heart shifted, the irregular beat pounding so hard he thought Nina would surely hear it. A sure sign of stress for him, as always. He had to get his mind on something else; there wouldn't be any sleep for a while.

Slowly he shifted to his side, letting Nina turn onto her back as he slipped his arm out from under. More than a thousand times he had been grateful for her propensity for deep, sound sleep. He stood, tightened the drawstring on his *calzones,* and walked barefooted down the broad curving stairs. Going into the kitchen, he squeezed the juice of two limes into a glass of crushed ice and added water. He took the drink into the library and turned on a single green-shaded lamp on the refectory table. He pulled the telephone to him and called the Vice Division. Mooney was out. They would get him on the radio and have him call.

Haydon turned off the lamp and stood in the dark, looking out at the terrace. The white tip of Cinco's tail made a splash of ghostly iridescence on the tile beside Nina's chair. Haydon sipped the lime and water, listening to the rich, thick sound of crushed ice in the glass, which was as pleasing in the tropical night as the drink itself. He waited.

When the telephone rang he picked it up before the first ring finished.

"Stuart? This is Ed. What're you doin', sleeping on the phone?"

"That was quick."

"What?"

"I just hung up from talking with the dispatcher."

"You just called me? I'm not in the car. What'd you want?"

"What do *you* want?"

"Well, okay. Look, I just wanted to tell you I don't think you're so crazy anymore about that theory of yours."

"This is a good time to let me know that, Ed."

"Yeah. Also I think I've got something else for you."

"What's that?"

"I'm standing about six feet from one of the best-looking call girls I've ever seen in my life, and she's naked." He paused for effect.

"And?"

"She's dead."

Haydon felt around on the table for a magazine and put the sweaty glass on it to protect the wood finish.

"Where are you?" he asked.

70

"Surprise. I'm in Sally Steen's condo over in West University Place."

"What?"

"That's right."

"What the hell's going on, Mooney?"

"It's a bit of a long story and I don't like hanging around alone in this place with this dead woman. Come on over, okay?"

"You're alone?"

"Right. Come on over, will you?"

"Have you called anyone else?"

"Nope. But I guess I'd better call the dispatcher and tell them I've gotten in touch with you or they'll send someone looking for me."

"No one else knows you're there?"

"There's an old woman across the way who knows. I'll tell you about her when you get here."

"Okay. I'll be there in about fifteen minutes."

Haydon touched the button and dialed Hirsch. He was home, watching a late movie on television. Haydon could tell from the way he talked he had a girl with him.

"I'm sorry, Leo," he said after he explained.

"No problem."

"Also bring your good camera, will you? I want you to shoot this one yourself."

Vanstraten was not at home, but his wife, Jean, told Haydon he was still at the lab. When Haydon called the coroner's office an assistant answered the telephone and put him on hold. It seemed like five minutes before Vanstraten picked up the receiver.

"This is Haydon. I'm sorry, but I've got another prostitute. I'd like you to take a look at her personally."

"Address?"

Haydon told him.

"I'll be there as soon as I can."

71

When Haydon hung up he felt Nina at his side.

"I thought you were asleep," he said.

"I was."

"I'm sorry."

"Oh, quit apologizing. That makes the third time you've said you were sorry in the last three minutes."

"We'll talk about it at breakfast," he said. He kissed her—too hastily, he thought later, when he had time to think about it—and ran upstairs to dress.

The condominium on Quenby was a duplex in the quarter-million price range. Ed Mooney was waiting beside a pale gaslight that illuminated an arbor of blooming wisteria whose clusters of lilac blossoms took on a waxy white hue in the aura of the lamp. Haydon parked at the curb and got out immediately. Mooney led him from the lighted arbor and they stood a moment just outside the wash of light as Mooney explained.

"Okay. First of all you'll be relieved to know I'm on duty. I was doubling tonight for Simpson, who's covering for me this coming weekend. After you'd gone home this afternoon, I thought about our talk and went back to the office and began fiddling with the CRT. Dialed up Judith Croft and got the scoop on her. Then I dialed up this Quenby place to see if we had any action on it. Turns out it's been under surveillance for about three weeks. A team from Vice had been trying to ferret out a little operation whereby some upper-class ladies are picking up grocery money during the day while the old man's gone to the office or on business trips.

"I was curious, so I came over here to chat with the stakeouts. Couple of special squads, real airheads. They say a girl named Theresa Parmer leases the place and that's all they know except they're supposed to keep tabs on the traffic. They don't know anything; just clocking time. Nothing come or gone from here in three nights. I agree to spell them

72

while they go grab something to eat. They've been gone about ten minutes when this blue-and-white pulls up and these two guys head for the door. I jump out and ask them what's up. They said the lady in the adjacent condo called in a checkout. Suspicious goings-on next door."

"She's the older woman you mentioned?"

"Right. I'm getting to it. I told them about the surveillance and got them to let me handle it. Seems Mrs. Vine steps out the front door this morning to get the paper from the yard and sees Miss Parmer's front door open about halfway. Didn't think about it. When she went to the store shortly before noon it was still open. She spent the afternoon at her son's in Piney Point and when she came back, just about dark, the same thing. She had supper, watched the telly. The news, Carson, and then halfway through the late movie she checks again. Same thing. She spooks, calls the police."

"Why didn't the stakeout see this?"

"From the street you can't actually see the front door. It's hidden behind a trellis and a wooded area. But you can see who comes and goes up the sidewalk to the door."

"So then you checked it out."

"That's right."

"Okay, let's see."

They started up the curving sidewalk through a thicket of blooming crape myrtle that provided a total screen from the street. They could see a second glass lamp blinking through the ribbing of the branches. The front door was still ajar and Mooney pushed it open with his shoe and turned on a single dim light in the entryway. The place had been designed with what an architect might call "imagination" and was constructed on several levels, which gave a cavernous effect to the whole.

The entrance was the lowest level and they stepped up from it into the living room. The floor was terrazzo tile and

73

the interior design was meticulously art deco, right down to the ashtrays. The fireplace had a clear glass mantel that allowed you to see through to the bricks and competed for attention with an old Wurlitzer jukebox that dominated a nearby corner, its carnival colors throwing moody hues of green and pink and blue against the stark white ceiling and walls. The furniture was new, but designed after the styles of the thirties: overstuffed armchairs and divans with pleated dust skirts and lots of piping. The fabric had gaudy floral patterns which were picked up on one wall by a mural that looked like thirties postcard art of a Mexican street scene.

Above them a mezzanine circled the living room, its walls hung with neon artwork, mirrors, and thirties kitsch. Small palms in painted Mexican pottery threw jungle shadows from the pastel lights onto the mezzanine's white balustrade.

They stood a moment while Haydon looked around, absorbing the deliberate ambience. He walked over to the Wurlitzer and looked at the songs handwritten on the strips of paper beside the illuminated plastic numbers. All the titles were in Portuguese. The artists were largely unfamiliar to him, but he recognized the names of the most famous ones: Chico Buarque, Maria Bethânia, Gal Costa, Antonio Carlos Jobim, Simone, Vinicius de Moraes, Elis Regina, Alcione. The artists and the music were all Brazilian. One song was printed in capital letters and underlined in red: "EU TE AMO," the theme music of a Brazilian film of the same name that had caused a sensation when it was exported to the U.S. and Europe. One other title was underlined in red. It was lettered in English and was cryptically titled "Burundi Black."

"There's a kitchen back that way," Mooney said, pointing toward an opening to their right. "And a bathroom there. That's all on this level. The mezzanine is on a level all its own. The three bedrooms all open off the mezzanine, but you have to step up three steps to get to them. They all have private baths. She's in the last one.''

He started up the stairs and Haydon followed, looking at the house from the different angles as he progressed upward and along the mezzanine to the last room. The doorway was dark and Mooney preceded Haydon up the three steps. He reached inside and touched a rheostat, which he turned slowly. The room became a glowing ember, then burst into a hot, dark flame as the lights came on full.

Everything in the room was mandarin red: the carpet, the walls, the furniture, the round bed in the middle of the room. In the center of the bed lay Theresa Parmer, her nude body like a frail white stigma in the opened scarlet blossom of the sheets. She lay with one leg extended, the other brought up in the fetal position. Her upper torso was twisted almost flat against the sheets, one arm under her, the other thrown out across the bed. Her long black hair was spread on the sheets as though she had been posed.

Haydon looked at the girl and then at Mooney. ''And the other bedrooms?''

Mooney nodded. ''Blue and yellow,'' he said.

Haydon walked around to the other side of the bed and found a red lamp that had fallen off the nightstand, its shade wedged between the bed and the table. A half-empty bottle of Johnnie Walker Red lay on the soggy carpet, where most of it had spilled. A red glass was shattered near the bottle. A trail of soiled red tissues littered the red carpet from the bed to the bathroom.

Stepping carefully over the clutter, Haydon went into the bathroom. Red tile, red enamel sink, toilet, and bidet. Red sunken tub big enough for several people and piled with dirty red towels beginning to smell musty with mildew. A pair of red panties lay in the corner by the toilet and a red negligee was wrapped around the pedestal of the sink. The medicine cabinet was open, revealing a crumpled toothpaste tube, mouthwash, dental floss, a wheel of birth control pills, Visine, Band-Aids. The bottom shelf held seven square clear plastic containers like those sold in gift shops. Each contained pills of a different color.

"Ed, come look at this."

The Irishman carefully eased into the bathroom with Haydon, looked into the cabinet at the confectionery colors, and began to recite.

"Yellow jackets, purple hearts, tooies, redbirds, peaches, speed, dexies, footballs. Barbiturates and amphetamines. Those're Nembutals and Tuinals scattered in the sink there." He reached down and stuck his finger into the mouth of a bottle of medicine sitting on the back of the sink and lifted it up. It was a bottle of Emetrol from Behrmann's Pharmacy.

"Emetrol?" Haydon asked.

"I guess she had an upset stomach."

"Didn't you say something about call girls generally not being dopers?"

Mooney pulled down one corner of his mouth and shrugged.

When they stepped back into the bedroom, Mooney went on through to the mezzanine and Haydon put his hands in his pockets and walked to the edge of the bed. He leaned over the body and looked closely at the girl's face. Foamy spittle had spilled from her half-opened mouth down her neck and onto the bed. A teaspoonful of it was congealing in the hollow below her Adam's apple.

Mooney's voice came along the mezzanine and then Hirsch's and Vanstraten's, the latter's deep and brusque.

"Well, I'll be damned," Hirsch said as he entered the room.

"Don't miss *anything*," Haydon said as he stepped past

Hirsch, who had squatted on the floor and was loading the camera and setting the appropriate exposure.

Haydon joined Mooney and Vanstraten on the mezzanine.

"You want me to call the lab van now?" Mooney asked.

"I guess we'd better," Haydon said. The first burst from Hirsch's strobe light flared red on the mezzanine. "Yeah, go ahead."

Vanstraten leaned patiently on the balustrade. Haydon offered him a cigarette but the pathologist shook his head.

"This changes things," Haydon said. "About my not wanting a rush on those tests."

"Of course," Vanstraten said. And then, "This is very interesting." He nodded to the opened door of the red room.

"Yes. There's a medicine cabinet full of junk in there. I haven't prowled around in the room much yet."

"It's nothing messy?"

"No. She's just dead."

"Just like the other two?"

"Just like the other two."

They waited in silence, each with his own thoughts.

11

When Hirsch was through, he came down the three steps lugging his camera and bags of equipment. Vanstraten picked up his black satchel and went in, followed by Haydon and Hirsch again. He put his satchel on the bed beside the girl and took out a pale-green surgeon's gown. Slipping it on, he wrapped it around and tied it in the front, the elastic wrist bands covering his white French cuffs. Then he took out a pair of surgical gloves and pulled them on.

"Will you turn the rheostat on high?" he asked. He walked slowly around the bed, looking at the naked girl from all angles. When he got to the side of the bed closest to her head, he abruptly bent over and put his face close to hers, which, at that position, was upside down to his own. He sniffed at her mouth, the side of her face, her hairline. Then he walked back around the bed and stood at her feet.

With both hands, he gently grasped the ankle of the leg drawn into the fetal position and drew it down slowly, feeling the degree of tension in the tightening muscles. He reached up and moved her head from side to side, being careful not to disturb the saliva as he tested the neck muscles.

He stood back and looked at the girl and then bent over and slipped his gloved hands under her naked hips and straightened them out so that she lay flat on her back. He checked the inside of her right thigh and hip for livor mortis, carefully noting the pattern of the rumpled sheets on her discolored flesh, and then looked closely at her hands, her fingernails, the insides of her arms and wrists. Taking a small vial from his satchel, he collected a sample of the saliva from the depression in her neck. With another vial he took a sample from her mouth, which he held open with one hand.

Once again he put his hands under the girl and expertly turned her over on her stomach. He raised her hair and examined her neck closely. He noted the livor on her back and on the back of the one thigh that had been lying out straight. Again he turned her over, examined her throat on the front and looked into her lifeless eyes.

He straightened up, his hands hanging straight at his sides as he wrinkled his eyebrows in thought.

From his satchel he took two disposable thermometers and tore the cellophane off them. He eased the girl over on one hip and deftly inserted the first for rectal temperature. The second was sheathed in an aluminum tube. He carefully placed the end of the shiny tube about three inches under the girl's right breast and whacked the haft of the thermometer sharply with the palm of his right hand, driving it directly into her liver.

There was more, but Haydon didn't want to watch. He walked away from the bed and pulled on a pair of his own latex gloves. Hirsch did the same and they began going through the closets and chests.

"She was a classy dresser," Hirsch said. He was pushing

aside hangers of clothes and checking the labels and pockets. "Some places I never heard of on these tags. Damn, look at the shoes. Wonder how long it took her to dress, match all this stuff?"

He rambled on, talking to himself as he covered the closet from top to bottom. The mumbling was the sound of Hirsch's computer. When he sat down to the CRT later that night to write out his report, his personal computer would feed back the information with astonishing accuracy. No one in the department, except maybe Pete Lapier, could match Hirsch's reports for accuracy and detail. When Haydon first began working with the young detective, he had a hard time getting used to the mumbling. Now he didn't even notice it.

There was nothing in the first chest but lingerie and provocative clothing. He found the cache of erotic paraphernalia in the top drawer of the second chest, and in the drawer below that he found the inevitable log of clients. He slipped the five-by-seven spiral notebook in his pocket and finished going through the drawers, which yielded nothing but more bras and hosiery. He walked to the bathroom door again.

"Did you get good shots in here, Leo?"

"Yeah, sure."

Haydon went in and picked up the towels in the bathtub, one at a time. There was nothing under them, but he noticed the detritus of hairs, long chestnut ones tangled in eely dampness and stuck to the sides of the red tub, and tightly coiled pubic hairs embedded in the towels and scattered around the drain. He looked behind the door and then came back into the bedroom. Vanstraten was standing beside the bed, pulling off his rubber gloves and regarding the girl. He looked up.

"I'll take samples of the drugs in the bathroom," he said, and carried a little packet of vials in with him.

"Anything in the closets?" Haydon asked Hirsch.

"Nothing besides clothes and some nifty little rubber and leather costumes."

The two of them walked out onto the mezzanine just as Mooney was letting the morgue and lab technicians in the front door. Walking to the next doorway, Haydon and Hirsch ascended the steps into the blue room. They duplicated the same search pattern through the same arrangement of furniture as in the red room and then went through the yellow room in the same way. Neither of the two rooms seemed to have been occupied. The medicine cabinets contained only incidentals and there were no clothes in the chests. The closets had scattered pieces of erotic leather and rubber clothing.

"Looks like the red room was headquarters," Hirsch said as they stepped out onto the mezzanine for the third time.

"I guess so," Haydon said. He heard the lab crew still working in the red room, and looking over the balustrade, saw Vanstraten sitting on a divan upholstered in a florid pattern of tropical orchids, taking notes. He had removed the green surgical gown. Haydon walked down the stairs and sat in an armchair opposite him. He waited, watching pink and green bubbles rise in the piping of the Wurlitzer.

In a few minutes Vanstraten closed his notebook and put his pen in the outside breast pocket of his suit.

"Rigor mortis is just now setting in around the neck and upper extremities," he said. "The first places where it begins to occur. There's distinct lividity. I'd guess—and it's just a guess—she's been dead maybe six, seven hours. If I'm right, considering the temperature in here, which is seventy-two according to the thermostat on the landing there, her body temperature should be about eight-eight, ninety. It's not. It's a lot closer to normal, which makes me think she was running a pretty high fever when she died.

"The position of the body indicates she had twisted or writhed at death. Not as if she had struggled with anyone; there are no bruises, and there would have been. It's as if she'd tossed about as one does unconsciously with a high fever, delirious. I don't think she's had sexual intercourse within the past twenty-four hours. I'll know for certain later. You noticed the marked salivation?"

"Yes."

"I didn't detect any perfume. That could indicate—I guess this is more in your field, but it could indicate she'd been ill for several days and hadn't bothered with it. If this had been sudden, interrupting the normal course of things, she probably would have been wearing some."

Haydon nodded. "What do you think?"

"I'll do my guessing after the autopsy. You want to see this one?"

"Should I?"

"I don't really think so."

Haydon crossed his long legs at the knee and leaned on one elbow in the armchair. "Three weeks ago your people did a postmortem on a call girl named Sandy Kielman. I don't know who did it. I'd like to pull her samples and duplicate the same tests you're running on this girl and Sally Steen."

"You'll have to send the special requests over. The paperwork."

"It'll be there before noon tomorrow. I'm also going to request priority on all three incidents."

Vanstraten tipped his head briskly. "Yes, I think you're right. These are curious enough to warrant it. But only in retrospect. Only because of the number of bodies in the brief period of time. Medically, taken separately at six- or eight-month intervals, you'd never have noticed anything unusual."

"You remember Kielman?"

"Yes. We don't get that many prostitutes."

"What do you think's going on?"

"I don't know, Stuart. It could be so many things. Could be an odd strain of virus communicated among these women. Something altogether without criminal impetus. Say there is criminal intent; poison comes to mind first, just from what I know so far. But if it's that, it's something exotic. We would have caught something common. The standard things. If this is homicide, I suspect the drugs in the Kielman death and in this one have been used as smoke screens. They complicate the chemical reactions, the fluids and tissues we work with. If it's homicide, Sally Steen will be our cleanest subject for research."

"They're homicides," Haydon said. "And there's something peculiar about them."

"Peculiar," Vanstraten said, seeming to mull over the sound of the word.

"When someone has a quarrel with a prostitute, it's often a pimp trying to deal with a rebellious girl, or in these cases with call girls, a frightened trick who thinks he's being set up for blackmail. They're going to use a gun, a knife, or simply beat the woman to death. Nothing imaginative. It's the banality of death you were talking about yesterday. But here we have some rather quiet deaths. Precise. Someone is being creative, very creative indeed. It could be a long time before we understand what's happening."

Vanstraten started to say something, but was distracted by the clattering movements of men and equipment on the mezzanine. The morgue attendants, in white, emerged from the red room with the body of Theresa Parmer, covered with paper sheeting and strapped to an aluminum stretcher. They were followed by the police lab technicians, carrying satchels and briefcases of evidence. The macabre conga line maneuvered its way toward the landing past the blue room, past the yellow room, and then slowly down the stairs through the watery carnival reflections that swam over the white walls from the bubbling jukebox.

12

The young man sat alone at the counter and stared at her over the glass sugar canister and chrome napkin holders. There were just the two of them in Reno Sweeney's Tenth Street Diner, except for Reno, who busily pushed his bony frame back and forth through the swinging doors to the kitchen. It was nearly four in the morning. In a couple of hours the sky would lighten across the street, above the tall shadeless second-floor windows of Diva's Academy of Dance, and the breakfast regulars would filter in, expecting the old man to do ten things at once. He was getting ready for them.

Actually, she had begun watching the young man first. She had come in off the dark street, exhausted after a marathon night, and the first thing she had seen in the diner's bright light was the man's back as he sat on the counter stool. She focused her bleary eyes just as his hand reached out and swept across the faded red Formica and caught a fly. She saw it, but the only thing that registered in her mind was a sense of relief that his back was to her. There would be no more tricks this early in the morning. Keeping her face turned away, she walked around to a booth next to one of the windows that fronted the gray street.

From the kitchen Reno saw her through the round windows in the swinging doors and came out with a menu and a cup of coffee.

"Hard night," he said. It was a statement, not a question, and she said, "You got it," and ordered hash browns, two scrambled eggs, and toast without even bothering with the menu. Reno did a fast crawdad back to the kitchen and she kicked off her shoes under the table and lit a cigarette. She let her eyes fall on the man at the counter. There was nothing else to do.

She saw him in profile. He was young, maybe twenty-six, twenty-seven, good-looking in an Italian sort of way, not Mexican, though he had a swarthy complexion. His hair was cut stylishly short and groomed like that of the male models in *Vogue* and *Mademoiselle*, shaved neatly around the ears. He wore good clothes, dress pants with a beige shirt open at the collar and a light-colored sports coat of European cut. From where she was sitting she could see one foot, a casual shoe that looked like a mat-woven summer slip-on.

His strong jaw was clean-shaven, with a cleft chin and a full lower lip that made him sexy as hell. But it was his expression that led her to watch him and what he was doing. It was a curious expression, one she did not actually understand until later. His upper lip rose minutely at one corner, the beginning, perhaps, of a sneer, while the nostrils of his handsome straight nose flared slightly as if detecting something malodorous and mildly offensive. His eyes were relaxed but seemed to reflect distaste at what he was doing, something that required his participation to the point of absorption.

On the old Formica countertop, where the brick red had been scrubbed away to white blotches by years of elbows

86

propped astraddle stoneware plates, the young man had mixed a runny puddle of sugar and water. When the flies came—and there was no shortage of flies in Reno's—he caught them and gently squeezed them to death in the cup of his hand. Although she didn't know it, she had seen him kill his fifth one as she came in the door. Now he was engrossed in shoving the little corpses around with a toothpick, putting them in first one arrangement and then another, sometimes in a circle, sometimes in marching order, working with them as if he were trying to accomplish a specific effect with the efforts of his strange expression.

It wasn't until Reno brought her food that the young man looked up and saw her. He fixed his eyes on her and did not move them the entire time she ate. His stare was frank and intense, like that of a mildly retarded person who had seen something interesting and proceeded to watch it greedily and openly.

She didn't care. Guys a hell of a lot worse than him had undressed her with their eyes before. When she finished and lit a cigarette to have with her coffee, he eased off his counter stool and walked over to her. She ignored him until he got right to her table and then she looked up. Hell, some nights you couldn't scare up a trick if you walked down the street naked, other nights they damn near stood in line for you.

"Excuse me," he said politely. "I was wondering if I might sit with you for a few minutes?"

"I don't mind," she said, and tilted her cigarette toward the seat opposite her. What the shit. At least he wasn't ugly.

He slid into the booth, his expression unchanged from the sour look he had had at the counter. She noticed, now that she looked at him straight on, that he had a long neck and sloping shoulders. His hands had no appearance of strength as he laced his tapering fingers together on the tabletop. She was disappointed by a slight air of homosexuality.

87

"I've seen you before," he said. "Do you live around here?"

"Maybe." She was aware of an unexpected defensive tone in her voice.

He tried to smile but it became a smirk instead. "I was only asking," he said. "I didn't mean to offend you."

His voice wasn't faggy. There was a slight accent, but she couldn't readily identify it.

She didn't say anything.

His smirk disappeared and his eyes dropped to her breasts and lingered there. She felt his stare as if it were actually tangible, touching, caressing, kneading her. She sensed a hidden emotion behind his eyes, something strangely akin to trepidation.

"Look," he said. "I'll be honest with you. I know where you live." He spoke carefully, as if he were afraid he might say the wrong thing. She hadn't expected this. He had appeared so self-assured. Maybe she had misinterpreted what she'd seen.

"I . . . I followed you home once." He raised a soft hand as if to stop her from thinking what she would inevitably think. "But . . . I just wanted to know where you lived. Just that."

"What the hell did you do that for?" She scowled at him and ran a restless hand through her hair, suddenly aware of its wiry texture. Too many gallons of bleach over too many years, but she had to do it; blond had always been best for her.

"I've seen you around Montrose," he repeated. "I wanted to . . . go with you, but I didn't want it to be ordinary. Not like you do with anyone else."

He was talking with his hands, earnestly trying to get her to understand. "Not the motel rooms. Not that kind of thing, but just like you were any other woman, an average woman, you know. A friend. So I followed you home. Then

88

I thought of you simply as a woman who lived on that street in that apartment. I knew you came here. I've been here the last two mornings, waiting to talk to you."

She looked at him. This guy had a problem and she had a sneaking suspicion she knew what it was. Poor son of a bitch. It was a shame to see these guys force themselves to do this. She had seen them before, and if guts made a man, she could go ahead and certify the poor bastards. You'd think in this day and age this kind of thing wouldn't be necessary. Damn, sometimes it seemed like half the world was queer, and here was this poor devil thinking he had to do this. She didn't know if she sympathized or what.

"I'm through for the night," she said coldly. And I don't do therapy anyway, she thought.

"Don't . . . don't think of it as work. Look. Look, just try to . . . try to think of it like we just met here."

Suddenly she was angry. "I know how to think of it," she snapped. "And you gotta be out of your silly mind. I don't give freebies to anybody, much less to some damn fag who wants to rub on me like—"

"No, no, no, don't say it. I want to pay. You don't understand."

"Shhh, dammit! Keep it down." She touched her straw hair with a reflexive pat. "Forget it," she whispered hoarsely. "No way am I going to take you home with me. You better get the hell outta here."

"I'll pay you double." He leaned toward her, unconsciously imitating her whisper. "Twice what you ordinarily receive."

She saw beads of sweat condensing on his upper lip. His eyes held her in a fierce effort to make her understand. Double? Would he really pay double? Well, he'd by God have to, because she wouldn't touch him for less than that, maybe even triple. She didn't have to do it.

"I ordinarily receive," she mimicked, "one hundred dollars for half an hour." It was a lie she figured would separate the men from the boys, so to speak.

"Two hundred? At your place? No motel?"

"That's right," she said stiffly, incredulous that he might go for it. "My place."

"And what can I do?" he asked. There was a tremulous intensity in his voice.

"For two hundred bucks you can do whatever you damn well please." She smiled. It couldn't possibly be much.

Without replying, he reached into his coat pocket and pulled out his wallet. She watched as he passed up a row of twenties to get to the fifties. He took out four and fanned them out on the table.

She looked at him, then glanced quickly toward the kitchen doors. "Your thirty minutes starts the second we walk into the bedroom," she said, scooping up the money.

"That'll be fine." He tried to smile again, but it didn't work. A sick expression crossed his face.

They walked three blocks together to a quiet old neighborhood near Cherryhurst Park and turned into the driveway of a two-story duplex. Behind a bank of oleanders with white blossoms that looked like tiny puffs of smoke in the early-morning darkness, an outside stairway led to the apartment in the back. He followed her up the stairs, watching her hips pump under her dress. He waited with her on the landing while she took out her key and let them in.

There was a single, smudgy night-light burning in a corner wall socket, warding off total darkness with a grudging jaundiced glow.

"Very nice," he said too quickly, looking around.

"Danish modern."

"It looks expensive," he said ingratiatingly.

It didn't and she knew it. "Bedroom's this way," she said.

He followed her across a hallway and into a darkened

90

room. There was no dim light here and she didn't turn one on. She slowly felt her way across to the window and opened the venetian blind. The pale aura of a mercury vapor streetlamp fell across the bed in thin bars of powder-blue light.

He looked around from where he stood, looked at everything as his eyes got used to the shadows. Then he began sniffing. She couldn't believe it at first, but then there was no doubt about what he was doing. He sniffed like a dog, looking around the room.

"I don't run the window unit when I'm not here," she explained defensively. "It costs too much. It gets pretty stuffy."

"I like it," he said.

She looked at him. Shit. Weird. Without speaking, she reached through the venetian blind and raised the window. The room wasn't going to cool off quickly. The air that seeped in through the window was warm, muggy, and coastal.

She turned to face him. "How do you want it?"

"You have any body powder?" he asked.

"Body powder?"

"Yes."

"Yeah, I got body powder."

"We'll need it."

She shook her head and walked into the bathroom and returned with a can of Fabergé.

"Is it full?"

"Yeah. I haven't had it that long."

"Good," he said. "Let's take off our clothes."

But he didn't move. He stood with his hands hanging at his sides while he watched her unbutton her blouse and take it off. She ignored him as she let her skirt drop and then her slip. She shrugged her bra off her shoulders and let it fall and then peeled her panties down her hips and let them slide to her ankles. She stepped out of them, left everything on the floor at her feet, and turned to face him.

As she watched, he began to undress. She decided this was part of the thrills. He didn't have an unattractive body. His olive complexion was uniform and had the tautness of youth. She could see that he took care of his body, and when he moved, it was with the grace of a dancer, agile and sure. Maybe this wouldn't be so bad after all.

He carefully folded his clothes over a chair, taking pains to preserve the creases and avoid wrinkling. He placed his shoes side by side in front of the chair, his socks folded and placed inside. When everything was properly arranged, he reached inside one of his coat pockets and took out a perfume atomizer. He walked to the bed and set the atomizer on the small glass-topped table next to it. Without saying anything to her, he sat on the bed and with slow deliberation lay down in the bars of blue light, stretching his legs out straight and close together, with his arms and hands pressed close to his sides.

She stood where she was, waiting for instructions.

"Sprinkle the powder on me," he said. His eyes were closed.

"Where?" she asked stupidly.

"All over." His voice was soft with emotion.

"Your face too?"

"All over."

She began. She dusted him with a light coat of powder, beginning with his feet and working her way up. She innovatively paused between his thighs and sprinkled an extra amount on his crotch because she thought he would like that, and then she continued upward until she had covered his face and head.

"Okay," she said.

"Keep it up. Until I'm white."

She hesitated.

"You're wasting *my* time now," he snapped. "Put it on."

She began again, this time sprinkling randomly until the powder piled up in the hairs on his legs and chest, and between his legs. She sprinkled until all the tiny wiry hairs on his body disappeared as he lay stone still, except for that one part of him which stirred in the whiteness like a leprous snake. She continued to sprinkle him until his body trembled, quivered with a sexual intensity she recognized as the pent-up fervor of kinky predilections too seldom expressed.

"Stop," he said suddenly, and she flinched.

He lay absolutely still, sweating profusely under the powder. Then, slowly, he moved his legs and then his arms as he rose off the bed in the rigid manner of a corpse rising out of a lime pit in a horror film. He stood beside the bed, the powder caked to his body like a coat of plaster, except for two dark spots where he had blinked away the white. His eyes stared out at her.

"Get on the bed," he said.

His voice had undergone a distinct change. The supplicant had disappeared behind the shroud of powder and in his place an aggressor was giving commands in a tone of explicit cruelty. She moved hesitantly to the bed, knowing instinctively that she was now dealing with another personality. This was not the man who had paid her the two hundred dollars. She lay down inside the outline of white where he had been and assumed the position he had taken. Warily, trying to read his mind in order to appease him, she lifted the can of Fabergé and started to sprinkle it on her own body.

"No!" he gasped, a black hole in the powder where his mouth moved. He took the can away from her and placed it on the floor. "Spread your legs. Your arms too."

She didn't want to do it. It was such a vulnerable position under the circumstances, almost sacrificial.

"Do it!"

She began slowly to move her legs.

"Wider."

It had been a horrible mistake. This wouldn't be over in thirty minutes. It wouldn't be over until he was through with whatever he had to do. She tried to think of the two hundred dollars.

"Close your eyes," he said.

She closed them only partially, and nervously watched him through the mesh of her eyelashes. He reached out a white arm and took the atomizer off the glass table and walked to the foot of the bed, out of sight of her vision.

Suddenly a cool spray hit the soles of her feet. He worked around her toes and slowly progressed up each leg, the cold spray sending chills to her groin and filling the room with the saccharine fragrance of lavender. He paused between her legs; she knew he would. The cold mist skirted across her stomach, causing her tendons to crawl as he moved up her waist to her breasts. When they were glistening and streaked with perfumed rivulets, he moved to her face.

"Inhale it," he said, and she felt the mist. The cloying fragrance sickened her. "Inhale . . . deeply," he demanded, drenching her face. She did, sucking the mist into her throat and lungs until she felt she would drown. When she started to gag he stopped.

"Keep your eyes closed," he cautioned.

She watched through lashes spangled with perfume as he circled her, spraying her from high above, then crouching, whispering rhythmically. He moved around her in a ghostly samba, so close she could hear the squish of the atomizer and her own deep breathing as she floated in lavender. She watched him, white as a dancing leper in the bars of blue light as he anointed her in a secret ritual that enthralled him and froze her in dread.

Suddenly he stopped. He put the atomizer on the floor be-

94

side the powder and she felt the bed move under his weight as he leaned directly over her. Then, slowly, like an insect clawing its way out of its cocoon, he began to scrape off the powder with his fingernails. He started with his face, letting the chunks of sweat-mixed powder fall on her face, where it dissolved in the lavender and the tears she could no longer restrain. His leprosy became her leprosy as he worked his way down their bodies, letting the caky powder fall from his neck to hers, from his chest to hers, from his stomach to hers. . . .

13

Lieutenant Bob Dystal had two identical chocolate-brown double-knit suits. Both had been purchased recently to replace his only other suit, a rust-colored leisure job with white stitching, which he had finally retired because its shabby condition had begun to attract attention. He bought the two identical suits for three reasons: they were on sale, he liked chocolate brown, and it was rare at any time in any store to find two size forty-eight long suits that looked middle-class enough for Dystal to feel comfortable in.

From the first day Dystal had shown up wearing one of his new suits and told Haydon what he'd done, Haydon wondered how he would manage it. How the hell did somebody wear two identical suits? Would Dystal wear one exclusively until it needed cleaning, then switch to the other? Would he alternate between the two by week? By day? Would he set one aside in a kind of self-imposed layaway plan until its mate had worn out completely, like the rust-colored leisure suit?

Luckily a triad of the inevitable double-knit snags soon appeared on the right shoulder of one coat. Haydon watched them with unfailing interest. In the six weeks since Dystal had bought the suits, he had worn them in no particular sequence. The snags showed up randomly. It seemed he simply reached into the closet every morning and grabbed one without any concern for whether it was the suit on the left or the one on the right. Actually, Haydon would have been surprised if the lieutenant had done it any other way.

This morning Dystal wore the suit without the snags as he sat back in his groaning swivel chair and unhurriedly read Haydon's report. Both men nursed steaming coffee, Haydon's in a styrofoam cup from the squad room and Dystal's from a squat wide-mouthed plaid Thermos.

Haydon rubbed his eyes, grainy from too little sleep, and wished he could smash the tiny Hitachi radio that sat behind Dystal on a filing cabinet. It played incessantly, its volume turned down to a muted stage whisper of country-and-western music so faint that only an occasional musical phrase or snatch of lyric was recognizable. This musicale of intermittent reception maddened Haydon as the Chinese water torture might. He tried desperately to ignore it.

Without taking his eyes off the report, Dystal reached for his plaid Thermos and took a long sucking swig of what Haydon knew to be the blackest, thickest coffee man could ingest. Dystal swallowed loudly and with relish and then, in a gesture that was almost childlike, laid his huge bear's paw alongside his head as he continued to read.

Haydon looked at the massive hand and remembered the night in a rank, narrow alley, slimy with garbage and drizzling rain, when he watched transfixed as Dystal, silent with rage, jerked a copulating dope pusher off the half-nude body of a fourteen-year-old junkie he had rendered unconscious with a stiff jolt of heroin. The burly detective had gripped the astonished pusher's face with one great beefy hand and held him at arm's length as he began to squeeze.

The man's face proved amazingly elastic, stretching like

a rubber Halloween mask until all his features were gathered in a moist wad in Dystal's paw. Grabbing the detective's loglike wrist with both hands, the pusher had struggled vainly, squealing like an agonized monkey. When Dystal finally released his victim, he did so with a cruel popping wrench of his fist that tore the pusher's face from his skull and made him drop cold and limp in the sludge of the alley floor.

The pusher's civil liberties lawyer had made the city pay more than five thousand dollars in plastic surgeon's fees. It had done the man very little good in the end. Dystal's grotesque frontier justice would stay with the pusher for the rest of his life.

"Well, this is pretty interesting," Dystal said in a rumbling drawl as he plopped the report on his desk and turned to face Haydon. He pulled a plain white pack of generic cigarettes from his shirt pocket and lit one with a time-burnished Zippo bearing a bulldozer insignia. He slipped the lighter into his coat breast pocket beneath the ever-present Stars and Stripes lapel pin. "What do you want to do?"

"I need your signature on the priority request form for the three postmortems. . . ."

"Three?"

"Sandy Kielman's fluid and tissues. I want them to have the same tests as the other two."

"Okay."

"I want to devote the next week exclusively to this. I'm not working on anything that can't be bumped for that long. Neither is Leo."

"I guess we could do that. What else?"

"And I want to borrow Mooney from Vice for the duration."

Dystal wrinkled his forehead and scratched his hairline with his thumb. He wore his muddy hair the same way he had worn it in high school in 1955 in the small west Texas town of Bronte, cropped close enough on the sides to reveal his scalp, neatly parted, and held in place with Brylcreem.

"I'll check it out," he said, and flicked the ash from his cigarette with the nail of his little finger. He sighed enormously as he pulled out one of the desk drawers with the pointed toe of his Nocona boot and reared back in his squeaky chair to prop both size fourteens across the top of the drawer. Squinting speculatively, he said, "What do you think's going on here?"

Haydon shook his head. "Van says they could be passing around some kind of viral infection, highly contagious."

"But you don't buy that."

"No, and I don't really think Van does either. If these girls were street hookers with a high trick turnover and sloppy hygiene, then maybe. But they don't even come close to that. They're high-class and so is their clientele." Haydon paused, then added, "Which means if these turn out to be homicides, we're going to have an unmerciful media show on our hands when it gets out."

"Yeah, I've thought of that too. Don't it depress you? So who's killing them?"

"Could be a dozen or more men with a dozen or more reasons."

"What do you mean, 'men'? I don't see a better suspect than this Croft woman."

"*If* she knows about the inheritance. And then that only accounts for Steen's death. What about the other two?"

"Maybe they knew something they shouldn't have."

"But Kielman died nearly three weeks before Steen."

"You never know," Dystal said.

"The thing that bothers me the most is the way all three of them died. Even if it's remotely similar to a viral infection, that means it's way out of the normal run of things."

"Poison?"

99

"Van says if it is, it's exotic. They'd have found the more common ones from the preliminary autopsy examination and tests they've done so far."

Haydon lit one of his own Fribourg & Treyer cigarettes so he wouldn't have to breathe the stench of Dystal's generics. "Let's say it turns out to be an exotic poison," he said. "How many people do these women know in common who have the technical capabilities to administer a poison like that?"

Dystal snorted. "Aw, hell, Stu. A smart high school kid could use a library to find out that sort of thing. Shit, if they can build atomic bombs from library books . . ."

"If they have plutonium. There's the matter of access. I know what curare can do, and what succinylcholine can do, but I can't get it from the neighborhood drugstore. And if I could, the library books don't tell me how to poison people with it without its being detected in autopsy. Most people would use a clumsier poison—cyanide, nicotine, strychnine—something that would have already shown up in Van's tests. Think of the exotic poisonings in criminal history. Who were the people who pulled them off?"

Dystal gave it some thought, breathing torpidly through his open mouth. "Yeah, I see what you mean." He stared at the toes of his boots and wiggled them, causing the leather to creak.

"We don't know what Vanstraten's going to find, but we do know all three women died after a similar illness that lasted several days. Granted, from the little we know, their illnesses seemed to be characterized by pretty common symptoms. But if I were going to kill someone this way, that's exactly what I'd want."

"I think so," Dystal said, nodding slowly, his eyes still on his boots.

"The next question," Haydon added. "How many call girls are out there right now developing a fever, getting a headache, having chest pains and 'flu' symptoms in the middle of the summer? I don't like to think about the possibilities.''

Bob Dystal ground out his cigarette in a clear Lucite ashtray in the shape of Texas and embedded with horny, discolored rattlesnake rattles from back home. He dropped his feet heavily to the floor and closed the drawer. Putting both elbows on his desktop, he listlessly flipped a computer printout of a patrol report that had been sitting between the two men.

"What're you leading up to?" he asked.

"There's always the possibility of a sociopath. If one more girl turns up, I'm going to lean in that direction.''

Dystal looked steadily at Haydon without speaking, a familiar catatonic stare that made most men uneasy. The big man held you with his eyes, and while you squirmed, his mind traveled at a fast clip in another direction. As was the case with many men of gifted intelligence, idiosyncrasies were a natural part of Dystal's complicated makeup. His good-old-boy dress and mannerisms were innocently deceptive, for his insight into the workings of the criminal nature far outdistanced his small accomplishments in the social graces.

"Well, Stu," he drawled, shoving the patrol reports across the desk toward Haydon. "It looks like you got your work cut out for you, then. Here she is.''

14

Peter Walther was taller than Haydon had expected. The young patrolman sat uncomfortably in the wooden chair, his stick and service .38 pushed around so he could sit back. His right cheek was humped up with bandages and the swelling that hadn't yet subsided.

"I appreciate your coming in early," Haydon said. "I apologize for calling you at home, but I thought you might not come in at all." He nodded at the bandages.

"I was coming anyway," Walther said.

"Good. Your report was well written, unusually good detail, but I'd like to go over a few additional points with you. Detective Hirsch and I are investigating what may possibly be a series of related homicides. The victims—we are aware of three at this time—are call girls. Each has died after an illness of several days. The symptoms of the illness seem to be little more than the symptoms of a common bronchial flu. Your girl may fall into this scheme somehow. We have no preconceived notions of how that may be; we're pretty much in the dark on this whole thing. Okay?"

Walther nodded.

"As I said, your report was thorough. I feel like I have all the facts you can give me. What I want more details about is your impressions of what happened. I want you to give me any feelings you might have that weren't concrete enough for you to have put in your report. I want your gut reactions about what happened, about the girl, the way she acted, the way the whole thing went down. You understand what I mean?"

"I think so."

"Good. Now, do you have any objections to my taping this? It's strictly for my own convenience."

"No objections. It's fine."

Haydon punched the buttons on the cassette recorder lying at his elbow on the desk.

"Do you have the postmortem on her?" Walther asked.

"No. I just learned about her this morning. I've sent for it."

Walther thought a moment. "We put in the report that we assumed the girl was having an adverse reaction to a drug. Possibly LSD or angel dust. But I've never actually seen anyone go nuts from a bad trip. I read about it in training, of course; we saw a film."

"I understand. But her actions conformed to what you'd learned?"

"Yes, sir."

"What made you think it was LSD or angel dust?"

"We knew people had this kind of reaction from bad trips on them. I mean, we knew that much."

"Can you describe again how she acted? Your impressions?"

Hirsch had been reading Walther's report at the next desk and was just finishing the last paragraph when Haydon asked his question. He folded the report and turned to listen.

Walther unconsciously touched the gauze on his face and shifted in the straight-backed chair.

"It was pretty weird. I've never seen anything like it. When she came flying at us out of the dark like that, her hair and skirt flapping, her eyes and mouth wide open, it was the most . . . well, it was shocking. I didn't realize this at the time. It happened too quick, and the adrenaline was really pumping. But I've thought about it a lot since." He turned his head a little to one side, pensively. "I don't remember her screaming, but it seems to me, looking back, that she was."

"She was crazed, you said. Just made a blind dash right into the headlights."

"No; she didn't run into the headlights blindly, like a dog or deer will do sometimes in confusion. She ran *at* the headlights. She saw them, all right. Which is strange, because only seconds later, when I was chasing her, she ran into a chain-link fence, twice, as if she *hadn't* seen it. Hell, it was eight feet high."

"What about when she bit you?"

"Well, I'd bent down to see how badly she'd been hurt by the car. She seemed kind of stunned. Just as I got down on one knee she lunged at me. The word 'bite' doesn't quite convey what she did. She really went after me."

"You hit her then?"

Walther hesitated half a beat. "Yes, sir, I did. It was reflexive. I swung and hit her hard enough to knock her head off. I jumped up and started pulling my revolver and then I kind of came to my senses. I realized she was crazy and wasn't going to calm down just because I was pointing my .38 at her. Then she was up and gone and I went after her."

"How was her condition?"

"Bad. Really, her running was more like a high-energy stagger. I mean, she made good time but she had a kind of sideways drift, as if she was running hard to keep from losing her balance and falling over in the direction she was going. I don't know how much of her disorientation was because of my having slugged her. Anyway, when I finally got her pinned down I had a heck of a time staying on top of her until Silva could give me a hand."

"What happened to her after you got the cuffs on her?"

"She tensed up. Didn't fight all that much because she was so rigid straining against the cuffs. Her eyes were still wide open. She seemed terrified. I suppose she was hallucinating. Thought I was going to kill her or something."

"She didn't say anything during all this?"

"Oh, no. She couldn't."

"Couldn't?"

"Her throat was too tight, I think."

"Why do you think that?"

"She was breathing through her mouth. She didn't seem to be able to get enough air. Her neck muscles were really standing out by this time, tight inside, and all that slobbering wasn't making it any easier. She couldn't talk. She was making sounds, all right, but it was just gurgling."

"Did you notice if she had a fever?"

"A fever? That'd be hard to tell. It was hot and we'd been running. I was sweating plenty and I knew she was hot too. It could've been a fever, I guess. She was sweating, that's for sure."

"Then what?"

"The rigidity increased and developed into what Roland and I realized was a convulsion. I've seen convulsions. I rolled her over on her belly. Tried to do something for her. She wouldn't let me clear her throat. She just bit me again."

He held up his right hand. A large adhesive bandage was wrapped around the outside of the hand to the palm. "Roland and I realized at about the same time that the seizure could be fatal. All of them look fatal, when you think about it. We got scared and Roland called EMS. She was dead by the time they got there."

Haydon sat back in his chair. "Do you have the feeling she was running from someone when she came at you?"

Walther shook his head decisively. "No. I think she attacked the car. She wasn't running *from* anything. She was running *at* us."

"Did you look around in the weeds where she came from?"

"Yes, sir. While we were waiting for the coroner's investigator, I took my flashlight and searched the area. I didn't find anything. I guess it could have been more thoroughly searched in the daytime."

"Anything else? Anything at all that sticks in your mind about this incident? You said earlier that you'd thought about it a lot."

"I have, yes, because it was eerie. You don't have too many women running into the headlights of your unit."

Walther looked at Haydon and then at Hirsch. There wasn't anything else to say.

"Okay. Thanks," Haydon said, snapping off the recorder. "I appreciate it. I hope your stitches will be out in a few days and you can forget about it."

The lanky patrolman stood up. "I wish it was going to be that easy."

"What do you mean?"

"Well, she bit a chunk out of my face about the size of a half dollar. The plastic surgeon said I could look forward to a series of skin grafts to fill in the hole."

"Jesus," Hirsch said.

Walther stepped to the door and then stopped and turned around. "There is one other thing. You haven't seen the morgue shots, I guess."

Haydon shook his head.

"The girl was . . . beautiful. Absolutely beautiful." He gave an ironic smile and walked out.

Haydon watched, without moving or speaking, as the

young patrolman crossed the squad room and disappeared. Suddenly he punched the rewind button.

"You know who she is, don't you, Leo?"

"The other Jane Doe Vanstraten had in the morgue yesterday morning."

"That's right."

The cassette rewound and clicked off. Haydon ejected the cartridge, jotted identification on the label with a felt-tip pen, and tossed the cartridge to Hirsch.

"Would you run this by the morgue on your way home? You might as well leave now. See that Vanstraten gets it personally. If he's not there, leave an urgent message with the girl you talked with yesterday. Then call his home and leave a message with his wife too. I want him to listen to this before he goes any farther. While you're at the morgue, be sure to fill out the papers to have Jane Doe added to our priority postmortem requests. Also fill out the forms for a makeup photo of her. Ask them to rush it. We'll need it tomorrow."

15

Thursday morning Haydon walked down the windowless and dull-lighted hallway on the third floor of the Houston Police Department on Riesner Street. At the end of the hall, inexplicably tiled in a baleful battleship gray, he could see the scattered desks of the Homicide Division. He shuffled sideways past two black women mopping the yellowed vinyl floor tiles with the same eye-burning disinfectant they used in the city jail, and continued past the rest rooms, where two coveralled plumbers had propped the doors open while they disassembled a urinal in the middle of the gritty floor.

He went around the four-foot-square tunnel fan that sat in the middle of the double doorway. The fan was used to pull a flow of warm, medicinal-smelling air from the corridor into the overcrowded and also windowless squad room, a stark and cheerless space that owed its dreariness to the 1950s architectural concept of "modern."

Haydon threaded his way through the maze of desks and arriving day-shift detectives, who dawdled in ragged groups trying to wear down the early-morning inertia. He went straight to the Mr. Coffee machine and poured a cup, added enough nondairy creamer to turn the oily brew the color of sludge, and took it into the cluttered cubicle he shared with Hirsch. Hirsch and Mooney were waiting for him.

The two detectives looked up from their grousing about the city's latest utility hike, said good morning, then turned to the subject of Houston's deteriorating streets. Haydon unclipped his Baretta from the waistband at the small of his back and put it in the top drawer of the filing cabinet, along with Hirsch's and Mooney's revolvers. He took off his coat and hung it on a wire hanger on the back of the door. Sitting at his desk, he tested the coffee, told himself he couldn't believe he was going to drink it, and then did.

"First things first," he said, looking at Hirsch. "You got the tape to Vanstraten?"

"Sure did. He was still there, so I gave it to him personally."

"Good." He looked at Mooney. "Any problems getting you transferred over for the next five or six days?"

"I guess not. Dystal had it all worked out when I came in this morning. He didn't mention anything about any five or six days, though."

"That's even better. Ed, I want you to start with Steen, Parmer, and Kielman. They must've had a fairly close network. Same customers, same routines, same friends. See if you can come up with some background on these colored rooms."

"Okay, but it's going to be tough getting skinny from the girls after last night," Mooney said. "They're going to clam up. You want me to catch Croft too? She's the one who's going to know."

"No. I want to follow up there."

"You think she's in any danger? She probably worked as closely with them as they did with each other."

"How do you feel about it?"

"I think she's a big girl. She knows the score. If she's afraid something screwy's going on, she can always shut down until the situation clears up."

"I agree."

"You saw the *Chronicle?*" Hirsch asked.

"They had a good time with the red room, didn't they?" Haydon said. "Who gave them the information?"

Hirsch looked uneasy. "One of the crime reporters latched onto a new lab man. The guy didn't know. It's understandable."

"But not acceptable. Anyone talk to him?"

Hirsch glanced at Mooney. "I did," he said.

"The reporter had just enough details to make it juicy. Can't really blame him on this one. It was flashy. Still, it's an isolated incident as far as they're concerned. Kielman was just a woman who got sick and died. Steen was a back-page item, and the Mexican girl never even made the papers. As long as no one snaps to their relationship, we'll be all right."

None of them said what each was thinking: The reprieve from the media wouldn't last long. They had to move quickly before the inevitable headlines brought on a different kind of pressure.

Haydon looked at his partner. "Leo, I want you to go by the morgue and get the makeup shots on the Mexican girl. Go to Magnolia Park and see what you can dig up on her. These other girls are obviously out of her league, so she may not have any connection to this investigation. On the other hand, she's Latin.

"Which brings us to the clubs. I'll check with them. These guys"—Haydon reached for a manila folder and flipped it open—"Paulo Guimaraes and Miguel de la Borda, listed on Steen's corporation papers, will have to be questioned too."

110

He tested the coffee again. Disgusted, he set the cup at the back of his desk, against the wall.

They sat in silence. Mooney absently probed the upper reaches of his stomach with his hand, communing with his ulcer, while Hirsch secretly dreaded the door-to-door campaign in the gummy back streets of Magnolia Park. He could already smell the rancid chemical effluent that hung in the barrio like an industrial fart.

Mooney was the first to realize Haydon wasn't going to say anything else. He looked at Hirsch, who raised his eyebrows in a puzzled shrug. Haydon was lost in thought, seemingly through with his instructions.

Mooney took the initiative and stood to get his revolver from the filing cabinet. He looked at Hirsch, who nodded and stood too, taking his revolver from Mooney's outstretched hand.

"We hate to eat and run . . ." Mooney said.

"Ed," Haydon interrupted him, still staring into space. "Why don't you get a copy of the makeup too? Take it with you and show it around. It's a long shot."

"Will do."

"Let me hear from you," Haydon said.

Mooney and Hirsch looked at each other again.

"Will do," Mooney repeated, and they walked out.

Before they had walked the length of the long gray hall to the elevators, Haydon had pulled out the box containing Steen's photo albums. He removed the three plastic pages of pictures taken in the colored rooms and carried them downstairs to the photo lab.

Pushing through the lab's swinging glass doors, he pressed the buzzer on the Masonite countertop that separated the three-sided waiting area from the rest of the lab. There were several desks on the other side of the counter, all deserted, and a wall covered with photographic curiosities, some old and yellowing, others in the dazzling, unreal colors of modern scientific photography—blow-ups, aerial photographs, microphotographs, and Kodak snaps. The pungent smell of developing chemicals assaulted Haydon's nostrils.

From one of the hallways that flanked either side of the wall of photographs, a gaunt young man in an ill-fitting blue uniform ambled around the corner, wiping his amber-stained hands with a paper towel. He looked at the empty desks and shook his head.

"I think Delores has bladder trouble," he said. "She's always gone to pee." He walked up and leaned on the counter. "Whatcha got?"

Haydon laid the sheets in front of Randal Murray, whose oily, shoulder-length hair was in direct violation of department regulations. The hair had been the subject of a running battle in which Murray's lieutenant defended the photographer's hairstyle to the captain with every defense that could be honorably justified by a grown man. He claimed Murray was a "photographic genius," the best lab man between New York and Los Angeles, and that sometimes you had to allow for creative personalities to get the best man for the job. He even claimed that Murray spent most of his time in the darkroom and that by the lieutenant's personal calculations only nineteen and one-half percent of the people who came into the lab would see him, and then, more than likely, they would get only a "glimpse."

The captain had remained unswayed. He said he didn't care if Murray spent a hundred percent of his time in the back drawer of a filing cabinet; if he wore the department's uniform, he was going to wear regulation hair. Either he cut his hair or the lieutenant could cut Murray's termination papers.

The beleaguered lieutenant persuaded the temperamental Murray to cut his hair . . . an inch, and then spent a lot of stomach-wrenching energy keeping the photographer out of

112

the captain's sight. This cautious insubordination was rewarded by the department's achieving the reputation for having one of the most outstanding law enforcement photo labs anywhere in the nation.

"Oh, good—live ones," Murray said, looking at the prints. He whistled. "Very alive. You not working murders anymore?"

"I'm still in homicide," Haydon said. Murders. Jesus.

"This's research, huh?" Murray said with a straight face.

"Right."

Murray laughed. "You guys."

"I need eight-by-tens of each of these. Will they hold together for that?"

"I think so." Murray brought them close to his face. "May be a little grainy, but not bad."

"Then I want every face blown up to five by seven."

"Partial profiles too?"

"Or even a portion of a face."

"Mmm. What about distinctive marks? Scars, moles on butts and tits? Things like that." He pulled a magnifying glass from a drawer and looped his stringy hair behind his ears to keep it from falling in his face as he bent down.

"Fine."

"Anything else?"

"Yes; I need them—"

"—as soon as possible," Murray said, nodding knowingly and looking up.

"It's urgent," Haydon said.

"Shit, I never had any doubt about that," Murray said. He shook his greasy head and put the glass to the pictures again.

Haydon ignored his impudence as if he were a petulant child. "When can I get them?"

Murray quickly looked over the prints, counting the number of blow-ups. He turned down the sides of his mouth.

"Will you take the flak if I bump something else?"

"You have other rush work?"

Murray gave Haydon a look of sarcastic indulgence.

"Okay," Haydon said. "Yes, I'll be responsible."

"Tomorrow morning. Say, ten-thirty."

Back in his office, Haydon filled out the paperwork to have the fingerprints from the Quenby house run through the computer. He processed the paperwork requesting data from Crime Analysis on persons convicted or suspected of homicide by poison, persons convicted or suspected of assaults on prostitutes, homicidal sociopaths cross-referenced with prostitution, and suspects of multiple homicides.

After he had put the last manila envelope in the interdepartment mail pigeonhole in the squad room, he walked back into his office and called Marvin Farris, Sally Steen's attorney, whose name Hirsch had eventually located among Steen's papers. He introduced himself to Farris's secretary, who put him on hold with a Muzak version of "Moon River." When Farris came on the line he was reserved but polite.

"This is Marvin Farris, Sergeant. What can I do for you?"

"I'm investigating the death of a client of yours, Mr. Farris. Sally Steen." Haydon paused but there was no response. "Were you aware of her death?"

"Uh, yes, I am. However, I didn't know there was anything in it that would be of interest to the Homicide Division."

"I didn't say I was with Homicide."

"You're not with Homicide?"

"I am."

Again there was no response, so Haydon went on.

"We've obtained copies of Miss Steen's legal papers from her home . . ." Farris gave a little snort, which Haydon didn't quite know how to interpret. ". . . and we've

114

found that a Miss Judith Croft is Miss Steen's chief beneficiary. We were wondering if you had already contacted Miss Croft about her inheritance.''

"I have spoken to Miss Croft; yes.''

"Was she aware that she was the beneficiary prior to your conversation with her?''

"I really couldn't say, Sergeant.''

"You don't know?''

"I mean I really couldn't say.''

"Well, then, did Miss Croft call you in regard to this matter or did you call her?''

"That's a question I'm really not at liberty to answer. I'm sorry.''

"Mr. Farris,'' Haydon said patiently, "are you now representing Miss Croft?''

"As a matter of fact, I am.''

Haydon shook his head wearily. Now that that fact had been brought out in the open in spite of Farris's lawyerly circumlocutions, the attorney seemed to loosen up a little.

"Do you have a particular interest in Miss Croft? I'm sure she'd like to help you any way she could. She's extremely disturbed over the death. You can appreciate that, I'm sure. They were the closest of friends, you know.''

"Yes, I understand that.''

"Obviously you believe Miss Steen's death may have been a homicide. Is that correct?''

"Not exactly.'' Farris didn't have a monopoly on vagueness.

"I don't think I understand,'' Farris said.

Haydon resisted the temptation to spar with the lawyer.

"We don't have the ME's report yet, and until we can establish a cause of death we're checking into everything.''

"I see.''

"Do you know a Mr. Paulo Guimaraes or Miguel de la Borda?'' Haydon asked, changing his tack.

Farris hesitated a moment—trying to figure his angles, Haydon thought—and then acted as if his remembrance of the men's names was slowly dawning on him.

"Yes . . . yes, I believe I do. I recall that Miss Steen shared a partnership with them in several nightclubs. Her share was very small. But I suppose you know that already."

"Are they American citizens?"

"Neither of them are, I think. Mr. de la Borda is Panamanian, I think, and Guimaraes is Brazilian. Both have considerable investments here in Houston as well as throughout the South."

"Apparently they both have unlisted telephone numbers. I couldn't find them in the book. Would you mind giving me their numbers and addresses from your files?"

"Surely you realize I can't do that, Sergeant. I'll be glad to help you in any way I can, however, that doesn't violate any client or client-related confidence."

"No, I think that's all for now. I appreciate your help."

"Not at all," Farris said.

At lunchtime Haydon sent out for a sandwich and then spent the remainder of the day in front of the green display screen of the CRT. He compiled an alphabetical listing of every name thus far connected with the call-girl deaths and laboriously fed them into the computer, selecting a variety of data screens from the menu. If the response was positive, he keyed in a printout, which the computer spat forth with chattering efficiency. Haydon tore the perforated paper from the back of the machine and added the copy to the file bearing the subject's name.

By the time he went home Thursday night, he had gone through three-quarters of the list and had picked up several additional names from cross-references. Friday morning he came in early before the lines had a chance to load up and continued the search, breaking only long enough to talk to

Hirsch and Mooney, who called in at different times during the morning to report disappointing progress. He finished the name search in the afternoon and then, from Hirsch's and Mooney's oral reports, typed supplements to the main file, which he had set up in an accordion folder and titled, simply, "Call Girls." When he went home Friday night, he took the file with him.

16

Cinco lay on the terrace in a latticework of shadows, snapping irritably at the june bugs attracted by the light coming through the small panes in the library doors. Inside, Nina had just gotten up to change a recording of Chopin nocturnes and had returned to her armchair, where she pulled her feet up under her and opened the new July issue of *Town and Country*. Haydon sat at the refectory table with his back to her and started through the file for the second time.

When the chimes from the front gates sounded, Haydon raised his head. Knowing Nina would be looking at him to see if he was expecting anyone, he shook his head and raised his shoulders. He heard Nina set aside her magazine and go to the speaker located near the door that opened out into the hallway.

"Yes?"

"Nina, dear. It's Harl." The voice was deep, even over the intercom. "Are you alone? Do we have a few hours to be together?"

Nina laughed. "I'll let you in, Van, but you'll have to share me. *He's* here."

"Oh, damn."

She pushed the button that opened the gates and Haydon turned around.

"He's got something or he wouldn't be coming by."

"I'll let him in," Nina said. She was smiling as she went out into the hallway toward the front doors.

Vanstraten's voice preceded him, telegraphing his good mood. When they came into the library he had one arm around Nina and they were both laughing.

"I don't understand," he said, stopping at the door and rolling his eyes at Haydon. "She won't take me seriously. I know," he said, looking down at Nina. "I'm much more persuasive over sherry. Get us some and I'll prove it. Everything looks different over sherry."

"Three sherries?" she asked, still smiling and looking at Haydon.

Haydon nodded and Vanstraten came over to the refectory table and looked at what Haydon was reading.

"Mmm," he said.

"What have you got?" Haydon asked. He gestured to one of the red leather armchairs and turned his own chair around to face the pathologist.

Vanstraten sat down and immediately lit a Dunhill cigarette. He adjusted his clothes, pulled his white cuffs to let them show from his suit coat, and crossed his legs.

"I think I've got what you wanted, but I'll tell you, Stuart, it's bizarre."

Haydon waited.

Vanstraten was suddenly all business. "As it turns out, all four girls were remarkably clean. None of them seemed to have punished their bodies particularly, but a pure diagnosis of the organic changes brought on by the illness was considerably obscured in the cases of Kielman and Parmer by the presence of drugs. There wasn't much in either one, but it was enough to complicate things. Steen, as I told you, was a good subject because she was in fine health and had no drugs. But she had a few more years on her and the abortions and herpes were there to have changed some things.''

There was a pause while Vanstraten drew on his cigarette. Then Nina came in with the sherry and each of them took a glass. Nina settled in her armchair across from Vanstraten, who was turned in profile to her as he addressed Haydon.

''Delicious,'' he said, sipping the sherry. He allowed himself another conspiratorial smile at Nina. ''Okay. It turns out the young girl was the *perfect* specimen. Incidentally, I don't think she was Mexican. Latin for sure, but not Mexican. Anyway, she was so young you could read her like a map. A real blessing. She was about twenty-three, somewhere in there. No drugs, no alcohol. Nothing. She was three months pregnant. No smallpox vaccination scar, so maybe she wasn't a U.S. citizen. Isn't that a part of the immigration regulations? Anyway, that officer's description of the girl's actions prior to death was invaluable when we started working on her. Saved us hours.''

When Vanstraten paused for another sip, Haydon lit a cigarette of his own. Nina looked at him.

''Naturally the seizures and convulsions indicated some type of neurological disorder. Fine, but you can work on brain sections for months and still have a whole library of information you haven't approached. Microscopic examination of cell sections taken from various areas of the brain allowed us to eliminate some possibilities from the beginning. D.T.'s were out. We tested for tetanus. Nothing. Tested for Guillain-Barré ascending paralysis. Nothing. Poliomyelitis? Nothing. We kept going, up and down the scales of the most probable disorders. Viral encephalitis? Nothing. . . .''

Vanstraten went on to list a host of neurological disorders they had tested for, with negative results. Haydon inhaled deeply and listened patiently. Obviously Vanstraten had conducted quite a search. It was the sort of challenge the pathologist delighted in; it required the greatest creativity from both him and his staff.

"Finally we started playing some hunches," Vanstraten continued. "Oddly, what threw us at first, I think, was too much reliance on logic. We were trying to establish a paradigm of communicability. That is, we were trying to determine what it was they could have communicated to *each other*. But then it occurred to us that this young girl was different. You don't in the least suspect her of being a call girl, do you?"

"No."

"Then they couldn't have shared the virus with her, at least not on the basis of that theory. Perhaps, then, they hadn't shared it with each other. When we began thinking from the perspective of the virus having been communicated to each of them separately and individually rather than *among* them, then our method of research had to change.

"We listened again to the tape you gave us—it must have been about the fourth time—and someone picked up the patrolman's description of how the girl propelled herself. He said she 'attacked' the car, ran into the fence 'as if she hadn't seen it,' had a 'high-energy stagger.' That turned us around. We began to work with a whole new set of premises. We changed to a new series of stains and scored right off. These little bullet-shaped RNA viruses showed up immediately. Negri bodies! We couldn't believe it. We thought we'd made a mistake."

"Negri bodies?"

"Yes, Negri bodies," Vanstraten said, not stopping or thinking to explain. "Double-checking ourselves, we went back to the brain sections of the other three women and subjected them to the same specific stains: histologic, fluorescent antibody, and mouse inoculation tests. All were positive. All of them, Stuart. They *all* had hydrophobia.''

"What!"

"I told you it was bizarre. But there's no doubt. They all had *rabies*. Every one of them died like common mad dogs.''

17

Haydon sat in stunned silence, his eyes fixed on Vanstraten. He felt his back muscles tighten against the curve of the polished cherry armchair. The smoke from the cigarette in his right hand, which dangled from the armrest in a misleadingly relaxed fashion, rose in a blue ray of absolute stillness. With heightened senses, he could feel the drumming of his accelerated pulse in that same wrist and could hear, in what he knew was distorted amplification, the booming of the hard shells of the june bugs as they collided with the glass panes in the library doors.

"What are you telling me?" he said finally.

Vanstraten opened his eyes in an exaggerated gesture. "What am I telling you? What kind of a question is that? I'm telling you how they *died*, or rather, why they died."

"All four of them?"

"Exactly."

"How could they have gotten rabies?"

Vanstraten shook his head.

"Then how *might* they have gotten rabies?"

"From animals, I suppose."

"Dogs? Cats? Rats?"

"Not likely rats, oddly enough. They don't seem to be carriers. Squirrels, though, and skunks, are highly susceptible. And of course, bats."

Haydon looked at Nina. "Animals. Jesus."

"Your cigarette," she said.

He got it to the ashtray just before a long, limp ash fell away. He put it out. Taking up the glass of sherry, he tasted it, his mind elsewhere, then he turned to Vanstraten.

"All right," he said. "I know you've studied up on it. Why don't you tell me what it's like. Nina, would you mind bringing the sherry in here? I don't want to be interrupted any more than necessary."

Nina crossed into the dining room and returned with a Baccarat decanter, set it on a tea table between the two men, and settled into her chair again.

"You're a dear, Nina," Vanstraten said, lifting the decanter and filling his glass halfway with the amber liquor. He offered some to Haydon, who shook his head; he looked at Nina, who smiled and shook her head also. Then he, too, settled back.

"Rabies is an acute viral disease of the central nervous system. The virus itself is in the rhabdovirus group, which simply means the virus is bullet-shaped when viewed under a light microscope. To initiate infection, the virus must come into contact with nerve tissue, any nerve tissue. In a dog bite, for instance, the epidermis is broken, the nerve tissue exposed, the virus comes into contact by way of the saliva. At this point the virus may simply lie dormant for up to ninety-six hours and could conceivably be aborted by simply washing the wound thoroughly with soap and water. After this period of time, however, the virus begans replication in the muscle tissue, infects the neuromuscular and neurotendinal spindles near the area of exposure.

"The virus then spreads in a *centripetal* movement along

124

the nerves, reaching the peripheral nerves and the dorsal root ganglia, where it ascends the spinal cord to the brain. Once the virus reaches the brain, it replicates almost exclusively within the gray matter, and then passes *centrifugally* along autonomic nerves to reach other tissues, such as the salivary glands, the eyes, taste buds, nerve endings of hairs, adrenal medulla, olfactory neuroepithelium, pancreas, and on and on. This, of course, produces an encephalitis, which is what you see as the initial pathology. If you don't know the history of the infection, you will be seriously misled from this point forward. A doctor would most likely treat the patient for one of the many encephalitides I mentioned in our wayward postmortem examination.

"Incidentally, from the moment the virus touches the first minuscule piece of brain tissue and causes the first symptoms to appear, the disease is irreversible. It is always fatal. Well, that's not exactly true. In 1970 a six-year-old boy in Ohio survived after having contracted the disease from a rabid bat. They began a series of post-exposure inoculations immediately, which is usually always successful as long as the virus is still incubating, but he contracted rabies anyway. It was an extraordinary struggle, which lasted six months. There have been a few other reported recoveries, but they could not be documented.

"Now, the clinical manifestations of rabies can be divided into three stages. The prodromal period is marked by a low fever, around 102 degrees, headache, malaise, anorexia, vomiting, sore throat. Most of the time there is a prickling sensation at or around the site of inoculation—the bite or whatever. The encephalitic phase is recognized by a kind of nervous agitation, which may include confusion, hallucinations, muscle spasms, focal paralysis. The periods of mental aberrations are interspersed with completely lucid periods, but as the disease progresses the lucid periods grow briefer. The person will develop hyperesthesia, with sensi-

125

tivity to bright light, loud noise, touch, and even gentle breezes. Temperature may soar as high as 105 degrees. Abnormalities develop in the autonomic nervous system: pupils dilate and become irregular, eyes water, salivation becomes profuse and uncontrollable. This is the classic 'foaming mouth.' Vocal cords become paralyzed.

"The final stage actually overlaps, or is continuous with, the one I've just described. This is when brain stem dysfunction is severe. All symptoms previously mentioned are intensified. If the subject is lucid during this period, he avoids swallowing water and manifests classic hydrophobia. From this point the subject quickly lapses into a coma and the involvement of the respiratory centers usually produces an apneic death. The median period of survival after the onset of symptoms is four days."

Vanstraten stopped, took a mouthful of sherry, which he swallowed with slow relish, and then worked his mouth for the aftertaste. "It's a horrible way to die."

"Can you be more specific about what actually causes death?"

"Hell, everything just falls apart. There's cerebral swelling, hormonal imbalances, oxygen deficiency, bacterial pneumonia, irregular heartbeat, congestive heart failure, plummeting blood pressure, blood clots, excessively low and then excessively high body temperatures, secondary bacterial infections, gastrointestinal bleeding . . ." Vanstraten opened his palms in a gesture of hopelessness.

"All of these women died like that?" Nina asked.

"I'm afraid so. The disease ran its course in each of them. They probably experienced every bit of what I've described."

"Are there variations, different types of rabies? I mean, can you tell if the virus originated with a dog, or bat, or cat, whatever?" Haydon asked.

"Yes to the first question. No to the second. Actually,

there's only a gross difference. 'Dumb rabies' is used to describe that manifestation of the disease producing no aggressive behavior. 'Furious rabies' describes a form in which there is very pronounced excitement. In 'paralytic rabies,' paralysis is the dominant symptom. It affects different people in different ways, and the name of the type is simply a description of what happens.''

"And you can't tell, postmortem, which of the three caused death.''

"No. But from the taped description you gave me, the poor Latin girl obviously had 'furious' symptoms.''

"Do you have any idea how many animals get rabies in the Houston metropolitan area in a year's time?''

"Yes.'' Vanstraten grinned smugly. "When I realized what we had, I had our records division do an incidence search.'' He produced a small notebook and opened it. "In 1979 eleven animals contracted rabies. At least, that many were confirmed. Three skunks, four bats, one dog, two cats, and one horse. In 1980 there were four cases: one skunk and three bats. In 1981, eighteen cases: four skunks, fourteen bats. This year, up to this month, there have been nine cases: six skunks, two bats, one cat.'' He closed the notebook and put it back into his pocket.

"You know my next question.''

"Never been a case of human rabies in Houston. And damn few in Texas. I looked back twenty years. One in 1962, no details. One in 1972, an odd case of accidental inoculation. A fifty-six-year-old laboratory technician employed by a pharmaceutical firm in Temple was making rabies vaccine using a fixed rabies virus. 'Fixed,' or 'attenuated,' means the virus has been altered in some way so that it is not communicable to humans though it is still a live virus. At least, it was thought not to be communicable until this incident. The technician was homogenizing rabid goat brains in a blender. Apparently he inhaled aerosols from this fresh

127

homogenate while transferring portions of it to other containers. He contracted the disease and died. In 1976 a thirteen-year-old Mexican boy died after being bitten by a rabid dog in San Antonio. In 1979 a seven-year-old Mexican girl died of rabies in Eagle Pass on the border. No details. That's all.''

"Are there nationwide statistics?''

"Averaged about one case per year for the last twenty years. And that includes Guam, Puerto Rico, and the Virgin Islands, and those cases in which the individual contracted rabies outside the United States but was brought here for treatment and died here.''

"So the actual number of rabies cases contracted in the U.S. is much smaller.''

"Well, some smaller. Certainly damn few.''

Haydon finished his sherry and set the empty glass on the refectory table. He let his eyes slide away to the bookshelves. The only light in the library came from the three lamps sitting on side tables by each of them, and their glow illuminated the spines of the rows and rows of volumes. Some, with gold lettering, glistened in the lamplight as if they were bound in tapestry faceted with golden thread. They seemed so precise and orderly, waiting with a wise patience to be opened and learned from. But there were none he could open to answer the questions he had now.

He stood and walked around the table to look out onto the terrace. Cinco was asleep, having given up his snapping fight with the june bugs. Haydon could see one of the beetles crawling stiffly along the old dog's back. He heard the clink of the decanter as Vanstraten poured himself more sherry. He heard the snip of the Dunhill lighter.

"It's almost too ghastly to contemplate, isn't it?'' Vanstraten said.

"Considering the statistics and the situation, I don't know

how I can avoid it.'' Haydon was still facing the French doors.

"Surely there's something else . . . some other explanation for these cases,'' Nina said. "This is an old section of town. Many of the buildings have bats. There's all those towers at Rice.''

Haydon turned around. "And the bats only bite call girls?''

"But who could do something like that?''

"A good question,'' Haydon said, coming back around the table. "Van, how difficult would it be to infect someone . . . without their knowledge?''

"That's not what I meant,'' Nina protested.

"You meant that someone who would do this sort of thing would have to be . . . mad.'' Vanstraten smiled at Nina. "A little symbolism is always a good thing, in life or in death.''

"How about it, Van?'' Haydon pressed.

"Well, the virus is not all that potent from an infectionary perspective. Its virulency is what inspires all the horror. The sure death. Actually, the virus is not totally understood. Let's say you're bitten by a bat, you're inoculated. The virus may sit at the site of introduction for as long as ninety-six hours, as I mentioned. Then it begins to travel on nerve tissue toward the central nervous system, the brain. This period of travel is known as the incubation period. The virus does not replicate during incubation, it just travels. You have no symptoms. It's during this travel time that science loses track of it. It may stop somewhere along the way and sleep awhile, travel some more, stop awhile. There's no way of knowing how it will act during this time. It may shoot straight to the brain. Once it reaches the brain— 'invades the host,' in medical terminology—you show your first sign of illness, perhaps a slight fever or a mild headache. At that point you're a dead man. You've got about four days left."

"Even if you're being treated?"

"Oh, no. With medical intervention they can drag it out to fifteen, twenty, twenty-five days. But sooner or later the cumulative deterioration of organs will surpass medicine's ability to restore them effectively. *Finis.*"

"What are the variables of the incubation period?"

"Ten days to over a year."

"My God!"

"Yes, that's bad for you. There won't be any 'scene of crime' on these deaths. If you were to catch your 'madman' tonight, you could have people die a year from now from what he's already done. Hypothetically."

"How would he inoculate them?"

"In an unlimited number of ways. All he has to do is bring the live virus in contact with exposed nerve tissue. A creative mind could do a lot with such simple requirements."

"Such as?"

"If you had stomach ulcers, a few drops in any kind of drink would be enough. A few drops in a bottle of Visine for bloodshot eyes or in anything injected with a needle; any kind of aerosol distribution which would allow it to be inhaled and come into contact with the pulmonary alveoli; a few drops in a nasal spray, or a vaginal liquid douche, or an antiseptic mouthwash and gargle for sore throats. There are countless possibilities."

Haydon sat down. He hardly knew what course of questioning to pursue next. "What about prophylaxis?"

"Two ways," Vanstraten said, holding his cigarette by its tip so that it stuck straight up in his cupped hand. "For persons such as veterinarians, who are constantly at risk, there are pre-exposure immunization shots. I think they require annual boosters. For post-exposure situations, as when one is bitten by a known rabid animal, you can prevent the infection in most cases by administering immune rabies globulin together with a vaccination using a 'killed' virus— that is, literally, a dead virus. Once injected, it will not replicate, but will stimulate the immune system. The passive antibody against rabies neutralizes the virus while the body, in response to the vaccine, produces antibodies. They mostly use a human diploid vaccine now.''

"This incubation period—can it be affected?"

"What do you mean?"

"Can it be accelerated?"

"Mmm, that's a bit of a controversy. The briefer incubation periods do seem to have a similar history. The amount of the virus introduced and the condition of the wound would have an effect. For instance, a dog bite might cause a mangling that would traumatize the tissue and allow the introduction of a greater volume of virus and would be more difficult to clean. The defense mechanisms of the host would have an effect. If the victim was already ill, or was a dope addict with poor immunological integrity, the virus would be less likely to be impeded in its travel to the brain. Some even say the location of the site of inoculation is a determining influence. Someone bitten on the foot would have a longer incubation period than someone bitten on the face, which is right there at the brain."

Suddenly Haydon lurched forward in his chair. "Jesus Christ! Walther! What about Walther?"

There was a disconcerting silence. No one moved. Then Vanstraten turned quickly to the telephone.

"I'll have one of my staff waiting in the emergency room upstairs in Ben Taub with the proper inoculations." He dialed and spoke quickly, punctuating his words with plosive Germanic inflections. It was always a sign of Vanstraten's agitation when his speech lapsed into accent.

He slammed down the receiver and tossed off the last of the sherry in his glass as he stood. "I'm going down there. I want to examine his face when he comes in. I want to be sure about the inoculation. Stuart, make sure he gets there."

Nina walked out of the library with Vanstraten, the pathologist taking long strides down the hall, his shoulders slightly hunched. He kissed Nina goodbye at the door and walked alone to his car.

Haydon was talking on the telephone when she came back into the room. ". . . and take him there *yourself*. Understand, Silva? Vanstraten's waiting. And tell him who you are. You probably ought to take the shots too. No. I don't want to go into it now. Vanstraten will explain. When you get to Ben Taub with Walther, call me. I want to know. Good, good."

Haydon hung up and ran his fingers through his hair. He turned and Nina was standing, hugging herself with crossed arms. Haydon could see the tears.

"Can you believe this?" he said heavily.

Nina wiped the hair away from her face and took a deep breath. Haydon was standing in the center of the room with his hands in his pockets. Neither of them knew what to do. Haydon walked to the telephone and punched out a number.

It rang awhile before he spoke. "Sorry, Bob. This's Stuart. You awake enough? Okay. Something's developed in the Steen situation and I need to talk with you. No, no—not now. But how about breakfast? You have anyone lined up? Good. Yeah, I know. Good night."

"Do you want to wait here," Nina asked, "or upstairs?"

"I'll wait here. I need to think." He looked at her and his face softened. "Go ahead, honey. You need the sleep. Really, there's no reason . . ."

"I'll wait a little while with you. I want to hear about Walther too. I'll put on coffee."

"Good," he said, sitting down again. He lit a cigarette and crossed his long legs. His eyes already had begun to indicate a preoccupation with something else. "That sounds good," he said absently.

18

Bob Dystal polished off the last bite of his six sausage patties by smearing it around in the yellow remnants of his four eggs. He put a glob of strawberry jam on the last half of a piece of whole wheat toast and ate it in two bites. He filled his cup from the complimentary pot sitting on the table and sipped it as he looked out the restaurant window, streaked with smog and weeping humidity. Bumper-to-bumper morning traffic was stalled on the loop.

The burly lieutenant ate at the same Jojo's every morning. He arrived at seven-thirty with the two major Houston dailies tucked under his arm and sat at the same window table, looking out onto the freeway. The waitress brought his pot of coffee and the cook put his eggs and sausage on the grill, having been signaled by the waitress. Dystal would dispatch the food while catching the headlines and major stories, and then would settle back to talk business with whoever might have gained a slot at his legendary breakfasts. Sometimes his guests were in the headlines themselves, criminally speaking, or had been, or knew something about someone who was. His easygoing style had made him a favorite with informers who didn't want to be grilled for information beyond what they were already willing to give.

This morning it was Haydon who watched Dystal settle back and blow on his coffee.

"Well, hell, that's weird," Dystal said, smacking his mouth. He always put sugar in the coffee he drank after he had finished breakfast.

Haydon nodded. His head felt heavy at the back, his neck muscles tight. He had slept very little.

"So Walther's taking the shots?"

"And Silva. Walther planned on working his shift because they were supposed to switch over to days beginning this morning. His face seems to be doing fine, according to Silva. I didn't talk to Van again."

"Maybe this's some kind of health problem. Those gals have some kind of damned old house dogs or something? Cats?"

"Not that I can discover."

Dystal looked out at the loop. He liked to watch the traffic. If there was no one to talk to at breakfast he would simply watch the traffic. He looked at license plates, wondered about the drivers' occupations.

"I guess we ought to notify the metro health authorities."

"Vanstraten's doing that this morning."

"I don't know if there's anything in this for us," Dystal ventured. He leaned on the windowsill and looked casually around the restaurant. "What'd Van say?"

"He said he couldn't determine anything from a rabies diagnosis. He said he'd push the health authorities for a thorough investigation."

"Yeah. That'd be the thing to do." Dystal ballooned his cheeks as he sloshed coffee against his teeth.

Haydon nodded.

"You ever see a rabid animal, Stu?"

Dystal was the only person Haydon had ever known who

135

called him Stu. It sounded comfortably natural coming from him.

"Never."

"We used to see them out at home. Skunks mostly. Skunks are the worst. Then dogs and foxes. It's purty pitiful. And scary. Wild animals bein' aggressive is spooky. It even spooks other animals. They can sense when another animal has rabies and they stay out of their way. Tuck their tails and go around real cautious."

"How about human rabies?"

"Oh, no. Never that, though I've heard stories. People out there like to tell stories." He smiled a bit wistfully and then let it go. "Van doing any guessing?"

"He had the same idea you had about a common pet. That's really the most logical first reaction."

"What's the most logical second reaction?" Dystal knew perfectly well how Haydon was looking at it.

"Under the circumstances, you make an assumption . . . that the most logical first reaction is incorrect."

"Yeah. So what do you want to do?"

"It's hardly the first time I've been surprised by a postmortem. It doesn't change anything. Four women still have died in three weeks. Three of them call girls, maybe all of them. Three of them were acquaintances, maybe all of them." Haydon shook his head. "I'd like to continue as planned. See what the Health Department turns up, see what Hirsch and Mooney come up with, talk again to Croft, talk to Guimaraes and de la Borda . . . follow through a little further."

"Then we'll just leave it open-ended for now." Dystal drained his coffee and tossed two quarters on the table. It was always two quarters regardless of the size of the check. "We'll just see what comes up. Maybe all cherries." He heaved his big body out of the chair and headed for the cash register.

Haydon hung back a moment, unobtrusively put a dollar over the quarters, and then followed Dystal to the front of the restaurant.

The two men chatted a few moments in the parking lot, with the traffic roaring so loudly they had to raise their voices, and then Dystal sauntered to his car and drove off. Haydon returned to the restaurant and went into a telephone booth next to the men's room.

A black woman answered the telephone and in a flat, phlegmatic voice said Miss Croft had gone to St. Rémy's.

St. Rémy's was one of the most exclusive health spas in Houston and was located on a heavily wooded estate not far away from the River Oaks Country Club. It was, like Judith Croft herself, très chic.

In a few minutes Haydon was driving along the densely wooded lane approaching the estate, which catered to "executives" and wealthy others who wished to surround themselves with luxuries while remaining righteously health-conscious. The spa's variety of recreational facilities offered exercise with as little pain and loss of grace as possible. Designer jock attire was de rigueur.

Haydon stopped at the guardhouse, identified himself, and pulled into the narrow lane leading through the towering pinewoods that formed an arboretum over the entire estate. For a while the lane followed alongside the jogging trail, which was covered with Superturf and twisted through the forest like a mossy carpet. Occasionally the pines would open to a meadow, with cleanly mown emerald grass.

St. Rémy's appeared to his left, a white Mediterranean mansion shimmering in the streams of morning light that broke through the pines. Haydon circled the elliptical drive that fronted the spa's palatial crescent-shaped building, and found a parking place next to a bank of white Madagascar jasmine. The two wide-reaching wings of the building were connected to the central structure by pergolas of limestone

137

columns which overlooked a sprawling lawn that reached a hundred yards to the forests of Memorial Park. The two separate wings comprised completely independent spas for men and women. The central structure, with its indoor gymnasium and running track, restaurant, club, and a handball court, provided a social common ground.

Haydon walked along the flower-bordered sidewalk to the main building and then turned left and ascended the steps to the pergola that led to the women's wing of the spa. The sugar-white portico of the arched entrance was flanked by palmettos, evoking the Hollywood movies of the thirties. He opened the door and was stopped in the foyer by the arresting smile of a thin woman, serenely proper in a cream silk suit, who sat behind a gilded Louis XIV writing desk.

"May I help you?" she asked. Her voice was smooth, authoritative.

"I was supposed to meet Judith Croft here."

The woman consulted a book on her desktop. "She's jogging now."

"Yes, I know. I'm to wait for her."

"Oh?"

"Is that a problem?"

"Well, normally our guests do not consider themselves presentable for visitors after . . . vigorous exercising."

"If it's a problem, I'd like to speak to Mrs. Arnault."

The woman hesitated.

"Shall I go up and speak to Mrs. Arnault?" He gestured to the sweeping staircase to his left, which reached up to the second floor.

"No. I'm sure it's perfectly fine. . . ."

"Good. I'll wait by the pool."

"Oh . . . visitors usually wait in the drawing room. We have guests using the pool area."

Haydon looked at her steadily.

"It's irregular for men to go out by the pool, but . . . I'm sure it will be all right." Her smile was strained as she gestured toward the French doors that opened onto the poolside beyond the drawing room. Haydon turned and walked away.

The oval pool was surrounded by slate flagstones, a thick carpet of grass, and potted palms. Haydon walked to one of the glass-topped tables on the terrace and sat down in the cusp of the morning shadows. Three women in maillots with the legs cut almost waist high lounged in the pool's sunny turquoise water. They rested their arms on the tile edge, their legs extended in front of them, as they treaded lazily. They saw Haydon and were not particularly concerned. One woman climbed out of the water and casually pulled up the edge of her suit to examine the tan she had acquired around the legs at her groin. He could see the dark arch where her tan met the white flesh of her stomach. Satisfied, she rearranged the elastic band and reached for a towel, which she spread on the flagstones near the edge of the water. She lay down, pulled the top of her suit down almost to her nipples, carefully arranged the material to conform to the tan she had already started, and lay back on the towel.

Judith Croft approached from under a canopy of banana trees. She was wearing a pastel pink jogging suit which accented her high hips and long legs. She was dabbing her face with a matching pink towel. Her bobbed jet hair was silky clean, but there were patches of perspiration coming through the suit between her breasts. She frowned and looked toward him in the shadow. He saw not even a hint of hesitation in her stride as she recognized him.

He stood and she sat in the wrought-iron chair opposite him. She tossed her hair, looked at the women lounging in the pool, and then offered him a cold smile.

"It's good to see you," she said.

"Good morning."

139

"I'm glad to see you can be discreet if not altogether honest." She looped the towel around her neck.

"I could hardly be both under the circumstances."

A black attendant in a starched white jacket came out and Croft ordered a dish of fruit and a pineapple-orange drink. The attendant turned to Haydon.

Haydon looked at Croft. "What do you recommend?"

"Why don't you bring him a Philippe," she said to the attendant.

"Beautiful women," Haydon said, looking toward the pool, as he waited for the man to get out of hearing range.

"Of course," she said, following his eyes and then turning on him. "What do you want?"

"We've determined the cause of Sally's death."

She was surprised. "What was it?"

"Rabies." Their eyes met.

Her face did not change expression and there was a long silence as they stared at each other.

"What do you mean?" she said.

"I mean rabies. Hydrophobia."

Another silence.

"What are you doing?" she asked evenly.

"I'm telling you how she died." He heard himself echo the same words Vanstraten had spoken in response to his own incredulity.

"I've never met a policeman who truly knew how to be clever," she said. "You're certainly no exception." She looked away and dabbed the loose-fitting jogging suit against her chest, enlarging the dark pink stain of perspiration.

"And I've never met a whore who wasn't consumed with suspicion," he said. "And *you're* no exception."

Her head snapped around. "You bastard."

It was too loud. The women at the pool roused themselves from their languid stupors and looked their way.

The attendant came out with their orders. A tall green lime drink for Haydon that made him wonder, and an equally tall citrus-colored drink with a cherry for Croft. Her bowl of fruit was an assortment of colored melon balls with a cocktail fork and a napkin.

They each took a drink, Croft trying with difficulty to compose herself.

"Let's relax, shall we?" Haydon said. "I'm not trying to be clever. Sally actually died of rabies. It was determined just last night. Rabies hasn't got anything to do with homicide. That's a city health problem. It's been turned over to them."

"You didn't come here to tell me about a city health problem." Her voice quavered slightly with tension.

"No." Haydon wondered how far he could go with her. He was probably making a mistake. "No; there are extenuating circumstances. I believe you knew Sandy Kielman, who died several weeks ago." She didn't react. "And of course you knew Theresa Parmer."

With each name, Judith Croft's expression evolved from anger to nervousness. It was all in the eyebrows, the interestingly expressive forehead, and the graceful hands that toyed with the stem of the cherry. Haydon remembered how she had fondled her drink in her living room.

"They all died of rabies; and a fourth, a young Latin girl whom we can't tie in with the others." He left it at that.

The woman sunbathing by the pool turned over onto her stomach and laid her head on her crossed arms. She spread her legs in a V toward Haydon. One of the women in the water was doing a backstroke across the pool, her movement smooth through the turquoise ripples.

He drank his Philippe and watched the women.

Judith Croft didn't look anywhere. She played with the cherry.

"What do you want?" she asked finally.

"Did any of them have pets?"

"No. Well, Theresa had a cockatiel for a while but she gave it away. She didn't like the mess."

"It didn't die?"

"It hadn't died two months ago, when she gave it away."

"Who did she give it to?"

"Barbara Sinclair."

"She worked with Theresa?"

"No; she's not in the business. She's a hairdresser."

Haydon waited a moment, still looking at the women in the pool. "What do you think's going on?"

"Coincidence."

"Really?"

"I wouldn't have thought anything about it if you hadn't popped up. Just a run of bad luck."

"A run of bad luck with rabies?"

"I didn't know about the rabies."

"You do now."

"Look," she said, "this is absurd."

"How did Sally use the condo in West University Place?"

"She didn't use it. She leased it to Theresa."

"It's an interesting place."

"Theresa was an interesting woman."

"It looked like a party house to me."

"That's what it was." She pulled the cherry off its stem with her even white teeth. "Theresa's party house."

"What was the deal with the colored rooms?"

"A gimmick. Tricks love gimmicks."

"An expensive gimmick."

Croft smiled. She looked at Haydon, let her eyes go over his coat and shirt and tie. "Bug your eyes out, huh? I'll bet Theresa turned more there in one night than you make in two weeks."

142

"You're right. Until last night, of course. Now I've got the rest of my life to catch up with her."

He wanted to ask her about the photographs, but he didn't want her to know he had them. That seemed like something he should hold in reserve.

"Did Theresa make a regular circuit of the Latin clubs too?"

"I guess so."

"She had a little more interest in it than you, maybe?"

"What do you mean?"

"The Wurlitzer, the decor. She seems to have been preoccupied with things Brazilian."

"She liked it a lot."

"Did she know de la Borda and Guimaraes too?"

"I don't know."

There was a subtle stiffness in her reply, or maybe he imagined it.

"How long have you known you'd inherit everything Sally had?"

She didn't react at first, and then she took a deep breath and held it as she looked around the courtyard, bordered by St. Rémy's white walls, and the glistening pool, set in the center like a semiprecious stone.

"It took you a while to get around to it."

Haydon waited.

"I've known her almost three years. That's about how long I've known about the money."

"All I have to do is check with her lawyers."

"Go ahead."

"It doesn't look good that you contacted Marvin Farris the same afternoon I came by and told you about Sally's death."

"Jumping to conclusions: the policeman's Achilles' heel."

"How about observation and deduction?"

143

Croft smiled slowly, as though she had caught him in a fatal move in chess. She let her eyes take in his Armani sports coat, his custom-tailored shirt and silk tie, his immaculate trousers and Bally shoes.

"I'd say you spend practically every cent you make on your clothes. Am I right? Am I jumping to conclusions or making an insightful deduction from observation?"

Touché. To make her point, Croft had to know her deduction was wrong. There was no question she had been checking up on him. Detectives rarely have their investigative tactics reversed and when it happens the feeling of aggression is unmistakable. He wasn't quite sure why she had chosen to reveal that she knew more about him than he might have suspected, but he had to admit it took an admirable amount of gall.

The white-coated attendant approached them across the flagstones.

"Miss Croft, you have a telephone call. You may take it in the lounge above the racket-ball courts."

Haydon and Judith Croft stood and she extended her hand.

"I'm sorry. Did you have many more questions?"

"Nothing we can't cover later."

"I'm sure," she said, and turned and walked away.

Judith Croft entered the central portion of the mansion and proceeded past the pro shop, which sold designer sportswear, to the indoor track of terra-cotta carpet. She paused to look at the muscular young man helping two women with the Nautilus equipment in the oval center of the track. Two lights blinked above the jogging lanes of the track to pace the man and woman plodding around the course. She turned and hurried up carpeted stairs that doubled back to a second floor. As soon as she came into the dining area of the restaurant, she could hear the *thwack* of the rubber ball slamming against the Plexiglas wall of the courts that formed one wall of the dining room. She looked around the almost empty room and saw a man sitting alone at a table next to the courts, watching the players. She walked over to his table and pulled a chair around next to him.

"I thought you might want to be rescued, my dear," the man said. He kept his eyes on the players beyond the Plexiglas wall. His thick gray hair was carefully barbered, full and wavy. He wore a steel-gray jogging suit with burgundy chevrons on the shoulders. His voice was baritone, modulated, and accented.

"You were right as usual, Paulo."

"Who was he?"

"An old . . . former acquaintance."

The man laughed slowly, softly. "There are so many of those, huh?"

Judith Croft did not reply, but put her hand on the man's right thigh and rubbed it. Still watching the racket-ball players, he reached over with his left hand and slipped it under the top of her jogging suit.

"Sweaty," he said. He laughed softly again and kept his hand there.

19

Leo Hirsch walked back to the unmarked department car next to the curb on East Canal in the heart of Magnolia Park. He unlocked the door and opened it, letting the interior cool off before he got inside. Unbuttoning his collar, he worked loose his necktie and unthreaded it from his button-down collar, which was soggy with sweat. He squinted back in the glaring sun at the Marsden Court housing projects. Their cement-block dormitory-style architecture set the tone of hopelessness that smothered the barrio neighborhood like a stultifying tropical heat wave.

It was midafternoon and he had just spent nearly three hours knocking on doors here. As he looked back, the sun fell through the palms and the pecan trees in dappled patterns in the scrubby courtyards between the rectangular sections of the project. He could still hear faint jerky strains of *conjunto* music and smell the odor of stale onions wafting through the torn screen doors. With the photograph of the Latin girl in his sweaty hands, he had worked his way from apartment to apartment, waking babies and dogs and night-shift husbands until he could feel a pair of eyes within each darkened doorway watching him from both sides of the bare courtyard. No one had admitted knowing the girl.

He shook his head and got into the car. The steering wheel was still too hot to handle, so he took his handkerchief out of his pocket, and after wiping his forehead and neck with it, draped it over the wheel. He started the motor, made a U-turn, and headed toward Sixty-ninth Street, which he followed toward the barge channel crossing. He turned right at Harbor Street, then stopped a block away from Hidalgo Park. He was closer now to the wharves where the girl had been found.

The houses here were small, wood-framed, with peeling paint in pastel colors and bare yards fenced in by chicken wire. The dirt street had been beaten to a fine powder at the edges where a gutter should have been and a light talcum film covered the dull paint of cars sitting in front of the houses like giant roaches resting in the gauzy shade of mesquites. In many yards, lush banana trees and flowering oleanders testified to the enduring tropical climate, and geraniums and cactus flowers bloomed stubbornly on deep-shadowed porches.

Hirsch parked behind the hollow shell of an old wheelless Plymouth sitting on wood blocks, and stared down the narrow street. A mockingbird whistled and rambled in a pyracantha bush outside his window, and in the background the harsh roar of the harbor derricks was an additional irritation in the pressing heat.

He took the black-and-white five-by-seven picture out of his coat pocket and looked at it. Vanstraten's photographers had somehow managed to keep her eyes open, so that her face wore a passive expression as though she were daydreaming. Walther had been right. She was beautiful. Death hadn't taken that away from her. If she was an illegal, as he suspected, she was only one of thousands who crossed the Mexican border and headed straight for the great caldron of

Houston's barrio, where they sought, and found, anonymity and the tacit protection of every Mexican American who lived there. He was not likely to find her this way, and he knew it, as did every policeman who had had to do this sort of thing. It was, however, a place to begin.

He got out of the car and slammed the door. The butt of his Smith & Wesson had made a hand-sized sweaty spot in the small of his back, where it was hidden by the tail of his suit coat. He approached the first house through a picket gate attached to a rotting fence post with rusted wire hinges. The entire yard, bare of grass and swept clean as Saltillo tile, was shaded by half a dozen crooked and scaly mesquite trees. Mauve petunias bloomed on either side of a beaten path to the front porch.

Hirsch walked between the petunias and stepped onto the porch. Tomato plants flourished in coffee cans along the edge of the vine-covered porch, and tiny red tomatoes peeked out of the feathery green borders like berries on Christmas holly. There was a sudden, deafening whistle from the dark end of the porch and sweat sprang to Hirsch's forehead as if he had been slapped with a wet sponge. He spun toward the deep shade, his eyes aching to separate the shadows as his mind tried to interpret the danger. Adrenaline pumped in his veins as another shrill whistle pierced the afternoon heat.

Then he saw the myna bird. It pranced back and forth, with all the style of Mick Jagger, along a two-by-four suspended between the house and the porch post, jutting its head in and out at Hirsch and high-stepping to its own inner rhythms. It whistled again, with incredible clarity and volume, and stopped suddenly in the middle of its perch, which was crusty with its own limy droppings. A yellow string was tied to one of the myna's legs and hung in a bright loop from the board.

For a second Hirsch thought he was going to throw up,

but as he eased his hand away from the butt of the .38 the nausea passed. He slowly straightened up and walked over to the bird. He peered into the red orbs that blinked back at him.

"Shit," he said.

"Shut up!" The voice came through the dark screen door behind him. "You, bird." Two words to clarify the object of the command.

Hirsch tried not to let the confusion show in his voice. "Just looking at your bird," he said unnecessarily. "Myna bird." He walked to the screen door.

"My watchdog," the woman said. "Scared you, huh?"

Hirsch grinned sheepishly. He tried with no success to see beyond the screen as he took out his shield and told her what he was doing.

"You got the picture?" Her voice was raspy.

Hirsch's eyes were adjusting to the shadows now and he saw her standing with her hands on her hips, her legs comfortably apart. She was in her early fifties, long hair piled on top of her head to ease the heat, a thin cotton dress. She was holding a white handkerchief, which she smeared continuously around her mouth.

Hirsch pulled the picture out of his pocket and held it up to the screen. She looked at it in silence.

"Is she dead in this picture?"

Hirsch nodded.

The woman unlatched the screen and reached out and snapped her fingers for Hirsch to hand her the picture. He gave it to her, feeling like a little boy obeying a strict teacher. She stood with her foot holding the screen open and looked closely at the photograph. She began moving her head slightly and then more definitely, until the movement developed into a nod. A firm nod.

"I know her, *sí*."

The myna shrieked.

149

"You know her?"

The woman looked at him. "Didn't I say that, yes? I know this girl, this beautiful girl." She pushed the screen open and stepped out onto the porch. She looked up and down the neighborhood street and then marched back past Hirsch into the house. "Come in," she said.

He followed her into a small living room, one end of which served as her dining room by virtue of its having an old dropleaf table with a crocheted sash draped across its center. A bowl of mangoes and lemons sat in the middle of the table. She gestured for him to sit at one end so he could look directly into the kitchen.

"You need some ice tea," she said, and went into the kitchen to make it. He looked around at the sparse furnishings. There was the inevitable altar on the living room wall, surrounded with plastic flowers and pictures of her family, near and distant. The top of the altar was covered with tinfoil to reflect the light from the candles, which were now half burned and cold. Mary looked down from above, her head tilted, a blue mantle draped over her head and shoulders.

There was a television in the opposite corner, a soiled fabric armchair angled toward it, and a sofa. All the windows were open; two looked onto the porch. One doorway led into a bedroom, another down a short hallway to a bathroom, Hirsch guessed.

"You been tryin' to find this beautiful girl very long?" she said from the kitchen. He could hear her taking ice out of the trays.

"Two days," Hirsch said.

He noticed now a breeze coming from a green Eskimo oscillating fan sitting on a rag rug near the kitchen doorway. She came through the door carrying an enormous glass of tea, the ice still swirling. She set it down in front of him and laid a clump of wet green leaves beside it.

"Mint," she said. "I grow it outside the back door. I washed it 'cause sometimes the cats piss on it. It's good for cooking and makes the best tea." She stepped back and took her handkerchief from under her wristwatch and wiped her mouth.

"Thank you," Hirsch said.

"Crush it up with you fingers and put it in you tea."

Hirsch crushed it up with his fingers and put it in his tea.

She watched him, one hand on her hip and the other wiping the white handkerchief around her mouth, as he stirred his tea with a spoon she'd given him.

"Good," she said after Hirsch had finished stirring and sipped the drink. She sat in the chair opposite him, blocking most of the breeze from the fan, and began eating an orange that lay half-peeled on the table in front of her.

"Anybody know her?" she asked.

"You're the first."

"Ah, *Pendejos.*" She laughed scornfully, without humor. "Nobody knows nothing, huh?"

"That's about it," Hirsch said. She was not an unattractive woman even now, but at one time she must have been really striking. She had lost her shape, to be sure, and the flesh of her face had long begun to sag, but the unmistakable elegance of her bone structure was still there.

"Let me see the picture again," she demanded.

Hirsch put it down in front of her. She leaned over to look; she took her time, then started clicking her tongue against the back of her teeth.

"What happened to her?"

"We think maybe a drug overdose."

"Oh, sure. Drug overdose. Happens alla time. Musta been that," she said in a way that indicated she didn't believe it for a second.

"We're waiting for a coroner's report. How do you know her?"

"She's not Mexican, you know."

Hirsch raised his eyebrows.

"No. Salvadoran. But she's the exception. Most of them are something else."

"Them?"

"You like the mint?"

"Very good," Hirsch said, and took another sip to show how much he liked it. " 'Them,' did you say?"

"Them!" She shook her head and ate a section of the orange, absently breaking the rind into tiny bits. "Well, I can tell you they're not Mexican. Look at this face." She stuck her chin forward. "You think I don't know a Mexican when I see one? And they don't talk regular Spanish either. And not Tex-Mex. Except the Salvadoran. I could understand her."

Hirsch thought it might be best to start over at the beginning. He tapped the picture facing the woman. "You knew this girl?"

"No." The woman slid an orange section into her mouth and looked at the picture as she crushed the juice out of the slice and ate it.

"But you said . . ."

"I've met her, talked with her. And the others, too, some of them."

"Who is she?"

The myna shrieked.

"There are a thousand ways to learn things in the barrio. Gossip is our passion. But the best way, the safest way, is to keep your *ojos* open and your *boca* shut."

She grinned broadly, liking the way she had said that. Hirsch noticed her teeth. They were exceptionally white, straight and strong. He knew a lot of girls who had paid thousands to get teeth like that and still didn't have them. She rose from her chair and walked to the limp pistachio drapes that hung over the two front windows. She stooped and took something from behind them on the floor and returned to the table. She set a pair of powerful binoculars on the table in front of Hirsch.

"Army surplus," she said.

"Yes, ma'am," Hirsch said.

"From Hidalgo Park I can see the ships coming into the channel. I can read their names and see the dirty water coming from the tiny holes. I can see the men walking around the pipes and towers on the big tankers; I can see them waving to each other, talking with their hands.

"From this little front porch, I can see even better just down the street. Why should I be embarrassed to admit it? I can see in the opened windows at night and see the sweat staining their shirts and thin dresses. I can even read their lips. Harbor Street at night is like watching a silent movie."

She tilted her head sideways, pointing with it, holding the orange sections in her hands.

"Down the street and on the other side there's a house with three palm trees in the front, old trees. The house is kind of hidden by this big honeysuckle on the fence. In the front there is a living room like this one. I have seen this girl in that room. Her and others. All young. They come there looking like poor girls look from Mexico. Simple clothes. Innocent in their manner. Humbled by their new life. They do not stay long, maybe a week, and then they disappear and I do not see them again. That's all."

She peeled a section from the orange and ate it.

"You said you talked to her."

"There is a Kwik-Wash on Hedrick Street next to the railroad tracks, right off Navigation. The whole neighborhood use it. I met her there and we talked. Chitchat. It could not be more, even though I was curious." She grinned. "Perhaps it is a failing, but I am a curious woman. She was polite but she kept looking at a man sitting in a green chair. He was

153

looking at a sex magazine. She was responsible to him, I think."

"How often did you see her there?"

"Maybe three times. She said she was new to the States. She said she was going to get a good job, that some people were going to help her. That's where it stopped. Except she tell me she was from El Salvador. I show her what kind of soap to use, how to work the dryers. I notice she was washing men's clothes too. Shit work. Probably for the greaser with the magazine."

Hirsch sipped his tea again. "Who lives in the house?"

"I don't know. The Ramirezes used to, but they moved a couple of years ago."

"Did you talk to any of the other girls?"

"I tried, a few times. I only saw them at the Kwik-Wash and through the windows at night."

"You tried?"

"Yeah. They spoke a funny kind of Spanish. No English. It was not easy. I would only get them to understand stuff like 'soap,' 'hot,' 'cotton,' 'nylon.' You know, washing talk."

"Was the same man always with them?"

"Sometimes it would be somebody else."

"Did your friends in the neighborhood talk about the girls coming and going?"

"Sure. At first we was afraid the whores were moving into the neighborhoods from the dock area. Nobody liked that but nobody was going to say nothing. There are some pretty mean peoples working with those girls around the docks."

"You don't think they were prostitutes?"

"I don't know. They seem like pretty nice girls. Never any parties over there. They don't act like whores."

"What were they doing when you watched them through the windows?"

154

"Nothing. Watching television."

"How long has this been going on?"

"Six or seven months, maybe. Something like that."

"And when did you last see this girl?"

The woman cupped one hand and spit three orange seeds into her palm. She closed one eye.

"Couple of months."

"In the time you've been watching the house, how many different girls have you seen there?"

"Oh, that's hard to say." She tilted her head back, thinking, chewing. Hirsch watched her throat work as she swallowed the juice from the fresh orange slice and then swallowed the pulp. Her head came down and she looked at him. "A dozen."

"A dozen?"

"It seems like that, yes. Twelve. That's about right."

"How many would be there at one time?"

"Usually two. Never more than three."

"You don't know any of their names?"

"Sure. This beautiful one"—she put her elbow on the picture—"is Petra Torres. She's the only one whose last name I know. I remember Lydia, a Lilia, a Soyla. Let's see . . . mmm. One was named Cecilia. That's all I remember."

Hirsch had had his notebook out for a good while, taking notes. The woman would slow down occasionally when she saw she was getting ahead of him. Her assistance seemed natural, not strained. There was no reluctance at all to give any detail.

He flipped back through the pages, double-checking his notes, clarifying a point with a rephrased question. Despite the oscillating fan behind the woman, he could feel a drop of sweat start between his shoulder blades and proceed resolutely down one side of his spine. The waistband on his trousers was already soaked through and was beginning to chafe his skin. He knew the leather holster in the small of his back was black with perspiration. He kept dabbing at a persistent trickle coming from his hairline. For some reason he was reluctant to take his handkerchief out and wipe around his face and neck, as though to admit he was drowning in perspiration would be an insult to her.

"How many are living there now?"

"I haven't seen any girls there in over a month."

"Which of these girls did you see there last?"

"Probably Soyla."

"Have you noticed anything else down there that's caught your attention? Anything at all. A particular car showing up more than once or twice? A particular person?"

She thought about that awhile, having no reluctance herself to use her handkerchief to smear around and around her mouth to soak up the constant ring of perspiration that appeared there.

"No. Just the greaser with the magazine."

"Would you be able to identify him from a photograph?"

"Sure."

"What kind of cars did you see there?"

"I got no idea. I don't pay attention to cars. I can't even tell 'em apart. Buick? Ford? Olds? Chevy?" She shook her head.

"Colors?"

She shook her head again.

Hirsch took the glass of tea and drained the rest of it. The mint leaves stuck in his mouth.

"Chew 'em," she said. "Give you a sweet breath."

Hirsch chewed them. "You've been a tremendous help," he said. "I may come back and see you again in a day or so."

The woman stopped wiping her mouth and looked at him. She rested the elbow of her right arm on the table and leveled her finger at him.

"One thing. I ain't no dummy. Something's going on down there. I don't know what. But I feel sorry for those girls and nobody else is going to talk to you. I put my neck out. Now you gotta do this for me. I'm not going to talk to you no more. I'm not the only one who watches the street. By now three or four peoples know you been here long enough to learn something. It wouldn't be hard to find that out if you wanted to know who been blabbering. Huh?"

Hirsch nodded.

"So what you do is, you go on down the street knocking doors. Somehow you got to stay in one or two houses just as long as you been here. Maybe all you do is talk about the heat, gran'kids, whatever. But you stay awhile. Later, if anybody wants to know what they talked about and they say only the heat and gran'kids, then I can say the same thing. I'm not going to be the only one who spend some time with you. Okay?"

Hirsch groaned inside, but agreed. He knew she was right. He got her name and telephone number and an additional caution from her that she would not talk with him again. At least not in her home. He thanked her again and went back onto the front porch, where the myna immediately shrieked and began prancing and strutting nervously. The woman did not try to silence him as Hirsch walked out of the yard gate and started along the edge of the dirt street to the next house. He cast a casual glance down the street toward the house with the three palms. He felt a dozen pairs of army surplus binoculars watching him as he plodded along in the dust.

20

Ed Mooney stood on the third level beneath the colossal atrium and gazed down through the tiers below. Light from the fourth-floor skylight above fed the banks of plants and ficus trees along the walkways of each tier, which swarmed with foreign shoppers, tourists, gawkers, businessmen and women, and residents of the condominiums in the upper realms of this nuclear-age nautilus of luxury and endless expectation.

The Galleria. A forty-two-acre city under glass. The temperature was an unfailing 76 degrees, the atmosphere was unabashed wealth, the population of the throng moving along its tiers was twenty thousand, its arteries pulsed with banks, hotels, offices, restaurants, boutiques, salons, bars, shops, ice skating rink, movie theaters, confectioneries, gossip, sex, romance, and intrigue. The essence of Houston. Oh, so elegant, so intelligent, the Galleria Rag.

From Mooney's vantage point he could see half a dozen gleaming escalators angling off to other levels, above or below him. It was a great place to watch people. In the twenty minutes he had been waiting he had seen one drug transaction (level one), an Arab something-or-other with entourage (level three), a pickpocket (level one), one cheetah on a leash (level two), two prostitutes picking up tricks (level three), Goldie Hawn (level two), a man and a woman strolling, with the man's hand inside the back of the woman's black tuxedo pants (level three), a man in see-through pants and red bikini briefs (level two), a crowd-stopping style show of Russian furs (level two), and his landlord kissing a woman who wasn't his wife (level one).

Then, within this carnival stream which Mooney judged to be the richest and most diverse example of street life anywhere in the world, he saw the familiar face he had been waiting for. She had stopped, predictably, before the sparkling windows of Fred Joaillier. (Simply Fred's, of Houston or Rodeo Drive or Paris or Saint Tropez or Monte Carlo, to the initiated.) There was an emerald as big as a walnut and surrounded by diamonds as large as the buttons on Mooney's J. C. Penney shirt. She was looking at it, and Mooney knew she was growing as excited as if she were undressing for Burt Reynolds. Her heartbeat was racing, her juices flowing, her imagination fired with God knows what kind of thoughts, thoughts bold enough to drive old Burt into his own kind of panic, enough to shatter the emerald, enough to make Mooney shake his head and smile to himself at the absurdity of the whole damn world he walked around in.

Finally she pulled herself away from the window and moved, slower than the rest of the crowd, past a shoe store, a dress shop (lingering), past a lingerie shop (lingering), to Tiffany's. She stopped. Her teal-green silk dress hung from her shoulders and hips to midcalf in folds as still as marble sculpture.

Maureen Duplissey was the kind of girl Texas was famous for. She was blond, leggy, high-hipped, and foxy. She spoke with a twang and could have stolen the Miss Texas title from any girl who had captured it during the past ten

159

years. She had grown up in North Dallas, where Daddy had made a couple of hundred thousand a year fiddling with computer chips under a microscope and Mama had had a tennis tan and danced in Capezios in the Junior League Follies. Maureen had started wearing makeup before she had her first period, had started taking birth control pills before she had her driver's license (Mama wanted to "be realistic about it"), and started calling sexual intercourse "love" shortly after she returned from having her first abortion in the middle of her junior year in high school.

She matriculated at the University of Texas at Austin, spending four years in Polos and Izods as a smiling Pie Fie (Pi Beta Phi) majoring in business economics. She was a quick study, and learned the hidden values of her natural assets by putting in equal time on balance sheets and bed sheets. She soon learned that a man would cheat the government a thousand different ways and risk criminal prosecution to save five hundred dollars on his income tax, then turn right around and give it to her with surprising alacrity in exchange for one night between her legs. It was a lesson she never forgot.

When she graduated and moved to Houston, she concentrated on applied economics. What nature had given her and she had polished with collegiate experience, she now developed with the discipline and flair of a shrewd entrepreneur.

She charged a basic five hundred per night. More if it was all night, and fifteen hundred to two thousand if it was a weekender that required her to go to the trouble of packing a bag and being companionable for as long as forty-eight hours. She vacationed one month every year, usually on the Mexican Pacific coast. It was a very good life, made downright glorious by the fact that she possessed the libidinous appetites of a gourmet and the playful inventiveness of an epicure.

Abruptly Maureen turned from the small Tiffany display

case and walked to the nearest escalator. When she stepped on the first rising grid she looked at her watch. Mooney smiled. Women who worked by the hour knew the value of time. Punctuality was a by-product of the profession.

He stood up from the railing around the atrium and threaded through the crosscurrent of Galleristas to the entrance of Zucchini's Farm-to-Market Café just outside the doors of Neiman-Marcus. He waited under the green oval sign for the hostess and then followed her to the table he had requested beside the green iron railing that separated the cafe dining from the sidewalk traffic in the mall. Zucchini's resembled a European open-air market-café, with a black-and-white-checked ceramic floor, small tables with white cloths, and bone-handled tableware.

Mooney ordered a Guinness Stout and waited for Maureen. It didn't take her long. She came striding through the café entrance and the heads began to turn, but she seemed oblivious of them. She had already spotted Mooney and was making her way to him, her eyes not wavering, her smile genuine.

He stood as she approached and she kissed him on the lips. She had to bend a little to do it.

"God, look at you," she said, sitting down and giving Mooney a shot of her décolletage, which stopped well below the point of discretion. "You must've gained twenty pounds."

"Maybe fifteen since I saw you last."

"Oh, Moon, come on!" She laughed. "Too much of that stuff." She tapped the bottle of stout.

"Yeah. I need more tush to work it off."

"Well, you're in the right business to pick that up."

"Sure," he said. "What'll you have?"

They looked over the menu and ordered. Maureen had a bottle of Artesia and the Quiche Coquille and Mooney had another bottle of stout and the Lemon Pepper Burger, which he ordered with a combination of lust and regret. After three o'clock he'd have to hit the Maalox.

Maureen put her elbows on the table and gave him another shot of squeezed breasts.

"So to what do I owe this pleasure? The last time you bought anyone a meal was when you had to tell Beverly Thorp she was gonna have to stop screwing the senator's son or the old man was going to have all her fingers broken."

"It was a big account. She was losing a lot of income and she needed consoling."

"And she was falling in love."

"And she *thought* she was falling in love."

"You gonna tell me something like that too?"

Mooney shook his head. "You're going to tell me something."

"Like what?"

Mooney took the picture out of his pocket and handed it across. "Like who is this?"

Maureen looked at the picture and saw immediately it was a morgue photo. "Ooh, damn." She made a face and handed the picture back. "No idea," she said, shuddering.

"No idea?"

She shook her head.

Mooney turned the picture around and handed it to her again. "Look at it. You don't know her?"

"Hey, Moon." She turned her head away. "Come on, huh? We just ordered lunch, for Christ's sake."

Mooney returned the picture to his pocket. "I didn't know you were squeamish."

"Well, good Lord! People don't go around looking at corpses during lunch."

"You're right. That's bad," Mooney said contritely.

Maureen twitched her shoulders as if to realign her cleavage, which somehow had been disturbed by the intrusion of such a photograph.

"Okay," Mooney said. "Then maybe you can answer this. What kind of thing did Sally Steen and Theresa Parmer have going over in West University Place?"

"Oh."

"Oh?"

"I didn't know that's what you wanted to talk about."

"I can believe that."

"That's too bad about them. Did you know Theresa was a Tri Delt at UT when I was there? Yeah. We knew some of the same people up there, but we never met each other. Went to some of the same parties, even."

"Amazing."

Maureen looked down at the tablecloth and plucked at the tines of her fork with a red nail.

"Moon, I don't know anything about their operation. I guess the police think their deaths may have been . . . connected."

"Well, you know how the police are."

"I just don't know anything about it." The playfulness had gone out of her voice.

"Just give me a little overview, Maury. I'm not asking for names and numbers. What was the general setup?"

Their food arrived and Maureen was noticeably relieved to have a break in the conversation. They ate in silence for a few minutes, with Mooney paying more attention to his food than it warranted. He would give her some time to think. She knew what she had to talk about.

Finally she said, "You'll have to level with me first, Moon. Just how bad is this? Am I going to be talking about a major thing here? I mean, you should go that far with me."

Mooney swallowed a mouthful of stout. "In May, Sandy Kielman died. A few days ago these two, and then the girl in the picture. The first three are in the trade, but we don't know about the girl. We're just trying to find out if she's connected somehow. We don't even know who she is.

Homicide thinks that's too many call girls to lose in ninety days and they're looking into it. That's all. Theresa was leasing from Steen and so we're starting there. The place was a little unusual, so we figured the entertainment there might be a little unusual too. Is it?''

"Why don't you talk to Judith Croft?"

"Oh, gee, we hadn't thought of that."

"Smart-ass. I just don't know why you want *me* to go into this."

"Because you knew all three women fairly well, Maury. It's as simple as that. If it's any consolation, you're not the first or only one we've talked to. Okay? We're listening to a lot of stories and comparing notes. Okay?"

"Having any luck?"

"You'd be surprised." He had had no luck. For some reason there was a healthy respect for Sally among the girls in her profession and especially for the activities on Quenby. The women he had spoken to were willing to talk of just about anything except Steen's business. Everyone had seen the newspaper stories about Parmer, as Mooney had anticipated, but some of them still had not known about Sally's death. If they had been reluctant to talk about her alive, her death slammed a steel door on the subject. It seemed to confirm something to them. Discussing anything related to Sally was a clear-cut taboo.

"Yeah. A lot of people are upset about the three of them dying so close together."

Mooney nodded.

Maureen laid down her fork and pushed away the half-eaten quiche. She took a cigarette from her purse and lit it.

"What happened to Theresa?"

"We don't know yet. She was just dead in bed. Naked. We're still waiting for a final report from the coroner's office."

"And Sally drowned?"

164

"That's what it looks like."

"And Sandy had pneumonia?"

"Something like that."

Maureen made a face that said none of that sounded particularly insidious. She held the cigarette to one side, her elbow on the table and her wrist crooked back. Mooney had always thought that was a cheap-looking pose. The filter tip had a red ring around it.

She lowered her voice to the business level. "If you try to make me testify with this I'll swear it's all a lie, something you made up when I wouldn't go to bed with you. I'll go right down the tube with you on this."

"You mean you don't trust me?"

"You'll see what I mean." She swiveled the cigarette into her mouth and puffed. "And I'll bet a week's take you haven't learned a damn thing from anybody you've talked to up to this point. Right?"

"You'd be surprised."

"Christ." Maureen had crossed her legs and was nervously jiggling her foot as she looked around the café, thinking it over. She looked out to the mall, up to the fourth-floor skylight, at Mooney.

"You know about their Brazilian thing." It was a statement.

"I know they liked the music, that Sally owned a piece of a couple of clubs."

"You've been in Sally's condo?"

"Oh, yeah, and there's Brazilian music on the juke."

"Well, that's just the head on the beer."

"I see."

"About a year ago things started changing a little for Sally. For the better. She was still pretty much running the same traps but she was sort of moving into a madam situation, and it all started when she met these Brazilians. Well, really, just this one guy especially. Rich guy. Rich-rich.

165

Lives in the Shelbourne Tower. That kind of rich. He's a businessman. Owns part of the Amazon or something. Made a fortune in lumber. Hardwoods. His family still operates down there and supposedly he's come to the big H to diversify. There's a kind of colony of Brazilians here and I understand this guy Sally was close to is the hub of this whole society.

"Anyway, he liked her a lot and gave her a bunch of breaks. Financial tips, clients with serious dollars. Just a gold mine for her, everything's coming her way. When you get to be Sally's age you're looking for something like this, something that'll keep bringing in the money but doesn't require you to put your body on the line every night. Sally's sharp and can see the potential right off. She steps back, brings in the foxiest girls in the business, and gets a piece of everything, while she furnishes this whole Brazilian bunch with the best the old Sun Belt can offer. They went wild for it.

"Pretty soon Sally is at the top of the heap. I mean, in big money. All of a sudden everything's carioca, right? La Brasilia is the main hangout for this bunch. I think Mr. Important owns it."

"What's this guy's name?"

"You said I wouldn't have to name names."

"You're right. Fine."

"Look, this Artesia's fine for a tête-à-tête, but we've graduated to something else."

Mooney signaled the waiter and Maureen ordered a martini. Mooney asked for another stout. When the drinks came Maureen lighted another cigarette and sipped the clear drink. The waiter removed their plates and she relaxed a little.

Mooney prompted her. "So the Quenby place is where it all happened?"

"Not quite. Those guys are more subtle than that. But there were special occasions. That's what Quenby was for."

"Like what?"

"You saw the place. Orgy city. There was nothing so strange that it couldn't happen there."

"Were you ever there? For one of the sessions, I mean?"

"Once, for a groupie."

"And?"

"And nothing."

"Okay. Did Theresa live there permanently?"

"Right. Somebody had to be the dorm mom."

"Dorm mom? Other girls live there?"

"Uh, off and on."

"You knew them?"

"No."

"What do you mean, 'off and on'?"

"Sometimes."

"When? What can you tell me about them?"

"Not a damn thing," she said sharply.

"Okay, okay. Did Kielman, Parmer, Croft, and Sally all take part in these 'special occasions'?"

"Oh, no. Just Sandy and Theresa and the dormies."

"Why not Croft and Sally?"

"I told you. Sally was out of that for good. Judith was simply above it."

"How did she manage that?"

"Judith and Sally had a special relationship. Sally kind of adopted her, protected her financially, made sure she got the pick of what was available. You know, didn't want to taint her with an out-and-out trick situation, wanted to put her more in the category of being a kept woman, a mistress. Judith came to the business late and Sally groomed her as the crème de la crème."

Mooney ventured a little further. "Do you know anything about the photography sessions there?"

Maureen hesitated. "Well, I knew they made some photographs."

"Who did?"

"Theresa told me they did."

"You mean while she was participating?"

"No. She and Sandy took turns doing the shooting."

"For the clients?"

"No, for Sally's insurance. Sally always figured everything from two or three different angles. She thought it would be good to keep a record of some things."

No doubt, Mooney thought, and sipped his stout.

At the table next to them a man and a woman who looked to be in their mid-fifties were discussing Krugerrands. They were not being subtle about it. Should they buy more? Should they sell part of what they had? They were drinking St. Pauli Girl beer and every time the waiter brought them fresh bottles they clicked their glasses together. They were very satisfied with themselves.

Maureen gave them a withering look and finished her martini. "Houston's full of that kind of crap," she said loud enough. After exchanging frosty glances with her, the couple started talking again, their bodies angled in the opposite direction.

"I guess we need to go, huh, Maury?"

"I guess." She was a little huffy.

"One thing. Are all the songs on the Wurlitzer in the condo in Portuguese?"

"Yeah, I think so."

"But nobody spoke Portuguese?"

"Well, Sandy and Theresa didn't."

"Didn't you say the Brazilians went there only on special occasions?"

"Most of them."

"But not all of them?"

"I think you'd better get the rest of your information from

Judith. You already got more from me than this meal was worth."

Mooney made a pacifying gesture. Something about the "dormies" really made her touchy.

He signaled for the check and paid, while Maureen dug in her purse and did something to her face. They walked out of the café together and into the stream flowing toward the far end of the atrium. When they got to the escalator that would take Maureen down to other realms, they stopped.

"You were a lot of help, Maureen."

She shrugged.

"I guess I don't really know why you talked about it," Mooney said, looking at her.

"Theresa and I were good friends. I liked her. If something's going on, it wouldn't be right to hold out."

She looked away a little uncomfortably and Mooney waited.

"And there was never any love lost between me and Judith. That Brazilian thing was lucrative. I got a couple of shots at it and then Sally froze me out. Theresa tried to work me in, but Sally wouldn't hear of it. I always thought Judith had something to do with that. You guys might as well find out what's going on."

"Thanks," Mooney said.

She tossed her hair and gave him another kiss on the lips before she turned and put her foot on the first grid that came out of the floor and started down. He watched her descend and watched the heads turn on the adjacent escalator going up. When she got to the bottom she stepped on the terrazzo floor and checked her watch. Without looking back, she disappeared into the crowd that swept her out of sight.

21

Rafael slipped his key into the deadlock and let himself into the laboratory. The round electric clock above the cabinets said it was nine-thirty. At this hour he shouldn't be interrupted. By now the night wards had gotten used to seeing him work late. Medical students didn't keep time like the rest of the world. Everything revolved around their studies and their work in the teaching wards. Food, sleep, and any private life they might have ran a distant third in importance. Rafael was no exception. Odd hours were so routine with him that the word "odd" completely lost its meaning.

It helped, however, to be part of a select group who, because of demonstrated superior abilities, had been given the opportunity to work closely on special projects with professors of outstanding reputations in their fields. Rafael worked on a team that studied under Dr. Taylor Morton in the department of microbiology and infectious diseases. In the reflected light of Dr. Morton's brilliance, his students were given wide berth by other students, covered with perks by the administration, and forgiven sins by the hospital staff that would have demanded unusual restitution by any other student. It was in the context of this association that he was never questioned about his late or strange hours in the laboratory.

He laid his books on a cluttered desk beside the supply cabinet and took his long white lab coat off the coatrack. He slipped it on, buttoned it, and looked around. The laboratory of a modern medical school was an environment that required precision, passionless precision. There was no room for the maladroit or the unsure among these instruments of exactitude, there was no room for shoddy thinking or casual theories. His eyes circled the room, his vision reverently touching the hard chrome surfaces, the unyielding glass of test tubes, cylinders, and flasks. He smiled inwardly, always inwardly, at the dials, lenses, scales for calibration, the curving, looping tubes and vials reflected off the black mirrored surface of the laboratory tables. This was his world. The odors of alcohol and formaldehyde were oxygen to his lungs.

Tonight it was his world in a special sense. Tonight would be dedicated, not to the ends of a shared research project, but to his own obsession. It was fitting, he thought, that he should always do his own work in the dead of night.

He walked to the back of the laboratory and opened the chrome refrigerated locker. Grunting slightly, he reached in and lifted out a clear plastic bag, then took it to one of the black-topped counters. He bent over and looked at the dog's head. It was an Irish setter and he was damned lucky to have got it. The heads of animals suspected of having rabies usually went to the State Health Department in Austin, where the virus was verified. But he would get them occasionally through his own black market. There were a number of veterinarians in the city who knew he would pay three hundred dollars per head, provided the animal had rabies.

The bag began to fog over and Rafael rubbed the plastic against the dog's hair. He picked up the bag and set it down again so that it rested on the neck stump like a mounted head, staring at him. It was a good head. The big dogs were easier to work on. He patted the head and then went into the small necropsy room that connected to the laboratory by a door beside the refrigerator. Everything was laid out precisely as he had left it earlier that evening. He always came in beforehand and set out the instruments. He liked the way it felt to walk in with the head and begin immediately.

As he stepped out of the room he flipped on a ceiling fan that brought in air from the main laboratory. There was no exhaust fan in the necropsy room, a precautionary measure to lessen the risk of spreading aerosol contamination.

Rafael slipped on another, bulkier lab coat and then a stiff rubber apron which tied in back. He put on the Plexiglas face shield, which could be lowered like a welder's helmet to protect his face from splattered blood and brain, and then pulled on the heavy rubber gloves. He grabbed the plastic bag and went into the necropsy room and closed the door. Ripping open the bag, he rolled the head onto the stainless-steel necropsy table, next to the shiny instruments on a sterile towel.

He placed the setter's head in a restraining device made of two lengths of angle iron mounted on a board and pivoted together at one end to form a V-shaped vise. The two arms of the vise were affixed with sharp steel spikes. With the head in the crotch of the V, Rafael slammed closed the two arms of the vise, driving the spikes into the sides of the skull and holding it firmly in position. Opening the dog's mouth, he slipped a tongue and jaw depressor over the animal's lower jaw and bolted it down tightly on either side. He grabbed the setter's ears and shook the head to test its stability on the board.

Taking a scalpel from the collection of instruments, Rafael made a midline incision in the top of the head, beginning between the eyes and going to the back of the skull.

With a pair of tenaculum forceps, he peeled back the skin, cutting it away from the skull as he progressed, draping the hide over the setter's ears and eyes to keep stray hair from contaminating the rest of the operation. He cut away the remaining muscle tissue to reveal the bare skull, which now lay like a small white dome amid the salmon-colored muscle tissue and pearly-gray cutis of the red pelt.

Rafael double-checked the security of the head in the restrainer and picked up the electrical autopsy saw, which was attached to a small motor by a long flexible drive cable. The saw was about the size of a microphone and was tipped with a crescent-shaped fine-toothed saw blade about the size of a doorknob, which vibrated back and forth when turned on. He switched on the power and the blade hummed softly. He positioned the blade just behind the eye sockets and lowered it into the bone at an angle that made the cut slant in toward him. The saw whined but cut quickly and easily, filling Rafael's nostrils with the dampish odor of burned bone. He then placed the vibrating blade on either side of the skull and made similar cuts, followed by the final cut at the back, leaving a square piece of the skull sitting loose in its own socket. With the tip of his scalpel he pried away the square section of the skullcap and exposed the glistening meninges that protected the brain.

Laying aside the instruments already used, to avoid contaminating the next procedure, Rafael began to cut away the opaque white meninges sac. It was a tedious job, but he liked doing it. When the brain was exposed, he began to free it from the skull, first lifting it from the front and cutting underlying nerves, then cutting the brain stem at the point where the spinal cord enters the cranial cavity. When the brain was free, he lifted it with a wooden tongue depressor and a large pair of serrated forceps and placed it on a large, prelabeled petri dish.

He raised the blood-spattered face shield and looked at

the brain. It wasn't all that big. It would fit comfortably in his hand. He picked it up now, felt the heft of the globulous tissue in his gloved hand. Through the rubber, he could feel the coolness from the refrigeration. He closed his hand around it and pressed it slightly. Opening his hand slowly, he watched the sticky tissue cling momentarily to his rubber fingers, almost as if it wished to remain attached to him, not wanting to be torn away. He used the wooden tongue depressor to rake it off into the petri dish.

Now he turned from the brain to the dog. Only the snout was showing, since the setter's eyes had been covered with its own skull flesh like a blindfold. Rafael lifted the skin on all sides and flopped it over into the empty cranial cavity. The dog looked at him, bodiless, brainless, passive. Rafael took another clean scalpel from the cloth and held it in his right hand as he gently pulled back the lid of the setter's right eye with the fingers of his left hand. He placed the scalpel precisely at the top of the eye and with a quick flick of his wrist he slipped it around behind the eye, severing the cranial and optic nerves, and popped it out on the table. He bent down and looked at it. He always saved the eyes. He must have had forty eyes at home, all of them floating in formaldehyde in a laboratory jar. These were good ones. He quickly enucleated the left one, put them both in a plastic test tube with formaldehyde, which he capped, and set them on the edge of the table.

Moving quickly now, he removed the dog's head from the restraining device and put it into a plastic trash bag, along with the contaminated toweling to be incinerated. He dropped the bag into a special canister that would assure immediate disposal, and set it in the hallway. He called the custodial service. It would be taken away within the hour. He wiped the surface of the necropsy table with a disinfectant of 1:500 dilution of quaternary ammonium compound, band then washed it with soap and warm water. He gathered the instruments he had just used and put them in wire trays in the round chrome belly of the autoclave. Closing the front-loading door, he twisted the steering-wheel-type lock, and turned on the sterilizer. He would return later to finish cleaning the instruments with the disinfectant and soap and water.

He removed and cleaned the face shield, removed the gloves and second laboratory coat and put them into the special laundry bags used only by the virology section. Lifting the eyeballs to the level of his own eyes, he looked closely at them once again. They were greatly magnified by the fluid and seemed nearly to be bursting the test tube. He jiggled the tube and then slipped it into his lab coat pocket. Then he took the brain in the petri dish and went into the outer laboratory, turning the light out and closing the door behind him.

Now he had to determine if the dog did indeed have rabies. He put on a new pair of surgical gloves and laid out a second series of instruments on a sterile cloth on the laboratory table. He slid the petri dish containing the brain in front of him and switched on a fluorescent lamp. He turned the brain in the dish just as it would be situated if he were standing over the dog as it faced away from him. The tissue sections would be taken from the most important parts of the brain for rabies detection. The hippocampus was a small squiggle of tissue in the floor of the inferior horn in the lateral ventricle on both hemispheres of the brain. Using serrated forceps to spread the two hemispheres, Rafael inserted the tip of the scalpel in the crevice and severed a piece from each hemisphere. He lifted each in succession on the end of the scalpel and placed them in a properly labeled petri dish. One for each side of the brain.

Turning the brain over, he followed a similar procedure for removing tissue from both hemispheres of the cerebellum, at the posterior base of the brain behind the medulla, or brain stem, from which he also removed tissue. Again he placed each of these in separately labeled petri dishes. It was important to keep the tissues from the various parts of the brain separate because the rabies antigen was often distributed unevenly and all areas had to be tested to determine the severity of the infection.

Taking six sterile microscope slides, Rafael made two impressions of each tissue section on a slide, pressing it firmly against the tissue to make a moist spot. These he arranged on their edges in a slide tray, which he lowered into a staining bowl containing acetone cooled to -20 degrees centigrade. He put the bowl in a freezer he had regulated to maintain the temperature and checked his watch. They would have to remain there four hours.

After sterilizing the instruments he had just used, he returned to the necropsy room and completed the cleaning process there. He came back to the main laboratory and picked up a small electric clock on the cluttered desk and set the alarm for two o'clock in the morning. Then he stacked the textbooks, photocopied articles, and medical magazines along the wall at the back of the desk until he had cleared sufficient space in which to lie down. He checked the lock on the outside door and turned off the light. There was enough of a glow coming from the streetlamps at the shuttle bus stop outside for him to see his way back to the desk. He took off his lab coat, removed the test tube of eyeballs from his pocket, and put it on top of the books. After rolling the coat into a ball for a pillow, he crawled onto the desk and immediately fell into a sound sleep.

When the alarm went off, Rafael slapped his hand over it. For a minute he lay still, looking out into the room. The pale light from the windows cast a blue outline to one side of every object in the laboratory. It was a world of shimmering halves, with each object fading from sapphire to pearl to coal. There was a moment, a brief moment, when he thought he saw a microscope rise, wavering, from the black top of a lab table. It tilted, turned, the blue light faceting the chrome objectives, the stage, the stainless-steel binocular eyepieces. He closed his eyes and when he opened them again the microscope was in place.

He got up and turned on the lights. He unfolded his coat and put it on and washed his face in one of the stainless-steel sinks and dried with paper towels. The slides now absorbed all his attention. He removed them from the freezer and set them on the countertop to dry. The tissue impressions were now "fixed." Using a Martex ink pen, he circled each impression with a heavy layer of gummy ink, forming a microscopic wall around the specimen to contain the drop of liquid conjugate he would apply next.

From the refrigerator, he removed one of the vials of prepared conjugates which had been stabilized by rapid freezing and dehydration under a high vacuum. The conjugate consisted of rabies virus antibodies embedded with a fluorescein dye. When this antibody came into contact with the rabies antigen on a slide, an antigen-antibody reaction occurred, which caused the dye to fluoresce when irradiated with the light from the Leitz microscope.

He reactivated the conjugate by adding distilled water through its rubber-sealed top with a syringe. Putting the vial in a centrifuge, he spun it at seven hundred times gravity for ten minutes. Again using a syringe, he removed a portion of the conjugate and diluted it in two suspensions of homogenized dog brain: one normal, one rabid. A set of control slides was always necessary to ensure the specificity of the results.

With a Pasteur pipette, he covered each of the two tissue impressions on the six slides with a single drop of the diluted suspensions he had just prepared, being careful to keep track of the normal and the rabid conjugate. He placed the slides in a humid chamber and incubated them for thirty minutes, after which he rinsed them in a phosphate-buffered saline and then soaked them for ten minutes. He then mounted the slides for viewing under the microscope by placing a few drops of buffered glycerol over the impressions and gently lowering a thin slide cover slip onto the glycerol, being careful not to create bubbles.

The slides were ready. He looked at the clock on the wall. It was nearly three o'clock. Taking the tray of slides to another table, he set them beside the Leitz fluorescence microscope. He double-checked the filters and the dichromatic mirror in the tubular chamber that led to the lamp housing. He selected the lowest power objective, flicked on the power, and adjusted the transformer meter's red needle.

Slowly, carefully, he examined each of the six slides, looking at both the rabid and the nonrabid brain suspensions as he switched to the oil immersion objective with a higher power and adjusted the focusing, the mirrors, and the iris diaphragm. He was elated by what he saw.

The Irish setter's brain was virtually aglow with the apple-green luminescence of rabies antigen—oval, smoothly contoured inclusions in the cytoplasm of the cells, which were stained a more brilliant green around their periphery. He methodically examined each slide. There was a minimum of nonspecific staining and the integrity of the antigen was superior. He looked up from the microscope and turned toward the brain in the petri dish at the other end of the counter. That lump of tissue, variegated with veins and crevices, was as dangerous as the venom of the tiger snake, its lethality the most intense he had ever seen.

It was getting late. There were only a few hours left. Appreciating his own self-control under the increasing pressure of shortened time, he calmly returned to the brain and cut large sections from each of the areas he had tested, placed them in a mortar, and ground them to a gummy paste. He scraped the paste into a chrome blender canister and added the proper proportions of phosphate-buffered saline containing antibiotics and a concentration of bovalbumin to stabilize the virus. Connecting the canister to the laboratory's Omni blender, he homogenized the tissue and solutions, being careful to wrap the neck of the canister in a towel to avoid the release of aerosols. There was a thirty-minute wait after homogenization to allow the aerosols to settle, and then he poured the brain suspension into a plastic screw-cap tube and set the tube into the centrifuge basket. He flipped the centrifuge switch and spun the tube at two hundred times gravity for five minutes and then turned it off. With a syringe, he extracted the clear fluid that floated above the milky liquid in the tube and transferred it to a vial with a rubber-sealed top, piercing the rubber seal with the needle and expelling the brain suspension into the vial.

By four-thirty he had packed the vial in ice along with the dog's eyes and put them in a wide-mouth Thermos. It took him half an hour to clean the laboratory and rearrange everything as he had found it.

At five o'clock, with the night shift at the hospital dragging to an end, Rafael stepped out of the laboratory and locked the door. His clean laboratory coat unbuttoned, he carried his books in one hand and the Thermos tucked under his arm, as though he were leaving early from a tiresome night shift. He walked down the main corridor, passing the color-coded intersecting halls designed to give the students points of orientation in the miles of sparkling hallways. When he reached the orange section, he entered one of the elevators and rode down to the ground floor, alone and in silence.

He stopped by the wall of pigeonholed mailboxes and checked his nook for interdepartmental mail. There was none. He walked out the back door of the medical school and stopped in the landscaped courtyard to inhale the clean predawn air. The night watchman was sitting under a Plexiglas kiosk, visiting with a shuttle bus driver, whose bus idled at the curb with its door open. Rafael started along the sidewalk in front of the old entrance to Hermann Hospital and headed toward the medical center parking garage number 4. In the east, a glow was rising from the pines, a pink precursor of the coming day. But to Rafael the glow was not pink. It was a glaring apple-green fluorescence.

22

The four of them sat in Dystal's office, Mooney and Hirsch in straight-backed metal chairs they had dragged in from the squad room. The conference was attracting some attention—glances from the other detectives, a speculative conversation at the coffee machine outside Dystal's office.

Each of them told his story: Haydon first, then Hirsch, and then Mooney, who had just finished. Dystal had put his size fourteens across the top of a pulled-out drawer as usual, and the radio murmured on the filing cabinet. Haydon had listened carefully, his long legs crossed at the knee, his coat on, his tie knotted tightly. He hadn't taken a single note, he hadn't missed a single detail or implication. Hirsch, eating Certs, had taken notes closely as Mooney drank milk from a half-pint paper carton. They were all quiet after Mooney finished.

Finally Dystal spoke. "Well, shit, boys, I don't know. So far we got something for the Health Department to look into, something for Vice to look into, something for Immigration to look into. Pretty thin soup for a homicide investigation."

"I guess you checked on the bird?" Mooney said to Haydon.

"He's alive," Haydon said.

Dystal said, "Leo, when you checked out Petra Torres you came up with nothing in criminal history, nothing from Immigration on illegal aliens, and nothing from the Torreses in the telephone book, right?"

"Right. Well, I'm still checking the telephone listings. There are five hundred and twenty-three Torreses listed. So far, a little over a hundred of them say they don't know anyone named Petra."

"You made a check on this Arturo Longoria who owns the house on Harbor Street?"

Hirsch nodded. "Nothing."

"You made a location check on the house and got nothing?"

Hirsch nodded.

"This ol' boy's in the import business?"

"Right. He's kind of a wholesaler of all sorts of commodities. I think whatever's going, he's selling."

"And this Guajardo woman says there haven't been any girls there in about a month?"

"She hasn't seen any."

Dystal looked questioningly at Haydon, who simply shook his head and continued to stare at the floor. The lieutenant turned to Mooney.

"Can you get any more out of this Duplissey gal? I mean, she's the one who knows all the scoop on that fancy house."

"Sure, I can pressure her, if that's what you want."

"Well, she seems to be the best we got." Then to Haydon, "How about this Guimaraes?"

"I'm waiting for something from NCIC. I've also got a query in to São Paulo and Interpol. There's no way of knowing how long all that will take."

"Too long," Dystal said.

Haydon switched his crossed legs. "Ed, Maureen said Steen was furnishing these Brazilians with 'the best the Sun Belt can offer.' Do you have any hunches?"

"No idea. This caliber of call girl is so far out on the edge of Vice's regular operations that we usually come across them only by accident. Just like now. It's unusual for them to be set up in an 'operation.' They're usually one-on-one, make their customers feel as though they're buying a secret night with a fashion model. Supposed to be an exclusive experience for the trick. A real heady affair, so to speak."

He grinned, but no one else thought the pun was worth acknowledging.

"That doesn't jibe with what Maureen said, though," Haydon continued.

"How's that?"

"The girls she said lived there from time to time. This call-girl profile you describe doesn't sound like they would be the sort to be classified as 'dormies.' Surely Maureen isn't talking about 'the best the Sun Belt can offer.' She also said she didn't know them. Wouldn't she have known the call girls?"

"Maybe, maybe not. Probably if they were from Houston."

"The way you related the conversation, she got nervous when you asked her to give you details about these women."

"Yeah, she did. She got pretty uptight."

"Maybe what made her nervous was not the girls' identities. Maybe she was nervous because she was getting close to another kind of woman altogether." Haydon turned and picked up Dystal's telephone. He dialed an interdepartmental number and waited.

"This is Detective Haydon in Homicide. Murray was rushing some blow-ups for me. They should be ready. Can

183

you send them up to Lieutenant Dystal's office? Thank you.''

Haydon didn't explain anything, but simply continued staring at the floor. He was going to wait. Dystal was comfortable with that, and the toe of his boot began to jerk to the rhythm of a western song no one could hear but him. Hirsch looked up something in his notes. Mooney kneaded his stomach.

A chubby woman in departmental blues tapped on the office window and stepped in with a fat manila envelope. Haydon stood, took the envelope, signed for it, and thanked her. She left behind a distinct, almost visible fragrance of powder and lipstick.

Haydon unwound the string from the flap of the envelope and took out the bundle of pictures. The monochromatic photographs looked even more bizarre in eight-by-ten formats. Haydon looked at each picture carefully and passed it around the room. It was like looking at completely different photographs. Objects and people showed up that Haydon didn't remember seeing the first time. The photographs were clustered according to their color: four each of red, yellow, and blue. Each photograph had been identified with a number written on a round adhesive sticker placed in the upper-right-hand corner. Each color group was numbered one through four. At the bottom of the stack came the blowups of facial and "remarkable" details. These also had been identified, but with letters rather than numerals. They were not evenly divided because some of the group shots yielded more details than others, but they were arranged by color.

There was a note clipped to the first detail shot: "The grain was holding together better than I thought it would, so I went ahead and made them eight-by-tens. I'm not going to do any more rushes for you if you don't pick them up when you're supposed to. RM.''

Haydon looked at the details more closely than the group

shots. There were very few full-face shots of the men, but the women were often caught from the front. Oddly, Sandy Kielman was an exception. Her face showed only partially in the one blue-room shot in which Mooney had identified her. But there was another exception, and Murray had caught it too: a girl with a duskier complexion than Kielman's, whose body was graceful even in contortions of sexual intercourse—which often took on an awkward quality in Vice's photo files despite the lovely cinematic simulations in skin magazines.

Since her face was never exposed, Murray had concentrated on her body and had developed several detail blow-ups. One detail in particular showed up three times: an amoeba-shaped spot behind the girl's right knee. Murray had taken them from the red series, numbers 1, 2, and 4. He had circled the spots in each photograph.

In the first shot, the girl was lying on top of a man who was reaching around her and grasping one buttock with each hairy hand. The girl was pushing herself back with her hands on the bed, her head thrown back, her long black hair falling down her back. Her legs were spread out, providing the best shot of the three of the back of her legs. The second shot was the poorest. She was on her hands and knees and another man, different from the first, was behind her. The fourth picture was a squirm shot. The girl was mixed up in a pile of people and she was identifiable only from the same spot on the back of the extended leg. Haydon immediately formed a new appreciation for the skills of the controversial Murray.

Haydon had passed all the detail shots around except for the red ones. He had turned to the top of Dystal's desk and placed the three photographs of the girl's legs side by side. He studied them a moment and then turned and walked out of the room.

When he returned, Mooney, Hirsch, and Dystal were standing over the red details.

"What's this?" Mooney asked.

"A piece of the puzzle," Haydon said. He was leafing through a manila folder. "This is Vanstraten's postmortem on Petra Torres." He picked up a pencil from Dystal's desk and circled something. "Under 'Physical Description': '. . . back of right knee distinguished by a junctional pigmented nevus approximately three and one-half millimeters in diameter.' A birthmark."

"This is Petra Torres?" Hirsch picked up the red group shots and put them in a row above the detailed shots of the birthmark. "Goddamn."

Mooney shook his head and Dystal looked at Haydon expectantly.

"I suspected this when Leo said that Mrs. Guajardo couldn't understand the Spanish spoken by most of the girls who lived in the same house with Petra," Haydon said. "Torres was Salvadoran, but I'm guessing the others, at least the ones Mrs. Guajardo referred to, were Brazilian. They were speaking Portuguese, a linguistic collage of Spanish and French. The French influences were the reason it sounded funny to her."

"We'd better try to get identification on every girl in these photographs," Mooney said. "We need to find them pretty quick."

"I'm afraid we're going to find some of them in the morgue's Jane Doe files," Haydon said.

Hirsch looked up. "You think Longoria was furnishing girls to be Parmer's 'dormies'?"

"I think so. And I think they're Brazilian and have some connection to Guimaraes through the Quenby setup."

"Like what?" Dystal asked.

"It's possible he, or someone, has an underground system for getting these girls into the States illegally. Vanstraten had mentioned that Torres didn't have a smallpox vaccination scar. If she had come in legally she would have. God knows what's happening to them once they get here."

Haydon sat down and crossed his legs again. "Leo, I want you to take these women's facial blow-ups to the morgue and see if you can find any of them among the Jane Does who've turned up during, say, the last four months. No—six months. There can't be that many."

"We've got five full facials here," Mooney said. "They don't all look Latinish."

"It doesn't matter," Haydon said. "Take them all. Any of them could be down there. And I think Bob's right, Ed. You'd better interview Duplissey again and come down on her hard. She knows something. Get the information or bring her in."

"What about Croft?" Hirsch asked. "Shouldn't you do the same with her?"

Haydon shook his head. "She's the only one so far who's been connected to the condo who hasn't died. She may be at the bottom of it. I don't want to go straight at her like that until we know more about what we're doing."

"You'd better visit Guimaraes," Dystal said. "And I suspect we'd better look into Longoria's import business too."

Haydon chewed the inside corner of his bottom lip. "Yes, I need to see Guimaraes, and I need to go through the condominium again." He shook his head. "It's the rabies thing."

"Let's think about that a little bit," Dystal said, grunting slightly as he pulled at his crotch. "Who comes into contact with rabies? Wild animals. Domestic animals. And who comes into contact with animals? Vets. Zoo people."

"Hell, everybody who's got a poodle," Mooney said.

"True," Dystal conceded. "But who comes into contact with animals *and* rabies on a regular basis? Vets."

"That trick book you found in the red room," Hirsch said to Haydon. "We could check occupations."

"Good. There are no last names but there are telephone numbers. We could call and try to con our way into some information. Can you start on that when you get through at the morgue, Leo?"

"I've got this friend who owns a couple of bassets," Mooney said. "Guy's a tightwad and won't take them to the vet. Buys the rabies vaccine from a little drugstore near his house and vaccinates them himself. Can you get rabies from the vaccine?"

"According to Van, yes."

"Then shouldn't we check all the drugstores that sell that stuff? See who's bought it on a regular basis? Maybe in larger quantities than are normally purchased by individuals. Or more frequently than once a year. A dog only needs a shot once a year."

"Excellent. In addition, let's notify every clinic, emergency room, and emergency medical center in the city and have them get to us immediately if they treat a prostitute or suspected prostitute for *anything*. Let's do the same for Vice, Ed. Tell those guys to let us know about any prostitute who's ill, even if it looks like an out-and-out drug-related illness or flu or diarrhea or whatever. Get them to a doctor until they know what's wrong with them."

Haydon turned to Dystal. "Can you get someone else to work with us on the telephoning? There are the drugstores; this with the clinics, hospitals; the Torreses in the telephone book. That can eat up a lot of time. And we put a stakeout on Longoria's place?"

"I think we can justify just about anything at this point," the lieutenant said. He had taken out his pocket knife and was using the instep of his boot as a strop. "Ya'll better get this stuff into the computers as soon as you can. I'll pull a report pretty quick and let the captain know what's going on. This could get out of hand before you know it, and he'd raise ol' Billy hell if it just came out of nowhere. Okay?''

"Stuart," Mooney said, looking down at the pictures on Dystal's desk. "I'd like to take copies of these too. It might be profitable to make second calls on some of the girls I've already talked with."

"Fine. You and Leo go down and get what you need from Murray as soon as you leave. And tell him I appreciate what he did for me."

"You need anything else from me before I take off?" Hirsch asked.

"No, not right now."

The three detectives looked at Dystal, still reared back in his chair, who was using the knife to shave little patches of hair off his forearm. He looked up at the silence, and gave a twitch with his thick neck.

"No, I don't know of anything else. I'll take care of the stakeout and get some people on the telephones. Just you boys be sure to keep me posted. On everything."

They stood to leave.

"One thang," Dystal said. "Roland Silva radioed in about an hour ago and said Walther had started throwing up in the squad car. Silva was taking him to Ben Taub. That's all I've heard."

"Jesus H. Christ," Mooney said.

Haydon returned to his office alone. The place stank of old metal from the clunky gray institutional desks and of hot electrical wiring, an odor which came from the tiny exhaust fan that blew hot air out of the back of the electronics module of the CRT. There was also the inescapable stink of decades of stale smoke and spilled coffee that was never thoroughly cleaned up. Even now Haydon spotted a half-empty cup of cold coffee on the floor behind the door, left there for God knows what reason. It must have been there a couple of days; a paddy of green fungus floated in the middle of it. Haydon took it outside and threw it in the trash.

He returned to his desk with a damp paper towel and wiped off the sticky rings left by soda bottles. There was no private territory in a squad room, and when the going was slow the detectives visited around in each other's offices with all the aimless camaraderie of bored adolescents hanging on each other's cars at a drive-in. Haydon dried his desk with another paper towel and sat down with the envelope of photographs. Pulling them out in front of him, he separated the group shots from the blow-ups not taken by Hirsch and Mooney. They were mostly indistinct quarter faces, profiles, and the backs of the heads of the unsuspecting tricks.

He concentrated on them, pausing occasionally to study a clear feature, an ear, a shape of a head, before moving on to another. He wondered which of them, if any, was capable of killing in the way he believed the killing was being done. Sometimes it still seemed odd to him that men who did these sorts of things did not look different from other people, that there wasn't something, *something,* in their faces that made them appear different from the men he had just been sitting with. Perhaps it was there, too subtle for discernment except by a rare few we skeptically call psychics.

It was the anonymity of the shadow inside this man, and all the faceless men it was his job to search for, that intrigued him, even frightened him. It was not uncommon to wonder if you were capable of the crimes committed by others if you should find yourself in the same situation. It was a line of speculation he had heard other detectives explore on those rare occasions when they were given to talk of such things in a serious way. But how many men feared the shadows within themselves, shadows they knew they shared with men like the murderer Haydon sought?

Ultimately it was all a matter of degree. He knew that, and every time he was faced with clearly aberrant behavior the matter of degree nagged at him. It had nothing to do with theories of criminal behavior as viewed by the judicial system or the penal system or by law enforcement organizations. It had to do with him, and what he saw and felt in such an encounter. He knew that the concepts of the borders of normalcy had been exploded further and further as science had learned more about the human mind and human behavior. It was understood now that the sick and the healthy mind shared more commonality than differences. Modern psychiatry had placed modern man in the unique position of being allowed small perversions, in one form or another, without the burden of being labeled "mentally ill" because of them. His closet might be full of shadows, his mind an abattoir of fragmented realities, but he can still find himself among the walking, laughing population of the normal. And he can remain among the normal so long as he does not allow his shadows out of the closet, so long as he does not take them out and show them to his neighbors as though he expected them to find the same pleasures in them that he does. He cannot do this because his neighbors are the Real World and if he fails to function in a way his neighbors find acceptable, then he is approaching the cusp of psychosis. It matters not that his neighbors may have similar or different but equally strange shadows in their closets; they do not bring them out and show them to him.

The man with the rabid shadow had made the mistake of bringing it out of the closet. His shadow was loose among his neighbors, and his neighbors feared it. Haydon thought it was ironic that what the man may long have hidden from the world was all the world knew of him now. The shadow was all that Haydon saw. The man himself was not visible. But what if he had kept the shadow inside the closet; would his neighbors have suspected him of his present madness? That was the question that mesmerized Haydon, because he already knew the answer. It was no. There was no such thing as normalcy; there was only the appearance of normalcy. And the very appearance of normalcy that had kept the shadow hidden before was the same appearance of normalcy that would keep the man hidden now.

Haydon mulled over these thoughts in the cramped confines of his office, with the grainy photographic details of men's heads spread out in front of him like the images of so many disjointed souls that needed putting together. He didn't see Bob Dystal pause at his doorway at the end of the day and then walk on, nor did he see the squad room empty and half fill again with the smaller evening shift. He didn't see anything but the garish gold, sapphire, and ruby portraits of nameless men, or hear anything but his own inner self-examinations, until the telephone rang and Nina reminded him to come home.

23

Pauline Thomas lay on the sofa and stared listlessly at the angst-ridden faces of the actors in *The Young and the Restless.* The television screen had shadowy waves rising across it horizontally and distorting the heads of Ashley and Jack, who were struggling with a love/hate relationship they had thought was over but apparently wasn't. There were a lot of close-ups, which made Pauline's stomach even more nauseous.

She reached backward over her head and grasped a pink bottle of Pepto-Bismol. She screwed off the cap and swigged it like a bottle of beer. She was trembling. A surge of muscle weakness overcame her and she set the bottle beside the sofa without replacing the cap. For a moment she lay absolutely still, exhausted. Her blue rayon gown was thrown open and she looked at her protruding hipbones, which accented the concavity of her abdomen. Shit, she'd had the dry heaves for the past three hours and she could practically see her spine. Her skin looked and felt pasty. The dark-brown patch of pubic wool made her think of the wild shock of bleached hair on her head. It was dead to the roots and stood out from her head like that of a frightened cartoon character. She could see it reflected in the television screen.

Both window units in her upstairs duplex were on cold-high, and still she perspired. Her slit, from front to back, was slick with it and it rolled out from under sagging breasts in huge pearly drops that ran off the sides of her chest. Her lungs felt as if they were working with worms and her sore throat was covered on the outside with a thick, gelatinous layer of Vicks VapoRub, which she had rubbed in thoroughly and then spread thick. Every breath she drew reeked of it, and when it hit her lungs it made the worms squirm furiously. She coughed a dry, raspy cough.

She tried to watch Ashley and Jack. Jack was angry but she couldn't understand what he was saying. His forehead began to balloon toward Ashley until it touched her, and then the back of Ashley's head ballooned in response and ascended toward the top of the screen. It didn't stop there. It rose out of the top of the set and knocked over a figurine, which fell on the floor and shattered. Pauline was upset about the broken figurine and started to get up, just as Ashley's head shrank, followed rapidly by Jack's. Pauline raised her head to see the shattered pieces. She was startled to observe that her naked right leg had flung itself off the sofa and was splayed out on the floor, jerking uncontrollably. It had kicked over the Pepto-Bismol, which had shot from the bottle in a splash of pink foam that reached across to the wall. The leg stayed on the floor, bouncing up and down on the heel of her foot. She closed her eyes and lay back and let it jump.

Son of a bitch! She'd never been sick like *this* before, not without drugs. It was like having the weird tail end of an acid stint without the benefit of the good part. She tried to be objective about it. She'd had a headache and then the nausea. Okay, she always got that stuff when it went around. Aspirin, lots of it. She'd thrown it up. Oh, so it was going to be bad. She'd jammed one of those thumb-sized suppositories up her ass. She kept them in the butter compartment of her refrigerator because she was susceptible to this kind of thing and when it really got hold of her only the suppositories would stop it. Always had them on hand. They would knock her out solid. They didn't this time. Everything just kept getting worse.

She thought about the hallucination. She'd never done it without drugs before. It was spooky. She raised her head and looked at the television set. Perfect picture. Figurine in one piece on top. She looked down at her right leg and was horrified to see that it was flung out on the floor and still jumping. Pink foam streaked the carpet and puddled around the mouth of the overturned bottle. She tried to control the leg. It literally bounced on the back of her heel. She saw the flesh on her thigh jiggling on the rigid femur.

Her head flopped back onto the pillow and she closed her eyes. She could feel the leg moving all by itself, as if it belonged to someone else. She was conscious of the sweat oozing from under her breasts again. It got heavier, the droplets swelling to the size of marbles, then of small eggs, as they pushed out from under her breasts as though they were being born from there. The sweat grew to the size of lemons, then oranges, until she couldn't tell the difference between the weight of the balls of sweat and the weight of her breasts. Suddenly the breasts themselves pulled loose and rolled down her chest like the sweat and tumbled onto her thighs like water balloons that burst and splashed all over her and the sofa; she could feel the water running all around her, soaking her. She opened her eyes and saw it. What a mess. She would have to clean up.

Pauline Thomas awoke. She knew instantly she had been hallucinating and then had passed out. She lay very still, with her eyes closed. Her leg was no longer jerking, though it was still flung onto the carpet, so that she was almost sliding off the sofa in an uncomfortable sprawl. Opening her eyes, she saw two glass laboratory jars, filled with a sudsy liquid, being stirred by a man in a white lab jacket. The bubbles settled out of one jar more quickly than the other, which was proof of the power of the antacid he held in his hands and was pointing at her. That was all she saw before she squeezed her eyes shut. The brilliance of the screen was too much for her. Her eyes were supersensitive, as if she had had an eye examination and they had been dilated. She tried to see the screen again but her eyes filled with tears.

Gripping the cushions of the sofa, she pulled herself into an upright position. Her head wobbled on her neck like a newborn baby's. She tried to stand; it took two all-out efforts. Standing uncertainly as she bent to steady herself on the sofa arm, she reached out to the television and snapped it off. The light faded to a phosphorescent wire that stretched from one side of the screen to the other. She couldn't look at that either.

The breeze from the air conditioner was making her itch all over, giving her the sensation of being covered with spiders. She moved, doubled over like an old woman, to the window and fumbled with the dials until the compressor died with a shudder that rattled the wood-framed window. She looked around the room. It was a wreck. She could smell puke. She could taste it.

Still grasping the plastic frame of the air conditioner grate, she began to tremble. Her head bobbed rhythmically, and ultimately was thrusting up and down so violently she couldn't focus her eyes. The palsy moved down her neck to her shoulders, her chest, her waist, wringing her body like that of a small child being furiously shaken by an angry adult. She dug her fingers into the louvers of the air conditioner, trying desperately to stay on her feet, until the shaking descended to her legs and she collapsed, ripping the louvers off with her clenched fingers as she went down. She sat down hard on the floor, her whole body out of control though she was wholly lucid and was viewing with detached bewildered horror the spasms that kicked her around on the floor like an invisible demon.

Eventually, after a period of time she could not determine or estimate, the spasms subsided and left her as limp and helpless as the gown that was now wadded and tangled around her legs and arms. Unable to move from exhaustion, she began to cry. She made no sound—her throat and vocal cords would not allow it—but she opened her mouth wide and cried in miserable and anguished silence. For the first time in her life she felt completely helpless, the sort of helplessness that would not stop with a long regenerative sleep or with another injection or snort or toke of something to chase it away. She was afraid she was going to die. She didn't understand what was happening to her, but she had never anticipated that death would be like this, without cause or recourse. Alone. The tears were profuse, bursting from her eyes and running invariably into her gaping mouth. Through them she saw the other side of the room. The sofa, the ejaculate of pink foam, and the telephone sitting on a small table at the near end of the sofa. Slowly, slowly, she twisted, moving in its direction.

From the bed he could look through the opened door, across the white polished marble floor to the glass wall of the living room. He could see the telescope on a tripod from where he lay. He looked at the woman asleep beside him. She had powder in her hair and smeared across her shoulder. He felt nothing. She was simply there like the sheet and the pillow, like the bed.

He pushed back the cover and got up. Standing naked beside the bed, he lit a cigarette and then strolled into the living room. He inhaled the smoke and bent over the telescope. The twenty-first floor of the Carrington was a good vantage point. He swept the lens over the thick canopy of ancient trees along Main and trained it on the medical school. It was late afternoon and the shadows of the buildings were to his left. He could see the floor where the laboratory was, but he couldn't see the windows. They were on the east side and he was looking at the north end of the building. Turning the telescope slightly to the left, he looked over the top of the Astrodome to the southern section of Loop 610. A menacing yellow haze engulfed the freeway and scattered the rays of the westward-falling sun. It suffocated the city, seemed the major cause for the crawling traffic, weakened by the lack of oxygen.

Suddenly every stereo speaker in the luxurious flat surged with the husky voice of Alcione singing ''Força do Amor.'' He swung the telescope around to the bedroom just in time to see an oval navel blur into a mist of nothing as it approached. He looked up and she danced naked toward him to the music of the samba as the chorus joined Alcione's raspy feminine croon in a ratchety rhythm of unison voices in swelling and regressing undulation:

> Eu sou tudo isso
> E nada sou
> Sem o teu amor
> Viverei, viverei . . . viverei . . .

Smoking, he watched her as she rose on her toes and circled the room to the humping samba, her eyes half closed, her hair black and wavy, swinging and rippling through the brazen rays of the sinking sun that pierced the glass wall and ignited half the long room. Though he did not look through the telescope, he stood behind it indolently, following her with it as though he were pointing a machine gun at her. At her back, through the window, the chrome and glass of the cars on the freeway caught the sun in their moving facets, throwing sharp splinters of light through the smog to dazzle over her olive skin as she followed the samba through the brass bars.

Sem o teu amor
Viverei, viverei . . . viverei . . .

He put the cigarette in his mouth and squinted at her through the smoke as he absently picked at the flecks of powder still caked on him. Stupid bitch! The samba chorus vibrated the glass wall. She danced. He watched her, squinting, breathing smoke into his lungs from his mouth and nostrils. The cigarette was short enough to burn his lips. He took it out of his mouth, wedged it between his middle finger and thumb, and flipped it at her. Her arms were raised and it struck her just below her rib cage and showered sparks down across her stomach and landed on the floor. She didn't notice. She danced over the burning tobacco on the marble and kept circling the room.

She'd never had it so good. A dumb, stupid girl from *o morro* in Rio. No education, only beauty. Great beauty. At eighteen she had been plucked out of Rio's infamous slums, hand picked by a kind of talent scout *cum* Professor Higgins *cum* pimp. In Houston she was sold to a real Professor Higgins. Bruno de Gravacão bought her. Like most of the other Professor Higginses, he was a wealthy Brazilian expatriate. His particular fortune was made in real estate in São Paulo. Although Ninfa Pereira had undergone several weeks of "grooming" after she arrived in Houston, to enable her to make the transition from slum girl to society woman more easily, de Gravacão was a thorough man and began at the beginning.

The first thing he did was to take Ninfa to Dr. Gilson Gonzaga, also an expatriate, and have her checked out. Everything was fine; excellent, in fact. De Gravacão congratulated himself. Next important step was to take her to Jacques Dessange for a coiffure that would make her enviable anywhere in the city . . . or in Rio or Paris. Then to Neiman's for a wardrobe to suit the natural style of the young woman; to Fred's for a few pieces of appropriate jewelry; to a dozen stores for shoes; to Intimate Intrigue for designer lingerie that would do astonishing things for her body. At last to an optometrist (Dr. Gonzaga had noted she was nearsighted; her only physical fault) for contact lenses. Voilà! A lady. Well, at least a superior lay. All she had to do in return for this wonderful new life was to destroy herself, if that was his request, for Professor de Gravacão's personal gratification. It was not an excessive requirement. Any child of *o morro* would gladly have done as much to get out.

So he watched her. Obviously she had inhaled another lungful of Colombia's best after he left the bed. She would be preoccupied for a while. He could see her nose running in a glistening stream down to her chin as she lurched to the samba through the increasingly brazen and oblique rays of the sun. Bitch. Even the sun fucked her.

Viverei, viverei . . . viverei . . .

He laughed. She heard him and laughed too. He thought of her Professor de Gravacão. The old man had no idea he was sharing her. Some of them knew, he was sure; but the cowards would not speak out against him. He came and took them when he wanted, within certain limits. All of them were hungry for him; he had made sure of that from the beginning. They loved to see him. They all loved Rafael.

He let her dance and walked from the living room. He went to the bathroom and showered, washing the powder out of his hair, cleansing himself of the grave, of the lime pit, of the leprosy that ate at him when he let himself get too close to them. He lathered thoroughly three times, washed

200

three times with minute attention to every pore of his body. When he stepped out of the shower he wrapped himself in warm towels taken from the electrically heated cabinet. He used three huge ecru towels, luxuriated in them. There were only two left for Ninfa. These he took out of the warmer and stuffed into the commode.

By the time he had dressed, the stereo had run out of Alcione sambas. He walked down the hall and looked into the living room. The glass wall was a shimmering sheet of vermeil; the room was set afire by the dying sun. Ninfa had collapsed in the middle of the floor, her golden body swimming in the fading molten light.

He shrugged and walked to the stereo turntable. Removing the record, he blew off the dust, sprayed the disc with a vinyl cleaner and wiped it off. He examined the grooves for scratches, satisfied himself that there were none, and slipped the record into a glassine bag and then into the cardboard cover. Laying the record by the front door in the foyer so he wouldn't forget it when he left, he returned to the bedroom.

From the outside pocket of his silk Valentino sports coat, hanging in the closet, he took a small black calfskin pouch. He unfolded the pouch and removed a glass vial with a rubber-sealed cap, which he put on the marble top of the dressing table in the anteroom of the bath. Next he took out a syringe and, inserting the needle in the vial, withdrew enough liquid to fill half the syringe, then returned the vial to the pouch. It took him a moment to locate the flat container for her contact lenses amid the jumble of perfumes and cosmetics. He opened it, removed the two gelatinous lenses, and poured the solution into the sink. He replaced the soft lenses and squirted the contents of the syringe over the membranous discs until they floated in it. The water-permeable lenses would absorb the virus distillate. After her revel with drugs and drink, Ninfa's eyes would be raw and bloodshot, but she would wear the lenses. It was what she was supposed to do. He snapped shut the lens case and put it back where he found it. He injected the remainder of the solution into her small plastic bottle of Naphcon eyedrops. He rinsed the syringe in the sink and put it back into the pouch.

In the bedroom he put on his coat, put the pouch in his pocket, and walked back into the living room. Ninfa was in a heap on the marble, now stained by the bloody death of the sun. Night was spilling into the sun's death like black ink, and all the sparkling lights of the city broke through it and stretched to the horizon like an infinity of scattered diamonds.

He picked up his record and opened the door. De Gravacão was due into the private jet hangars at Hobby at nine forty-five. He would be home by ten-fifteen. Ninfa Pereira would have to explain herself to him the best she could.

24

On Wednesday evenings Gabriela prepared and served a full dinner with the help of a girl she brought with her for that purpose. Sometimes there would be guests, but more often Haydon and Nina dined alone. The Wednesday-evening dinners were something his mother had instituted when he was a boy, to give the family a special time together to talk and dine in a "civilized manner," to get beneath the trivialities she believed filled their lives. Cordelia Haydon had been a great one for "civilized conversation" too. It was at a Wednesday-evening dinner that Haydon first introduced Nina to his parents. They fell in love with her from the beginning and she became a favored guest on those evenings, and quickly a member of the family even before they were married. Haydon sincerely believed that if he had eventually married someone else, Nina would have continued to be with them on those nights. She became the daughter his parents never had, a special person to both of them.

Gabriela, who was also a family tradition, having been in the house longer than Haydon had lived, had just indignantly expelled Cinco from the dining room, where Haydon had tried to hide him by having him lie quietly in a corner. But she had spotted him—her eyes were not *that* bad—and had shooed the collie out by flapping her white apron after him as he tucked his tail, lowered his head, and fled down the hall to the terrace. He now looked at them with joyless eyes through the dining room windows, as Gabriela stewed back through the dining room on her way to the kitchen, muttering loudly enough for Haydon to hear that they had *never* allowed dogs in this house and they were not going to start now.

"You just make him feel worse by having him ejected like that," Nina said, looking out at the collie.

Haydon grinned. "She doesn't know that he's in here most of the time anyway. I always let him in when she's not around."

"She does know," Nina said, laughing. "She told me she'd been finding *pelos de perro* in the library."

They finished their dessert with small talk about the house, the work Pablo had planned with the citrus trees, whether or not they should have the roof checked where Haydon had seen the stain. Afterward Gabriela brought fresh coffee. Haydon got up and took a cigar from the humidor sitting on the sideboard, clipped the end, and lighted it as he came back to the table. He inhaled the smooth dark smoke of the Marca de Oro corona, allowing himself this indulgence just once; the rest of the cigar he would merely taste. He began to relax for the first time since Vanstraten had come by with his startling diagnosis.

"Going to bed early?" she asked. She was leaning on her elbows, smiling at him.

"Late," he said.

"What? You didn't sleep two hours last night."

"I'll have to make it up some other time. I've got to go over to Parmer's place."

"Surely that can wait until tomorrow."

"There are other things to do tomorrow."

Nina looked at him. He recognized the expression and knew what she was thinking. It was a strange symbiosis they shared. He dreaded the fear in her eyes as much as he dreaded the inimitable deepening anxiety that grew within him and that she recognized almost before he did. They feared it together without ever speaking of it, he pretending nothing was any different than it ever was, and she watching him more closely, monitoring every change in mood like a telepathic barometer. Together they watched the dark season approach until, suddenly, he descended into its black vacuum, where he lost both time and space, and, inevitably, another small piece of himself. Both of them were increasingly afraid of what these descents might someday mean.

Like a guilt-ridden alcoholic who angrily refuses to think of his certain relapse, Haydon restlessly suppressed a secret resentment against Nina for her stability in the face of his own recurrent weakness. His success in repressing it was due to his own talent for unflinching self-examination, which could be critical to the point of morbidity, and a sense of profound respect and gratitude for her absolute fealty.

"When will we ever talk about it?" she asked. Her voice had softened, her face bore a sad, faint smile.

"Not tonight."

"Why?"

The cigar tasted good. He didn't want her to continue, hoped she would stop.

"Stuart?"

"I wouldn't know what to say," he answered truthfully.

"I didn't expect that you would. But we could talk anyway. You don't have to know. It wouldn't hurt you to explore this thing."

"This thing?"

She hesitated. "Yes. That's the way I've come to feel about it."

205

He looked at her. His eyes saw her but his mind was falling back on itself, retreating but keeping balance.

"I can understand that," he said. "I guess I feel the same way."

"Then let's talk about it, Stuart. I'm concerned about this investigation, about what it's beginning to do to you. You need a vacation now, not intensified involvement in this case."

"There's nothing I can do about it. It's here."

"You need a leave of absence."

She said it hurriedly, as though it was a harsh truth that she knew would hurt but needed to be said. It was the tone one used to tell a heart patient he must quit his job or it would kill him. Heart patient. He was quick to see the symbolism in the example he drew for himself.

He sipped his coffee, picked up the half-empty bottle of Chablis on the table, and pushed back his chair to stand.

"Let's go outside," he said.

They went out into the hallway and together approached the glass doors. Haydon held the door open and they walked onto the terrace, where Cinco immediately came to them for reassurances that he was still loved. Nina knelt to comfort the old dog with a hug, while Haydon filled Cinco's bowl with the Chablis and put it down in front of the grateful collie. As Cinco lapped at the wine, Haydon walked to the balustrade and leaned his elbows on it, looking out to the citrus trees and blowing a thin stream of blue smoke into the heavy, humid night air.

When he felt Nina at his side, lacing her arm through his, he said, "You're going to force me to wax philosophical about it."

He felt her shrug.

"It's true," he said. "I recognize . . . the old symptoms. An honest confession. I've never denied the reality of it to myself, only to you. We never really discussed it together as

206

I had once promised we would, and I don't want to now. It's one mystery I'd rather not explore, though I acknowledge its presence and I acknowledge the pain and the damage it inflicts on both of us. But now is the wrong time to talk about it.''

"Why?"

"This particular investigation is important. This man —I'm sure it's a man—is unlike anyone I've ever encountered. A genuine madman. What he's doing is not on such a grand scale numerically, though it may prove to be when we finally get to the bottom of it. But I'm intrigued by his . . . approach. Multiple or serial murderers have many common denominators. There is the semblance of a syndrome, historically, psychologically. Most of this can be seen in retrospect, but not necessarily before the murderer is stopped or caught. In this case there's something observable from the beginning, something that differentiates him from other men of his sort.''

He turned the cigar in his mouth, rotating it back and forth with his fingers as he tasted the tobacco. It seemed to him richer in the open air, as if the tropical humidity enhanced the flavor of the dark, moist leaves.

"The serial murderer often enjoys a fierce hate. That hate drives him, impels him to murder repetitiously and brutally. The object of his hate is made to suffer and the murderer savors the power of being the agent of that suffering. He wants to see the object suffer; he wants to hear the object cry, whimper; he wants actually to feel the object's suffering with his own hands and experience the life being drained or wrenched away. It's a visceral violence, unbelievably intense and horrifying. It's awesome. He may be the classic quiet guy whose neighbors are always so astonished to discover is a demon in disguise, but ultimately the disguise is shed to allow for that grand moment of violence that must eventually be satisfied.

"The man we are looking for seemingly has no such visceral need. He simply inoculates the victim, by whatever devious manner he decides is best, and walks away. Apparently the victims don't realize what has happened to them. His moment of contact with the victim not only lacks the elements of pain and fear, but it may lack the very appearance of violence. Since there is no way of determining exactly when the victim will die of the disease, he can't even have the vicarious pleasure of witnessing her death from afar. He lacks that white heat of passion which I imagine must consume the multiple murderer in those final moments when he physically encounters his victim and destroys him."

Haydon was quiet, his mind searching in a multitude of directions, grasping at ideas, traces of ideas, memories and paraphrases of ideas, trying to relate concepts heard, and read, and dreamed. His calm demeanor, the long casual pull on the cigar, belied the agitation within.

"I remember something I underlined in one of my father's books. It was a quote by Justice Brandeis that struck me as strange and has come to me from time to time in conflict with, oddly enough, ideas of another kind, from Carl Jung. Brandeis was writing of the dangers of letting our prejudices so deceive us that we come to give them the status of legal principles. He wrote, 'If we would guide by the light of reason, we must let our minds be cold.' I wondered then, and still wonder, whether a cold mind is an admirable goal for attainment. I suspect that behind these murders we will find a very reasonable man, a man whose mind is so cold that even the passions of murder cannot warm it."

Nina didn't say anything for a while. She simply stood by him, her arm in his, her head lowered slightly. In the splash of light that fell on the terrace from the dining room windows, a soft and lumpish toad appeared from the shadows. He sat placidly in the light as if he had made a stage entrance from the wings, the first actor in the scene, who must wait alone for the action to begin. Cinco saw him too, but he had dealt with toads before and had no desire to play the fool at his age. Besides, the wine made him sleepy. The toad croaked once, a rare soliloquy in the limelight, which drew only a yawn from the collie, lying with his wrists crossed in the shadows of the opposite wings. There being no further action or monologue, the toad made three mushy bounds past Cinco into the darkness.

"So this is an exceptional case," she said. It was not a question.

"Yes, exceptional."

"Why?"

He watched a wraith of smoke twist and float away from him, gray against the darkness, until it became the darkness and was lost.

"I get an actual sensation of evil from this person," he said. "It's the kind of presentiment you can't ignore. It follows you about like a vague premonition, an ominous uneasiness hovering at the back of your mind that causes you to wake up suddenly in the middle of the night and lie still with pounding heart, wondering what it was that woke you and knowing it was *something*. It can be the closest thing to encountering the unknown, this side of death. When one senses that kind of experience standing off in the dark waiting for you, it is an opportunity to encounter an aspect of one's self that shouldn't be denied. Encountering an evil of this purity is like approaching a milestone in psychoanalysis. It's archetypical; you come face to face with a piece of yourself."

"A piece of yourself?"

"Yes. I don't know how to explain it, but that's what it seems."

"That's frightening."

"Exactly."

"You've talked with Leo and Ed about this?"

"Of course not."

"Van?"

"We've touched on these sorts of things before."

"What does he think about it?"

Haydon gave a grunt of amusement. "You don't want to know."

"It's odd," she said after a moment. "The longer I know you, the less I understand you. It doesn't seem that it should work that way."

"I've often thought the same of you."

"Really? I don't believe it."

"It's true. It only proves how much there is to all of us. And I'm sure there are vaster dimensions than we're imagining now, but we simply lack the vision to conceive of it."

She pulled herself closer to him, almost snuggling.

"Stuart, do you ever just sit and think of nothing?"

"What do you mean?"

"I mean, does your mind ever . . . relax?"

He flipped the rest of his cigar out into the damp grass, where for a few seconds it was a single burning eye before it died.

"Never," he said.

"I didn't think so." She laughed.

He turned to her and smiled and kissed her lightly on the lips. She made a comfortable moaning sound in her throat and returned his kiss and then pulled back.

"You stink," she said.

"No, it's the cigar."

"That's what I mean."

"Oh."

"I don't know whether to try to seduce you into staying and run the risk of your getting up in the small hours of the morning and leaving me asleep, or to shove you out of the house now, hoping you'll be home early enough for me to seduce you before you have to leave again in the morning.''

"Now whose mind is working overtime?"

"I'm trying to keep up with you."

He held his watch up to catch the glow from the dining room. "It's ten o'clock. Give me a couple of hours. It's not far over there and I'll give you the telephone number."

"In case someone calls."

"Yeah, that too."

They turned and walked back into the broad hallway together, their arms around each other's waists. He took the keys to the department Ford off the marble-topped side table and kissed her again.

"I won't be long," he said.

"I'm sure."

He felt her watching him as he walked across the porte cochere and got into the car. He waved to her as he drove out of the light. When his headlights hit the gates he pushed the button on the electronic switch and they swung open slowly as he approached. Once through, he turned on the radio, which stayed on the classical music station. It was playing Mozart's "Eine Kleine Nachtmusik."

25

Haydon parked the car at the curb a block away from Parmer's condominium and walked back to the sidewalk that led up through the crape myrtle grove. Shining his flashlight on the front door, he saw the black-outlined red sticker that said the house was under police superintendence and must not be entered without written permission from the Homicide Division. He recognized the new police-department-issue deadbolt and fished in his pocket for the key. Before he unlocked the door he checked the mailbox. It was empty.

Once inside, he turned on the lights and locked the door behind him. Looking around from where he stood, noting once again the cavernous effect created by the tiered floor plan, which rose from the lowest point at the front door, he sensed the hollow feeling of vacancy that overcame unoccupied houses even though they remained fully furnished.

He stepped up into the living room, looked toward the mezzanine, back toward the kitchen, and then at the glass fireplace and the old Wurlitzer that stood beside it. He walked over to the Wurlitzer. It was a carnival in a box, horseshoe-shaped, with the arch at the top; an elaborate lyre design formed the basic shape of the plastic-and-chrome fili-gree between the two arms of the shoe, and through it an am-ber light issued from the bowels of the machine. Framing all this was the multicolored plastic piping, alive with rising bubbles that disappeared into a crown of shattering light which hid behind another frieze of filigree. Inside the glass compartment, half a hundred records were stacked in back of chrome guards.

Once again he reviewed the titles and the artists, then he punched the first two plastic keys. He watched the arm come for the record, slide it out of its slot in the stack, flip it over, and lower it onto the turntable. Quickly, but accurately, the needle arm placed itself on the spinning vinyl. When the song began, Haydon quickly recognized the surging rhythms of a carnival samba.

He listened for a few seconds and then began to explore the house. There was nothing in the living room that might help him but a small writing desk. He went through it and found only a few stamps, stationery from several hotels in Houston, pens, books of matches from more hotels, picture postcards from Mazatlán. He looked through a stack of magazines on a coffee table between the two sofas.

Walking back to the kitchen, he checked the cabinets, which were stocked with the usual canned goods. There was an assortment of cooking utensils as well as china, pottery, and tableware. The dishwasher was full of dirty dishes and roaches. A door led out to a washroom with an electric washer and dryer, and another door led from there to a ga-rage, which had to be entered from a driveway that came in from the rear of the condominium. It was empty and showed no signs of having been used regularly or recently.

He came back through the washroom, pausing to check the contents of the washer, dryer, and clothes hamper, mov-ing the dirty clothes around with the end of his flashlight. When he got to the living room again, he crossed to the

Wurlitzer and pushed several more buttons. As he ascended the steps to the mezzanine, the house was filled with a serene, sophisticated arrangement of a song called "India," sung by a clear-voiced woman named Gal Costa.

He walked past the potted palms to the red room. As he went up the three steps that led into the room, he took careful note of the thickness of the wall that was common to the mezzanine. It was, he calculated, a little over three feet thick, the approximate depth of the clothes closets. The room was still a mess; no one had been allowed to clean it.

Haydon went to the opposite wall, near the bath, and turned to look above the closet door. Two air vents from the air conditioning fed into the room. Two more vents entered from the wall to his left. He walked around the bed to the closet and opened both folding doors. Shoving aside the clothes at one end, he searched the wall seams and then moved along the back wall, shoving clothes as he went until he reached the other end, which was lined with shoe shelves. He snapped on his flashlight and shone it on the ceiling. It was a few seconds before he located the hairline seams that formed a square above the shoe racks. He touched the racks. They were solid and permanent wooden shelving. Looking closer, he saw that the center of each shelf was slightly scuffed. He began to remove the shoes.

Using the shelves as steps, he reached the trapdoor, which was well seated into the ceiling but easy to lift off. He shoved it back out of his way and stuck his head and flashlight up into the hole. It was a long, empty chase about three feet wide and four feet high, enough room to let you move along it in a crouch. Haydon checked the pair of bogus vents he'd observed below. They could be removed easily and were more than large enough to be used as ports for taking photographs. He crawled to identical vents above the other two rooms and checked their positions, which were analogous. The chase was otherwise empty.

Haydon returned to the hatch and, after replacing the trapdoor, climbed down. He had left the bedroom and was halfway along the mezzanine when another samba started on the Wurlitzer and the telephone began to ring. He got to it after four rings. It was Hirsch.

"Stuart, you need to get down here to Ben Taub. We've got a woman with rabies."

"Where?"

"Intensive care."

"Can she talk?"

"She's coming and going."

Haydon slammed down the telephone and hurried to the door. He turned off the lights and stepped outside. The pounding rhythms of the samba came to him through the door as he locked the deadbolt.

Hirsch and Mooney were standing inside the glass quadrangle of the nurses' station in intensive care, looking across a highly polished floor to another glassed-in room, where several doctors and nurses were working busily over a patient Haydon could not see. He knocked on the glass and a nurse let him in as Hirsch and Mooney looked around.

"What's the situation?" Haydon asked.

"Emergency vehicle brought her in a little after noon today on a 911 by her. Name's Pauline Thomas, a prostitute from the Montrose area. They didn't know what to do for her and had been experimenting when the notice from the department came through emergency. She's in pretty bad shape. Ed tried to talk to her while I was on the phone to you and by the time I got off they'd hustled him back in here when some buzzers went off in there."

"Shit, you ought to see her, Stuart," Mooney said. "She's in isolation. Weird. They've got her strapped down. She starts slobbering and they have to suck the stuff out of

215

her mouth to keep her from choking. She bites the aspirator, chews on it. Goddamn.''

''You didn't get anything from her?''

''Oh, hell, no. No way.''

''What does the doctor say?''

''Just wait and see if she clears up again. As soon as she does, they'll let someone in until she freaks out again.'' He turned to the window again. ''Wait'll you hear what Leo's got.''

Haydon looked at Hirsch.

''First of all, Walther died. Right here in this same unit at six-thirty this evening. Lieutenant Freed has already seen his wife. Silva's still on the shots and scared to death.''

Haydon didn't miss a beat. ''What about the media?''

''There was an official warning about that in the department's notice alerting medical facilities. Ed and I have talked to the proper administrative chiefs here and they understand, but it's inevitable that—''

''Yes, I know that. What else?''

''I found two more in the morgue. Vanstraten's people pulled their samples and confirmed the rabies. They're Latin, young.''

''Incredible. How long have they been there?''

''One six weeks. One eight.''

''When she clears up, who's going in?'' Mooney said, still facing the glass.

Haydon looked at him. He could tell Mooney wanted to talk to her. The whole thing was beginning to get to the rough-edged Vice officer, so much so that he wasn't able to hide it anymore.

''You can, Ed.''

''What do you want me to ask her? I'm not going to have long.''

''See if you can get any connection to the Quenby thing. See if she knows any of the women who have died. Ask

216

about Brazilian men or music or anything. Hell, ask her how she got sick, if she knows what's wrong with her.''

"This really is pissing in the wind, isn't it?" Mooney said. "That woman's in bad shape. You should have seen her."

Haydon noticed his old friend was massaging his stomach, with both hands in his waistband.

"Did you get to Duplissey?" he asked.

"Didn't find her until tonight. I've got an appointment to meet her in the morning."

Haydon had been oblivious of his surroundings, but now, as they stopped talking to wait, he became aware of the blipping of electrocardiographs lined up behind him. They monitored each of the intensive care rooms circling the glassed-in nurses' station. There was the squishing of rubber-soled shoes as the nurses moved in and out of the doors; there was the inescapable odor of alcohol mixed with the fragrance of night-shift coffee. The station looked like a control room at NASA, with blinking lights, dials, meters, computer printouts, and pulsing red LEDs.

Inside Pauline Thomas's room, one of the nurses responded to a remark by the doctor and moved to the door, where she began pulling off her green isolation gown and mask. When she stepped outside the room she was wearing a pale-yellow sweater over her white uniform. She pushed the sleeves up to her elbows as she walked across the fluorescent glare that separated the room from the nurses' station. She was young, perhaps in her late twenties, and had a cheerful face. She opened the door and leaned in, her stethoscope dangling around her neck.

"The doctor says two of you can come in now."

Haydon looked at Hirsch, who shook his head.

Haydon and Mooney followed the nurse back through the white light that seemed to drain the blood from their faces as they passed through it. They stopped outside Thomas's door, where two chrome trolleys were stacked with green clothing and packages of sterile rubber gloves.

"You're going to have to suit up," the nurse said, smiling and taking two surgical gowns off the trolleys. She helped each of the detectives into the gowns, which pulled on from the front and tied in back. She made sure the elastic wrists on the gowns were pulled down over their sleeves and then helped them with the surgical gloves that came up over the gown sleeves to mid forearm.

"There's a gray barrel lined with a red plastic sack that sits just inside the door," she said, tying their face masks. "When you start out, untie your gowns and take them off. Be careful not to touch your clothes with your gloves. Just peel the gown off wrong side out and the gloves will come off automatically with the ends of the sleeves. Throw everything into the barrels."

She opened the door for them and they went in.

As the door closed behind them, the doctor stepped over to them and shook hands. "Dr. Hammond," he said and then crossed his arms as he looked at the woman in the bed. He had on a short-sleeved scrub suit over which he wore an isolation garment like the detectives', except that it was a transparent plastic material. Haydon noticed that the doctor's pale arms were devoid of muscle definition and were covered with thick glossy black hair. He seemed incredibly clean. Although Haydon could not see the man's features behind the surgical mask, he noted that the dark bushy eyebrows dominated the unlined forehead of a young man.

"You may have one more shot at her," Hammond said, looking at his patient with a nod. "We're going to give her something that should bring her around, but it might not last long, and we might not be able to do it again."

"Have you ever treated anyone with rabies before?"

"One. The young policeman who died earlier today. I'll

218

be in charge of any more of the cases that might come through here. I've talked with Dr. Vanstraten.''

They watched a nurse wrap and tighten a length of rubber surgical tubing around the woman's arm. She waited until the large vein swelled and then she lifted a syringe and slipped in the needle. As she slowly pushed in the clear liquid, Haydon looked at the woman in the bed. Her strawy, bleached hair stood out from her head in matted tufts, stiff and unforgiving. Her face was flushed and her eyes, half open and beginning to flutter, were swollen and red. She was strapped to the bed and implanted with wormy tubes that descended to her from plastic bags dangling from aluminum racks. Other bags hung off the side of her bed, some filling with fluids that should not be leaving her, others with fluids that had to.

A second nurse, wearing thick rubber gloves, stood at the head of the bed. When the woman's eyes began to open fully, the nurse quickly flipped on a machine and with deft strength pressed pressure points in the woman's jaws and opened her mouth. She inserted a clear blue aspirator, which with a loud liquidy sucking sound extracted the overabundance of saliva. The patient tried to resist, but the nurse was firm and quick about it. The machine went off and whined to silence.

The woman looked at them with unseeing eyes. "Oh, God," she said. She hardly moved her lips.

Mooney moved up. "Do you know where you are?"

Haydon heard a kindness in his voice he had not thought possible.

The woman nodded.

"We want to help you. Do you know what's the matter with you?"

She shook her head wearily.

"Somebody has made you sick. Given you something. Did you know that?"

She shook her head.

"You don't have to move your head unless you have a 'yes' answer. Okay?"

A short nod.

"Do you know a woman named Sally Steen?"

Nothing.

"Judith Croft? . . . Theresa Parmer? . . . Sandy Kielman? . . . Petra Torres?"

Nothing.

"Do you know any Brazilians? Men or women?"

Nothing.

"Do you go to any nightclubs that play Brazilian music?"

The woman frowned.

"Do you know what Brazilian music is?"

She continued to frown.

Mooney looked at Haydon, who moved up. "Samba, bossa nova . . ."

She nodded.

"Where?" Haydon pursued.

Her frown became a hard look, which grew to a slight shudder as her eyes pulled back at the corners. She was fighting a convulsion.

"Where?" Haydon urged. "It's very important."

She began to hiss, her mouth flattening out as she struggled.

"Sss, ah, ssss . . . sshssh . . ." Her head began to bounce on the pillow and the veins in her neck tightened and sprung out from her throat like guy wires. "Ssss . . . shsssshh." Her eyes locked on a point at the foot of the bed as she pulled against the straps on the side rails.

"Brasilia? Club Havana? Christ!" Haydon said as the woman's eyes filled with oily tears that overflowed and streaked her face while she strained against the straps.

"Copa's?"

Her head began thrashing wildly, bobbing, jerking.

220

"Copa's?" he repeated.

She flung her head forward and backward, pounding it against the bed.

The doctor came up and moved next to the woman. He held her head on either side and steadied the jouncing.

"Shit," Mooney said. "Is that a nod? Is she controlling that?"

"She can't stop it," the doctor said. He let go and it began again.

"If it's Copa's make a noise," Haydon said.

The noise began like a rumble in her chest, an unreal sound like a low-toned synthesizer that gradually crawled to her throat, where it grew to a higher pitch that throbbed and undulated like the sonar communications of whales. The tears literally streamed from her eyes and she rattled the rails violently as a thick, clear syrup emerged from the sides of her gritted teeth. It, too, became a stream as her eyes rolled and swelled wide.

"All right," the doctor said quickly. "Excuse me." He pushed them back, and he and the two nurses bent over her. The whine of the aspirator picked up but could not drown out the rattling rails or the hysterical ululation that issued from Pauline Thomas.

The two detectives quickly removed their gowns as they had been instructed, and stepped outside.

"Did she do that deliberately?" Mooney asked as they crossed over to the nurses' station.

"Who knows?" Haydon said. His voice was low; he was angry.

"What was that 'sss . . . sshssh' business?"

Haydon shook his head and barged into the nurses' station. Hirsch had just gotten a cup of coffee from the cheerful nurse.

"Let's go," Haydon said, and without breaking stride, left by the opposite door, which led out into the hospital cor-

221

ridor. When he got outside he stopped and turned to Hirsch and Mooney.

"Leo," he said. He was speaking very softly. "Get those two Jane Doe photos to Mrs. Guajardo. If she identifies them I want the two of you to go over to the docks and talk to Longoria. Pull a routine on him. I want to know what he knows. Do whatever is necessary to get it out of him. I want something of significance from him or I want him booked. Don't let him get away from you.

"Ed, I'll talk to Duplissey. Where were you supposed to meet her?"

"In the tunnels downtown. At the Shale restaurant under Pennzoil Place. Ten o'clock."

"How will I know her?"

"I'll give you a picture in the morning."

"Good. I'm going to call Dystal. See you tomorrow."

He turned and walked quickly away from them, to an alcove with telephones. It rang awhile; Dystal slept hard. When he answered, Haydon made sure he was fully awake.

"I'm listenin'," Dystal said.

"You heard Walther died?"

"They called me."

"Hirsch found two Jane Does in the morgue files who turned out to be rabies victims. Latin girls. I'm at Ben Taub and there's a Montrose hooker dying in intensive care right now with the same thing."

"Son of a bitch. Okay. Okay . . . I'll get with the captain in the morning. You better be thinking about what you want to do. We're on for the ride now."

"Thanks," Haydon said.

"Try to get some sleep."

26

The morning bells of the Immaculate Heart of Mary Catholic Church across from De Zavala Park floated through the opened door of Los Chinos neighborhood grocery as Hirsch turned his back to the stacked gallon cans of La Padrino olive oil and offered the two photographs to Mrs. Guajardo. A red plastic-mesh shopping bag hung from a string looped over the crook of her arm. She took the photographs, checked the aisles of the grocery with an arched eyebrow, and then looked at the pictures she held in each hand. She studied them, looking from one to the other as her face clouded over.

She clicked her tongue. "Dear God," she said.

"You've seen them?"

"Oh, yes." She handed him one. "Her name was . . . it was the Soyla, I think. Yes," she said, still looking at the picture in Hirsch's hand. "Soyla." She looked at the picture she was still holding. "This one I saw at the Kwik-Wash several times, but I did not know her." She handed the picture back to Hirsch.

"Are you sure?" he asked. "You've got to be sure."

223

She nodded. "Oh, yes. So young, so young." She shook her head. She made a sign of the cross so vague she could have been warding off a fly.

"You were kind to meet me here," Hirsch said. "I'll be in touch."

She nodded again and turned to inspect a stack of oranges as if they had never spoken. Hirsch made his way to the front of the store, stepped out into the bright morning sun, and crossed the street. He walked around the corner and down half a block on the side street to the dirty beige department car parked in the shade of a chinaberry tree beside the drainage ditch. He got in on the passenger side and left the door open for air. Mooney was finishing his third doughnut and sweat was already oozing from the short hair at his temples.

"Well?"

Hirsch reached into the cardboard box and got the last jelly roll. "She knows them."

"Positively?"

"That's what I asked. She said yes."

Mooney burped violently. Hirsch turned away and looked out the window toward the ship channel. It was only five blocks away at its closest point, down the street beside them, past two blocks of clapboard houses, across the railroad tracks and a span of dry, reedy coastal grass. But it was twelve blocks to the Turning Basin, where they would have to go.

"Smells good down here," Mooney said. "I could even taste it in my doughnuts." Reaching up, he took a half-pint carton of milk off the dashboard. He drained it and threw it out the window, into the drainage ditch. Then he reached down for his notebook. "Warehouse number forty-one. That sounds about right. What else? Maybe he even wears a tie."

"It's not his private place, Ed. Just happens to be where

224

his goods are being stored right now. That warehouse could hold bananas next week, or oilfield equipment, or cotton, or cinnamon. Depends on what's coming in or going out and who gets the space first.'' Hirsch finished his jelly roll and wiped his fingers on a napkin and put it in the empty box. ''You ready?'' he asked.

Mooney started the car. ''Now, this guy's supposed to be there, right?''

''That's what his office told me. He's filling up warehouses forty-two and forty-three with leather. He's supposed to be down here this morning, all morning, doing paperwork or something. He's supposed to be in an office over number one.''

Mooney eased the car along the drainage ditch, his window rolled down and one arm resting on the sill as he scanned the dirt yards of the clapboard shanties shaded by overgrown ligustrums and chinaberry trees. He turned right on Seventy-fifth Street and drove the few blocks to Navigation, which looked empty and steamy in the morning sunshine. He crossed Navigation and then the Houston Belt and Terminal railroad tracks, and began the approach to the basin. The air was rank with the smell of the ship channel. A webbing of electrical wires crossed over the street from leaning creosote poles, one of which was now being used as a urinal simultaneously by a wino and a dog. There wasn't an exposed piece of metal on the street that wasn't rusted. The weeds along the cracked sidewalks were filled with trash.

The street dropped sharply and they entered the double-width chain-link gates of the basin. The Turning Basin itself was a ballooning hernia in the intestine of Buffalo Bayou, which trailed a wormy path through the center of Houston and became known as the barge channel when it reached the sewage disposal plant at Lockwood Street. When the barge channel reached the Turning Basin, it officially became the

Houston Ship Channel. It ran another twenty-two miles through marshland and bays before it emptied into Galveston Bay at the mouth of the Gulf of Mexico.

After passing through the gates, Mooney pulled into an open parking area on the quayside. The first two warehouses in the basin were to their right. The others circled to their left around the basin and continued on the north side of the channel until they were out of sight. They got out of the car and, like little boys, instinctively walked to the edge of the quay and looked over. The harbor water was gray and the consistency of milk. Buoys of clustered trash bobbed on the ripples and a bunch of black bananas waited at the foot of cement steps which disappeared into the water.

Mooney passed judgment. "Shit."

They turned and walked to the end entrance of warehouse forty-three. They looked the length of the building and out its other end to the mouth of warehouse forty-two in the distance. The cavernous corrugated-tin building had a cement floor and steel girders crisscrossed its ceiling. There was one broad center aisle, flanked with wooden pallets laden with bundles of fresh hides wrapped with twine. The animal hair on the exposed hides still glistened with blood serum, which leaked into the liberal quantities of salt used to preserve them and produced a thick syrup, which oozed from the bundles and formed fragile white stalagmites. The humid morning heat added strength to the stench and made Hirsch's stomach turn over.

They began walking the length of the aisle, passing every twenty or thirty feet into the light and cross breeze of openings on either side of the building. To their right, black railroad tank cars sat in a fog as they off-loaded tallow, using steam to melt the residual fat. On the other side, a Brazilian freighter lay alongside the quay while shouting and sweating stevedores using forklifts loaded her with hundreds of pallets of hides. The freighter was named the *Filomena,* its mother port, Recife.

When they reached the far end of the building they looked into the door of the next. More hides, more stevedores. To the right of the door, a wooden stairway outside the warehouse climbed to a landing with a metal door and a window, whose sagging air conditioning unit dripped water onto the hood of a shiny emerald Lincoln.

"I would of parked it over a little," Mooney said, and started up the stairs.

The office door was open and they stepped into a small closed room, almost cold from the efforts of the overworked window unit. Two men sat at desks; one was conducting an earnest conversation on the telephone, holding his forehead with his free hand as though he were receiving terrible news, while the other was casually going through a stack of pink bills of lading. Both men were Mexicans in their early forties. A third man, an Anglo in his late fifties, wearing the gray work uniform of the Houston Port Authority, was sitting on top of a third desk with his feet in a wooden swivel chair, sipping coffee from a red Thermos cap. He had the nonchalant look of a veteran loafer and was the only one who took notice of them.

"Howdy," he said briskly. He held a filterless cigarette between yellowed fingers and looked at them with rheumy eyes set in an incredibly wrinkled face. "What can I do you for?"

"I want to speak to Mr. Longoria here," Mooney said, nodding toward the two Mexicans and waiting to see which one would react to the name. The man with the bills of lading looked up.

"Well . . ." the old man said.

"Arturo Longoria?" Mooney asked the Mexican.

For a second the man hesitated, then stood slowly, trying to make up his mind how to handle it. It was enough time for

227

Mooney to look him over. His thick black hair had a twenty-dollar cut and his thick mustache drooped slightly at the corners of his mouth, which slowly began to reveal long teeth as he decided to smile. He wore a long-sleeved white shirt, unbuttoned at the neck to reveal a heavy-link gold chain which Mooney thought looked more like a dog collar. The shirt sagged to one side from the weight of a dozen varicolored ballpoint pens packed into its pocket. In another few years he would be a fat man.

Longoria extended his hand. Mooney ignored the proffered hand, whipped out his shield, and held it up so Longoria could see it as he introduced himself and Hirsch.

"Police?" Longoria dropped his hand.

Mooney looked at the shield he was holding out, examined it.

"Uh, yeah, *policía*," he said, overpronouncing the word.

The use of the Spanish word took away what was left of the smile that was already fading from Longoria's face.

"Got a minute?" Mooney asked, sitting down in one of the two chairs in front of the desk Longoria had been using.

"Do I got a choice?" Longoria asked, looking at Mooney.

Mooney shook his head and grinned.

"Alberto." Longoria addressed the man on the telephone but kept his eyes on Mooney. Alberto started talking frantically to end his conversation. He was speaking Spanish in a stage whisper.

"Alberto." Longoria barked again.

"Chinga tu madre!" Alberto yelled into the telephone, and slammed down the receiver hard enough to ring the bell. He looked at Longoria's back, trying to figure out what was going on.

"Go smoke a cigarette," Longoria said.

Alberto took in both Mooney and Hirsch, seemed to come to some kind of understanding, and stood up. He was built

228

about like Longoria, but was bullish, and tougher in manner. As he walked by the old man, he slapped him on the back. The old man climbed down from his perch and followed him out the door.

"What do you want?" Longoria asked. He did not sit down and he addressed his question deliberately to Hirsch, who was still standing.

Mooney responded. "Just some routine questions," he said, making himself sound like a television cop.

"Routine about what?" Longoria asked Hirsch.

Mooney turned and looked up at Hirsch. "You talkin', Leo?"

"No."

"I didn't think so. Hey, I'm down here, Mr. Longoria."

Longoria looked at him but didn't say anything. He looked as if he was trying to decide whether he was going to take this kind of crap.

"Routine about that place where you live over on Harbor Street."

"I don't live on Harbor Street."

"You *don't?*" Mooney said with mock surprise.

Longoria stared coldly at him. He was thinking. He picked up a pack of cigarettes, put one in his mouth, lighted it. He threw the matchbook on the desk and blew the smoke at Mooney.

"Fuck you," he said.

"Ooh, a real *bad* bean," Mooney said, grinning. "Jesus and Mary!"

"You own the place on Harbor Street," Hirsch said quickly.

"You know that," Longoria said.

"Who do you rent it to?"

"That's my business."

"There have been questionable activities at that house,

229

Mr. Longoria. It would be best for all concerned if you co-operated with us," Hirsch said.

Longoria reached down and pulled out his desk drawer.

"Careful there . . ." Mooney said quickly, leaning forward.

Longoria looked at him sarcastically and pulled out a business card. He flipped it across to Mooney.

"This is my lawyer's card. He'll know who lives in the house."

Mooney picked up the card and read it slowly, mouthing the words as if he were simpleminded.

"By this I see you are a big man," he said. "Big men have lawyers." He turned and held the card up for Hirsch to see. "His lawyer."

Mooney stood slowly and handed the card back to Longoria, who didn't reach for it, so Mooney dropped it on the cluttered desk.

"What the shit is this about?" Longoria was glowering.

Hirsch spoke. "Your house on Harbor Street has been used for some months as temporary living quarters for young girls brought into the States illegally from various Latin American countries for the purpose of prostitution. Three of these girls have turned up at the city morgue and we think we'll be finding others. We were hoping you would cooperate with us by answering a few questions. If you refuse, we can only assume complicity on your part and will have to take you downtown and book you."

"For what! Book me for what?"

"Aggravated promotion of prostitution, conspiracy to violate the immigration laws, murder in the first degree."

"Bullshit!" Longoria's head was thrust forward and there was as much dismay in his expression as defiance.

Mooney's hand shot across the desk and grabbed a fistful of chain, which he twisted taut so that his knuckles pressed against Longoria's Adam's apple.

"You fuckin' taco," he said through clenched teeth. His face was scarlet. "You're wasting our *time.*" He let go of the chain by shoving Longoria backward as he reached into his pocket and pulled out a small blue card and began to read from it. " 'You have the right to remain silent and not make any statement at all and that any statement you make may be used against you and probably will be used against you at your trial; any statement—' "

"What are you doing? Hey!" Longoria's voice was hoarse.

" '—you make may be used as evidence against you in court; you have—' "

"Goddamn it, wait!"

"Hold on, Ed," Hirsch said.

"Huh?" Mooney looked up.

Longoria sat down heavily in his chair. He pulled a red plastic comb out of his pocket and raked it through his layered hair. He held his cigarette clenched between his front teeth as he desperately tried to salvage his tough-guy image.

"What's this about murder?" he asked. He was breathing heavily.

"We've told you all we're going to tell you," Mooney said. "You're supposed to tell *us.*"

Longoria looked at them, his mouth set hard. "Shit. Guy named DeLeon rents the house."

"How do we get in touch with him?"

"I got a card." He looked at Mooney and said, as though he were explaining himself to a child, "It's in my wallet. I'm going to reach in and get it, okay?"

Mooney just looked at him. While Longoria was going through the jumble in his fat wallet, Mooney leaned across the desk and picked up the matchbook. There was a dancing Carioca embossed on the cover, with the words Club Bragança underneath. Mooney showed it to Hirsch and tossed it back on the desk.

Longoria gave a white card to Hirsch. The name and address on the card read: "Robert J. DeLeon, Bahia Properties, Inc., Two Houston Center."

"How well do you know Mr. Guimaraes?" Mooney asked.

Longoria lowered his head with a slight tilt and looked up at Mooney, offering an open-handed gesture of innocence.

"Now listen, I hardly know the guy. I don't know what you heard, but I always deal with DeLeon." He shook his head. "Guimaraes? No."

"How many times have you met him?"

"Once. One time."

"When?"

"About six months ago, I guess. DeLeon was here. I walked out to his car with him, talkin', and he's in this big Mercedes. Big one with tinted windows. I start laughin' about it—I mean, you know, joking—and he says it's not his but Mr. Guimaraes'. We get to the car, the window comes down, and he introduces me. We shake. The window goes up. That's it."

"Letting you rub palms with the big man, huh?"

Longoria shrugged.

"Is that when you worked out the deal for getting the girls through customs?"

Longoria looked anxiously from Mooney to Hirsch and back. "Hey," he said.

"Hey," Mooney said back.

"I don't do that."

"We think you do."

"No way. No fuckin' way."

"Oh, we may be confused. Straighten us out on it, will you?" Mooney said.

Longoria took one of the dozen ballpoints from his shirt pocket and began popping the point in and out. He was one of those men for whom thinking was a visible activity that seemed to require a good deal of effort. Hard work, not mental acrobatics, had gotten him the gold choker and emerald Lincoln. His bottom teeth raked at his mustache.

"All I do is a favor for DeLeon," he offered, and then paused to see how that was sitting. Mooney and Hirsch just looked at him.

"See, I import all type goods from Brazil. Not a lot, but I got a license. You got to have a license to book space on the freighters. There's all kinds of space on freighters. I kind of . . . sublease my license to DeLeon. Sometimes. What the hell, I ain't usin' it. I mean, it ain't illegal so far as I know."

"And DeLeon's Bahia Properties belongs to Guimaraes?" Hirsch asked.

Longoria looked sick. He nodded.

"Does he own your business too?"

"Oh, no. No. This's all mine. I done all this myself and I own all of it. Nobody helped me with this."

"DeLeon made the arrangements to bring the girls by freighter?"

Longoria nodded again.

"How?"

The agony was written all over Longoria's face. Whether he was involved a little, a lot, or not at all would remain to be seen, but for now he had decided to save his own neck by telling the story. The first thing you do when you're put on the spot is to get off it. You worry about *how* you got off later, when there is more time to think and more room to maneuver.

"You got to pay a lot of people," he said. "At both ends. DeLeon takes care of the *mordidas* in Rio or Belém. He flies down there. Here he takes care of it too, but he uses my . . . some people I know."

"This DeLeon is pretty busy for a realtor. What is he, the big man's go-fer?" Mooney interjected.

"More than that. He's his lawyer."

233

Mooney grinned maliciously. "No shit."

"He's got another card says that. I don't have one of those. That real estate thing, it's not his main deal. He's a lawyer."

"Who are these 'people' you know that he uses?" Hirsch asked.

"A customs agent. A ship agent. People who have to check the bill of lading against the freight."

"How do the girls actually come over?"

"Crates. It's not bad," he said quickly. "They're four-by-four-by-five crates, padded real good and with handles and straps on the inside in case they get bounced around some. They're only in it for maybe six hours. Once they get on board and the ship's in international waters, there's a merchant sailor who lets them out and takes care of them somehow. I don't know no details about that. There's an officer and a sailor on each freighter in on the deal. There's not much risk. It's easy."

"Then they get back in the crate for unloading here, your people check it in, and DeLeon picks up his 'freight.' "

"Yeah. At night."

"How many have been brought in that way?"

"Maybe twelve, maybe fifteen. I'm not countin'. They come sometimes two at a time."

"Over how long a period of time?"

"About eighteen months."

"Where do they get these girls?"

"I think most of them come from Rio. They're slum girls. They got this big slum in Rio, millions of people in it. People will do anything to get out of there."

"What happens when the girls get here?"

"They go to the Harbor Street place a few days. They get photographed. Close-ups of the face. They're all good-looking. Without clothes; they're all young. The shots are showed around to the customers."

234

"Who takes the photographs?" Mooney asked quickly.

Longoria paused. "Hey. I spelled it out for you. I mean, there's a limit."

"That right?" Mooney asked. "A limit? You going to tell that to the judge: 'Hey. Ten yeers iss too mush! Hey!' "

Longoria looked as if he wanted to take Mooney apart. He didn't like the detective's José routines.

"How do I know you're not goin' to haul me in anyway?" Longoria said. "You think I'm just goin' to jabber away on your say-so?"

"You been doing pretty good," Mooney said.

"We'll walk out of here alone," Hirsch assured him. "But you can't just pick and choose your information."

"Let's just call it a little free-lance plea bargaining," Mooney said. "Believe me, you'll get a better deal from us than your lawyer will get from the DA's office."

Longoria was thinking again. He stood and walked over to the air conditioner and looked out the window above it. He had both hands in his trousers pockets, jangling change.

"DeLeon, he once told me Guimaraes' nephew takes the shots. He's real good at it. Makes them sexy, you know."

"Does he work for his uncle?"

"Hell, no. He's in school."

"Where?"

"Medical school. University of Texas Medical School."

"What's his name?"

"I don't know," Longoria said, turning around. "Honest. All I know is what I hear from DeLeon. If he don't tell me, I don't know."

"Why do they bring them all the way from Brazil?"

"Well, you can't sell American girls like that. Besides, lots of these guys are Brazilian. They like that kind of woman. Some of them are real knockouts. These old farts fix 'em up like high society. Keep 'em set up real nice in fancy condos. It's a great deal."

"What does a customer have to pay for these girls?"

"Twenty-five thousand."

"Shit!" Mooney shook his head.

"Hell, those guys don't even blink. I mean, they're getting this young, beautiful girl. Classy, sophisticated, sexy. They take 'em around and show them off to their frien's and let ever'body wonder what it's like to crawl into the sheets with what he's got. There's never no shortage of takers."

"These girls from the Rio slums are real sophisticated, huh?"

"They don't just take 'em off the freighter, give 'em a bath, and collect a check. Guimaraes has some additional investment in training them."

"Training?"

"Yeah. He's got some high-class call girls that teaches these little things how to act like ladies. Take off the rough edges."

"Who does this?"

"I don't know their names."

"Ever see them?"

"Once."

"You meet everybody once, don't you?" Mooney said. Longoria ignored him.

"Could you identify them from photographs?"

"I guess."

"Where did you see them?"

"Over on Harbor Street. They'd come over to look at some new girls."

"Do they train the girls there?"

"Hell, no. They took 'em somewhere for a coupla three weeks. It was no hit-and-run thing. They'd polish these girls real good. You wouldn't know they was the same girls when those hookers got through with them. Shit. They were *really* fine women when they were ready to sell."

236

"How much of that twenty-five thousand was profit for Guimaraes?"

"About twenty, I'd guess. He pays out about five in *mordidas*. I don't know what the overhead is on the training part of it."

Mooney sat still, his head lowered as he stared into his lap, seemingly contemplating the fate of one Arturo Longoria in light of Longoria's heinous crimes and the mitigating circumstances of his born-again cooperation. Hirsch didn't move. The air conditioner's compressor kicked in and the window shuddered. Mooney sucked loudly at a doughnut shred in his teeth.

"Tell you what," he said suddenly, looking at Longoria, whose white shirt was billowing slightly from the vents behind him. "You get your fancy lawyer and the two of you go down to the Harris County District Attorney's building on Fannin and talk to a guy named Russ Million. He's the assistant district attorney. He'll know you're coming in and he'll get this plea bargaining thing straightened out. In the meantime I guess I don't have to tell you that if you breathe a word of this to DeLeon, you can forget any damn plea bargain. Besides that you'll find yourself in goddamned hot water with Guimaraes, and he don't go strictly by the law, as you well know. I mean, you're a material witness as of now and if he don't want you to witness, he may try to take care of you. Hypothetically. I'm talkin' hypothetically, right?"

Longoria didn't respond.

"Right?" Mooney repeated.

Longoria nodded. His grim expression made it clear that he understood.

27

The tunnels that honeycomb almost fifty blocks of downtown Houston and interconnect a fraternity of corporate buildings can be attributed not to a single Daedalus, but to a host of architects employed by the city's billionaire corporate powers. Because each building owner is responsible for excavating his own tunnel and joining it to those of the adjacent blocks—most buildings downtown occupy a full city block—the disparity of the design from block to block produces a true subterranean labyrinth.

One might enter the tunnels by a network of polished steel escalators in the lobby of one building and proceed along corridors of travertine marble that turn in oblique angles until they join the ownership of the next block. At that point the corridors will change colors, with walls, perhaps, of ecru carpeting, and the turns will become serpentine and subtle, with slight rises and falls in elevation until one emerges in another lobby in another block by way of chrome capsules, illuminated from an unidentifiable source, through tubes that burst up through silent space and slide open in an arbor of ficus trees amid vaulted ceilings of glass. Sometimes the tunnels run straight and lonely, while at other places they will be broken by small plazas surrounded by tobacco shops, delicatessens, drugstores, barbershops, restaurants, liquor stores, and newsstands. Computerized bank teller machines are the most frequently recurring sight.

Oddly, there are few signs or directories telling the underground traveler where he is, or is about to go. There is, however, one unwavering element of consistency: the evidence everywhere of wealth applied to the latest in architectural technology and design. The tunnels are air conditioned, the lighting is soft, the appointments are always tasteful, deliciously new, and immaculately clean. The city of the future has gone underground in an elegant manner, far away from the thrum and roar of the streets above, which simmer in equatorial humidity and heat.

Haydon parked in a street-level lot adjacent to the Southwest Tower, on the corner of Milam and Walker. He walked across Milam to the lobby of the Bank of the Southwest and entered the tunnels. He crossed under Walker to the Esperson Building, under Rusk Street to the Houston Club, turned left and headed toward Milam again. In the middle of Milam he approached the smoked-glass gates at the entrance of the corridors of Pennzoil Place. At this juncture the corridor floors became red granite and the walls were covered with a cinnamon-brown carpet that lent an additional softness to the sweeping serpentine curves. Recessed canned lights ran in two tracks from the ceiling, throwing soft diamond patterns on the walls.

When he entered the underground lobby of Pennzoil Place he immediately looked to his right at the Shale restaurant. Maureen Duplissey was supposed to be waiting at a table next to the bronzed plate glass that looked into the lobby. He passed the length of the restaurant but did not see her and crossed to the windows of the travel agency across the lobby. He studied the travel pictures, all of which were dominated by a large poster of a dark and heavy-breasted Jamaican beauty standing waist deep in the blue Caribbean in a wet T-shirt, water beading her smiling face. It was a moment before he realized that the two girls standing behind the sales counter inside were smiling at him too, as he looked up at the lusty Jamaican.

He turned away and walked to the escalators, ascending to the main lobby, which rose twenty stories above the floor from six converging walls of glass. Behind the walls, office cubicles looked down over the lobby and across at angles to one another. A sloping crystal ceiling supported by white tubular lattice girders allowed the lobby's plants and flowers to be flooded with sharp, clear light, which sparkled from the glass flues and partitions of the main offices of the Texas Commerce Bank.

Haydon looked up and saw an office worker in shirtsleeves standing at his glass wall five stories over the lobby, looking across with his head tilted up at another office, far above him. The fluorescent squares of office ceiling lights above grew smaller and closer together as they ascended to the top of the lobby. The entire structure could have been a Spielbergian set for an orbiting space city. Haydon looked outside to the glare of summer light, and stepping on the descending track of the escalator, returned to the lower lobby.

She was not difficult to spot. She had just sat down and was digging in her purse as a waiter placed a frothy cup of Irish coffee in front of her. Haydon walked into the restaurant, rounded the cashier's desk, and approached her.

"Miss Duplissey?"

She looked up from her purse, a cigarette bobbing from her lips, and squinted at him as she quickly ran her eyes over his clothes and ruled out police work. She nodded.

"I'm Detective Haydon. I work with Ed Mooney. May I sit down?"

She removed the cigarette from her mouth and laid it on the table beside her steaming cup. "No."

He sat down.

"Please do." Her eyes leveled on him. "Where's Moon?"

"I'm afraid I cheated him out of this appointment. We're working on the same case and I felt since I'd already had two conversations with Judith Croft, I'd like to follow up on your conversation with Ed."

"I'm not going to talk about it anymore. Period."

"Then I'll have to take you in and book you."

"You've got to be joking."

"No."

She was wearing a dove-gray Qiana dress with a surplice neckline, which she traced with a middle finger as she studied him. When she got to the diagonal overlap, she plucked the material lightly with her fingers, unaware of what she was doing.

"This is really serious, huh?"

"It couldn't be more serious."

Her eyes broke away from his and she lit the cigarette.

"This is my first one today," she said. "And my first cup of coffee," she added. She tested the coffee. "I try not to use much of either one. In the long run they put wrinkles on you." She looked around. "Well, this is a nice place to talk anyway, isn't it." She wiggled her shoulders.

Haydon waved off the waiter. "Ed told me you'd been to Parmer's only one time, for one of their big parties. But you were there on other occasions, weren't you?"

"Mmm, yeah. I didn't get along with Judith, and after she and Sally got tight I didn't get along with Sally too well either. But Theresa and I were close. She'd have me over occasionally for combos, some little parties, until Sally found out and cut me out completely."

"Were there any young Brazilian girls there when you were?"

She sighed. "Yeah, there were."

"Did they live there?"

"Not these, but others did occasionally."

"What others and how occasionally?"

She frowned slightly, her eyes looking down at the table as she slowly exhaled smoke through slightly parted lips.

"Ed said I wasn't the only one you're talking to. Is that right?"

"Yes."

"Then I might tell you things you've already heard."

"It's possible. But it helps to hear the same story from different perspectives. Sometimes it doesn't sound like the same information when it comes from a different source."

She looked at him, thinking, nodding. "I see. Well, you know about them running a sort of 'Miss Manners' thing there at Theresa's?" she asked cautiously.

"Something to put a little polish on the Brazilian girls?"

"Yeah. Sandy and Theresa did the work, but it was Judith who ran the whole thing. She was the one who made the arrangements and decided when a girl was ready to go. She was sort of headmistress and communicated with the Brazilian guy. Actually, I think they're an item."

"Judith and Guimaraes?"

"Yeah. I think that's a deal Sally cut early on. Judith was taken care of no matter what."

"I'm still confused about what girls were at Theresa's, and when. Did these new girls take part in the group sessions with prospective buyers?"

"Definitely not. They were protected like sacred objects while they were in training. Top secret. But the condo parties were a little confusing, all right. For the two or three weeks the dormies were there, it was all business. No fooling around. But when they were in between 'classes,' when

242

there were no trainees living there, anything might go on. Sometimes these old buzzards would get together and agree to meet there with their girls and it was wide open."

"You mean these were the same girls who had previously trained there but now had been sold to the men?"

"Right. It was kind of like a fraternity party. Everybody kind of felt they had a common background. It could be a real melee. And then when that wasn't going on, this nephew of . . ." She fluttered her fingers, not wanting to say the name.

"Guimaraes."

"Yeah. He would come over with one or two of the girls for his own bash."

"He'd bring the mistresses?"

"That's right." She grinned. "That's something, huh? He's a gally bastard. See, these businessmen traveled a lot. These girls weren't kept half busy. This nephew would take up the slack. It was one of those open secrets and if any of the johns knew about it they never let on. Uncle is *the* big banana in this Brazilian crowd and I think nephew just did what he wanted to and everybody kept quiet."

"You've been around him?"

"Oh, yeah."

"What's he like?"

"A certified nut. Weird. Really 'mad, bad, and dangerous to know.' "

Haydon smiled.

Duplissey thrust her head forward. "You know that quote?"

"Yes, do you?"

She grinned slowly, a big grin of real pleasure. "Listen, I went to UT. Business major, but I got a kick out of a few English courses. I remembered that quote because I thought it was so goddamned clever. Lady Caroline Lamb, said of

Georgie Byron.'' She laughed. ''God, I can't believe you know that.''

''This guy's like Byron?''

She sputtered smoke. ''Hardly. George may have been kinky, but this guy's perverted. The guy would come about three times a week, sometimes alone, sometimes with one or two of those Brazilian girls. Let me tell you, those girls may have come from the slums, but once they sank their teeth into the good life they took to it with *style*. They were naturals. Dressed like fashion models. Gorgeous. All of them.''

''They would party with the nephew . . . what was his name?''

''Rafael. Oh, would they party! They'd crank up the old Wurlitzer that Rafael kept stocked with the *greatest* Brazilian music. We all loved it. They'd get that thing cranked up to Rio carnival level and break out the champagne. Rafael was addicted to the music. If he was there it was going from the moment he cleared the door. Sometimes the real romantic stuff, then sambas, and when things got hot he'd jam on those carnival *batucadas*. Wild. Those broads were insatiable. This creep nephew just toyed with them. He'd hooked them all on one kind of dope or another almost from the beginning, and that's more or less how he controlled them. Theresa thought it was too much. It scared her. When it got like that we backed off. Sometimes we even left.''

''Was he the one responsible for all the drugs in Parmer's place?''

''Oh, sure. Theresa wasn't a doper. Nephew left all that stuff around. And he's the one who got the idea for the bedrooms being different colors, furniture and all.''

''Did they ever take pictures of this action?''

''I don't know. I never saw any.''

''You know that pictures were taken at some of the sessions where the johns were involved.''

''Yeah.''

"Do you know where they were taken from?"

"Yeah."

"I crawled up there and looked around. You know anything about that?"

"Yeah. That was the weirdo's favorite cozy hole. He had this fetish about powder. He took photographs from up there and . . . he had this powder. It was that kind of thing, the sick stuff, that weirded Theresa out."

"Did he ever use the powder with the Brazilian girls?"

"I understand he did. I never saw it, though."

"Did Theresa ever see it?"

Duplissey shook her head sadly. "Yeah. The fool did it to her one time. Made her. Got mean about it."

"When was this?"

"Oh, I guess a couple of months ago. She wouldn't stay around him if she could help it after that."

"What would he do?"

"I don't know the details. She just said it was ritualistic. She wouldn't go into it, but I know it shook her up."

"You have any pictures of this man?"

"Me? No."

"Do you know anyone who does?"

"No."

"Who else was there the times you were, besides this nephew and the Brazilian girls?"

"Some men Theresa had lined up."

"Brazilians?"

"No."

"Remember their names?"

She did, after giving it some thought, and Haydon wrote them down.

"Would you recognize the girls if you saw them again?" he asked.

"Oh, I think so. . . . Wait. You're not going to show me some more of those morgue shots."

Haydon leaned toward her on his forearms. "Maureen, we've identified two more girls who've died like the others. I'd like to know if you've seen them at Theresa's. We've got to get a handle on this somehow. You might be our best chance. None of us like it."

She frowned. "God, you guys have grisly work." She held her hand out and Haydon gave her the two morgue shots.

She covered her mouth with one hand and frowned at the pictures, looking back and forth between them.

"God, they're even pretty dead," she said behind her hand. She shoved one picture across to Haydon and studied the one left in front of her. "This girl was there. I remember her. Beautiful girl, the classic type." She picked up the picture and handed it over. She sipped her coffee and made a face because it was cold. She reached for another cigarette and Haydon lighted it.

"This whole thing sounds like it's pretty rough to me," she said. "Can you give me a little idea of what's going on? I heard a good bit of talk after Theresa died. Everybody knew her and Sally and Sandy. But the scare died down. Nobody knows about these Brazilian girls, and there's been, what, four of them?"

"Three of them and a Montrose hooker." He wouldn't try to explain Walther.

"Shouldn't you be warning people? Girls?"

"Frankly, we don't know who to warn. We don't think every girl in the city is in danger. Seems Theresa's condo is a common denominator. We don't really understand much beyond that. That's where we were hoping you could help us. You know who the victims are. With the exception of the Montrose woman, they've all been at that condominium."

He saw it in her eyes the moment he spoke. He didn't know where in the hell his mind had been.

"Here," he said, taking a Mont Blanc pen from his coat pocket and scribbling Dr. Hammond's name and office address on a piece of paper. "I'll call him. He'll start a series of prophylactic inoculations. I don't believe you're in any danger, but don't go around anyone you ever met at that place. Men or women."

"Inoculations? How have they been dying, anyway?"

"A rare virus."

"My God. What does it do?"

He told her what the symptoms were without telling her what it was, and he told her to get in touch with Hammond if she felt as if she was getting sick. He didn't envy her the hypochondria she would go through until she was safely into the series of inoculations. The cigarette was jiggling between her fingers.

"Am I in more danger because I've talked with you?" she asked soberly.

He shook his head. "I wouldn't think so. I don't think it's that sort of thing." He had absolutely no grounds for saying that. "You should be careful, though. I'm in no position to anticipate this person."

She pulled hard on the cigarette.

"Well, how do you like that," she said to herself. She looked out through the bronzed glass to the underground lobby.

Haydon felt sorry for her. She was shaken to the point of not being able to hide it, nor caring whether it showed. He watched her face as her eyes absently wandered over the businessmen hurrying in and out of the tunnels into the Pennzoil underground lobby. He would have liked to ask her what she was thinking.

He took a card out of his wallet and laid it in front of her.

"If you want to call me, for whatever reason, please do. They can reach me anywhere at any time."

"I'll do that," she said. Her mind was still somewhere else.

Haydon got up and paused beside the table.

"Oh," she said. "I think I'll stay awhile."

"Fine. I appreciate your taking the time to talk with me." It sounded like "Thank you, ma'am. Come see us again."

"Sure, sure," she said. She was polite but preoccupied, and her eyes drifted back out to the lobby.

He walked away and paid the cashier for her Irish coffee on his way out. She didn't even see him through the glass when he walked in front of her on his way to the tunnels.

28

Rafael Guimaraes sat alone in the noisy cafeteria on the ground floor of Hermann Hospital. He was not eating or drinking anything and was drawing disgusted glances from students with hands and arms full of books and food trays, who were looking for a place to eat as they came out of the cafeteria lines and into the crowded dining room. He gazed idly out to the driveway that came off Fannin Street and went through the medical school as a covered drive and then out again into Sterling Circle, where the medical center shuttle bus made its rounds.

Rafael had just made his own rounds, with a team consisting of himself, another gifted senior student, a fellow in infectious diseases, a medical resident, and Dr. Morton. It was a special project of Dr. Morton's, intended to stretch the abilities of the overachievers who excel in a society of overachievers. Afterward Rafael was supposed to have gone to a lecture on gastroenterology, but he had skipped it and come to the cafeteria, where he had been for the last hour. With an air of total preoccupation, he picked his nose and looked across the manicured grass and crisp brick landscaping to the tall triangle of the Dunn Interfaith Chapel, which sat high on a football-field-sized berm. Two people walked out of the chapel's front door wearing white coats and headed toward the old elliptic rear entrance of Hermann.

It was, he supposed, inevitable that the police should get onto it. After all, he had killed several now. If he had stayed with the little Cariocas they wouldn't have got wise. But the others had to be killed too; he would simply have to be more careful. He wondered if the police knew what they were dealing with. If anyone connected with the investigation had any brains, they would find out.

Then what would they do? They would spend a lot of time trying to track down rabid bats and dogs. The little Cariocas would probably never be discovered, so they would think the call girls had had a dog in the house that had had rabies. (They would surely discover the women were all related to the house. Too bad about the condo. He missed the rooms and the Wurlitzer.) When no more call girls died, they would surmise that the dog had died of the disease but not before infecting the women, and that when they had died the chain of infection had burned itself out.

But suppose the very worst. Suppose they suspected him. There would be nothing substantial for them to work with. Circumstantial? Yes, of course. The same kind of circumstantial evidence they would have on fifty other men who had relationships with those women. Dr. Morton's laboratory was kept scrupulously clean of Rafael's rabies operations. The dog heads were incinerated the same night and none of the equipment was unique to his needs. The stockpile of the virus he had accumulated was well hidden in the research virus locker under the name of another lethal virus that only he and Dr. Morton had access to. Dr. Morton never used the virus under which name it was hidden.

He looked at his watch. He took off his white coat and draped it across his books on the table to signal it was taken, and walked out to the telephones in the hall. He called his ward clerk, who told him there were no new patients to work up. Great. He would have the afternoon off and tonight he was not on call. He would be off until seven forty-five the next morning. He walked back to his table, slipped on his coat, took his books, and left the cafeteria through the covered drive and headed for parking garage number 4, on the other side of Sterling Circle. Another perk. Most students had to park in the blistering sun in lots so far across the complex they had to ride the shuttle.

As he held the Mercedes 380 SL in a tight turn coming down from the sixth floor of the garage, he already knew what he wanted to do. He wanted to see *Eu Te Amo* for the sixth time. It was showing at a theater on Richmond Avenue, not far from Greenway Plaza. He wanted to see Sonia Braga again, watch her respond to the violence, watch her calculate, watch the animal in her that was so near the surface of the woman. Sometimes she looked straight into the camera and he saw her eyes sizzle around their edges and his own mind held the scene on screen longer than it was actually there and he watched her face go white and then her shoulders, and eventually her whole body would go white and he would be able to make love to her.

The Mercedes burst out into the sunlight and the brightness woke him. He slammed on the brakes just in time to avoid crashing through the wooden arm that hung across the drive at the ticket gate.

As it turned out, he watched the film twice. He liked to go to the cinema in the middle of the afternoon because the audiences were sparse. There were fewer distractions. He could become the characters on the screen, absolutely a part of the story, so deeply immersed that often he sat in the theater seat for as long as five minutes afterward to reorient himself. It was a phenomenon that became increasingly easy for him, so that now he could literally leave his body for

251

those on the screen within minutes after the film had begun. Often his cinematic reincarnation was born through a visual tunnel, his sight constricting to obliterate first the audience, then the perimeters of the screen, until it grew so narrow it exerted a gravitational pull that sucked him into the screen and out again into the other world. Time was altered. Favorite scenes were prolonged and took on a life of their own, others were accelerated, but none were left out. In his mind the film was edited to allow him to savor those scenes that inspired him.

Braga had been redolent. He smelled her from the first moment she appeared on the screen and the fetor of her presence smothered him with the sweetest anxiety she had ever inspired. Throughout the first showing his agitation grew to an unbearable level. He sat in his seat during the break between features, frustrated, sweating, savoring the lingering staleness of her presence, left hovering about him in the silent, empty theater.

As soon as Chico Buarque began singing the opening lyrics of the film's theme and the yellow credits rolled up from the bottom of the screen, the mephitic precursor of Braga's presence rushed at him through the constricting tunnel and sucked him with it into the images of her sizzling eyes as the sophisticated tremors of the piano notes emerged behind Buarque's urbane voice.

> *Ah, se já perdemos a noção da hora*
> *Se juntos já jogamos tudo fora*
> *Me conta agora como hei de partir*

He was with her in the penthouse at night, overlooking the shattered stars that lined the curving beach of Ipanema. The lights of Rio dazzled below them as they coaxed the end of one another's lives from the darkness. The moments gathered above them like a cloud as they stood nude in the

252

darkened window before the sheen that was Rio. The cloud of moments paled like a growing mist, its presence known by its rotten breath, which thrilled him beyond expression. In the gloam between them the cloud iridesced, each scintilla candent above them, each growing heavy with its own moribund mission.

Se, ao te conhecer, dei pra sonhar, fiz tantos desvarios
Rompi com o mundo, queimei meus navios
Me diz para onde è que ainda posso ir

The cloud sank, like the dust of lime it covered them as they sambaed like marionettes whose strings were attached to the other's corresponding arms and legs. They grew white from the moments burning into them, the gases rising from their smoldering heads as they danced in the glow of one another's phosphorescent dying. Outside, the stars from Ipanema detached themselves from the beach and rose en masse to the black sky outside the penthouse and hung there, casting their shimmering light through the glass. Then he stood still and she circled him, her fiery breasts swaying with her hair to the crying *cuica* as the chorus picked up the refrain of the samba and he saw the dead Cariocas descending, dancing together through the stars as though through fields of burning flowers.

Suddenly the dancing woman stopped. Her face was a death's head, her phosphorescence faded to yellow, then brown, and henna, and the cloud of moments became ash. The voices of the dead Cariocas quavered in the samba chorus and the stench of ordure flooded the penthouse and the Woman embraced him and he became ash as she held him close, the stench of her breath filling his lungs. Oh, the pleasure of it! The ecstasy of her song and the singing of the dead Cariocas who were also ash and who began to blow

253

away though they sang in absolute stillness amid the field of henna stars. He felt the ultimate sickness that was Death and knew it was the essence of the Woman who smothered him to her conflagrant breasts in the henna night.

He wanted it to be the end.

But it wasn't. Though his eyes were open the vision faded and he began to see the actual film again, the samba was gone and the closing strains of "Eu te Amo" ceased with the tinkling light notes of the piano. Wrung out and stunned, he watched the film to the end.

It was six o'clock when he walked out of the theater and returned to his car. The fire from the sun had permeated the streets and sidewalks, which would reflect it back into the atmosphere long after the sun had died. The city would be hot until midnight and the five o'clock rush hour traffic would last until seven-thirty.

Rafael drove toward downtown on Richmond and turned north on Kirby. The leather seats of the Mercedes quickly brought sweat to his back. He knew the perspiration was making a dark spot on his powder-blue linen sports jacket as he pulled back the sun roof now that the fire was low on the horizon. He turned in at a tavern near Avalon in River Oaks and went inside.

Alone at a table for two, he drank two Smirnoffs, straight up, and thought about what had happened. The music from the film kept running through his head. He was admittedly disconcerted by the vision. It had never happened quite like that before. It wasn't the content of the vision that disturbed him; it was natural and appealing, a sensual pleasure beyond description. No, the vision had been a gift to him from his subconscious and he accepted it with gratitude. He was disturbed because it had come unbidden, had burst upon him with a life of its own. It was true, in a sense he had invited it, but then in another sense he hadn't intended an experience of such intensity.

254

Another Smirnoff.

What specifically did he fear? That it might possibly be a sign of . . . what? Madness? He had often willfully fled from reality, but he had never *lost* touch with it. There was too much yet to do. He had to maintain his reason at all costs. There were so many more inoculations to be made.

Another Smirnoff.

He smiled as his thoughts turned to the girls. He had been amused at the reaction of the men who had bought the girls and were later baffled by the deaths of their relatively new acquisitions. The first one, Antonio Vianna, turned out to be one of the few exceptions among the lot. He had come home from Mexico City and found her violently ill. He called the good doctor Gonzaga, who of course was unable to save her. Vianna flew her body across the border and buried her in an elaborate shrine in a small village near Cuernavaca. He truly mourned her passing. He was a widower and had fallen in love with his new purchase.

Ross Wilson, the oilman who lived in Louisiana and kept a separate residence in Houston, was less romantic. When he found his Carioca dead, he resorted to the American Way. A friend who owned a funeral home smuggled her in at night and cremated her. What was left was hauled away by the garbagemen the next morning. Wilson had confronted Rafael's uncle about the poor merchandise. After he tallied everything up, he had lost a fifty-thousand-dollar investment. He put his name on the list for another one, however.

Luis Guerreiro had his mistress dumped in a drainage ditch in the heart of the barrio. He knew she would end up in the Jane Doe file and her identity would never see the light of day. Another man had friends bury his mistress in a salt grass field among the petroleum refineries of Pasadena. Another girl became ill and died while on a holiday cruise on her man's private yacht off the Florida Keys. Unable to take her back, the man had considerable difficulty explaining to his other guests why she had to be buried at sea. It had been a strained return voyage and might yet be brought to the attention of the police.

Rafael reached into his coat pocket and pulled out a calendar. On this date he had marked "Lunde in New Orleans." Charles Lunde was a shipping executive who owned a condominium on the fringes of River Oaks, six blocks from where Rafael was now. Lunde had been one of the first participants in Paulo Guimaraes' importing operation. His girl, however, still had very little facility with English, though Lunde was not in the least disturbed by this. It seemed to him she communicated quite well and with considerable talent despite her halting language.

Rafael called her. She was delighted to hear from him and he agreed to be there in twenty minutes. He paid for the Smirnoffs and left. It had been simple to party with the girls whenever he wanted. In the first place, he was practically the first person they met after arriving in Houston. Since he spoke Portuguese he quickly gained their confidence, and it was easy to renew their acquaintance once the girls had been placed and were established. His ability to contact the girls frequently and with ease was aided by one consistent fault shared by the men who purchased the girls (with the notable exception of Vianna): they ignored their mistresses eighty percent of the time. Though the girls lived in luxury, theirs was a life of isolation broken only by those occasions when their men were in a partying mood and were not afraid to be seen with them in the chic places of the city or at parties of privilege. Rafael's visits were a welcomed treat in more ways than one. He introduced them to drugs, which made the long days bearable, even when he wasn't around.

Stephany Bedaque had called down to the guard in the portico of the entrance and cleared Rafael's name and car license. He pulled into the courtyard just as the electronic timers illuminated the globes surrounding the quadrangle to a lustrous glow. Night had fallen on the city and only a mauve stretch of sky over the towers of Post Oak reminded him there had ever been a day at all.

Stephany answered the door at the seventeenth-floor private lobby. She was carrying a rare but corpulent Abyssinian cat. The creature looked strange, like a mutant, because Abyssinians were supposed to be thin animals. The girl's luxuriant carbon hair was washed clean and fell full around her face, which epitomized all the beauty that had ever come out of Brazil. She wore a long-sleeved blouse of amethyst shantung silk, and amethyst earrings dangled from the folds of her hair. She was naked from the waist down. She did that sometimes. The woman was bored.

He followed her into a large room that overlooked the western skyline of the city. The bejeweled skyscrapers of Greenway Plaza shone off to their left, and straight ahead the magnificent spectacle of the Post Oak section on Loop 610 provided a stunning display of coruscating architecture, marvelous towers built by a city gone wild with the vision of its own future.

They stepped down into the sunken living room amid furniture of chrome and glass. A thick white carpet climbed up the steps and spread across the floor of the rest of the rooms. Stephany sat in a transparent free-form Plexiglas chair that showed her bottom nicely, and tucked her legs up under her, Indian style. Rafael settled in a chrome-and-leather chair directly across from her. She made an interesting image. He noted she had anticipated him; the clear voice of Gal Costa came out of the surrounding walls.

Neither of them spoke. Neither was going to. He unzipped the leather bag he had with him and took out the syringe. He laid it on the glass table between them, along with a glassine packet of heroin. Her favorite. He set a vial with a rubber-sealed cap beside the other objects and began the ritual mixture of the heroin with matches and spoon from the bag.

When the heroin was ready, he inserted the syringe into the rubber cap of the little vial and withdrew most of the solution there. She didn't ask what he was doing, though she greedily watched every move. All the girls knew he was a medical student, and never questioned what he gave them. When the syringe was ready, he rose and walked to her. She remained in the transparent chair and extended a long honey leg, which she raised with the assured ability of a ballerina. He grasped it with one arm, supported it against his side, and inserted the needle in the large blue vein behind her knee. He emptied the syringe there.

When he let go, she continued to hold her leg aloft for a moment before she began lowering it with a peaceful and almost invisible slowness of motion. By the time it touched the floor she was feeling the heroin. Her arms fell to her sides and the obese Abyssinian jumped heavily from her lap. In slow motion, her eyes rolled toward the top of her head, one leg straight out on the white carpet, the other still bent up under her.

Gal Costa sang the beautiful "India" as Rafael walked to the bar and poured a Smirnoff. He glanced to the Plexiglas chair, where Stephany had begun to slide toward the carpet, removing her blouse as she snaked onto the floor. She didn't quite have it all the way off when she curled into a fetal ball and was still. Rafael went to the glass wall and sipped his cold vodka as he watched the mauve sky grow to a dark bruised purple behind the spangled face of the city.

29

The telephone calls Dystal had overseen had determined that about one-third of the drugstores in the city carried the rabies vaccine and that Petra Torres didn't belong to any of the city's Torreses. At least, no one claimed her. Hirsch, too, had conducted a telephone marathon, to determine the occupations of the men listed in the trick book Haydon had found in the red room. It was a touchy effort, at best, and about a quarter of the seventy-eight names in the book couldn't be located at all. Of the persons they were able to locate, nearly a third were duly protected by cautious wives and secretaries, who were suspicious of Hirsch's bogus inquiries, and the rest were businessmen, with one exception: a Bellaire veterinarian whom no one considered a serious suspect after he had been questioned.

Captain Mercer pulled at the loose skin at his neck and looked up from under the thick, unruly shock of gray hair.

"I think the implications are pretty strong. I'll wager my next pay raise you've found your man. But . . ." He shook his head and thought about it. Mercer had been around a long time and was a cautious man. They all knew what he meant. It was going to be incredibly difficult to get hard evidence against Rafael Guimaraes.

"What do you guys want to do now?" Dystal asked, looking at Haydon. They were in his office again, bringing Captain Mercer up to date, following procedure.

"First thing is to put a tail on Rafael. I'd like Leo and Ed to start today. I want to talk with Dr. Morton at the medical school. At some point soon we're going to have to bring somebody over there into this. It may be that he's not going to be the right person, but I won't know until I've met him. Then, depending on how that shapes up, I want to call on Paulo Guimaraes about his prostitution racket."

"You want to hang on to that? You don't want to turn it over to Vice or Immigration?" Mercer asked.

"We'd like to keep it awhile longer. We don't think it goes beyond these fifteen or so girls and we don't think it goes beyond Guimaraes. We've been in touch with Russ Million over at the DA's office and he's advising us on how to keep it tight. If it looks like it's going to spread out and take us away from the homicides, then we'll turn it over. We're just not sure about it yet."

"Then you think Longoria is going to be a solid witness? He's not going to bug out on you?"

"We don't think so. He's never been in trouble before. We're relatively sure he'll plea bargain and spill everything for a slap on the wrist. He sees the handwriting on the wall for DeLeon and Guimaraes and he's got no loyalty there beyond the *mordida* he receives in exchange for 'leasing' his import license. He's certainly not going to protect anyone and risk going up for murder one. With what he can give us, we have a solid case. And we have Mrs. Guajardo's testimony."

"Yeah, I see this big-shot Brazilian as a touchy spot publicity-wise," Dystal said. He had not put his fourteens on the desk drawer, in deference to the captain. "We been so damn lucky about these gals. If any more call girls had turned up, the press woulda been on us like a duck on a june bug. But it's just been these poor ol' gals and I suppose their sugar daddies have been dumpin' them out like garbage on the streets. No telling how many more there are that just haven't turned up. Vice is trying to put together a list of these gals based on what we've already given them. I'd sure like to sit that Guimaraes down and get the names of all those he's brought in. I'd like to know how many are left out there."

Captain Mercer sat forward in his chair and put both hands on his lower back, astraddle his kidneys. He bowed his back and stretched.

"Where does this Rafael live?" he asked, carefully keeping his eyes on the floor in front of him.

"The Carrington," Haydon said. "Twentieth floor facing the medical center."

"Uh-huh," Mercer said, working his back from side to side now, keeping his eyes focused on nothing against the wall. He stood up. "Well, you'd better keep me posted pretty closely." He looked first at Dystal and then at Haydon. "You've done fine. Let's be cautious, let's don't forget he's a nut, and let's don't give him any room. Good luck," he said, nodding to Hirsch and Mooney, and left the room.

Dystal lit one of his stinky generic cigarettes and groaned mightily as he raised his boots onto his desk drawer. Mooney set an empty milk carton on the floor, put his foot on it, and slowly eased his weight down to flatten it. Hirsch was thinking about how difficult it was going to be to tail Guimaraes, and Haydon was seeing Mercer in his mind's eye as he massaged his back and asked where Guimaraes lived, only to respond with an "Uh-huh" when he was told. Haydon hoped he understood Mercer's question and response.

261

He hoped he understood, because he already knew what he was going to do.

"What if Rafael and his uncle are in this together?" Hirsch said. "What if several people are involved?"

"I guess we'll find that out," Mooney said, picking up the squashed carton and tossing it in Dystal's metal trash can. "But they're not."

"How close do you want this tail?" Hirsch asked Haydon.

"While he's at the medical school, I just want to know that he's there for sure. His schedule there, when he's in lab, when he's in class, when he makes his rounds. He's in this special project with Dr. Morton, so his schedule is likely to be different from other seniors. I'll get his recorded schedule from Morton's office, but I want to know if he sticks to it. When he's not at the university, I want to know where he goes and who he sees. He may lead us to other Brazilian girls and they in turn could lead us to still others. Be *very* careful. If you have to lose him to avoid being spotted, then let him go and pick him up later. Just don't let him know you're there."

From a distance, the buildings of the Texas Medical Center looked like an architect's model of how the complex would appear upon completion, including the landscaping. The sharp summer light threw shadows from the angles of the white, straight-lined buildings in just the precise manner the architects must have predicted. The bronzed and smoke-gray windows appeared as square and rectangular dark bands or dotted lines dividing the alternating striations of niveous stone. It was, in a sense, comforting to know that concepts of so grand a scale could be completed according to plan. It was an impressive sight, even by Houston standards, and it was not difficult to grasp the fact that more than forty institutions of applied and research medicine were lo-

262

cated here in this solid square mile of Houston real estate, offering the world their collective skills, power, influence, and hope.

Haydon turned off Fannin at the entrance of the University of Texas Medical School and drove through the covered drive out into Sterling Circle and then to the seven-story parking lot number 4. He was lucky to find a space on the first floor. Students streamed in and out of the rear entrance of the medical school, stopping momentarily to exchange a few words in the landscaped courtyards like ants touching antennae briefly and then moving on. The younger students still carried the ubiquitous backpacks of bright-colored nylon and wore faded denim jeans as if to prove they could still do that in medical school. They seemed to Haydon to be incredibly young. The older ones did less loitering. They wore their white coats over casual cotton trousers, or skirts, and seemed to be more aware that there was something serious about what they were doing.

Haydon entered the rear doors of the building, walked past the long file of open-ended mailboxes, and emerged into the muted lighting of the lobby. He rounded the security station, which overlooked an expanse of ginger carpet and several levels of modern seating modules of polished kid leather, and entered the administration office. When he had called Morton earlier that morning, the doctor told Haydon to check at the office when he arrived and they would locate him wherever he was in the building or in Hermann Hospital. After several calls to both buildings, the secretary found him in a lecture hall on the fourth floor. He asked that Haydon meet him there, since he had just finished one lecture and was due to give another in half an hour in the same room.

When Haydon pushed open the shiny walnut door of the lecture hall, he found himself on the landing of the top tier of a bright semicircular amphitheater. Dr. Morton, hearing the door open, looked up from his conversation with a girl, nodded slightly, and continued talking as Haydon made his way down the aisle through the tiers of desk seats. By the time he got to the floor of the stage, Morton was making a concluding point to the student, who thanked him and walked past Haydon, frowning.

Haydon introduced himself and Morton extended his hand. A small man in his mid-fifties, he wore glasses on a strong, solid nose and looked through them with subdued heavy-lidded eyes. He was not a man who exuded a great deal of enthusiasm, but Haydon immediately got the impression of innate kindness. His white medical coat was heavily starched and its pocket contained only a vermeil Cross pencil and pen set.

"Tropical parasites," he said in a low, comfortable voice that Haydon was sure was rarely raised a decibel in excitement or anger. "Give students trouble from the beginning. They are grudging organisms and will continue to give that young lady trouble long after she is an experienced physician."

He stepped around from behind the laboratory table where he had been lecturing and the two of them walked to the first row of desk seats and sat down. Dr. Morton removed his glasses to rub his eyes, which seemed even more lugubrious when unprotected. He returned his glasses and looked at Haydon.

"You've got some questions? You weren't too enlightening on the telephone."

"I'd like to ask you a few questions about one of your students, Rafael Guimaraes."

"All right. Is he in trouble?"

"We hope not. I'll be glad to explain it to you before I leave."

"What do you want to know?"

"First, your general impression."

264

Morton launched right into it. "A brilliant student. High achiever with a true talent in his chosen field. Virology. You may know he's an honor student in a special program which I direct. He is not an extrovert, but he gets along well with the other students with whom he works. He is not aggressively egocentric—a certain amount of that goes along with the profession, I'm afraid—but is well aware of his considerable abilities. I do not know him socially, though I do bring my senior students together a couple of times a year in social situations so as not to remain totally aloof from them. He comes from a wealthy Brazilian family, has plenty of money to spend. I don't know of any particularly outstanding personality traits, positive or negative. I've seen no change in his work habits nor any decline in his research performance lately." He paused. "Am I anticipating your questions accurately?"

Haydon smiled and nodded. "What is the nature of the special program he's participating in?"

"I have a grant from a private foundation which allows me to conduct research involving the genetic induction of viruses and their influence on the production of interferon. Interferon is a class of small soluble proteins which are produced and released by cells that are invaded by viruses. This released interferon then travels to other cells, noninfected cells, and induces in them the formation of an antiviral protein that inhibits viral multiplication. Now, man has always produced interferon, of course, but we produce it in such minuscule amounts that it's never attracted that much attention. In fact, its influence was believed to be as minuscule as its volume. Recent discoveries about the nature of interferon, however, have led medical researchers to believe that if produced in larger amounts, perhaps even synthetically, this humble but potent protein could become a new 'wonder drug,' capable of promoting the cure for innumerable dis-

265

eases, including cancer. We are most interested in its effect on specific kinds of viruses.''

He stopped. ''That's probably more than you wanted to know.''

''What kinds of viruses?''

''Encephalomyelitis, specific strains.''

''Does that involve working with live animals?''

''Certainly.''

''What kinds of animals?''

''Rats. Occasionally mice and hamsters. During one aspect of the research we spent six months working with primates, but that was a kind of side trip in regard to the specific problem we're investigating.''

''Do you ever work with rabid animals?''

''Rabid? No.''

''Does anyone in the building work with rabid animals?''

''Not to my knowledge.'' Dr. Morton turned slightly in his chair and looked evenly at Haydon. ''Detective Haydon, I would appreciate it if you would explain to me what it is you want to know and why you want to know it.''

30

Haydon outlined the investigation in chronological order, explaining as much as he could without revealing specific details that he thought it wiser to withhold. Morton's impassive face showed little movement as he slowly realized the implications of what he was hearing. When Haydon finally brought Guimaraes into it, Dr. Morton's eyes tightened into wrinkles at the outside corners. It was his only concession to the pain and anxiety he must surely have been feeling. Haydon did not tell him that it was Rafael's uncle who was the man behind the smuggling of illegal aliens, but he made it quite clear that Rafael's involvement with those aliens and call girls was extensive and long-standing.

Morton was quiet for a long time, his eyes staring solemnly at the blackboard behind his lecture table. "You're quite sure Rafael is . . . doing this?" he said finally, continuing to stare at the blackboard.

"Not at all," Haydon said. "I have no direct, tangible, or testimonial evidence. Nor am I likely to have any. Everything is circumstantial."

"But you, personally, believe he's doing it."

It was a remarkably perceptive observation. Haydon was not aware that he had done or said anything to inject his personal feelings into what he had told Morton.

"Yes. I believe he's doing it." It wouldn't do to be evasive with a man like Morton. "I'll tell you directly, Doctor, that this is the kind of investigation that drives a detective crazy. It often leads to one of the most frustrating aspects of our work: that is, being absolutely certain that an individual is guilty of a homicide, or some other felony, and seeing that individual continue to live his life as though he had never committed a crime against society and caused anguish, and pain, and heartbreak—solely because we are unable to collect enough evidence that could be considered 'court admissible.' It happens more frequently than the public would ever imagine."

Dr. Morton was looking at Haydon again now, his eyes still pinched at the corners, giving a curious intensity to his lazy-lidded gaze.

"But haven't I heard something about 'overwhelming circumstantial evidence'?"

"Yes. Usually on television that's the sort of thing the prosecuting attorney pummels the 'suspect' with when he takes the stand, which usually brings about a distraught confession. That's about as realistic as *Trapper John*. In the first place, it's difficult to get circumstantial evidence admitted in great enough volume in a trial to convince a jury of someone's guilt beyond a reasonable doubt. In the second place, no defense attorney worth his salt would let his client take the stand to testify in a case built only on circumstantial evidence, for the very good reason that he would be risking an otherwise watertight case on the often shaky personality of his client.

"And from the prosecutor's perspective, it would not be wise to risk a trial under these conditions because once the suspect is acquitted, which is probable if *only* circumstantial evidence is available, he can never again be tried for the same crime should substantial evidence present itself at some future time."

"A dilemma," Morton said.

"An odd one, yes. If the district attorney's office were allowed to present to a jury every tiny piece of circumstantial evidence we were able to accumulate against individuals in such cases, I do not doubt that we could convince those twelve people of that suspect's guilt. Often such evidence is, indeed, overwhelming. They would be as sure as we are of the defendant's guilt. They would be angry. They would be furious. They would be disgusted and frustrated. And they would render a verdict of 'not guilty.' Circumstantial evidence, in whatever volume, does not constitute proof beyond a reasonable doubt, and that is the point the defense attorney will drum into their heads. Damn few juries will convict in the face of the 'reasonable doubt' exhortation from the defense in these kinds of cases."

Above and behind them, the door to the amphitheater swished open and two students came in talking and started down the aisle. Dr. Morton turned and addressed the taller of the two boys, who was drinking a diet Dr. Pepper. He had the thick bull neck of a football player.

"Mr. Jackson."

The boy stopped talking to his gangly companion and looked down at them. "Yes, sir."

"Do me a favor, will you?"

The boy waited.

"Take a piece of notebook paper and write on it that the eleven o'clock lecture has been postponed and put it outside the door. Tell them I'll notify them of a reschedule."

"Yes, sir." Both boys grinned and hurried out.

"Thank you," Morton said to their backs, but they didn't hear it. He turned to Haydon again. "How do you believe I can help you?"

269

"Because of Guimaraes' standing here and because of his professional future, I felt an obligation to notify you of his involvements and to inform you that he was the subject of an intense homicide investigation. Beyond that, I was hoping you, because of your association with Guimaraes, would be able to enlighten me, as you partially have, as to his habits and proclivities from this side of his life. I had hoped your observations would throw additional weight on our side of the scale. The more we know about him, the better our chances of getting something substantial."

Dr. Morton listened attentively and nodded. "You know," he mused, "though it's not common, it certainly isn't rare to run across this kind of Jekyll and Hyde personality among your colleagues. You would think you would build up a philosophy about this sort of thing to allow you to deal with it without its having a debilitating effect on you. I suppose doctors and clergymen . . . and detectives see the Hyde in people much more than others do. And yet I never fail to be struck hard by these sorts of discoveries. Deep down in the subconscious, one harbors a yearning that people will turn out actually to be what they appear to be. I suppose that is a kind of primitive yearning, like the yearning for an earthly paradise. It has no place in reality, but persists in living anyway in the hope of dreams."

Morton came very close to smiling. "That's an admission of weakness. An unforgivable thing in our profession."

He stood slowly and thrust his hands deep down in the starched pockets of his white coat. With his head bent down and his eyes looking at the floor, Dr. Morton moved unhurriedly around to the back of the laboratory table and returned with his lecture stool. He placed it a little to one side in front of Haydon and sat down.

"Rafael Guimaraes is probably even stranger than you have imagined," Morton said. It was not what Haydon had expected to hear. "The medical community in general, and especially *this* medical community, is as demanding of the apparent integrity of their people as the CIA. This is increasingly the case with those individuals who rise to the top of our profession and, whether we like it or not, come to represent the profession's persona to the general public. You notice that I said 'apparent integrity.' This kind of pressure often has the unfortunate effect of creating two kinds of individuals—the constipated moralist and the genuine hypocrite. It can even promote the Jekyll and Hyde syndrome I just mentioned.

"In medical schools, professors are ever vigilant in their search for gifted students to be mentors to and thereby receive some sprinkling from the clouds of glory these young men and women may trail behind them on their rise to fame. Rafael was recognized as a student of singular abilities from the very beginning, and there was no little competition among the professors looking to sponsor him. I wasn't vying; I had some good people already working with me. However, virology was his passion, and he asked if he could work with me in microbiology. I had directed the program of clinical infectious diseases before I received my grant and devoted myself to this particular research. I had a full staff, but he was exceptional and I made room for him.

"Another factor that made Rafael attractive to professors here was his wealth. His uncle was widely known to have given millions to the medical school and also privately supported several research grants. He is not the source of my grant moneys, incidentally. Anyway, all this is to say that the mantle of respectability had already fallen on Rafael when he came to me, and he was an enviable acquisition."

"Only he wasn't."

"That's right. I wasn't totally honest with you when I said earlier that I didn't know of any particularly outstanding personality traits. I detected something peculiar about him from the beginning, but I couldn't put my finger on it. He did his research assignments quickly and thoroughly. He *was* brilliant. He's demonstrated this over and over. But he wasn't a comfortable person to be around. In conversation he was generally lifeless and seemed continually bored and made no pretense to hide that boredom for the sake of common good manners. He was cold and aloof. He never laughed—I've never seen him laugh—and he never smiles. He smirks. His facial expressions often gave the impression he smelled a putrid odor.

"More than a few times at night I've come into the offices we share here among ourselves, those of us working on the grant, and turned on the light, to find that he'd been sitting in the dark, alone for no telling how long. He doesn't seem to have been brooding; he simply seems to like the dark. When discovered in such a situation, he speaks to you as though he'd not been doing anything unusual and then he either leaves or sets about doing some work that is always waiting on his desk. He apparently never sees the need to explain anything he does.

"These might seem like small things, and they are when taken separately and incidentally. But when they are a constant given in a single personality, they are signals of an unusual psychology."

Morton looked at Haydon appraisingly, as if he were weighing what he was about to say on the same scale with the detective's anticipated reaction. Haydon imagined this conversation was costing the doctor a considerable price, which Haydon could not fully appreciate.

"Recently we smelled a foul odor in the laboratory, which persisted for several days," Morton continued. "It smelled like a dead animal. Rats we've inoculated are kept in locked cages, but healthy rats are kept in another part of the lab, in simple portcullis cages. The cleaning people have accidentally, or as a practical joke, let them out before and we can't find them until they die somewhere and we detect the odor and search them out. That's what we assumed this time. We turned the lab upside down. No rat. Finally we asked the custodian to please clean the place out over the weekend and get rid of the smell.

"That Friday night, late, I decided to do about half an hour's work at the lab so I wouldn't have to go in on Saturday morning, when my grandson was having a birthday party. I drove to the school and went upstairs. I slipped the key in the lock, opened the door, and flipped on the light. Standing across the room at an angle and at the end of one of the lab tables was Rafael. He was looking up at me in only slight surprise, holding something in both cupped hands, which were held close to his face. I didn't say anything, nor did he, as I came around the end of the table and approached him. I suddenly smelled the fetid odor of putrescent flesh and recognized the dead rat in his hands. The animal was in a fairly advanced state of decomposition. It had already swollen and burst, the flesh was slipping away from its organs, which were exposed and jellied, and its hair was sloughing away from the tissue in damp wads. His hands were sticky with it. When I looked away from the rat to Guimaraes, I was stupefied by what I saw. His eyes were glassy and flecks of spittle dotted his lower lip. Particles of rat hair clung to his skin in various places from his forehead to his chin, as did reddish-gray smears and daubs of the rotting animal. He'd been rubbing his face in it.

"He managed to say 'Dead rat,' and then I turned and walked out of the laboratory."

Morton stopped and simply sat quietly. Haydon suddenly felt a sense of acute discourtesy to be watching the doctor's face. He looked down at the tip of his highly polished shoes and said, "How do you interpret what you saw?"

"I am not a psychoanalyst, Mr. Haydon, but I can't help drawing my own conclusions. I believe Guimaraes is a necrophile. He is more interested in death and things dead than in life, and I do not believe his is a passive sickness. I sense a strong malignant tendency in his character. This is all a very general reading on my part. His personality is obviously vastly complicated."

"Doctor, do you remember what, if anything, may have been on top of the lab table as Guimaraes stood there?"

Morton's expression did not change. "Yes, I do. There was a plastic bag, for the rat, maybe. There was a scalpel and, oddly, there was a can of talcum powder. Johnson's baby powder, I believe it was."

"How did Guimaraes react to you the next day?"

"Both of us acted as though nothing had happened."

"Was that the end of it?"

"For him, I suppose so. For me it was the beginning. I resolved that this young man would never be a physician. Not one who ministered to people, at least. He's shown no inclination that he cares for humanity or for nurturing life. You see, Mr. Haydon, the mainstay of medicine is, after all, biology. The prefix *bio* is from Greek, meaning 'life.' That's what we are all about. Rafael is not a biophile, a lover of life. He is a necrophile. Death is his passion. His interests in medicine are purely intellectual and largely aberrant."

Morton stopped, his mind wandering over ideas only hinted at by the tension at the corners of his eyes, which had floated away from Haydon and fixed themselves somewhere in the space beyond him. Haydon could see the man had already given a good deal of thought to the special case of Rafael Guimaraes.

"What did you do?" Haydon asked.

"I composed a long report in which I explained in detail essentially what I've outlined to you. I strongly recommended that Guimaraes' file be reviewed by an examining board and that he undergo an extensive psychological examination. I personally recommended that he be denied a medical degree and gave my reasons in detail. I've already submitted my records to the proper administrators.''

"When was this?''

"About three weeks ago.''

"Have they discussed it with you?''

"I have a meeting with them tomorrow.''

"You'll have to tell them about my visit?''

"Without a doubt.''

"You'll make it clear he's only a suspect? He's been found guilty of nothing.''

"Of course.''

"What will happen?''

"I anticipate an investigation of our own that will be laborious and tedious. At the end of it I suspect Guimaraes will be called in and advised to withdraw from medical school or the school will begin expulsion procedures. All this will be prolonged by those who are sensitive to his uncle's considerable financial influence. We will see a total end to that, I'm sure. And there will be those who will be afraid to move on this at all for fear of a scandal. There's nothing quite like the fear of scandal in the medical community.''

Haydon could no longer justify concealing the elder Guimaraes' involvement.

"I haven't been totally forthcoming with you either, Dr. Morton,'' he said cautiously. "I think you should know, and the school should know, that Paulo Guimaraes is also under investigation. We *do* have court-admissible evidence against him for organizing the smuggling of Brazilian girls to the U.S. for use as prostitutes. He is the one behind the business Rafael is involved in.''

Morton's face was absolutely without emotion. "My God,'' he said.

"I'll have to ask you not to take any action against Rafael within the next few weeks which might cause him to change his regular habits. Any major disruption of his life at this point could make it impossible for us to gather any kind of substantial information against him. Can you guarantee me that you'll hold off? For a few weeks, at least?''

''I can try. I'll have to deal with the committee. It'll be their decision.''

''Would it help if I spoke to them? Explained the situation?''

''No, I'll handle it. If I can't give you what you want, I'll let you know. Then you can try.''

''Fair enough,'' Haydon said.

31

The last week of July passed slowly from the calendar and August came in sultry, with record temperatures scalding the potholed streets until they became soft and blistered, shimmering with heat waves from midmorning until well after dark. The Gulf breezes that brought the ashy clouds in across the bays disappeared, seemingly sucked out across the gray whitecaps into oblivion. The flags at the Astrodome hung limp and fading in the laser light that burned the city, vapor locked cars on the expressways, and drove tempers in the barrios and wards to the exploding point, assuring that once again August would see the most homicides of any month of the year.

Hirsch and Mooney had spent the last ten days alternating with another team tailing Rafael. They pulled double shifts, both evening and night, after they established that Guimaraes' days were a totally predictable routine at the medical school and Hermann Hospital. But in the evenings, when he prowled aimlessly, Hirsch and Mooney stayed with him. Twice he visited call girls in expensive hotels. Both girls were picked up afterward and "debriefed" in detail.

Each girl was given a bogus story and started on a series of prophylactic rabies inoculations.

The great fear was that Rafael would eventually meet with another Carioca. Haydon judged them to be in the greatest danger. Clearance for a wiretap was sought and obtained. The tap yielded nothing for days. Rafael made most of his calls from pay telephones at the medical center. Then on August 5 he made a call from his residence and arranged to spend the next night, Friday, with one of the Cariocas. The call was traced and the girl's residence identified. She lived in yet another condominium, on Buffalo Speedway. The place was owned by Raymond Evans, an oilfield-tool manufacturing executive. His office verified that he was out of town for a week.

At nine-thirty on the night of the sixth, Hirsch and Haydon were sitting in the Steak & Eggs diner on the corner of Oakley and Montrose, waiting for a call from Mooney that would verify that Rafael was safely settled in the Buffalo Speedway address with the Brazilian girl. They were only fourteen blocks from the Carrington. When the call came, Hirsch paid for their sandwiches while Haydon made a quick call. Since Haydon was driving, he satisfied a personal whim, taking them a dozen blocks out of the way into the elegant circular intersection of Fannin, San Jacinto, Main, Montrose, and Hermann, on the north side of Hermann Park. The fountains were spangled in their own mist, which hung heavily in the sultry night, and the lamps along the drives that laced the park were like bright white pearls on strings that wound into the dark lanes within the woods. They turned past the opulent old Warwick Hotel and headed north again toward downtown.

Within a few blocks they turned into the terraced ramp that took them up one story off the street to the Carrington's open-air courtyard and lavishly landscaped gardens surrounding the condominium. They parked in a far corner of the compound and crossed the parking lot in the coppery glow of tall sodium-vapor lamps to the lobby entrance. Hirsch lingered near the door while Haydon went to the lobby telephone and placed a call. After a brief conversation, he replaced the receiver and motioned to Hirsch. They followed a broad hallway that turned twice before they approached an unmarked metal door without handles. There was a buzz and a click, Haydon pushed open the door, and they entered an un-air-conditioned corridor that took them to a service garage, where a security guard was waiting for them.

"Frank," Haydon said, smiling, and shaking hands with a uniformed man in his late fifties who wore his shiny-billed hat cocked over one eyebrow. "This is Leo Hirsch," Haydon said. "Frank Winters."

The older man shook hands quickly but did not speak.

"This looks like retirement to me," Haydon said.

"It sure as hell beats driving one of those smelly blue-and-whites," Winters said with a sideways grin. "This's a big deal, I guess."

"It is," Haydon said. "I'll owe you one, Frank, and I won't forget it."

Winters was flattered to be taken into Haydon's confidence and tried to act soberly responsible.

"I go off at midnight," he said. "You gotta be out of there by eleven-thirty."

"No problem."

"You got your tools?"

Haydon nodded.

"Okay, like I told you. I've cut the electronic security in that place. After I get you up to the twentieth floor, I'm coming back down here to my cubbyhole so nobody wanders in and sees what I've done. Your man here stays in the lobby on the twentieth to catch anything unexpected that might wander in there. If you need to call me from upstairs,

279

dial one-eleven. If I need to get in touch with you, I'll let the phone ring once, hang up, ring once again, hang up, and then call again." He looked at Hirsch. "There's a house phone in each lobby if you need it. Ya'll going to keep in touch with walkies?"

"Right," Haydon said, patting his coat pocket.

"Okay, let's go," Winters said.

They walked to a service elevator and Winters opened it with his key and they started up.

"Naw," Winters said, watching the floor lights flash above the door. "I've never regretted leaving the department. I wasn't going nowhere, and Betty's not scared all the time that I'm going to get blown away. I had to think about her, you know. And to tell you the truth, being a cop in this city ain't what it used to be. I didn't sign up to be a garbage collector, especially when the same garbage keeps getting dumped right back onto the streets. And the pay? Shit, the department never paid like this. Here we are."

The door slid open to a handsome lobby.

"There's actually two towers here, you know, sitting kind of cockeyed to each other. They're connected at intervals by three or four floors of hallways. That's one of them right there. Go down to the end of this and it'll put you in the other tower. His place is off the next lobby on the right. Call me when you're ready to come down."

They stepped out of the elevator and the doors closed behind them as they strode to the end of the corridor and entered the second lobby. Haydon took out his soft leather pouch of brass tools and went to work on the door while Hirsch paced the lobby. Much to Haydon's surprise and frustration, it took him nearly fifteen minutes to pick the lock. When he finally succeeded, he unlocked the door from the inside so Hirsch could come in quickly if he had to, and then closed it.

It took a minute for his eyes to adjust to the low light. He walked through a wide entranceway to the living room with the inevitable view of Houston's skyline. In this respect all the condominiums in the city were the same: a main room designed to accommodate the city's dazzling views. Haydon found the drawstring on the drapes and pulled them closed. He had to do this to three separate panels along the glass wall. In the pitch dark he made his way back to the entrance and felt on the wall for the light switch. He found it and flipped it on.

It was as if he had turned on a light in the center of the earth. Everything was black: the walls, the marble entrance, the carpet, the ceiling, the drapes. And the rooms were practically empty. A formal dining room to the left of the entranceway was totally empty. Beyond that the kitchen glistened with shiny ebony tile, and where metal had to be used it was made of highly polished chrome that reflected the blackness around it like reflections in a bottomless pool. There was one stool at the bar in the kitchen, no table or chairs. The entrance to the living room, where he had just drawn the drapes, was cambered in such a way as to blend into the ceiling of the larger room.

He turned toward other rooms which he could see along a hallway with a concave ceiling. Where the walls met the floor, the angle was curved rather than square, so that the corridors became elliptical tunnels. None of the rooms opened directly off this main artery. Instead, their doors were approached through five or six feet of similar, but smaller, black veins. Through the first oval doorway to the right there was another empty room, which might have served as a library or a study in a normal home. It, too, had a window that looked over the park, but there were no drapes, only bare glass.

Haydon passed to two other rooms, also black, each with one mirrored wall. Nothing else. Finally he came to Rafael's bedroom. Again, one wall was mirrored, but the opposite side of the room was a surprise. It was completely covered by an enormous etching in black and white. Haydon moved back against the mirrors for a better view and immediately recognized a reproduction of Goya's *El Sueño de la Razón Produce Monstruos*. A brooding artwork of Goya's later life and one of a series of etchings called "Los Caprichos," it portrayed a distraught individual slumped over a desk in fitful sleep as ugly winged creatures descended out of the darkness to haunt his tortured dreams. There was one difference in this reproduction, which Haydon found intriguing. The inscription, which was the title of the etching and appeared on the end of the desk upon which the subject was slumped, was written in mirror image so that in order to read it one had to face the opposite wall of mirrors. As one did this, the monsters of Goya's psyche descended from the shadows to haunt the viewer as well. Haydon himself became a part of the Capricho and the demons of unreasoned sleep fell upon him from the darkness at his back.

He turned again to face the room. Going directly to the closet, he flicked on a small penlight and began searching the pockets of Rafael's suits, sports coats, and trousers. He found only a stray coin and a partially used matchbook from a drugstore across from the Medical Center. There was a low chest beneath the hanging clothes with underwear, socks, laundered shirts, handkerchiefs, and other accessories. Haydon went through each of the drawers, probing the clothes and feeling into the corners. He crouched on the closet floor and felt into the toes of each of the eight pairs of shoes.

The bathroom, covered entirely in black tile, with black towels and washcloths, contained the usual toilet articles. The medicine cabinet held no drugs as Haydon had thought it might. In fact, there were so few personal items it reminded him of a hotel room. Returning to the bedroom,

Haydon walked to the water bed encased in a black-lacquered frame. He stared a moment at the unmade shiny coils of black silk sheets, and then bent down and circled the water bed, feeling next to its frame with his hands. Nothing. Then he saw the powder in the corner.

It looked, at first, like a blurred splash of pale light on the black carpet. But Haydon knew instinctively what it was. He moved toward it, its configuration becoming more distinct as he approached. It was scattered in a radius of about five feet from the corner where the large artwork converged with a black wall. On the outer edges of the radius, the powder was thinly distributed, sprinkled like hoarfrost, but quickly grew thicker toward the corner until it was heaped an inch thick where the floor met the two walls. Within this area, a thin film of white dust clung to the pimpled texture of the two walls up to a distance a little above Haydon's head. The powder itself had been violently disturbed, as if something had thrashed and scrabbled about in it and worked it deep into the carpet and then layered it again with more powder. Not all of it was fresh. Some of it was old and soiled. It looked as if it long had been the bedding ground for an animal.

But there had been no animal. On the floor, close up to the baseboard under the artwork, a narrow path issued from the powder wallow and followed under the looming nightmare to the doorway of the bathroom. The trail was thick with powder at first, but quickly grew thinner until it disappeared altogether halfway along the wall. Rafael's footprints were clearly visible in several places near the end of the path.

Haydon backed away from the corner until he stood near the middle of the room. He looked at the painting on the wall and then he turned again and looked in the mirror: The Sleep of Reason Produces Monsters. He walked out of the room.

The only sources of light in the living room were three lamps, one of which sat on the floor. Haydon turned on each of the lamps, but the claustrophobic black sapped every ray of illumination so that he still had difficulty gaining his perspective and distinguishing dimensions. A feeling of vastness was enhanced by the scarcity of furnishings: a black coffee table, large and squat, with a smoked-glass top and a flask of marbles sitting in the center of it; a long black table cluttered with books, obviously schoolwork; a black cabinet, its glass shelves loaded with a disarray of incidentals such as papers, used and unused syringes with and without needles, a dangling stethoscope, a partially empty pack of cigarettes, some pocket change, a comb, a coffee mug. Two black lucite chairs sat on one side of the coffee table opposite a small sofa covered in black leather. That was all. Haydon had anticipated an elaborate stereo system and hundreds of records, but they weren't there. There were no vases, plants, or keepsakes, the small things people surround themselves with to make a house an extension of their persona.

Except for the Goya paintings.

The two largest walls in the room were again covered with the moody Spanish artist's works. On the wall to the left as Haydon faced the windows he recognized *The Dog*, in many ways one of Goya's strangest works, portraying the small head of a dog looking upward from the bottom left of the picture. The rest of the gray-and-black painting was empty except for a vague shadowy area in the upper right corner which gave Haydon the feeling that the dog was looking out over the rim of the earth into an empty cosmos. The painting was an object of constant speculation by Goya experts. The artist himself left no clue.

The other wall was filled with the grisly etching called *Nada*. It depicted a decaying corpse sinking back into the grave it had risen from, after having written the Spanish word for "nothing" in the dust with its bony finger. It was a work of profound hopelessness.

Haydon backed away toward the entrance hall and surveyed the funereal scene of Rafael's home. He had seen the living quarters of many murderers, and while each was generally reflective of the economic status of its occupant, they were in every case unexceptional. This was the first he had ever seen that could be described accurately as a "lair." These dark rooms gave off a noxious feeling, one could even say an actual vibrating aura of the mind that occupied them. It was incredible to Haydon that Rafael Guimaraes slept, worked, and dreamed here. It was not an environment imposed upon him by the circumstances of dingy poverty, such as Raskolnikov had had to endure and which added to his gloomy perspectives. It was not an environment that could be forgiven for misguided bad taste. No, everything in this hell had been painstakingly designed. It was an exercise in malevolence, born of a sick mind and designed to feed that mind its own mutations so that they lived one within the other in a state of psychic cannibalism. These rooms had a moribund essence of their own which Haydon sensed and could not shake off any more than the sleeping woman of legend could shake off the incubus that lay upon her in her dreams. Haydon's own dark season stirred in response to these walls and his heart raced, his ears rang, his vision narrowed.

He turned and walked quickly, fled, to the front door and jerked it open. Hirsch whirled around.

"What's the matter?"

Haydon looked at the bright lobby and Hirsch's young face as though their brilliance and youth were talismanic. He wondered what was showing on his own face. He was sweating profusely and was afraid his eyes were reflecting the horror he felt in Rafael's moonless den.

"Nothing." He partially closed the door. "Give me another fifteen minutes and we'll get out of here."

He closed the door and tried to put everything from his mind but what he had to do. Returning to the kitchen, he opened the refrigerator. It was practically bare. There was a carton of orange juice, some cheese in a bowl, half a bar of butter still in the foil wrapping, five or six pieces of rye bread in crumpled cellophane, and two bottles of Heineken beer. The freezer was empty. Haydon had thought Rafael's collection of viruses might be kept there. The pantry was equally bare. Rafael did little eating in this gloomy place.

Haydon walked into the living room and went through the papers and books on the study table. There was nothing personal there; it all appeared to pertain to his medical studies. The cabinet with glass shelves revealed nothing of more importance than he had seen on his first cursory glance. He looked around the room. The place was so pitifully devoid of superfluities that there were few places to search. He walked over to the coffee table and knelt on one knee as he ran his hands along its wooden frame. One hand supported his weight on the table as the other skimmed along its bottom edge. He turned his head sideways and his eyes fell on the flask half filled with marbles. As he moved, he jiggled the table and one of the marbles separated from the others and floated upward a little and then sank. Haydon stopped. He stared hard at the flask. Slowly he straightened and reached out both hands and drew the flask toward him. The eyeballs stirred in the jar and stared back at him from a hundred different angles, their bulbous whites the only brightness in all the room as they oscillated in the viscous liquid that preserved them.

Haydon was unable to suppress a shudder as he gaped at the pile of eyes. How many were there? Not human, surely. None of the girls had been mutilated. God, what a macabre centerpiece!

He stood and went into the kitchen. Opening the cabinets, he rummaged through the various boxes and cans until he found a small spice jar of black pepper, which he emptied into the sink and washed down with water. He rinsed out the pepper residue in the bottle. He went to the cabinet in the living room and took down one of the needled syringes and walked over to the coffee table. Removing the stopper from the flask, he carefully lowered the syringe into the liquid and withdrew a syringeful. This he emptied into the pepper bottle. Next he extended the plunger on the syringe and, holding it by the very end of the plunger, lowered the needle into the flask and eased it into one of the eyeballs, which he hauled up like an olive from a jar. He slid it off the needle into the pepper bottle.

He quickly recapped the flask, returned the syringe to the shelf and, making sure the top was tight, slipped the pepper jar into his pocket. Passing back through the apartment one last time, he turned off all the lights until he got to the living room again. He dialed the telephone and told Frank Winters to come up and get them. He turned off the lights, opened the drapes, and stepped out into the lobby.

"How long was I in there?" he asked. He felt as though he had been resurrected.

Hirsch looked surprised. "You through?"

"Yes." Haydon wiped his face with his handkerchief. His hands were shaking as if he had been pumped full of caffeine.

"What's the matter?"

"What do you mean?"

"That was the quickest search on record." Hirsch looked at his watch. "Twenty-three minutes."

"You mean since I looked out the door?"

"No. The whole time."

Haydon felt the pepper bottle in his pocket. "When we get out of here let's go straight to the morgue. Van may not

287

be there, but any of his people can answer my question. Let's get Mooney on the radio and meet him back at the Steak & Eggs on Montrose.''

The three of them occupied the booth next to the front window. Haydon sat quietly beside Hirsch, looking past Mooney's pudgy shoulders at the car lights going by in the street. He could see two of the sidewalk umbrellas, with ''Cinzano'' and ''Gancia'' printed on their fringes, that belonged to Zimm's sidewalk café next door. He felt drained after recounting his search of Rafael's rooms in as much detail as he could recall. The recitation had been punctuated by one-word obscenities from Mooney.

''So,'' Mooney said suddenly. ''The eyeballs are probably from dogs. I mean, that's what Van's people guessed, and he's going to give it the rabies test because that's where a lot of the virus piles up, right?''

Haydon nodded.

''Okay. Let's say he's got a jarful of rabid dog eyeballs. So what?''

''It's more supportive evidence,'' Hirsch said.

''Which is circumstantial, and we can't use it anyway because you broke into the place,'' Mooney retorted.

''Too bad you can't arrest people for being weird,'' Hirsch said.

''Listen, if that was the case, the population of this city would be cut in half.'' Mooney opened his eyes wide and rolled them around the diner. He hated this particular diner, which was a favorite of Haydon's because it was extraordinarily clean. Mooney hated it because it was predominantly patronized by homosexuals. He wore a perpetual scowl and narrowed his eyes menacingly whenever he caught someone looking at him.

''Well, we can't let it go on like this,'' Haydon said. ''We can't keep close enough to him and he's going to kill

288

again without a doubt. It's impossible to clean up after every encounter by giving the girls crazy stories and a series of prophylactic inoculations. He's going to reach women we know nothing about. And he's *not* going to slip up and give us anything substantial to use against him.''

"What about the girl he was with tonight? We're going to have to do something about her, aren't we?" Hirsch said.

Haydon nodded. "We'll have to. And that puts us in an entirely new situation. That puts us right in the middle of the whole thing.''

"Hell, I'm ready for that," Mooney said. "That sicko's got to be put away somehow.''

Haydon sipped his coffee and watched a young couple at the second umbrella table on the sidewalk. They were dressed in formal evening clothes. The young man had removed his jacket and draped it over a chair and his white shirt almost glowed in contrast to the dark hues of the street at night. Haydon suddenly felt overwhelmingly depressed. He wanted to be absolutely alone, to have time to think. He wanted to think for a week, and then go away somewhere with Nina. He had seen less and less of her during the past month, but he could tell when he was with her that she hadn't stopped worrying about him. He was sorry. It was a waste of time.

Again, suddenly, he was aware of Mooney and Hirsch looking at him, waiting.

"I think I've worked something out," he said. "A way we can go after him and make it stick. It's a little complicated, maybe, but the alternative is impossible. We can't wait him out.''

32

The Shelbourne Tower was one of Houston's most audacious showplace condominiums, designed by an architect of worldwide reputation whose risk-taking convex matched the gaudy dimension of his commission. Rising fifty-six stories from the center of a palm-studded block in the prestigious Galleria–Post Oak area, the Shelbourne Tower was a marvel of vertical architecture. In the daytime it appeared as a shaft of subtly tiered pale-blue ice that glistened as though perpetually melting in the white intensity of the Southern sun. As it was seen now, at night, it resembled a monumental obelisk of Lalique frosted crystal illuminated from within by a pale glow that grew fainter as it rose to the tower's summit.

Hirsch sat in the front passenger's seat as Haydon guided his royal-blue Jaguar Vanden Plas through the San Felipe entrance into the park. The headlights of the car picked up a uniformed guard, who stopped them and came around to the driver's side.

"Yes, sir?"

Haydon showed his shield and gave his name. The guard

checked a piece of paper on a clipboard, found Haydon's name, tipped the bill of his cap, and backed away from the car. They circled the plaza, which formed a huge wheel of banked flowers between the covered driveways of the two towers, and stopped under the canopy of the tower adjacent to South Post Oak Lane. Valets opened their doors and asked if they wanted the car parked. Haydon said no, tipped them, and the two detectives walked into the lobby of marble and glass.

They stopped at the circular desk, behind which a fashion-model concierge smiled at them.

"Would you please call Señor Paulo Guimaraes, forty-seventh floor, and tell him Mr. Haydon and Mr. Hirsch are waiting?" Haydon then took Hirsch aside and reviewed their procedure.

"When they get here, you get in behind the wheel so I can look at both of them in the back seat. Russ Million said to go ahead and try to get a verbal plea bargain commitment. I'll simply introduce you as Mr. Hirsch. You know the terms we want. I'll spell them out and from time to time look to you for confirmation. If DeLeon asks you for any assurances, give them to him, but be careful of the technicalities. We'll just let them assume what they want about you. As long as you don't impersonate a DA's attorney with the authority to negotiate plea bargains, we're all right. If they happen to agree to certain terms under the misconception they *are* dealing with a DA's attorney, then they've made a mistake. And we're not bound to any agreements discussed. I'll never refer to you as a DA's man and you should never reply to any of DeLeon's questions if he should frame them in such a way as to cause you to reply as though you were a DA's man. Okay?"

"Fine, but I don't think they're going to go for it," Hirsch said. "They're going to be pissed because you refused to meet them upstairs."

"He should be happy I'm not making him come downtown. I got points for understanding his desire for 'discretion.' A compromise is a good way to start off."

The elevators opened and the sound of hard leather heels on the marble floor echoed in the lobby. Haydon and Hirsch turned as a barrel-chested man with wavy gray hair approached them briskly. He wore a pearl-gray suit with tiny pale stripes. His cuff links were platinum ovals with diamonds that sparkled against his white cuffs. He wore platinum-framed glasses tinted a light smoke at the top and going clear at the bottom.

"I'm Paulo Guimaraes," he said quickly, without extending his hand. "This is Robert DeLeon."

DeLeon was taller than the stocky Guimaraes and had none of the other man's Latin appearance. He was in his forties and seemed more tense than his companion.

"I'm Detective Haydon. This is Mr. Hirsch. Our car's outside."

Haydon led the way out to where the alert valets were opening the Jaguar's doors. Haydon indicated that Guimaraes and DeLeon were to get in the back seat. He and Hirsch got in the front as planned. The doors were closed and Hirsch started the engine.

"I hope this is more suitable than our departmental cars. When you're with Mr. Hirsch you always travel in style. He's a man of good taste."

Neither Guimaraes nor DeLeon replied, but Haydon could tell they were clearly relieved to be seen driving away in a Jaguar rather than one of HPD's unmarked Fairlanes. They settled in for the drive.

Hirsch pulled out from under the lighted awning and started around the huge plaza circle. Halfway around the other side, he turned out of the drive and pulled under a canopy of oak trees at the edge of the main parking area and just out of the spill of light of the plaza lamps. He turned off the motor and lights.

"Hey." Guimaraes' face reflected belligerent suspicion. "What's this? I thought we were going someplace neutral. What is this shit?"

DeLeon didn't say anything. He was trying to figure it out.

"This is as far as I go in accommodating you, Mr. Guimaraes," Haydon said, his voice devoid of courtesy. "If you want to save face any more than this, you're going to have to bark for it."

"You're crazy," Guimaraes said. He grabbed the door handle and popped it open. "To hell with you." He started to get out, but DeLeon reached over and placed a hand on his arm.

"Why don't we listen to what he has to say?" He spoke calmly.

Guimaraes replied quickly in Portuguese and looked fiercely at Haydon. DeLeon remained composed as he responded, also in Portuguese, and nodded at Hirsch. Guimaraes said something else, which must have been a curse, and closed the door.

"Tell us what you think you have to say to us," DeLeon said.

Haydon turned half around in his seat so he could see both men. Guimaraes glared squarely back at him.

"I told you over the telephone, Mr. DeLeon, that we had some serious allegations against Mr. Guimaraes that we would like to clear up. Since our conversation this morning, those allegations have taken a more serious form."

"Get to the point." The words came from deep within Guimaraes' barrel chest. It was his tried and proven scare-the-hell-out-of-subordinates tone of voice.

"Mr. Guimaraes," Haydon said, addressing him. "In the course of investigating the murder of several call girls

293

during the past six weeks, we have brought to light your scheme to bring young girls in from Brazil to be sold as prostitutes to wealthy persons here in the States. Our documentation of this operation is sound. Since these girls are being killed by someone who seems to be systematically picking off every one of the girls you've smuggled in, we have suspicions that you may somehow be involved.''

Guimaraes' eyes narrowed and he fastened them on Haydon. His jaws rippled with tension as he clenched his teeth, and Haydon could almost believe his nostrils flared.

"It is our intention," Haydon continued, looking at DeLeon, "to indict Mr. Guimaraes in the morning on three counts. One: aggravated promotion of prostitution, which is a state offense and carries a two-to-twenty-year sentence. Two: conspiracy to violate the immigration laws, which is a federal offense and carries a two-to-twenty-year sentence that is *not* to be served concurrent with the sentence for the aggravated promotion of prostitution. And three: murder in the first degree, which carries two to life.''

Guimaraes made a sound in his throat, which Haydon did not know how to interpret. He thought the man might be having a stroke. He didn't care.

"Let me clarify the last indictment," he said, speaking to DeLeon. "Even if Mr. Guimaraes has nothing to do with the murders, he is certainly by any definition an accessory to that crime by virtue of being guilty of the previous two allegations. You know that some time back, Texas did away with the lesser charge of accessory to a felony. It is all viewed by the courts now as an equal offense.''

Haydon paused and looked at each man in turn.

"And?" DeLeon said.

The lawyer was quick, Haydon thought. "And since you are an integral part of this operation, we intend to indict you

294

also on all counts." Haydon turned to Hirsch. "Did I get all the points right, Mr. Hirsch?"

"You did."

"I don't believe a fuckin' thing he says," Guimaraes said to DeLeon. Then to Haydon, "End of discussion." He looked cockily at DeLeon, who was still staring at Haydon, but he didn't move.

"What have you got?" DeLeon said.

"Arturo Longoria. He plea bargained. Everything he knew for a probated sentence. Raymond Evans. His girl is still alive, so he's not going to get caught in the murder situation. He plea bargained. We've got a call girl named Maureen Duplissey, who turned out to be quite helpful. She just didn't like your setup."

"Jesus Christ!" Guimaraes' belligerence was knocked out of him as if he had been hit in the stomach with a sledgehammer. He slumped slightly and looked unblinkingly at Haydon, his mouth sagging open.

"What do you want?" DeLeon asked. "You didn't call us for a gentlemanly preview of our indictments."

"I know you've been aware that the girls have been dying. We've got a suspect in mind and we are relatively sure he's going after the Brazilian girls who are left. We know fifteen girls have been brought in up to this point. We want to know the girls' names and the names of the men who bought them. We want to know how many have died—we know of three in addition to Sally Steen, Sandy Kielman, Theresa Parmer, and a Pauline Thomas. If we have this information, we can prevent more deaths. If we don't get the information, it will be difficult to do, and I can assure you that if one more life is lost for lack of the information, I will dutifully add it to your account. In simple language, we want you to spill your guts."

DeLeon glanced stoically at Guimaraes, who now appeared comatose as he sat hunched into the corner of the back seat. In the space of eight minutes the blustery Brazilian had been stunned and reduced to silence. His barrel chest was slack on his stomach and he stared out the side window. Haydon studied the dramatic change in his appearance. His face was full of lines invisible only minutes before, his suit, which fit with the care and elegance of hand-tailored clothing, now lay like cotton sheeting over his dumpy body. Even the sparkle in his diamond cuff links seemed dulled to the glint of chipped glass.

"You realize how powerful these men are, don't you?" DeLeon said.

"Yes, like Mr. Guimaraes here," Haydon replied, nodding at the badly shaken man beside the lawyer. DeLeon followed Haydon's eyes. His face was impassive; he and the Brazilian had switched roles. His initial tenseness had become tempered steel. He understood the odds and was determined to make the best of them.

"Mr. Guimaraes and I will talk it over tonight and be ready to meet with you in the morning," he said.

Haydon shook his head. "No. We're filing at eight in the morning and how we file depends on what we settle right here, right now. You're free to fight it out, of course. If you make a deal with us it'll make the rest of our investigation easier, but I can assure you it will not make the results any less sure. As I said, we'd like to save some lives."

"These men are very important. When they're confronted, they're going to come out swinging," DeLeon said with cool authority. "It's their way. We don't want to be dragged through it. We want total immunity from the three charges you outlined."

Guimaraes roused himself. He'd been listening after all. He spoke to DeLeon in Portuguese and then the two of them exchanged a few remarks before Guimaraes went back to staring out the window.

"We'd like some assurances of protection from any suits

296

that might be brought against us issuing from those men who
. . . whose names we will give you.''

Haydon looked at Hirsch. Hirsch answered DeLeon.
"We can't do that. We're prepared only to make arrangements regarding those indictments we've already mentioned. The other would be beyond our involvement."

DeLeon spoke to Guimaraes in Portuguese again and the
older man merely snorted and continued looking out the
window.

"But you are prepared to give us total immunity on those
issues?''

Haydon looked at Hirsch, who did not respond to DeLeon
immediately, but finally nodded. "Yes, we'll agree to
that.''

"We would like one further agreement," DeLeon said.
"We do not want our names mentioned by the police department in regard to these issues. We do not want to be made
media spectacles by your crowing police department. If we
assist you in this, we want to be referred to only indirectly as
'police sources.' If we are discovered by someone else at a
later date . . ." He made a shrugging gesture. "But *you* do
not give our identities to the press.''

"Okay," Haydon said. "But I want to make this clear to
you. If any part of the information you give us is incorrect,
any small part of it, every assurance we've given is null and
void." He looked DeLeon directly in the eyes and added,
"So be circumspect, Mr. DeLeon.''

"Agreed," DeLeon said. "How shall we give them to
you?''

"Mr. Hirsch has a tablet and a pen. Simply tell him the
girls' names, ages, the names of the men who paid you for
their services, who the men are, and whether or not the girls
are, to your knowledge, dead and the dates of their deaths. It
would help if you could give them to us in the order in which
they arrived from Brazil.''

DeLeon withdrew a small notebook from his vest pocket and leaned slightly to the window to catch the lamplight as he flipped through a few pages to find what he wanted. Then, as dryly as if he were listing car parts from an inventory check, he called out the information Haydon had specified. Because many of the names were Brazilian, he kindly provided the spelling. When he was asked about incidental details, which Hirsch was clever in asking so that much more was learned than was seemingly intended, DeLeon freely complied with the information requested.

During this banal listing of data, Guimaraes continued to gaze out the window. He seemed only to be passing the time, waiting for DeLeon to carry out some dutiful task to which Guimaraes had accompanied him for lack of something better to do. Haydon wondered at the man's sudden detachment. Had this wealthy and obviously clever man some small touch of his nephew's madness that enabled him to be so blasé in the face of an investigation which, despite the assurances he might believe himself to be in possession of, would surely bring him considerable misery, if not ruin? Was he thinking about the destruction he had wrought upon others and, finally, himself? Did he have any sense of remorse, or was he simply disgusted with himself for being caught? Did he struggle with the question at all?

Haydon found it odd that neither Guimaraes nor DeLeon had questions about the murderer, though it was the answer to what must have been a mystery to them during the past several months as they watched the Brazilian girls die one by one. Perhaps the deaths were only a passing piece of peculiar information for them. Perhaps they didn't really know about as many deaths as Haydon thought, or perhaps they were so absorbed in saving their own skins that the deaths of poor slum girls held no substance for them at all.

DeLeon droned on. Hirsch stopped him periodically to clarify a point. Haydon was sorry he had let them ride in his car. He would always remember them there, men who had risen to the top. It was well to remind oneself that cream is not the only thing that rises. Dross does too, and it must always be skimmed off and thrown back into the fire.

"I believe that's it," DeLeon said at last. "Count them."

Hirsch turned back the pages and counted out fifteen names. "Let me double-check this. Three of these are out of state and are still living. Eight are dead. Four are living here in Houston."

"That's correct."

Hirsch handed the list to Haydon, who looked over it briefly. He noted that two of the girls were eighteen, the others were between twenty and twenty-three.

"This will do for starters," he said, turning around. "We'll be in touch with you and follow up on our discussions."

Hirsch started the car, pulled out into the lamplight, and returned across the plaza to the covered entrance. The valets came to the two rear doors and opened them. Guimaraes crawled out into the driveway and walked around the back of the car and entered the lobby. DeLeon got out and then stuck his head back in and looked at Hirsch and Haydon.

"You'll get back to me and firm this up?" he said.

"You can bet on it," Haydon said. He didn't even look around.

DeLeon paused uncomfortably at the opened door. "I'll be waiting to hear from you," he said.

"We'll call," Hirsch said.

DeLeon looked at him. It seemed there was something more he wanted to say, but he wasn't sure he should say it. He seemed, perhaps, suspicious.

"Let's go," Haydon said to Hirsch, and DeLeon backed out of the doorway as the car began to roll.

Neither Haydon nor Hirsch looked back as they circled the wheel of flowers in the plaza beneath the luminescent tower that rose imperiously into the night and added its splendor to the fires in the sky.

33

When Haydon walked into Jojo's the next morning, Dystal, Mercer, and Russ Million were already having coffee at Dystal's table. Million flashed a smile clear across the restaurant as Haydon started toward them. As a young assistant district attorney, he had won Haydon's total trust in the brief two years he had been on the staff downtown. He was soft-spoken, about Haydon's height, had longish chestnut hair with fawn streaks. His clothes had a slightly western flair and he kept them, and his handlebar mustache, militarily neat. He had the ramrod-straight posture of an old-time Texas Ranger and a disarmingly gentle smile that unintentionally obscured the fact that he was savvy, hard, and loved to prosecute. Haydon's mother would have considered him, in every respect, a gentleman.

Haydon took the only chair available and the waitress was already there with his coffee.

"How did it go?" Mercer asked.

"Fine. Hirsch could get an Oscar for it."

"You mean they talked? DeLeon didn't give you the third degree?" Million grinned.

Haydon opened the manila folder he had in his hand and gave each of them three sheets stapled together.

"You sure ya'll didn't leave yourselves open for entrapment?"

"It'll stick," Haydon said. He sipped his coffee in silence while the others read over the list.

Million spoke first. "Scandal time, boys."

"Yeah, I know of a couple of these names," Dystal said.

"We can make murder one stick with some of these for sure," Million said. "Juries don't like to hear about little dead girls just thrown away like garbage. I'm glad 'accessory after the fact' is not on the books anymore. That would be to good for some of these guys."

"How do you want to go from here?" Mercer asked Haydon.

"For the three girls out of state, we just turn the files over to the appropriate DAs. That gets them out of our way. Which leaves us with eight dead. We have bodies on three of those: the two Leo turned up in the morgue and Petra Torres. If we're going to prosecute for these deaths and go for murder one like Russ wants, we're going to have to establish a relationship between these girls and the men who bought their services. We can do that with Guimaraes' and DeLeon's help. If we want to clear up the cases quickly, we can plea bargain with the men who supported them, and close the cases. We still can plaster these men's names all over the media for weeks and get lesser convictions.

"That leaves five dead girls and no bodies. Well, maybe we can come up with Antonio Vianna's girl, but I'm not inclined to stick him with murder one. The way DeLeon told it, Vianna fell in love with the girl and was distraught when she died. He treated her well while she was alive and gave her a respectable burial in Cuernavaca. That leaves four missing girls. Same choice. We plea bargain and clear the cases or we go for murder one and see if we can find the underlings who actually disposed of the bodies and can lead us to them. If bodies exist. If bodies don't exist, those people are going to be even more valuable. All of this is going to take time.''

"Can't the testimonies of this Guimaraes and DeLeon cinch those for us?" Dystal said.

"Not unless they actually witnessed the disposal of the bodies," Million said, shaking his head. "All this is hearsay on their part.''

"What about this Ross Wilson?" Mercer said, referring to his notes. "He came to Guimaraes complaining because his girl died. That's not hearsay.''

Million nodded mechanically. "Yeah, it sure is. It's sure as hell hearsay in the court.''

"But we can get them on conspiracy to violate the immigration laws and aggravated promotion of prostitution, can't we?" Mercer insisted.

"Sure, with Guimaraes' and DeLeon's testimonies. But to get that you're going to have to bargain with them. Stuart and Leo have just gone to a lot of trouble to avoid making a plea bargain commitment so he could charge them with murder one. You can't get them all with murder one. You're going to have to pick and choose. Decide which ones you want the most and go after them.''

"Oh, goddamn," Dystal said.

Haydon's neck was aching. These were just preliminary sparrings. The discussions in such cases could go on endlessly for weeks at a time, and in multiple murder cases, even for months. The legal maneuverings were sure to be intricate and extensive, and there was plenty of time to make the most of them. He faced the windows and the expressway. The traffic crawled its inexorable course along the ridges of steel and concrete beyond the scummy glaze on the windows. He wondered when, exactly, the management had last washed the windows.

303

"I'm not that concerned about the dead girls right now," he said. He could not believe he was actually reaching into his pocket for a cigarette. Coffee and cigarettes and no sleep. He was killing himself. He remembered what Maureen Duplissey had said about coffee and cigarettes and wrinkles. "What I want to do is stop Rafael, and we're going to have to do it with the four girls who are still alive."

"How?" Mercer again.

Haydon was ready for that. He had thought about it and discussed it with Hirsch and Mooney.

"Call in the four guys and lay it out flat. They're in it for conspiracy to violate the immigration laws and aggravated promotion of prostitution. If they cooperate with us, we'll talk about reducing those charges. If they stall and another girl dies, whoever she belongs to gets slapped with murder one.

"If they cooperate, we want to tap their telephones so we can see where Rafael will move next. When we find out where that will be, we want to have the guy take his girl out for the day while we wire every room in the place, put in video cameras where we can. We let him come to the girl, do what he does, and move in while he's at it."

"Whoa! Now let's talk about this a little bit," Million said, laying aside the list. "First of all, we don't have to waste any plea bargaining with these four guys. Just tap their wires. We can just do it. That means we can give the full count to the three who don't have to help us further. With the fourth guy, whoever it turns out to be, we'll have to bargain."

Million's mind was working like a trap. The other three men were listening as he looked at each of them in turn, knowing each would have to agree on what was to be done.

"The setup in the room is going to be touchy. You're really going to jeopardize your case if you sit out in the street in a TV van or in the next condo and watch and listen to this weirdo give the girl a lethal dose of rabies virus. How's that going to look to the jury? 'What? You let this man endanger this girl's life just so you could charge him with attempted homicide?' Defense is going to get red in the face and indignant. 'Entrapment,' he'll scream. Okay, that's arguable, and I doubt if he can sustain that kind of objection, because you did not induce him to come to this girl. You didn't invent her like you'd invent a bogus warehouse for a stolen-goods sting or dress a lady cop in fishnet stockings and put her on a street corner. He would put us on the defensive to prove him wrong about his objection, but I think we could do it. But . . . to *not* step in and prevent this creep from giving the girl a lethal dose of something, when it's in your power to prevent it, is going to be tough to explain.''

Haydon shook his head. ''Russ, we don't know how he's going to give it to her. We don't know how he does it. How are we going to stop him from doing something when we don't know what he's going to do?''

''I don't know,'' Million said. He stroked his handlebar, shaped it with his fingers. ''I don't know. These things are so risky when you set up something like this. It wouldn't be much of a problem if you could catch him in aggravated attempted murder. If you could catch him committing a felony along with the attempt. Maybe raping her. Stealing something. I don't know, but it's stronger that way.''

''Oh, goddamn,'' Dystal said again. ''This isn't a game of checkers.''

''Sorry,'' Million said. ''I'm just telling you what you can look forward to in court on this kind of thing.''

''A legal screwing,'' Dystal said.

''What's the alternative?'' Mercer asked.

''The alternative is to let Rafael just keep on going the way he's been going and watch him kill some more girls until we have a mountain of circumstantial evidence to eventually submit to a jury that will acquit him,'' Haydon said softly. He was angry, not at Million but at the system, the same system he had defended and expressed frustration with to Dr. Morton. This was precisely what he had been trying to get across to the physician. It drove you crazy.

"You know," he continued, in a low voice that all the others recognized for what it was, "when you are looking at this from the ethical perspective, I wonder which is the more morally questionable: watch him shoot one girl with a lethal dose of rabies, which we know we can counteract with a prophylactic inoculation, or wait until he kills two or three more girls while we try to gather the exact, specific legal evidence to conform with the letter of the law and convince a judge and jury beyond a reasonable doubt that this madman is killing people. As far as I'm concerned, it's a rhetorical question for which I've already got an answer."

There was a dead silence around the table.

"I'm with Stu," Dystal growled. "Shit, let's do it."

Mercer looked steadily at Million. The traffic on the loop moved behind his profile like the endless flowing blood of the city. Stop the traffic and the city gets sick; stop it long enough and the city dies.

"Okay, we'll go ahead. Set it up," Mercer said. "Russ, you do the best you can to anticipate our problems. You go with them when it's ready and watch the whole thing. You tell them when to go after Guimaraes and you stay on top of it all the way through, to prevent as many loopholes as possible." He looked around the table. "You all have to admit that it's not a solid thing anyway. He could spend the night with whichever girl he chooses and not do anything but brush his teeth."

"Fine," Haydon said. "I'll get the paperwork ready for the indictments and we'll plea bargain with whichever john draws Rafael's black-bean telephone call."

"What about Guimaraes and DeLeon?" Russ asked.

"Throw everything at them," Haydon said quickly. "I'd

rather nail them and let one of the others go through plea bargaining as long as he can help us put them away. I want them if we have to let *all* of the others off the hook."

Everyone agreed.

"But," Haydon added, "I want to hold off on everything until we move on this wiretap thing and get our shot at Rafael. If we make a lot of noise with those indictments now, he could get antsy and change everything. Let's just keep quiet and go after him."

Within eight hours of the breakfast meeting, taps were installed on the telephones of the four remaining Brazilian mistresses. The most difficult part of the setup was finding eight men who could operate in shifts and were capable of understanding Portuguese. They found four officers who worked the Chicano squads and could understand varying degrees of Portuguese, but they had to hire the others from the language departments of Rice University and the University of Houston.

Homicide officers were pulled from less pressing cases and placed on a twenty-four-hour tail of Rafael, freeing Hirsch and Mooney to begin the paperwork on the indictments. There still remained the problem of sorting out which of the two Jane Does Hirsch had found in the morgue belonged to which businessmen. Because the bodies existed, they had to be properly identified; this meant the beginning of extensive correspondence with the Rio de Janeiro police, who began working the slums with photographs. A hopeless task that no one believed in. At the same time, Arturo Longoria had provided them with the names of the three merchant ships used for the smuggling and the names of the officers and merchant marines who had been in on the scam. Warrants were put out for their arrest at their next scheduled ports of call. The customs officer at the Houston

Ship Channel who had been in on the deal was picked up and booked.

At four o'clock in the afternoon, Mooney, Hirsch, and Haydon were bunched up in their tiny office off the squad room, their gray metal desks covered with paperwork, their CRTs glowing green as each brought the reports up to date. The telephone rang and Haydon picked it up. It was Dystal. Haydon rolled his chair back to the opened door of the office and looked across the squad room through the plate-glass window in Dystal's office. He could see the lieutenant hunched over the telephone like a bear, his back to the squad room.

"Stu, we just got a call from the security people at the Shelbourne Towers. They want a 'discreet' plainclothes team to come out and investigate an apparent suicide. Looks like it's Guimaraes."

Haydon looked at the squad room clock and then rolled his chair back out of the doorway.

"Thank God they did the right thing. We can keep this quiet. Leo and I will take it."

Haydon called Vanstraten to meet him at the Shelbourne Towers and left with Hirsch.

Paulo Guimaraes was indeed dead in his bedroom overlooking Houston's sprawling skyline. But he had not committed suicide. Vanstraten said it was a stroke. The uncapped bottle of sleeping pills beside the bed, which the maid had seen and which had therefore caused her to offer her expert opinion of suicide, was virtually full, lacking two tablets. Paulo Guimaraes had wanted to sleep, not die. But fate proved once again to be mercurial and not without a sense of drollery. She let him sleep.

Haydon was in complete sympathy with the Shelbourne management in wanting to keep Guimaraes' death quiet. He asked the management to bring everyone into Guimaraes' living room who knew about his death and there informed them that the late Mr. Guimaraes had been the subject of a police investigation for some time and it was the wish of the Houston Police Department that his death be kept a total secret. There were implications of dire actions against anyone who even whispered of this to any person outside the room. Everyone understood.

A morgue van came without its flashing lights and went down a concrete ramp in the back of the tower to the basement. A police officer was left in Guimaraes' rooms in anticipation of anyone who might enter unannounced and it was agreed that the Guimaraes' telephones would not be answered until the police said they could be. The Shelbourne management would leave the notification of relatives to the police, and they were to display open-faced innocence and ignorance to anyone who might inquire of them regarding Mr. Guimaraes' whereabouts.

Finally it was all settled and everyone left except Haydon and Hirsch and the policeman charged with staying in the suite. Haydon wandered around the living room and stopped at the windows. The condominium faced east over downtown, so the coming of night was not accompanied by a brilliant Texas sunset. Rather, it came almost imperceptibly, as perhaps death might have come to Paulo Guimaraes in his sleep. But from the forty-seventh floor it was clear that here darkness was not eternal. In fact, almost as quickly as it began to cover the city it was pierced through, permeated, and conquered by the ever-increasing fulgence of billions of individual lights, the very symbols of life, that stretched all the way to the lapping water's edge at Galveston Bay.

34

During the next forty-eight hours Rafael's schedule did not deviate: ward rounds at the hospital, lectures at the medical school, laboratory duties with Morton's research grant. Home to his black lair in the evenings. Hirsch and Mooney shoved aside their paperwork and insisted on alternating shifts tailing him. Everyone felt the building tension and wanted to be close to the crucial events leading to Rafael's arrest.

With Dr. Morton's cooperation, a team from the police department's Bureau of Technical Services was allowed into the laboratory. They gathered fingerprints from equipment used only by Rafael, hair samples from a comb in the pocket of one of his lab coats hanging in his locker, saliva traces from chewed pencils in his desk, and whisker samples from an electric razor also found in his desk. There was no way of knowing if any of this would be useful to them, but Haydon insisted on having as much physical evidence about Guimaraes as possible. They searched, too, for traces of the rabies virus among the inventory of viruses Rafael used in his section of Dr. Morton's research.

By the afternoon of the second day they had identified the virus in samples taken from six vials in a freezer storage compartment shared by Rafael and Dr. Morton. They were taken from test tubes labeled as a strain of arbovirus causing Venezuelan equine encephalomyelitis. The test tubes were photographed and marked with a tracing dust and their contents replaced with a harmless saline solution having the same appearance and consistency as the original. The virus was saved as evidence. Being able to replace Raphael's cache of viruses with an innocuous substitute without his knowledge was a stroke of luck Haydon had not anticipated. If Rafael used the contents of one of these tubes with the next girl, there would be no charge from the defense counsel that the prosecution had acted recklessly in allowing his client to infect the girl with a lethal virus.

That same afternoon, Robert DeLeon called Haydon. He had been trying unsuccessfully for nearly two days to get in touch with Paulo Guimaraes. He was furious, thinking the police had arrested the old man. Haydon assured him they had not and calmed the lawyer after a lengthy conversation. When he finally got off the telephone, Haydon radioed the two detectives he had assigned to tail DeLeon, and told them to bring him in. Later that afternoon DeLeon was informed of Guimaraes' death and quietly indicted on all counts previously outlined. Within hours DeLeon had hired Dane Massey, the most powerful criminal lawyer in Houston. Both readily agreed with Haydon's request to keep the indictment under wraps.

While Haydon and Russ Million were going through the procedures with DeLeon and Massey, Leo Hirsch was sitting at a small table in the Hermann Hospital cafeteria, watching Rafael make a telephone call from a bank of pay phones just outside the cafeteria doors. At the same time, Rice University language professor Sergio Thomases was sitting in a Southwestern Bell utilities van outside the

Sutherland luxury condominiums overlooking Buffalo Bayou and Memorial Park. The van was steamy hot. Thomases, and the detective and electronics technician with him, were dripping with sweat despite having partially opened the van's back door for circulation. It did no good. Outside, the night air was dead still.

Thomases and the technician had cocked their headphones back on their heads and were drinking cold diet Cokes from an ice chest when the telephone line clicked and rang. The technician flipped the toggle switch on the recorder and big chrome wheels began to spin behind them as Thomases leaned forward, elbows on knees, and listened.

Rafael's voice was low and inflectionless, making the normally lyrical Portuguese sound lifeless. He spoke to the girl without identifying himself.

"I want to come over tonight."

There was a moment's pause as the girl recognized his voice. Thomases held his breath. He knew the police needed four or five hours lead time to prepare the room.

"Ah, Rafael." A throaty laugh. "No, no. He is in town. Tonight he is going out with his wife. He may come over after they have finished dinner. Late. But tomorrow, huh? He is leaving town tomorrow."

"I know that," Rafael said. "No, not tomorrow." He didn't offer any explanations.

"Tomorrow night?" she asked hopefully.

Rafael did not reply. In the background Thomases heard people talking. Their voices loud, then fading. He had been informed that Rafael might call from the hospital cafeteria and that he might find it difficult to hear. It was, however, no problem.

"I have good snow," he said finally.

She laughed and growled softly, playfully. "Tomorrow night, then?"

Rafael did not respond.

312

Thomases, unused to wiretapping, wondered if Rafael could tell something was going on. He looked at the technician in the dim glow of tiny winking lights. The young man shook his head and grinned.

"Tomorrow night?" the girl asked again.

The tape reels turned steadily, collecting only silence, an occasional distant voice, a snatch of laughter.

"Hey, Rafael," the girl said.

"Okay," he said. "But not there. At a hotel."

"I don't care where we are," the girl said casually.

"There are suites in the Hyatt Regency that have stereos," Rafael said. "I'll get one in your name for tomorrow night. I'll be there at nine."

"I'll bring the records," she said.

"Good." Rafael broke the connection.

The technician quickly replayed the tape for Thomases, who recorded it word for word in English on a small recorder provided by the police. The actual conversation was recorded on another cassette. The detective dropped both cassettes into his pocket and slipped out the van's back door. In minutes he was speeding down San Felipe, nearly five miles from the police station.

Haydon listened to the brief tape four times. It was the first opportunity he had had to hear Rafael's voice. As he listened he looked at the photographs of him Leo had taken during one of his afternoon surveillances. They had been made at too great a distance for Murray to do anything about the grainy results. There was a fuzzy profile with the blurry grids of the medical school parking lot in the background. Another profile of Rafael standing at the mailboxes in the corridor near the school's rear entrance. A front-on facial was the best; Rafael appeared to stare straight into the camera. Leo had crouched in the shadows of the third floor of the parking garage and photographed him with a telephoto lens. He was in the sun. In a series of shots taken seconds

313

apart, Haydon was able to see the rhythm of the young man's stride, the way he carried himself. He did not shamble along but moved well, though the fact that he had narrow sloping shoulders was not altogether hidden by the padding and extreme cut of the European sports coat. There were definite furrows between his eyebrows as he frowned in the sunlight. His lower lip was full, there was a dimple in his chin. Haydon did not know why, but he was surprised to be looking at a handsome man.

Haydon stationed Pete Lapier in the Hyatt Regency with the reservations clerks. At seven o'clock the next morning, Lapier called Homicide Division and left word that a stereo-furnished suite had been reserved in the name of Dolores do Bandolin. Within an hour all the technicians scheduled to install the proper equipment had been contacted and were on their way to the hotel. At eight-thirty Haydon was sitting in the coffee shop, looking out onto the sunken lobby. He recognized the first team of technicians as they entered the lobby from the covered driveway. As previously arranged, all of the equipment had been packed in regular travel luggage. Two men and a woman entered together, but one of the men went to the telephones instead of registering. The man and the woman were handed the keys to their suite on the twenty-sixth floor by Lapier, who was working behind the desk wearing a Hyatt blazer. They took their suitcases and walked to the elevators, where they had to wait for a few moments with an elderly couple who were already there. When an available elevator arrived, the two waiting couples stepped inside and were joined at the last moment by the second man, who had just completed a telephone call. He pretended not to know the others.

Haydon sat at his table and watched the glass capsule, surrounded by bright lights like a theater marquee, shoot up twenty-six floors, with his first team of technicians staring

314

out the glass bubble at the passing tiers of floors like goggle-eyed conventioneers.

The second team arrived twenty minutes later in a similar fashion. The only thing that distinguished them from the other registrants was that Lapier saw to the paperwork and handed them their key. Fifteen minutes after the second team ascended in the sparkling tube, Haydon paid his check at the cash register of the coffee shop and followed them up.

Two of the suites were on a short angle of the twenty-sixth floor and could not be seen from the long balconies onto which most of the rooms on each floor opened, over-looking the lobby far below. This gave the technicians more freedom of movement back and forth to the center suite. The technicians who worked in the suite on the left had to turn up their television volume while they were drilling, because the room on the other side was occupied.

Marty Rangel was in charge of the installations and took Haydon into the suite where Rafael would be staying. Rangel was a small man with a salt-and-pepper mustache and clear eyes almost totally lacking in pigmentation. He talked and moved quickly and had the habit of fibrillating his tongue against the edges of his upper teeth when he wasn't talking.

"Your man will be in 2639 here," he said, preceding Haydon into the suite. "Okay, we got the sitting room here first thing. Bedroom to the right. We're going to spend your whole budget on this thing. Four video ports, two cameras in each port. The tapes we'll be using are expensive, top of the line, with thick oxide coating. We can put them through a lot of punishment without threatening the integrity of the picture quality."

Rangel stepped into the center of the sitting room and faced the wall adjoining suite 2638. "Okay, we're lucky here. This port's behind a mirror." He pointed to a hole in the wall over an armchair. "Janet's got the mirror frame and is putting in a two-way glass. This camera will take in everything from the windows, the table, that long sofa against the wall, and up to the bedroom door. The other port's over this L-shaped sofa. It'll take in part of the sofa under it, part of the wet bar, and the doorway to the bedroom. This one's a booger. We're going to have to disguise the wallpaper somehow. Janet's working with some cellophane sheeting to match the pattern. We're lucky the tech freaks have developed these small lenses. We wouldn't be able to do this with the old kind."

Darting his tongue against his teeth while Haydon looked around, Rangel then walked into the bedroom.

"In here we have an easy one too. These cameras will be coming from 2640. One behind the mirror facing the bed. Nice place for a mirror, huh? So they can comb their hair the second they wake up, I guess. It'll get from the windows to the bed and up to the doorway. The other camera is directly across from the one over the L-shaped sofa in the sitting room. A good shot of the sofa right through the doorway. We'll get the closet in here with this one too.

"Now. We get ninety-eight percent of the suite with these cameras. What we don't get is the front entrance, the entrance closet, the whole wet bar, and the bathroom. We can put one in the bathroom from 2638 if you want."

Haydon nodded and walked out to the bathroom. "I'm afraid we'll have to, Marty," he said, looking into the bathroom doorway.

"My pleasure."

"When do you think you'll be through?"

"By lunch. Well, maybe a little after, now that you want to put a peeper in the bathroom. We'll have to replace this big piece of mirror here. It'll take a little while to get the two-way glass cut and sent up here. We'll vacuum up our own mess, so when we leave it'll be ready. I'd suggest you have housekeeping come in with air fresheners, though. Get

316

rid of the sawdust smell, the smell of fresh plaster. We've got good cameras and good recorders, so I'd suggest they put smaller watts in the lights too. No use in putting spotlights on our wall work."

"You take care of that. You'll know best about that."

"Okay."

"How will we watch this?"

"A television monitor for each port. That way we can see everything at the same time. If they walk out of view of one port, all we have to do is look at the other monitor. That will keep us from having to switch electronically from port to port. If she stays in the viewing area of one port and he walks out of the viewing area of that port and into the viewing area of another port, we won't have to make the decision as to which camera to turn on. We can watch them both at the same time. The bathroom will have a separate monitor. Course, the whole place is bugged like the damn space shuttle. No problem there. We'll have lots of headsets."

"Great. I'm going back to the station. Call me when you're finished. I'd like to do a walk-through before your people leave."

"I'll be in touch."

35

On a moment's impulse, Haydon had called Nina for a late lunch at Cody's on Montrose. It turned out to have been a mistake. He was preoccupied and distant, irritated at her efforts at conversation. After a while she stopped trying. The truth was, he didn't want to talk but he hadn't wanted to lunch alone either. Selfishly, he simply wanted her to be there. After nearly an hour of Haydon's surliness, Nina said she had to get back to the studio.

Outside, he leaned through the window of her car and kissed her, then told her he would be late coming home. A surveillance had been set up and he would have to be there. She smiled, leaned out to kiss him again, and drove off. Haydon walked to his car and sat with the door open to let out the swelling heat as he called in on the radio. Dystal said Rangel had just checked in and was ready for the walk-through. Haydon said to tell him he was on his way over.

Rangel and his technicians had done an excellent job improving on the original plan. They had first thought that the monitors for 2640 would have to be in that suite, requiring the detectives to be split into two groups, one monitoring the sitting room on one side, one monitoring the bedroom on the other. Since Million had the decisive word about when to move against Rafael, it was going to be a toss-up about which suite to put him in. However, Rangel's technicians probed the furring above the entrance of each suite and found a way to run the thick cables through it, enabling them to put all the monitors in 2638. It solved a crucial logistics problem.

Haydon watched the monitors as two of the technicians wandered around in different parts of suite 2639. Rafael and Dolores do Bandolin would be visible at every moment. Two technicians would be left in 2640 during the entire operation in case something happened to the cameras. They could communicate by microphone. Haydon thanked Rangel and asked him to be there during the operation.

When he got back to the office, Haydon checked with Mooney. Rafael was making his afternoon ward rounds in Hermann Hospital. Hirsch was home asleep and had left word that he wanted to be wakened in time to go to the hotel with them. Dystal, Haydon, and Mercer sat in Dystal's office, reworking the possible scenarios Haydon might face during the surveillance. Mercer was still worried about the technicalities.

At four-thirty, Lapier called and said Dolores do Bandolin had just registered and was on her way up to her room. She was carrying a single overnight bag and a train case. Haydon called Hirsch and told him to meet him at the Hyatt at five-thirty. Mooney would stay with Rafael until he came to the hotel. Next Haydon called Million and told him to come to suite 2638 at a quarter to six. He placed a third call to Professor Thomases at Rice University and made the same arrangement for six o'clock. The technicians already at the Hyatt would stay there.

Haydon hit downtown in the midst of rush-hour traffic. The heat that had collected in the pavement and sidewalks was still boiling up to join the exhausts of buses and cars. But the sun had been blocked out. Though it was as still as the equatorial doldrums and you had to fight to draw a breath of befouled air, a gray sheet of clouds had formed high in the sky, obscuring the late-afternoon sun. The humidity rose into the nineties along with the temperature, until it was difficult to tell whether you were dripping with perspiration or salty Gulf vapor. With the sun lost in the nebulous slate, the canyons between the downtown monoliths became gloomy. The neon lights came on early and found a dull reflection in streets that glazed over in the clammy air like frosted glass.

He was a few minutes early when he entered the brilliant lobby of the Hyatt, but Hirsch was already there, waiting in the sunken lounge. A bar had been set up and the pit was filled with drinkers. Leo had seen him come in and was already heading toward him.

"Get enough sleep?" Haydon asked.

"Sure," Leo said. "Anything new?"

"No. But it's looking good, Leo. It's a good setup."

"Have you heard from Ed?"

Haydon looked at his watch. "He's supposed to call as soon as he can after six. We'd better go on up."

By six-fifteen everyone was there and Rangel was softly explaining the setup to Hirsch, Million, and Thomases. As he spoke, they watched Dolores do Bandolin lounging on the sofa in the sitting room with a glass of champagne in her hand and *Little House on the Prairie* on the television. She wore a slinky dress which she gathered up around her thighs as she concentrated on the television.

When the telephone rang, Haydon turned away from the group and answered it.

"We're sitting in this damn cafeteria again," Mooney said. "He's absentmindedly picking his nose and staring out at this shit weather. If something else hadn't already

320

screwed this turd's brain, his god-awful routine around here would've eventually driven him crazy. We've been here an hour! Same chair. No food, no drink. He's been glued to this damn gloomy weather.''

"We're ready for him here.''

"The baby doll's there?''

"Yes.''

"Is she a real honey?''

"Yes.''

"Good. Listen, I'd feel a lot better if you'd call Dystal and have him send someone over here to help me tail this guy once he gets in his car. The weather's going to turn nasty and I'd really hate to lose him.''

"Fine; I'll do it.''

"I'll check in. Let you know when we're headed your way.''

Haydon had sandwiches along with extra coffee and hot plates sent up to both suites. They settled in for the evening, talking and glancing now and then at Bandolin on the monitors. They had pushed the sofas and chairs to one side of the room and lined up the five monitors against the wall across from them. The two showing the sitting room were on the left, the two in the bedroom were on the right, followed by the one in the bathroom. At times, as Bandolin rose to get more champagne or to go into the bedroom to brush through her hair or apply a dab more of perfume, she would show up on two monitors at once from different angles. A testimony to Rangel's expert planning for overlapping coverage.

Bandolin stayed glued to the television all through *Dukes of Hazzard* and was well into the first quarter of *Dallas* when the telephone beside Haydon rang again. It was Dystal.

"I've got Ed and Crowley on the radio here. Rafael's on the move. They're just now leaving the medical center.''

"They've been there all this time?''

321

"Yeah, mostly in that cafeteria, just sittin' there in a daze. Ed says the old boy went up to the laboratory before he left. Figures he got some of his brew. I'll get back to ya."

At the half hour commercial of *Dallas*, Bandolin got up from the sofa and went into the bathroom. She urinated in the presence of three electronics technicians, two detectives, a language professor, and an assistant district attorney. Looking directly into camera number five, she examined her face in the mirror, looked closely at her eyebrows, smoothed them with her fingers, and shook her head of bouncy black hair. She smiled, turned her head at different angles as she looked into the mirror from the corners of her eyes, appraising herself. Then she turned and walked into the bedroom. She brushed her hair again and then went to the bed and took several record albums out of her overnight bag. Humming and swaying slightly, she walked back into the sitting room, holding the albums to her breast. She was graceful and beautiful. Impossible not to watch.

Pouring herself more champagne, Bandolin put one of the records on the stereo. As the needle lowered on the disc and the beautiful voice of Elis came clear and smooth through the microphones, she stood with her wine and peered out the window at the city, its lights now shattered by mist that had crept in from the Gulf. She looked at her watch and as if it were a signal, the men in the suites on either side of her looked at theirs.

"Is he supposed to be punctual?" Million asked softly.

Haydon shrugged. It was nine o'clock.

The telephone rang and Haydon picked it up.

"He's not going to be on time," Dystal said. "Ed says he's been circling the hotel for the last fifteen minutes. Just going round and round. You think he smells a rat?"

"Who knows? Is Ed sure he hasn't been spotted?"

"Says he is. What's she doin'?"

"Listening to records. Killing time."

"She seem nervous?"

"Not really."

"Well, if he— Hold it." There was radio static and Dystal rumbled in the background. "He pulled into the hotel garage. Ed's parking in the street and going into the lobby. Crowley's going to wait by the garage exit. I'm goin' to hang on to Crowley until you've got him inside for sure."

Haydon could hear Dystal breathing. Everyone in the suite was looking at Haydon, who was looking at the second telephone. It seemed like five minutes before it rang and he picked it up.

"This is Lapier. Ed's down here now. We're looking at each other across the lobby but he hasn't seen the man and I haven't either."

"Can he get to the elevators without your seeing him?"

"Yeah."

Haydon told Dystal and continued to sit with one telephone to each ear. He stared hard at the monitor with Bandolin. The music was too loud for him to hear a knock next door, but he was expecting her to react to it instantly. Both telephones were silent and Bandolin was still looking out the window, her back to the cameras. Rangel got up and fiddled with the contrast on one of the monitors. It was an invisible adjustment, a nervous movement. Million sat with one booted leg crossed over the other, his back flat against the straight-backed chair as he balanced a cup and saucer and slowly caressed his handlebar with a forefinger. Hirsch nervously scanned all five monitors as if he expected Rafael to spring out of any one of them.

Then Dolores do Bandolin turned around slowly, a smile parting her perfect lips as Rafael emerged simultaneously from opposite sides of monitors two and three.

"He's in," Haydon said into both telephones.

"I'm off," Dystal said, and disconnected.

"Hang on, Pete," Haydon said to Lapier. "Have Ed wait a second."

Rafael walked into the sitting room wearing a raincoat, both arms hanging limp at his sides. One hand held a small leather bag. Bandolin swayed toward him to the music, still smiling, her arms reaching out to him, one holding an empty champagne glass. Rafael approached her without expression and she wrapped her arms around him. He reached up with his hands and unwrapped them and walked to the champagne in an ice bucket. He poured himself a glass and she approached him, still smiling, holding hers out for him to fill. He ignored her, stuffed the bottle back down into the ice, and walked past her again to an armchair. He removed his coat and threw it on the floor and sat in the chair.

"Okay, he's staying," Haydon said to Lapier. "Have Ed wait another five minutes to be sure before he comes up. Tell him just to move our doorknob slightly. We can hear it."

Bandolin refilled her own glass and turned back to Rafael, her smile unwavering. Something about the smile seemed familiar to Haydon. He concentrated on it as she moved toward Rafael in the armchair. She stood in front of him and slowly knelt on the floor, her eyes fastened to his passive orbs. Kneeling, she continued to smile as she lowered herself even further in front of him until she was almost nestled between his feet in a crouch, smiling. Then Haydon recognized the expression. He had seen it on the faces of dogs who wished to ingratiate themselves with someone or with another dog. She twisted her body in the same whining, fawning manner in which he had seen bitches present themselves in sexual foreplay, a desperate effort to make themselves pleasing, a self-degrading offering of oneself.

"What do you want?" Rafael asked. It was the first either of them had spoken. Thomases translated quickly and effortlessly, without prompting.

324

"Anything," she said. She dipped the fingers of one hand into her champagne and sprinkled it onto her chest, massaging the tops of her breasts, running her long, narrow fingers deeper into her dress. When she withdrew them, wet with champagne, she traced them across her lips, her neck, her smooth cinnamon shoulders, pushing away the straps of her dress to let the watery material slide down the slope of her breasts. Leaning forward slightly, she let the material fall away to her waist. Still on her knees, she picked up the wineglass by its stem and slowly poured the rest of the wine over her chest until she glistened with it and tiny rivulets ran into her navel, and disappeared into the folds of the dress in her lap. Then she rose, gradually arching her back as she bent toward him dangling her dripping breasts in front of his face, touching first one and then the other to his lips.

He didn't move a muscle.

She backed away, smiling, and stood straight as she worked the dress down over her hips and let it fall around her ankles. She wore only high-legged lace panties, now soaked with champagne and transparent. Cocking her hips slightly, she ran her fingers into the sides of the panties and peeled them off.

At this point the doorknob of the room rattled. No one moved except Haydon, who got up and let Mooney in.

Rafael drained his glass, set it on the floor, and picked up his leather bag. He stood and walked past the tall and lovely Bandolin without touching her, a feat of restraint every man in the room found incredible. He sat at the table next to the windows and began to empty the bag. The girl turned to watch him, the dimples above her hips more prominent on one side as she rested most of her weight on her left leg.

"Anything?" Rafael said. "Okay." He placed two glassine bags side by side. A spoon, a candle, syringe, rubber tubing, matches, a vial.

"There's the stuff," Mooney whispered. "He brought it.

Looks like coke, some heroin. Shit, the turd's making a speedball. I hope she's used to this."

There was silence as Rafael continued brewing the drugs.

"Goddamn, Stuart," Million said. "This could snuff her."

No one else spoke, but the tension was electrifying the room.

"We going to watch this, Haydon?" Million asked. His voice was tight.

Haydon's heart had lost its rhythm and was bouncing all around his rib cage. Million turned away from the monitors and stared at him. Haydon could feel his eyes.

"He's not going to kill her," Haydon said. "She's had speedballs. She's young. He wants the virus to do it."

No one asked him how he knew.

Rafael added the contents from the vial with the finally prepared solution and drew it all into the needle. From the back the girl showed no emotion, except that her fingers had begun to work. When the syringe was full, Rafael laid it on the table and turned to the stereo. He put on a new record.

"Samba," Haydon said when the music began to vibrate the walls. Rafael had turned up the volume.

He sat down again and picked up the rubber tubing. The girl approached and held out both arms, the insides of her elbows upward. Rafael quickly wrapped the tubing, picked up the syringe, and slipped it into the swollen vein of her right arm. When he pulled it out he looked at her. He touched the rubber tubing, then suddenly popped it off with a single jerk.

Everybody in the room flinched. He was sending it to her in a single rush like a shot to the heart. The girl stood still. She raised her arms above her head, spread her legs to steady herself, and then fell with a whump as if she'd been poleaxed.

Million grunted.

326

Haydon dialed the telephone. "Pete, get a doctor over here, ready to deal with a speedball. Keep him with you until I call. Hurry!"

The girl had fallen like a rag doll, her arms and legs twisted awkwardly under her. Rafael stood and stepped around from behind the table. He stood over her and then reached out with the toe of his shoe, slipped it under her cheek, and shoved her head around with a little kick. He bent over and opened her eyelids. He took a penlight from his jacket pocket and played it over her eyes. He lifted an arm and felt her pulse. Standing, he poured himself another glass of champagne and drank it all at once.

He stepped over the girl and went to the other end of the sofa, where he began to undress. He hung his jacket on the back of a chair, and spread his shirt over that. After slipping off his pants, he folded them neatly, taking pains to get the crease straight before he hung them over the back of another chair. He removed his shoes and socks, placed the shoes side by side in front of one of the chairs, the toes pointing outward, and put the socks inside. He spread his undershirt flat on the floor and directly below that, as if it were on a manikin, he spread his Jockey shorts.

Completely nude now, he wrestled the girl around until he had her by the ankles and then he began dragging her into the bedroom.

"Son of a bitch," Hirsch said. He started to stand, but Haydon put a hand on his shoulder. "Goddamn, isn't this enough?" He looked at Million.

Million kept his eyes glued to the monitors. He was breathing like a long-distance runner, his mouth clenched shut.

"You know what's coming?" Haydon asked, looking at Million.

Million snapped his head once.

When Rafael got the girl into the bedroom, everyone's

head moved in unison to another monitor. Rafael jerked the bedspread off the bed, leaving only the white sheet. He lifted the girl under the arms and dragged her onto the bed, taking care to position her in the very center, her legs together and straight, her arms close at her sides. He took some time with her hair, smoothing it around her face so that it flowed over the pillow like ink.

He returned to the sitting room and took a handful of candles out of the leather bag and then went back to the bedroom. These he positioned on the floor all around the bed and then lit one by one to form a rosary of flickering lights. He walked to the door and turned out the lights, proceeded to the sitting room, and turned off the record. He slipped a cassette into the recorder and snapped it on.

It was a second before Haydon recognized the ratchety, African drum slaps of "Burundi Black." It had been the second of the two songs marked in red on the old Wurlitzer in Parmer's condo. Rafael turned off all the lights and made his way toward the glow coming from the bedroom.

"We're getting a good picture in here." Rangel was hoarse as he spoke to his technicians in the other suite. "Maybe you should boost the gain a little. Good. Hold it right there." He looked around at the others. "Good pictures." No one paid any attention.

Suddenly Rafael was beside the bed. The room was dark except for the glow that fell over the girl and lit the front of Rafael's body inside the ring of candles. He raised his arms and began to flutter his hands, which were obscured in the penumbra above them. A cloud descended, a constant falling fog of powder. The tempo of the music quickened as a swelling chorus of tribal voices joined the syncopating drums in a counterpoint rhythm that had a compellingly hypnotic effect on Rafael. He moved to it around the bed, his body pulsing, gyrating, bucking, as the powder fell and fell and fell and the girl grew as pale as a corpse beneath his wild attentions. With her increasingly cadaverous appearance, he grew more excited until his sexual arousal made them all want to turn away.

There was the double thump of an overturned chair in the room as Thomases rushed to the bathroom. They could hear him retching.

"You have the keys, Leo?" Haydon asked. Hirsch stood quickly. "Ed?"

The two detectives opened the door to the suite and waited, watching the monitors.

Rafael trembled and shambled around the girl, her hair white strands, her face a death mask beneath the powder. The music was taking over his movements, he became tied to it, a part of it. They grew wild together, frenzied. Without warning he flung himself violently onto the girl.

"Get him!" Million screamed, leaping out of his chair. "Get him!"

Hirsch was already gone.

"Get the doctor up here," Haydon yelled into the telephone, and then watched the monitors in astonishment as Hirsch burst through the door of the suite, his silhouette an instant cutout in the doorway backlighted from the balcony outside. Haydon froze, his eyes locked on the other monitor as he watched Hirsch's figure fly through the candlelight at Rafael, who was already pulling himself up. They disappeared. Instantly the lights came on and Mooney was stumbling across the room, screaming, "Leo! Leo!"

Someone screamed horribly—it could have been anyone's voice—and Haydon could see Hirsch's arms pounding, he could hear the blows and see the black butt of the .38 pounding, pounding. In the bright lights he saw a squirt of blood shoot up the side of the wall. Then Mooney was on them, fat and huffing and fighting. A candle had caught fire to a trailing sheet and Million came on the monitor, fighting it, knocking out the other candles. There was another scream and Haydon recognized Hirsch's voice, and then Mooney yelling, "Leo! Leo! Goddamn it, you'll kill him!" and then, "Million! Million!"

Lapier appeared on the monitor with someone else and carried the girl out of the room, covering themselves with powder. They laid her on the sofa and the doctor began clearing her nostrils.

On monitor number three there was a pile of men in the corner of the bedroom, absolutely still.

36

Cesar Guimaraes flew into Houston from Rio de Janeiro with an entourage of family and servants to support his son. Dane Massey found himself backed with enough financial resources to build a defense of extravagant proportions for both Rafael and Robert DeLeon, and that was exactly what he set about doing.

Massey's initial moves subsequent to indictment were to get Rafael released on a $750,000 bond and initiate a flurry of delays. Because Rafael was Brazilian and DeLeon's case involved the activities of Brazilian citizens, Massey pleaded for time to obtain information from Rio and São Paulo that was pertinent to both cases. With little effort at all, he quickly was able to guarantee that the case would be bogged down for months before the prosecution would be free to make any serious moves toward preliminary trial procedures.

Million and his staff did not squabble about moves they had fully anticipated. They filed the papers needed to meet Massey's delays and then turned their attention elsewhere. Judith Croft was indicted for aggravated promotion of pros-

331

titution and conspiracy to violate immigration laws. She also was immediately released on bail. Million then began building the cases against the wealthy men involved in the purchase of the Brazilian girls. The case against DeLeon was so strong at the outset that Million did not immediately extend plea bargain feelers to Massey. Instead the DA's office and the police made an all-out effort to locate those persons actually employed in the disposal of the bodies of the five girls who had not yet been found.

Vianna was not a problem. He readily took investigators to the little village of Yautepec near Cuernavaca, Mexico. There, in the center of a small cemetery where most of the graves were marked with homemade wood or cement crosses, the girl lay in comparative opulence in a narrow whitewashed crypt embedded with seashells painted blue. Raymond Lyles had had skittish friends on his yacht off the Florida Keys. Sworn affidavits were enough to indict him. That left three missing bodies. It took months of additional research and cultivation of informants before investigators were led to the middle of a salt grass field near the Pasadena refineries, where they dug up the skeletal remains of Soyla Villas. It was even longer before they were able to successfully indict oilman Ross Wilson for the cremation of Lydia Pinheiro. The body of one girl was never found and no indictment was brought forward for her murder. Nearly four more months passed before the trials began in the deaths of Petra Torres and the two girls Hirsch had found in the Jane Doe section of the city morgue. Including Sally Steen, Sandy Kielman, Theresa Parmer, and Pauline Thomas, twelve girls in all had died.

Three days after Rafael's arrest at the Hyatt Regency, Nina called Bob Dystal to tell him Haydon had suddenly come down with the flu. His doctor said he might be away from work for several days. Nina refused to let anyone from the office or the news media talk to him for nearly a week, and when he finally returned to work, hollow-cheeked and quiet, Hirsch and Mooney were already carrying the burden of the follow-up investigations, providing Million with the constant flow of documents from their files that were necessary for his trial preparations. Haydon's lassitude persisted for weeks, and he was slow to gain back the weight he had lost during his illness. Those who worked closely with him were too preoccupied to notice any changes out of the ordinary, and by the time things let up enough for them to take note of his depression, he had begun to recover to the extent that the subtle alterations in his personality were well camouflaged.

For a little more than a year the deaths of the girls and the prominent men involved with them dominated the front pages of the Houston dailies intermittently and surfaced repeatedly on the national evening news. As the primary investigating detective, Haydon was continuously referred to in the news media. It was the kind of attention he detested, but the department had few men as articulate as Stuart Haydon and the administration well knew the value of such a spokesman. They insisted he remain accessible to the press to field questions about his successful investigation. Knowing of his natural reticence with reporters, they had no fear he would overstep departmental confidentialities.

Summer plodded reluctantly into fall, which meant the temperatures stayed predominantly in the eighties. Winter made a brief appearance, which meant it rained frequently and sometimes the temperature wandered into the fifties. The famous Texas Northers blew down from the Panhandle and wore themselves out on the Gulf Coast. A few nights the thermometer sank into the thirties. Then winter was gone. Spring was fragile and short-lived, and summer returned, rightful owner of the city. It seemed never to have left at all.

As Massey accumulated volumes of material for the defense of DeLeon, it became apparent that the indicted attorney was in trouble. Longoria's testimony was damning. Massey approached Million about plea bargaining in exchange for information regarding several of the girls who were, at that time, still missing. Million wouldn't even consider it. By the time of the trial date it was clear little could be done for DeLeon. He received a life sentence with no possibility of probation.

For Massey, DeLeon's case had represented an instance of triage in criminal defense. He did what he could, but the results were a foregone conclusion. There was little hope and Massey did not spend an excessive amount of time trying to develop extraordinary stratagems for his defense. Rafael's wounds, however, did not appear to be mortal, though Russ Million had thrown the book at him. He was indicted for aggravated attempted capital murder of Dolores do Bandolin, aggravated promotion of prostitution, conspiracy to violate the immigration laws, and illegal possession of dangerous drugs. Everyone knew from the outset that there would be no possibility of trying Rafael for the murder of the twelve women. As one newspaper reporter pointed out, though the indirect evidence against Rafael was awesome, there was not a shred of direct evidence. In the concrete matters of jurisprudence, "awesome" was not a sufficient or valid claim.

From the defense position, Massey felt he could see several cracks in the prosecution's case into which he could possibly drive wedges. The videotape was a seemingly insurmountable piece of evidence, but Massey planned to turn it to his advantage. The whole point in making such a film had been based upon Haydon's belief that Rafael would somehow attempt to administer a lethal amount of the rabies virus to Bandolin. When the police saw Rafael give the injection to the girl, an injection they believed Rafael thought contained lethal amounts of a live virus, why did they then wait an additional seventeen minutes before breaking into

334

the suite? Hadn't they seen what they set out to see? Since Bandolin was rendered unconscious by the powerful speedball, did they not endanger her life by delaying her medical attention in the hope of catching the defendant in an act of rape? In allowing the defendant to remain alone in the suite for more than a quarter of an hour with the beautiful, unconscious, and nude young woman, did they not perpetrate an act of entrapment for the purpose of obtaining evidence of a crime the defendant might not have contemplated had the police not allowed the situation to continue? Did they not, themselves, commit a crime in allowing the unconscious girl to serve as bait for a possible crime, a crime they easily could have prevented? Further, how could they have known whether the girl was unconscious or dead when she collapsed on the floor? In either case they should have acted quickly to prevent any further crimes against her person they may have anticipated. If the girl had died, would not the police themselves have been guilty of criminal negligence? As it stood, weren't they already guilty of passive negligence and the most shameful kind of voyeurism? In addition, Massey would maintain his client had been brutalized at the time of arrest, having sustained a broken nose and cuts and lacerations requiring thirty-two stitches. Countersuits were filed.

Million, of course, had anticipated this tack from the defense and had prepared an elaborate defense of his own. It was going to be a difficult case no matter how you looked at it.

In the end, however, neither defense nor prosecution would be required to parade their painstakingly constructed cases before the court. Though Dolores do Bandolin had been closely guarded and nurtured at great expense by the DA's office during the year's wait for the case to come to trial, ultimately they were not diligent enough. One evening three weeks before the trial was to begin, she was driven to

Jamail's for some last-minute shopping before dinner. She disappeared from the store. Two days later she took a cab from a cheap motel on the city's south side to the international airport, and boarded a direct flight to Rio de Janeiro. She disappeared into the wastes of *o morro* from which she had come nearly two years before.

Haydon took the telephone off the cradle to stop the ringing. He didn't want to talk into it. He laid the receiver beside him on the sheet and looked over at Nina. She was awake, looking at him.

"Don't you think you'd better speak to them?"

He lay flat on his back and looked across the foot of the bed to the tall windows that overlooked the terrace and lawn below. The large panes were thrown open and a faint tangy fragrance of lime came in from the trees.

Nina ran the long fingers of her hand across the hair on his chest. She picked up the receiver and held it to his ear.

"Hello? Anybody there? Hello. Detective Haydon?"

"This is Haydon," he said huskily.

"I guess I woke you up."

Haydon looked at the oval Cartier clock beside the bed. It said it was two-fifteen.

"Who is this?"

"Detective West, sir. We've got a problem over at that place you dealt with on Quenby."

Haydon couldn't believe it. He felt a surge of nausea.

"There's a guy here with his face blown to shit. Can't recognize him. Woman here says she wants to see you. I don't know who she is either. Won't give her name."

"I'm coming," Haydon said. Nina hung up the telephone and they lay for a moment in the dark, looking at the blue light coming in through the windows.

"My God," he said after a few minutes. Then he got up and dressed.

336

All the furniture in the condominium was covered with white dust covers and the place smelled musty. It had been unoccupied for over a year now. West and his partner were the only ones on the scene. They stood quietly as Haydon crossed the living room to the woman. Judith Croft sat on the edge of one of the sofas, smoking a cigarette. Her jet bob framed her face as precisely as the first time he had seen her, the perfect contrast to her light-blue eyes, pale skin, and the deep mandarin of her lips.

They looked at each other a moment and then Haydon turned and walked over to the body in front of the Wurlitzer. West pulled back the dust cover they had taken off an armchair and thrown over the victim. Rafael's face was gone. Something powerful had shoved it right off his head by way of his hairline.

"A nasty little handgun that shoots a single .410 shell did it," West explained. He held it out to Haydon. Haydon just looked at it in the other detective's hand, and then went over to Croft.

"You all right?" he asked, looking down at her.

She nodded, and blew a stream of smoke.

Haydon sat down at the other end of the short sofa and lit a cigarette too. The ritual.

"What happened?"

She sighed a jerky kind of sigh.

"I was the only one in all this . . . this sad collection of women who hadn't slept with him. I just wouldn't do it. I called him earlier tonight. Told him we should get together, drown this damned past year in one nice evening together. It's been rough on him, you know, even if he never shows it. He was ready for some sympathy. When he got here I just walked up to him and put the barrel right under his chin." She cleared her throat.

"Where'd you get that kind of weapon?"

337

"Paulo gave it to me a long time ago. For 'protection.' It was absurd for me to have a gun like that."

Haydon couldn't help it; he looked up at the ceiling. There were chunks of hair in the mess there.

"Why?"

"I could see where it was going," she said. "He never would have gotten what he deserved. I heard Massey was going to switch to an insanity plea. The man was evil. There was no justice in excusing him because he was mad."

Her hands were properly folded in her lap and she looked over at Rafael's body under the dust cover.

"I know how this must sound coming from me, but . . . there is a moral question here. I didn't want it just to be swept away in a flood of legal technicalities."

Haydon looked at her. She was immaculately dressed. He could smell her perfume. Bal à Versailles. He remembered the lithe body he had seen beneath the tea-rose peignoir on the sunny morning he met her.

"So now you think he's gotten what he deserved?"

"I knew what I was doing," she said.

"Why did you have them call me?"

She looked at him. A small glycerol tear formed in the inside corner of each eye. They did not overflow and run down her cheeks, but stayed there, perfect and still like diamonds.

"I want you to take me through this. It started with you and I want it to end with you."

There wasn't anything he could say about that. He just nodded.

Neither of them spoke for a little while. Haydon knew he should take her and go, but he didn't move. He felt West's curiosity. He didn't care.

Judith Croft leaned over and ground out her cigarette in a side-table ashtray. The hem of her crepe de chine dress slipped past her knee. She stared down at the floor in front of her.

"Did you know Sally was my mother?"

The question hung in the musty air, among the ghostly dust sheets and Rafael's corpse, like a misspent thought searching for a reason to exist. Haydon felt sorry for her.

"No," he said.

"It was all in a sealed document as part of her will. I was her first pregnancy. Instead of getting an abortion, she went through with it and then gave me away. It was all in the document, the whole story. Eight pages, single spaced. She kept track of me, through school, through college."

She turned her eyes on Haydon again. He could tell from the look on her face that she knew there was no sense in going into it.

"Shall we go?" she said.

Haydon was very tired. As he stood and took her hand to help her up, he caught again the fragrance of her perfume. He would have given anything to have been allowed to cry.

Home delivery from Pocket Books

Here's your opportunity to have fabulous bestsellers delivered right to you. Our free catalog is filled to the brim with the newest titles plus the finest in mysteries, science fiction, westerns, cookbooks, romances, biographies, health, psychology, humor—every subject under the sun. Order this today and a world of pleasure will arrive at your door.

POCKET BOOKS, Department ORD
1230 Avenue of the Americas, New York, N.Y. 10020